PENGUIN BOOKS

THE PENGUIN BOOK OF
THE MODERN AMERICAN SHORT STORY

John Freeman is the editor of *Freeman's*, a literary annual of new writing, and executive editor at Alfred A. Knopf. His books include *How to Read a Novelist* and *Dictionary of the Undoing*, as well as *Tales of Two Americas*, an anthology about income inequality in America, and *Tales of Two Planets*, an anthology of new writing about inequality and the climate crisis globally. He is also the author of two poetry collections, *Maps* and *The Park*. His work is translated into more than twenty languages and has appeared in *The New Yorker*, *The Paris Review*, and *The New York Times*. The former editor of *Granta*, he teaches writing at New York University.

THE PENGUIN BOOK

of the

MODERN AMERICAN

SHORT STORY

Edited by

JOHN FREEMAN

PENGUIN BOOKS

PENGUIN BOOKS
An imprint of Penguin Random House LLC
penguinrandomhouse.com

First published in the United States of America by Penguin Press,
an imprint of Penguin Random House LLC, 2021
Published in Penguin Books 2022

ISBN 9781984877826 (paperback)

THE LIBRARY OF CONGRESS HAS CATALOGED
THE HARDCOVER EDITION AS FOLLOWS:

Names: Freeman, John, 1974–, editor.
Title: The Penguin book of the modern American short story /
edited by John Freeman.
Description: New York : Penguin Press, 2021. |
Includes bibliographical references. | Identifiers: LCCN 2020056441 (print) |
LCCN 2020056442 (ebook) |
ISBN 9781984877802 (hardcover) | ISBN 9781984877819 (ebook)
Subjects: LCSH: Short stories, American—20th century. |
Short stories, American—21st century.
Classification: LCC PS648.S5 P47 2021 (print) | LCC PS648.S5 (ebook) |
DDC 813/.0108—dc23
LC record available at https://lccn.loc.gov/2020056441
LC ebook record available at https://lccn.loc.gov/2020056442

Printed in the United States of America
5th Printing

Designed by Amanda Dewey

CONTENTS

Introduction by John Freeman   ix

THE LESSON · Toni Cade Bambara, *1972*   1

A CONVERSATION WITH MY FATHER · Grace Paley, *1972*   10

THE ONES WHO WALK AWAY FROM OMELAS ·
Ursula K. Le Guin, *1973*   17

BICYCLES, MUSCLES, CIGARETTES · Raymond Carver, *1973*   25

THE FLOWERS · Alice Walker, *1973*   36

GIRL · Jamaica Kincaid, *1978*   38

THE RED CONVERTIBLE · Louise Erdrich, *1981*   40

THE REENCOUNTER · Isaac Bashevis Singer, *1982*   51

TAKING CARE · Joy Williams, *1982*   58

STORY · Lydia Davis, *1983*   69

CHINA · Charles Johnson, *1984*   73

PET MILK · Stuart Dybek, *1984*   96

THE WAY WE LIVE NOW · Susan Sontag, *1986*　　102

SALVADOR LATE OR EARLY · Sandra Cisneros, *1986*　　123

THE THINGS THEY CARRIED · Tim O'Brien, *1986*　　125

RIVER OF NAMES · Dorothy Allison, *1988*　　146

EMERGENCY · Denis Johnson, *1991*　　157

STICKS · George Saunders, *1994*　　170

FIESTA, 1980 · Junot Díaz, *1996*　　172

SILENCE · Lucia Berlin, *1998*　　188

THE TWENTY-SEVENTH MAN · Nathan Englander, *1998*　　201

BULLET IN THE BRAIN · Tobias Wolff, *1998*　　221

THE HERMIT'S STORY · Rick Bass, *1998*　　227

A TEMPORARY MATTER · Jhumpa Lahiri, *1998*　　242

THE PENTHOUSE · Andrew Holleran, *1999*　　262

THE FIX · Percival Everett, *1999*　　292

WATER CHILD · Edwidge Danticat, *2000*　　310

THE AMERICAN EMBASSY · Chimamanda Ngozi Adichie, *2003*　　322

THE CONDUCTOR · Aleksandar Hemon, *2005*　　334

ST. LUCY'S HOME FOR GIRLS RAISED BY WOLVES ·
Karen Russell, *2007*　　354

THE LAST THING WE NEED · Claire Vaye Watkins, *2010*　　373

THE PAPER MENAGERIE · Ken Liu, *2011*　　389

THE DUNE · Stephen King, *2011*　　405

DIEM PERDIDI • Julie Otsuka, 2011   419

THE GREAT SILENCE • Ted Chiang, 2015   432

THE MIDNIGHT ZONE • Lauren Groff, 2016   437

ANYONE CAN DO IT • Manuel Muñoz, 2019   449

About the Contributors   467

Credits   477

INTRODUCTION

John Freeman

For a long time, the 1960s have been seen as a pivotal point for the modern short story. Not just the actual time period, but a version of the 1960s in popular culture. These 1960s are a time of tumult and expansion. Sexual freedom, suburbanization, growth, and wealth. It was when a great nation lost its innocence and began its march toward greater liberties.

More than fifty years on from this period, the 1960s seem a very different era. One in which it took riots, assassinations, and televised public beatings to wake up white Americans. Towns and cities across the country fought desegregation with violence, and even federal legislation couldn't end discriminatory practices. It just started a new movement. From the moments of their passage, the Voting Rights Act of 1965 and the Civil Rights Act of 1968 met concerted pushback. Indeed, they jump-started a right wing movement in its ascendancy today.

Even more interesting than uprisings are their aftermaths, when norms and laws resettle, and the imaginations of people adjust to new horizons. In recent years, the 1970s have begun to seem like one of the most fertile periods of American life, grim as they were with stagflation, war, and the financial collapse of cities. It was also a time of environmental activism, a rising Black Arts Movement, the emergence within film and literature of genres for reimagining society. In one five-year period, Toni Morrison, Stephen King, Maxine Hong Kingston, and Rudolfo Anaya all made their debuts.

This anthology, though it tracks the high points of the short story, is enabled by spaces these writers opened up. For some this was not a metaphorical activity. Starting in 1967, Toni Morrison began editing fiction for Random House, a post from which she nurtured books by new Black voices, including Toni Cade Bambara's *Gorilla, My Love* (1972), which included the first story in this collection, "The Lesson," about school kids on a trip from Brooklyn into Manhattan, to a fancy toy store.

American irreality took on a new cast in 1972, as the separation between official life and actual life in America began to yawn. The Dow closed over 1,000 for the first time, yet indicators of malaise defined the US economy. Nixon was reelected in a landslide with historically low turnouts; a year later he'd be gone. Angela Davis was released from prison, finally pronounced not guilty of murder, and was able to begin her next half century of activism.

All across America, community spaces evolved to educate and create storytellers, citizens. In her memoir, Vice President Kamala Harris describes Maya Angelou and Alice Walker coming to her after-school program in Oakland. June Jordan ran poetry workshops at Church of the Open Door in Fort Greene, Brooklyn.

In the meantime, in the country's center, a new journal called *Science Fiction Studies* dedicated a whole issue to the work of Ursula K. Le Guin. By the time "The Ones Who Walk Away from Omelas" was published, Le Guin had been setting tales in Orsina, her fictional country, for over a decade. This classic dystopia disassembles one of the founding engines of so many nations, real or imagined. Whose suffering gets to be invisible for the sake of everyone else?

The 1970s also saw the aftermath of second-wave feminism. One hears its questions in Grace Paley's "A Conversation with My Father," in which her narrator adapts the weave of a story to make it more believable to him, then changes course, giving it a happy ending.

What children learn is beautifully dramatized across several stories. In Raymond Carver's "Bicycles, Muscles, Cigarettes," a child's father tries to officiate a dispute between two boys over bikes and winds up in a fight himself. In Alice Walker's triumphantly brief "The Flowers," a young girl playing outdoors stumbles upon the remains of a person, not unlike how the past mulches right in front of us. Jamaica Kincaid's "Girl" tells all the lessons a young child in the Caribbean is meant to learn from her mother. Meantime, across the country, in a desert, the child protagonist of Lucia Berlin's phenomenal "Silence" pays attention to what she's not supposed to know, growing up in the shadow of unhappy people.

How much more fresh air there is in the American short story when it's not presumed to be realistic. When it isn't bent toward an American Dream. Louise Erdrich's "The Red Convertible" sets fire to such expectations with its tale of two Native American brothers and the car meant to symbolize their happiness. Isaac Bashevis Singer often made humor from the bleakest threads of American life, as he does in "The Reencounter," where a man meets his mistress in the afterlife. The hero of Joy Williams's "Taking Care" stands between his wife and that next stage, whatever it be, facing down an overwhelming loss.

It would take us decades to appreciate what a time the 1980s were for writers. In "Story," Lydia Davis puts down the driving, intense prose style that became her signature, and for which she was rediscovered—"overnight"—in the 2010s. Andrew Holleran hasn't had this moment yet, but "The Penthouse," his fabulous and devastating long story, should make clear he deserves one. It's as if Maupassant were set loose on downtown New York as it careened toward the AIDS crisis.

Love, in all its angles, animates these stories. In "Pet Milk," Stuart Dybek carries two young Chicagoans aloft with the same natural grace of a new love affair. Meantime, in "China," Charles Johnson crawls inside a decades-old marriage that's begun to crack. In "The Way We Live Now," Susan Sontag's story pours from one voice to the next, launching a daisy chain of concern among friends, some of whom were terrified of contracting HIV—and, then, did.

The stakes across so many stories are unbearably high, even when they chronicle why a child comes to school late, as in Sandra Cisneros's masterpiece of flash fiction, "Salvador Late or Early." In his Vietnam War story, "The Things They Carried," Tim O'Brien returns individuality to his soldier characters in dehumanizing circumstances. And in "River of Names," the narrator of Dorothy Allison's tale of growing up poor in the rural South—of all the things she's had to carry—steps through the scrim of fiction to ask if this suffering has moved us yet.

To choose these stories, I read about a thousand works of short fiction over two years. Allison's question to the reader—*Is this enough, have I flayed you?*—is an apt one. How can a story move us and remain somehow true to itself, not a trick? For this reason, when a story made a mark on me, I read it aloud, and often then the difference between manipulation and magic became very clear. Sadness alone never made a story great.

In some stories, though, hilarity and melancholy approach a provocative meeting point, as in Denis Johnson's "Emergency," which unfolds overnight in a hospital as orderlies and nurses try to maintain their sanity. At one point the main character—high and going for a drive—believes he's wandered into a land of gargantuan angels. Actually, it's an all-night drive-in theater playing a film as snow begins to fall.

How hard it is in a tale to capture the unexpected, the clobber of time. George Saunders does both in just 392 words in "Sticks," maybe the best piece of flash fiction of all time; fast on the heels of which is Tobias Wolff's "Bullet in the Brain," wherein a book critic mouths off during a bank robbery and watches his entire life flash before his eyes as he pays the consequences.

America is a violent country, and brutality does seep into these tales. Nathan Englander's "The Twenty-seventh Man" reimagines Stalin's round-up of poets, depicting the denial, absurdity and terror of a state at war with truth. Sometimes a family is the territory of the pain, as in Junot Díaz's "Fiesta, 1980," which churns around a punishing father. Sometimes danger comes from the landscape itself. In Rick Bass's "The Hermit's Tale," a naturalist tells of how she and a hiking companion got lost under a frozen lake, then navigated back to land from beneath the ice by lighting pockets of trapped gasses on fire, detonating their way home.

Here also is the twice-told tale; the story that unfolds on a cold night. Some of the '90s best fiction used sturdy old tools to talk about modern conditions. In Jhumpa Lahiri's "A Temporary Matter," a heart-sick couple from Calcutta now living outside Boston spend a candle-lit snowstorm cooking and telling stories. When the weather finally breaks, they find they haven't rescued a marriage but performed its wake. Percival Everett's "The Fix" effects a similar reversal: introducing a mechanism loaded with potential that leads to tragedy.

During the fifty years these stories span, trends arose that were thought to change writing forever: the rise of television and the internet would make stories short and stupid. This clearly hasn't happened. The explosion of creative writing programs, some argued, would create an army of clones. One need only read Karen Russell and Chimamanda Ngozi Adichie, with their MFAs from Columbia and Johns Hopkins, to see the canard in this claim. Adichie's scorching "The American Embassy" is a powerful fable of the cost of performing pain;

Russell's "St. Lucy's Home for Girls Raised by Wolves" a coming-of-age tale in surreal furs.

Surely this debate was more about migration and class than it was about writing. Can a person leg their way up into a better America with an advanced degree? If their fiction's part of that climb—is it bankrupt? These questions fall hard on the narrator of Aleksandar Hemon's "The Conductor," in which the man's mentor turns up in Iowa City from Bosnia and acts—as Hemon's hero cannot, because he left Sarajevo before the siege—like someone broken by the shock of war.

Societies that fancy themselves in constant motion can be prone to accidents and envy, drift and collateral damage. In Stephen King's "The Dune," a man who learns to predict the future discovers that with the gift come some attendant horrors. The hero of Claire Vaye Watkins's short story looks into the swerve of life out West and spins a note of longing, writing letters to a stranger whose belongings he discovered along the side of a road.

Memory loss is a powerful theme throughout American literature. *What if I un-become myself?* a society that adores movement makes us ask. In Julie Otsuka's powerfully sad story, a woman sinks into the oblivion of Alzheimer's. Ken Liu delivers an exquisite fable of immigration: a man who grows up Chinese American and learns to hate his heritage realizes that his mother spoke to him through a paper menagerie she'd taught him to imagine was real, when her story was the unbelievable tale.

In the future, perhaps much of this work will face one major question: Should it have chronicled the various ecological collapses we now know are underway? In the 2010s, such environmental ethics moved to the center of American fiction. Ted Chiang's story from the voice of a bird, "The Great Silence," imagines what one of its kind might say to us. "The hush of the night sky," the bird warns, "is the silence of a graveyard."

What does one do in the face of a possible apocalypse? Lauren Groff's fiction channels the sound that question makes when it caroms around a domestic space. In "The Midnight Zone," a woman brings her kids on a cabin retreat; everything that can go wrong does, and she waits tensely for things to get worse.

There are many families in America for whom the apocalypse *has* come. It chased them here, or it caught them at the border. Soberly, elegantly, Manuel Muñoz has been telling their stories. In "Anyone Can Do It," he imagines the life of a family of undocumented migrants in an America where any one of them can be taken away, at any time, with no warning and little recourse.

When the heroine of Muñoz's story is tricked by a fellow field hand who makes off with her car, the woman hitches a ride from a foreman back into town. Dropping her off, the man hands her a twenty-dollar bill. "It's not your fault," he says. "And I'm not defending her for what she did. But I believe any story that anybody tells me. You can't be to blame if you got faith in people." And so we turn to tales to lift us up, to make things brighter, to remind us that so much depends on where you start from.

THE LESSON

Toni Cade Bambara • 1972

Back in the days when everyone was old and stupid or young and foolish and me and Sugar were the only ones just right, this lady moved on our block with nappy hair and proper speech and no makeup. And quite naturally we laughed at her, laughed the way we did at the junk man who went about his business like he was some big-time president and his sorry-ass horse his secretary. And we kinda hated her too, hated the way we did the winos who cluttered up our parks and pissed on our handball walls and stank up our hallways and stairs so you couldn't halfway play hide-and-seek without a goddamn gas mask. Miss Moore was her name. The only woman on the block with no first name. And she was black as hell, cept for her feet, which were fish-white and spooky. And she was always planning these boring-ass things for us to do, us being my cousin, mostly, who lived on the block cause we all moved North the same time and to the same apartment then spread out gradual to breathe. And our parents would yank our heads into some kinda shape and crisp up our clothes so we'd be presentable for travel with Miss Moore, who always looked like she was going to church, though she never did. Which is just one of the things the grown-ups talked about when they talked behind her back like a dog. But when she came calling with some sachet she'd sewed up or some gingerbread she'd made or some book, why then they'd all be too embarrassed to turn her down and we'd get handed over all spruced up. She'd been to college and said it was only right that she should take responsibility for the young ones' education, and she not even related by marriage or blood. So they'd go for it. Specially Aunt Gretchen. She was the main gofer in the family. You got some ole dumb shit foolishness you want somebody to go for, you send for Aunt Gretchen. She been screwed into the go-along for so long, it's a blood-deep natural thing with her. Which is how she got saddled with me and Sugar and Junior in the first place while our mothers were in a la-de-da apartment up the block having a good ole time.

So this one day Miss Moore rounds us all up at the mailbox and it's puredee hot and she's knockin herself out about arithmetic. And school suppose to let up in summer I heard, but she don't never let up. And the starch in my pinafore scratching the shit outta me and I'm really hating this nappy-head bitch and her goddamn college degree. I'd much rather go to the pool or to the show where it's cool. So me and Sugar leaning on the mailbox being surly, which is a Miss Moore word. And Flyboy checking out what everybody brought for lunch. And Fat Butt already wasting his peanut-butter-and-jelly sandwich like the pig he is. And Junebug punchin on Q.T.'s arm for potato chips. And Rosie Giraffe shifting from one hip to the other waiting for somebody to step on her foot or ask her if she from Georgia so she can kick ass, preferably Mercedes'. And Miss Moore asking us do we know what money is, like we a bunch of retards. I mean real money, she say, like it's only poker chips or monopoly papers we lay on the grocer. So right away I'm tired of this and say so. And would much rather snatch Sugar and go to the Sunset and terrorize the West Indian kids and take their hair ribbons and their money too. And Miss Moore files that remark away for next week's lesson on brotherhood, I can tell. And finally I say we oughta get to the subway cause it's cooler and besides we might meet some cute boys. Sugar done swiped her mama's lipstick, so we ready.

So we heading down the street and she's boring us silly about what things cost and what our parents make and how much goes for rent and how money ain't divided up right in this country. And then she gets to the part about we all poor and live in the slums, which I don't feature. And I'm ready to speak on that, but she steps out in the street and hails two cabs just like that. Then she hustles half the crew in with her and hands me a five-dollar bill and tells me to calculate 10 percent tip for the driver. And we're off. Me and Sugar and Junebug and Flyboy hangin out the window and hollering to everybody, putting lipstick on each other cause Flyboy a faggot anyway, and making farts with our sweaty armpits. But I'm mostly trying to figure how to spend this money. But they all fascinated with the meter ticking and Junebug starts laying bets as to how much it'll read when Flyboy can't hold his breath no more. Then Sugar lays bets as to how much it'll be when we get there. So I'm stuck. Don't nobody want to go for my plan, which is to jump out at the next light and run off to the first bar-b-que we can find. Then the driver tells us to get the hell out cause we there already. And the meter reads eighty-five cents. And I'm stalling to figure out the tip and Sugar say give him a dime. And I decide he don't need it bad as I do, so later for him. But then he tries to take off with Junebug foot still in the door so we talk about his mama something ferocious. Then we check out that we on Fifth Avenue and everybody dressed up in stockings. One lady in a fur coat, hot as it is. White folks crazy.

"This is the place," Miss Moore say, presenting it to us in the voice she uses at the museum. "Let's look in the windows before we go in."

"Can we steal?" Sugar asks very serious like she's getting the ground rules squared away before she plays. "I beg your pardon," say Miss Moore, and we fall out. So she leads us around the windows of the toy store and me and Sugar screamin, "This is mine, that's mine, I gotta have that, that was made for me, I was born for that," till Big Butt drowns us out.

"Hey, I'm goin to buy that there."

"That there? You don't even know what it is, stupid."

"I do so," he say punchin on Rosie Giraffe. "It's a microscope."

"Whatcha gonna do with a microscope, fool?"

"Look at things."

"Like what, Ronald?" ask Miss Moore. And Big Butt ain't got the first notion. So here go Miss Moore gabbing about the thousands of bacteria in a drop of water and the somethinorother in a speck of blood and the million and one living things in the air around us is invisible to the naked eye. And what she say that for? Junebug go to town on that "naked" and we rolling. Then Miss Moore ask what it cost. So we all jam into the window smudgin it up and the price tag say $300. So then she ask how long'd take for Big Butt and Junebug to save up their allowances. "Too long," I say. "Yeh," adds Sugar, "outgrown it by that time." And Miss Moore say no, you never outgrow learning instruments. "Why, even medical students and interns and," blah, blah, blah. And we ready to choke Big Butt for bringing it up in the first damn place.

"This here costs four hundred eighty dollars," say Rosie Giraffe. So we pile up all over her to see what she pointin out. My eyes tell me it's a chunk of glass cracked with something heavy, and different-color inks dripped into the splits, then the whole thing put into a oven or something. But for $480 it don't make sense.

"That's a paperweight made of semi-precious stones fused together under tremendous pressure," she explains slowly, with her hands doing the mining and all the factory work.

"So what's a paperweight?" asks Rosie Giraffe.

"To weigh paper with, dumbbell," say Flyboy, the wise man from the East.

"Not exactly," say Miss Moore, which is what she say when you warm or way off too. "It's to weigh paper down so it won't scatter and make your desk untidy." So right away me and Sugar curtsy to each other and then to Mercedes who is more the tidy type.

"We don't keep paper on top of the desk in my class," say Junebug, figuring Miss Moore crazy or lyin one.

"At home, then," she say. "Don't you have a calendar and a pencil case and a blotter and a letter-opener on your desk at home where you do your homework?" And she know damn well what our homes look like cause she nosys around in them every chance she gets.

"I don't even have a desk," say Junebug. "Do we?"

"No. And I don't get no homework neither," say Big Butt.

"And I don't even have a home," say Flyboy like he do at school to keep the white folks off his back and sorry for him. Send this poor kid to camp posters, is his specialty.

"I do," says Mercedes. "I have a box of stationery on my desk and a picture of my cat. My godmother bought the stationery and the desk. There's a big rose on each sheet and the envelopes smell like roses."

"Who wants to know about your smelly-ass stationery," say Rosie Giraffe fore I can get my two cents in.

"It's important to have a work area all your own so that . . ."

"Will you look at this sailboat, please," say Flyboy, cuttin her off and pointin to the thing like it was his. So once again we tumble all over each other to gaze at this magnificent thing in the toy store which is just big enough to maybe sail two kittens across the pond if you strap them to the posts tight. We all start reciting the price tag like we in assembly. "Handcrafted sailboat of fiberglass at one thousand one hundred ninety-five dollars."

"Unbelievable," I hear myself say and am really stunned. I read it again for myself just in case the group recitation put me in a trance. Same thing. For some reason this pisses me off. We look at Miss Moore and she lookin at us, waiting for I dunno what.

"Who'd pay all that when you can buy a sailboat set for a quarter at Pop's, a tube of glue for a dime, and a ball of string for eight cents? It must have a motor and a whole lot else besides," I say. "My sailboat cost me about fifty cents."

"But will it take water?" say Mercedes with her smart ass.

"Took mine to Alley Pond Park once," say Flyboy. "String broke. Lost it. Pity."

"Sailed mine in Central Park and it keeled over and sank. Had to ask my father for another dollar."

"And you got the strap," laugh Big Butt. "The jerk didn't even have a string on it. My old man wailed on his behind."

Little Q.T. was staring hard at the sailboat and you could see he wanted it bad. But he too little and somebody'd just take it from him. So what the hell. "This boat for kids, Miss Moore?"

"Parents silly to buy something like that just to get all broke up," say Rosie Giraffe.

"That much money it should last forever," I figure.

"My father'd buy it for me if I wanted it."

"Your father, my ass," say Rosie Giraffe getting a chance to finally push Mercedes.

"Must be rich people shop here," say Q.T.

"You are a very bright boy," say Flyboy. "What was your first clue?" And he rap him on the head with the back of his knuckles, since Q.T. the only one he could get away with. Though Q.T. liable to come up behind you years later and get his licks in when you half expect it.

"What I want to know is," I says to Miss Moore though I never talk to her, I wouldn't give the bitch that satisfaction, "is how much a real boat costs? I figure a thousand'd get you a yacht any day."

"Why don't you check that out," she says, "and report back to the group?" Which really pains my ass. If you gonna mess up a perfectly good swim day least you could do is have some answers. "Let's go in," she say like she got something up her sleeve. Only she don't lead the way. So me and Sugar turn the corner to where the entrance is, but when we get there I kinda hang back. Not that I'm scared, what's there to be afraid of, just a toy store. But I feel funny, shame. But what I got to be shamed about? Got as much right to go in as anybody. But somehow I can't seem to get hold of the door, so I step away for Sugar to lead. But she hangs back too. And I look at her and she looks at me and this is ridiculous. I mean, damn, I have never ever been shy about doing

nothing or going nowhere. But then Mercedes steps up and then Rosie
Giraffe and Big Butt crowd in behind and shove, and next thing we all
stuffed into the doorway with only Mercedes squeezing past us, smoothing out her jumper and walking right down the aisle. Then the rest of
us tumble in like a glued-together jigsaw done all wrong. And people
lookin at us. And it's like the time me and Sugar crashed into the Catholic church on a dare. But once we got in there and everything so hushed
and holy and the candles and the bowin and the handkerchiefs on all
the drooping heads, I just couldn't go through with the plan. Which
was for me to run up to the altar and do a tap dance while Sugar played
the nose flute and messed around in the holy water. And Sugar kept
givin me the elbow. Then later teased me so bad I tied her up in the
shower and turned it on and locked her in. And she'd be there till this
day if Aunt Gretchen hadn't finally figured I was lyin about the boarder
takin a shower.

Same thing in the store. We all walkin on tiptoe and hardly touchin
the games and puzzles and things. And I watched Miss Moore who is
steady watchin us like she waitin for a sign. Like Mama Drewery
watches the sky and sniffs the air and takes note of just how much slant
is in the bird formation. Then me and Sugar bump smack into each
other, so busy gazing at the toys, 'specially the sailboat. But we don't
laugh and go into our fat-lady bump-stomach routine. We just stare at
that price tag. Then Sugar run a finger over the whole boat. And I'm
jealous and want to hit her. Maybe not her, but I sure want to punch
somebody in the mouth.

"Watcha bring us here for, Miss Moore?"

"You sound angry, Sylvia. Are you mad about something?" Givin
me one of them grins like she tellin a grown-up joke that never turns
out to be funny. And she's lookin very closely at me like maybe she
plannin to do my portrait from memory. I'm mad, but I won't give her
that satisfaction. So I slouch around the store bein very bored and say,
"Let's go."

Me and Sugar at the back of the train watchin the tracks whizzin by large then small then gettin gobbled up in the dark. I'm thinkin about this tricky toy I saw in the store. A clown that somersaults on a bar then does chin-ups just cause you yank lightly at his leg. Cost $35. I could see me askin my mother for a $35 birthday clown. "You wanna who that costs what?" she'd say, cocking her head to the side to get a better view of the hole in my head. Thirty-five dollars could buy new bunk beds for Junior and Gretchen's boy. Thirty-five dollars and the whole household could go visit Granddaddy Nelson in the country. Thirty-five dollars would pay for the rent and the piano bill too. Who are these people that spend that much for performing clowns and $1,000 for toy sailboats? What kinda work they do and how they live and how come we ain't in on it? Where we are is who we are, Miss Moore always pointin out. But it don't necessarily have to be that way, she always adds then waits for somebody to say that poor people have to wake up and demand their share of the pie and don't none of us know what kind of pie she talkin about in the first damn place. But she ain't so smart cause I still got her four dollars from the taxi and she sure ain't gettin it. Messin up my day with this shit. Sugar nudges me in my pocket and winks.

Miss Moore lines us up in front of the mailbox where we started from, seem like years ago, and I got a headache for thinkin so hard. And we lean all over each other so we can hold up under the draggy-ass lecture she always finishes us off with at the end before we thank her for borin us to tears. But she just looks at us like she readin tea leaves. Finally she say, "Well, what did you think of F.A.O. Schwarz?"

Rosie Giraffe mumbles, "White folks crazy."

"I'd like to go there again when I get my birthday money," says Mercedes, and we shove her out the pack so she has to lean on the mailbox by herself.

"I'd like a shower. Tiring day," say Flyboy.

Then Sugar surprises me by sayin, "You know, Miss Moore, I don't think all of us here put together eat in a year what that sailboat costs."

And Miss Moore lights up like somebody goosed her. "And?" she say, urging Sugar on. Only I'm standin on her foot so she don't continue.

"Imagine for a minute what kind of society it is in which some people can spend on a toy what it would cost to feed a family of six or seven. What do you think?"

"I think," say Sugar pushing me off her feet like she never done before, cause I whip her ass in a minute, "that this is not much of a democracy if you ask me. Equal chance to pursue happiness means an equal crack at the dough, don't it?" Miss Moore is besides herself and I am disgusted with Sugar's treachery. So I stand on her foot one more time to see if she'll shove me. She shuts up, and Miss Moore looks at me, sorrowfully I'm thinkin. And somethin weird is goin on, I can feel it in my chest.

"Anybody else learn anything today?" lookin dead at me. I walk away and Sugar has to run to catch up and don't even seem to notice when I shrug her arm off my shoulder.

"Well, we got four dollars anyway," she says.

"Uh hunh."

"We could go to Hascombs and get half a chocolate layer and then go to the Sunset and still have plenty money for potato chips and ice-cream sodas."

"Uh hunh."

"Race you to Hascombs," she say.

We start down the block and she gets ahead which is O.K. by me cause I'm goin to the West End and then over to the Drive to think this day through. She can run if she want to and even run faster. But ain't nobody gonna beat me at nuthin.

A CONVERSATION
WITH MY FATHER

Grace Paley · 1972

My father is eighty-six years old and in bed. His heart, that bloody motor, is equally old and will not do certain jobs any more. It still floods his head with brainy light. But it won't let his legs carry the weight of his body around the house. Despite my metaphors, this muscle failure is not due to his old heart, he says, but to a potassium shortage. Sitting on one pillow, leaning on three, he offers last-minute advice and makes a request.

"I would like you to write a simple story just once more," he says, "the kind de Maupassant wrote, or Chekhov, the kind you used to write. Just recognizable people and then write down what happened to them next."

I say, "Yes, why not? That's possible." I want to please him, though I don't remember writing that way. I *would* like to try to tell such a story, if he means the kind that begins: "There was a woman . . ." followed by plot, the absolute line between two points which I've always despised. Not for literary reasons, but because it takes all hope away. Everyone, real or invented, deserves the open destiny of life.

Finally I thought of a story that had been happening for a couple of years right across the street. I wrote it down, then read it aloud. "Pa," I said, "how about this? Do you mean something like this?"

Once in my time there was a woman and she had a son. They lived nicely, in a small apartment in Manhattan. This boy at about fifteen became a junkie, which is not unusual in our neighborhood. In order to maintain her close friendship with him, she became a junkie too. She said it was part of the youth culture, with which she felt very much at home. After a while, for a number of reasons, the boy gave it all up and left the city and his mother in disgust. Hopeless and alone, she grieved. We all visit her.

"O.K., Pa, that's it," I said, "an unadorned and miserable tale."

"But that's not what I mean," my father said. "You misunderstood me on purpose. You know there's a lot more to it. You know that. You left everything out. Turgenev wouldn't do that. Chekhov wouldn't do that. There are in fact Russian writers you never heard of, you don't have an inkling of, as good as anyone, who can write a plain ordinary story, who would not leave out what you have left out. I object not to facts but to people sitting in trees talking senselessly, voices from who knows where . . ."

"Forget that one, Pa, what have I left out now? In this one?"

"Her looks, for instance."

"Oh. Quite handsome, I think. Yes."

"Her hair?"

"Dark, with heavy braids, as though she were a girl or a foreigner."

"What were her parents like, her stock? That she became such a person. It's interesting, you know."

"From out of town. Professional people. The first to be divorced in their county. How's that? Enough?" I asked.

"With you, it's all a joke," he said. "What about the boy's father?

Why didn't you mention him? Who was he? Or was the boy born out of wedlock?"

"Yes," I said. "He was born out of wedlock."

"For Godsakes, doesn't anyone in your stories get married? Doesn't anyone have the time to run down to City Hall before they jump into bed?"

"No," I said. "In real life, yes. But in my stories, no."

"Why do you answer me like that?"

"Oh, Pa, this is a simple story about a smart woman who came to N.Y.C. full of interest love trust excitement very up to date, and about her son, what a hard time she had in this world. Married or not, it's of small consequence."

"It is of great consequence," he said.

"O.K.," I said.

"O.K. O.K. yourself," he said, "but listen. I believe you that she's good-looking, but I don't think she was so smart."

"That's true," I said. "Actually that's the trouble with stories. People start out fantastic. You think they're extraordinary, but it turns out as the work goes along, they're just average with a good education. Sometimes the other way around, the person's a kind of dumb innocent, but he outwits you and you can't even think of an ending good enough."

"What do you do then?" he asked. He had been a doctor for a couple of decades and then an artist for a couple of decades and he's still interested in details, craft, technique.

"Well, you just have to let the story lie around till some agreement can be reached between you and the stubborn hero."

"Aren't you talking silly, now?" he asked. "Start again," he said. "It so happens I'm not going out this evening. Tell the story again. See what you can do this time."

"O.K.," I said. "But it's not a five-minute job." Second attempt:

Once, across the street from us, there was a fine handsome woman, our neighbor. She had a son whom she loved because she'd known him since birth (in helpless chubby infancy, and in the wrestling, hugging ages, seven to ten, as well as earlier and later). This boy, when he fell into the fist of adolescence, became a junkie. He was not a hopeless one. He was in fact hopeful, an ideologue and successful converter. With his busy brilliance, he wrote persuasive articles for his high-school newspaper. Seeking a wider audience, using important connections, he drummed into Lower Manhattan newsstand distribution a periodical called *Oh! Golden Horse!*

In order to keep him from feeling guilty (because guilt is the stony heart of nine tenths of all clinically diagnosed cancers in America today, she said), and because she had always believed in giving bad habits room at home where one could keep an eye on them, she too became a junkie. Her kitchen was famous for a while—a center for intellectual addicts who knew what they were doing. A few felt artistic like Coleridge and others were scientific and revolutionary like Leary. Although she was often high herself, certain good mothering reflexes remained, and she saw to it that there was lots of orange juice around and honey and milk and vitamin pills. However, she never cooked anything but chili, and that no more than once a week. She explained, when we talked to her, seriously, with neighborly concern, that it was her part in the youth culture and she would rather be with the young, it was an honor, than with her own generation.

One week, while nodding through an Antonioni film, this boy was severely jabbed by the elbow of a stern and proselytizing girl, sitting beside him. She offered immediate apricots and nuts for his sugar level, spoke to him sharply, and took him home.

She had heard of him and his work and she herself published, edited, and wrote a competitive journal called *Man Does Live By Bread Alone.* In the organic heat of her continuous presence he could not help but become interested once more in his muscles, his arteries, and nerve connections. In fact he began to love them, treasure them, praise them with funny little songs in *Man Does Live*...

> *the fingers of my flesh transcend*
> *my transcendental soul*
> *the tightness in my shoulders end*
> *my teeth have made me whole*

To the mouth of his head (that glory of will and determination) he brought hard apples, nuts, wheat germ, and soybean oil. He said to his old friends, From now on, I guess I'll keep my wits about me. I'm going on the natch. He said he was about to begin a spiritual deep-breathing journey. How about you too, Mom? he asked kindly.

His conversion was so radiant, splendid, that neighborhood kids his age began to say that he had never been a real addict at all, only a journalist along for the smell of the story. The mother tried several times to give up what had become without her son and his friends a lonely habit. This effort only brought it to supportable levels. The boy and his girl took their electronic mimeograph and moved to the bushy edge of another borough. They were very strict. They said they would not see her again until she had been off drugs for sixty days.

At home alone in the evening, weeping, the mother read and reread the seven issues of *Oh! Golden Horse!* They seemed to her as truthful as ever. We often crossed the street to visit and console. But if we mentioned any of our children who were at college or in the hospital or dropouts at home, she would cry out, My baby! My baby! and burst into terrible, face-scarring, time-consuming tears. The End.

First my father was silent, then he said, "Number One: You have a nice sense of humor. Number Two: I see you can't tell a plain story. So don't waste time." Then he said sadly, "Number Three: I suppose that means she was alone, she was left like that, his mother. Alone. Probably sick?"

I said, "Yes."

"Poor woman. Poor girl, to be born in a time of fools, to live among fools. The end. The end. You were right to put that down. The end."

I didn't want to argue, but I had to say, "Well, it is not necessarily the end, Pa."

"Yes," he said, "what a tragedy. The end of a person."

"No, Pa," I begged him. "It doesn't have to be. She's only about forty. She could be a hundred different things in this world as time goes on. A teacher or a social worker. An ex-junkie! Sometimes it's better than having a master's in education."

"Jokes," he said. "As a writer that's your main trouble. You don't want to recognize it. Tragedy! Plain tragedy! Historical tragedy! No hope. The end."

"Oh, Pa," I said. "She could change."

"In your own life, too, you have to look it in the face." He took a couple of nitroglycerin. "Turn to five," he said, pointing to the dial on the oxygen tank. He inserted the tubes into his nostrils and breathed deep. He closed his eyes and said, "No."

I had promised the family to always let him have the last word when arguing, but in this case I had a different responsibility. That woman lives across the street. She's my knowledge and my invention. I'm sorry for her. I'm not going to leave her there in that house crying. (Actually neither would Life, which unlike me has no pity.)

Therefore: She did change. Of course her son never came home again. But right now, she's the receptionist in a storefront community clinic in the East Village. Most of the customers are young people, some old friends. The head doctor has said to her, "If we only had three people in this clinic with your experiences . . ."

"The doctor said that?" My father took the oxygen tubes out of his nostrils and said, "Jokes. Jokes again."

"No, Pa, it could really happen that way, it's a funny world nowadays."

"No," he said. "Truth first. She will slide back. A person must have character. She does not."

"No, Pa," I said. "That's it. She's got a job. Forget it. She's in that storefront working."

"How long will it be?" he asked. "Tragedy! You too. When will you look it in the face?"

THE ONES WHO WALK
AWAY FROM OMELAS

(VARIATIONS ON A THEME BY WILLIAM JAMES)

Ursula K. Le Guin · 1973

With a clamor of bells that set the swallows soaring, the Festival of Summer came to the city Omelas, bright-towered by the sea. The rigging of the boats in harbor sparkled with flags. In the streets between houses with red roofs and painted walls, between old moss-grown gardens and under avenues of trees, past great parks and public buildings, processions moved. Some were decorous: old people in long stiff robes of mauve and grey, grave master workmen, quiet, merry women carrying their babies and chatting as they walked. In other streets the music beat faster, a shimmering of gong and tambourine, and the people went dancing, the procession was a dance. Children dodged in and out, their high calls rising like the swallows' crossing flights over the music and the singing. All the processions wound towards the north side of the city, where on the great water-meadow called the Green Fields boys and girls, naked in the bright air, with mud-stained feet and ankles and long, lithe arms, exercised their restive horses before the race. The horses wore no gear at all but a halter without bit. Their manes were braided with streamers of silver, gold, and green. They flared their nostrils and pranced and boasted to one another; they were vastly excited, the horse being the only animal who has adopted our ceremonies as his own. Far off to the north and west the mountains stood up half encircling Omelas on her bay. The air of morning was so clear that the snow still crowning the Eighteen Peaks burned with white-gold fire across the miles of sunlit air, under the dark blue of the sky. There was just enough wind to make the banners that marked the racecourse snap and flutter now and then. In the silence of the broad green meadows one could hear the music winding through the city streets, farther and nearer and ever approaching, a cheerful faint sweetness of the air that from time to time trembled and gathered together and broke out into the great joyous clanging of the bells.

Joyous! How is one to tell about joy? How to describe the citizens of Omelas?

They were not simple folk, you see, though they were happy. But we do not say the words of cheer much any more. All smiles have become archaic. Given a description such as this one tends to make certain assumptions. Given a description such as this one tends to look next for the King, mounted on a splendid stallion and surrounded by his noble knights, or perhaps in a golden litter borne by great-muscled slaves. But there was no king. They did not use swords, or keep slaves. They were not barbarians. I do not know the rules and laws of their society, but I suspect that they were singularly few. As they did without monarchy and slavery, so they also got on without the stock exchange, the advertisement, the secret police, and the bomb. Yet I repeat that these were not simple folk, not dulcet shepherds, noble savages, bland Utopians. They were not less complex than us. The trouble is that we have a bad habit, encouraged by pedants and sophisticates, of considering happiness as something rather stupid. Only pain is intellectual, only evil interesting. This is the treason of the artist: a refusal to admit the banality of evil and the terrible boredom of pain. If you can't lick 'em, join 'em.

THE ONES WHO WALK AWAY FROM OMELAS 19

If it hurts, repeat it. But to praise despair is to condemn delight, to embrace violence is to lose hold of everything else. We have almost lost hold; we can no longer describe a happy man, nor make any celebration of joy. How can I tell you about the people of Omelas? They were not naïve and happy children—though their children were, in fact, happy. They were mature, intelligent, passionate adults whose lives were not wretched. O miracle! but I wish I could describe it better. I wish I could convince you. Omelas sounds in my words like a city in a fairy tale, long ago and far away, once upon a time. Perhaps it would be best if you imagined it as your own fancy bids, assuming it will rise to the occasion, for certainly I cannot suit you all. For instance, how about technology? I think that there would be no cars or helicopters in and above the streets; this follows from the fact that the people of Omelas are happy people. Happiness is based on a just discrimination of what is necessary, what is neither necessary nor destructive, and what is destructive. In the middle category, however—that of the unnecessary but undestructive, that of comfort, luxury, exuberance, etc.—they could perfectly well have central heating, subway trains, washing machines, and all kinds of marvelous devices not yet invented here, floating light-sources, fuelless power, a cure for the common cold. Or they could have none of that: it doesn't matter. As you like it. I incline to think that people from towns up and down the coast have been coming in to Omelas during the last days before the Festival on very fast little trains and double-decked trams, and that the train station of Omelas is actually the handsomest building in town, though plainer than the magnificent Farmers' Market. But even granted trains, I fear that Omelas so far strikes some of you as goody-goody. Smiles, bells, parades, horses, bleh. If so, please add an orgy. If an orgy would help, don't hesitate. Let us not, however, have temples from which issue beautiful nude priests and priestesses already half in ecstasy and ready to copulate with any man or woman, lover or stranger, who desires union with the deep godhead of the blood, although that was my first idea. But really it would be better not to have men wear her flowers in their shining hair. A child of nine or ten sits at the edge of the crowd, alone, playing on a wooden flute. People pause to listen, and they smile, but they do not speak to him, for he never ceases playing and never sees them, his dark eyes wholly rapt in the sweet, thin magic of the tune.

He finishes, and slowly lowers his hands holding the wooden flute.

As if that little private silence were the signal, all at once a trumpet sounds from the pavilion near the starting line: imperious, melancholy, piercing. The horses rear on their slender legs, and some of them neigh in answer. Sober-faced, the young riders stroke the horses' necks and soothe them, whispering, "Quiet, quiet, there my beauty, my hope. . . ." They begin to form in rank along the starting line. The crowds along the racecourse are like a field of grass and flowers in the wind. The Festival of Summer has begun.

Do you believe? Do you accept the festival, the city, the joy? No? Then let me describe one more thing.

In a basement under one of the beautiful public buildings of Omelas, or perhaps in the cellar of one of its spacious private homes, there is a room. It has one locked door, and no window. A little light seeps in dustily between cracks in the boards, secondhand from a cobwebbed window somewhere across the cellar. In one corner of the little room a couple of mops, with stiff, clotted, foul-smelling heads, stand near a rusty bucket. The floor is dirt, a little damp to the touch, as cellar dirt usually is. The room is about three paces long and two wide: a mere broom closet or disused tool room. In the room a child is sitting. It could be a boy or a girl. It looks about six, but actually is nearly ten. It is feeble-minded. Perhaps it was born defective, or perhaps it has become imbecile through fear, malnutrition, and neglect. It picks its nose and occasionally fumbles vaguely with its toes or genitals, as it sits hunched in the corner farthest from the bucket and the two mops. It is afraid of the mops. It finds them horrible. It shuts its eyes, but it knows the mops are still standing there; and the door is locked; and nobody will come. The door is always locked; and nobody ever comes, except that sometimes—the child has no understanding of time or interval—sometimes the door rattles terribly and opens, and a person, or several people, are there. One of them may come in and kick the child to make it stand up. The others never come close, but peer in at it with frightened, disgusted eyes. The food bowl and the water jug are hastily filled, the door is locked, the eyes disappear. The people at the door never say anything, but the child, who has not always lived in the tool room, and can remember sunlight and its mother's voice, sometimes speaks. "I will be good," it says. "Please let me out. I will be good!" They never answer. The child used to scream for help at night, and cry a good deal, but now it only makes a kind of whining, "eh-haa, eh-haa," and it speaks less and less often. It is so thin there are no calves to its legs; its belly protrudes; it lives on a half-bowl of corn meal and grease a day. It is naked. Its buttocks and thighs are a mass of festered sores, as it sits in its own excrement continually.

They all know it is there, all the people of Omelas. Some of them have come to see it, others are content merely to know it is there. They all know that it has to be there. Some of them understand why, and some do not, but they all understand that their happiness, the beauty of their city, the tenderness of their friendships, the health of their children, the wisdom of their scholars, the skill of their makers, even the abundance of their harvest and the kindly weathers of their skies, depend wholly on this child's abominable misery.

This is usually explained to children when they are between eight and twelve, whenever they seem capable of understanding; and most of those who come to see the child are young people, though often enough an adult comes, or comes back, to see the child. No matter how well the matter has been explained to them, these young spectators are always shocked and sickened at the sight. They feel disgust, which they had thought themselves superior to. They feel anger, outrage, impotence, despite all the explanations. They would like to do something for the child.

But there is nothing they can do. If the child were brought up into the sunlight out of that vile place, if it were cleaned and fed and comforted, that would be a good thing, indeed; but if it were done, in that day and hour all the prosperity and beauty and delight of Omelas would wither and be destroyed. Those are the terms. To exchange all the goodness and grace of every life in Omelas for that single, small improvement: to throw away the happiness of thousands for the chance of the happiness of one: that would be to let guilt within the walls indeed.

The terms are strict and absolute; there may not even be a kind word spoken to the child.

Often the young people go home in tears, or in a tearless rage, when they have seen the child and faced this terrible paradox. They may brood over it for weeks or years. But as time goes on they begin to realize that even if the child could be released, it would not get much good of its freedom: a little vague pleasure of warmth and food, no doubt, but little more. It is too degraded and imbecile to know any real joy. It has been afraid too long ever to be free of fear. Its habits are too uncouth for it to respond to humane treatment. Indeed, after so long it would probably be wretched without walls about it to protect it, and darkness for its eyes, and its own excrement to sit in. Their tears at the bitter injustice dry when they begin to perceive the terrible justice of reality, and to accept it. Yet it is their tears and anger, the trying of their generosity and the acceptance of their helplessness, which are perhaps the true source of the splendor of their lives. Theirs is no vapid, irresponsible happiness. They know that they, like the child, are not free. They know compassion. It is the existence of the child, and their knowledge of its existence, that makes possible the nobility of their architecture, the poignancy of their music, the profundity of their science. It is because of the child that they are so gentle with children. They know that if the wretched one were not there snivelling in the dark, the other one, the flute-player, could make no joyful music as the young riders line up in their beauty for the race in the sunlight of the first morning of summer.

Now do you believe in them? Are they not more credible? But there is one more thing to tell, and this is quite incredible.

At times one of the adolescent girls or boys who go to see the child does not go home to weep or rage, does not, in fact, go home at all. Sometimes also a man or woman much older falls silent for a day or two, and then leaves home. These people go out into the street, and walk down the street alone. They keep walking, and walk straight out of the city of Omelas, through the beautiful gates. They keep walking across the farmlands of Omelas. Each one goes alone, youth or girl, man or woman. Night falls; the traveler must pass down village streets, between the houses with yellow-lit windows, and on out into the darkness of the fields. Each alone, they go west or north, towards the mountains. They go on. They leave Omelas, they walk ahead into the darkness, and they do not come back. The place they go towards is a place even less imaginable to most of us than the city of happiness. I cannot describe it at all. It is possible that it does not exist. But they seem to know where they are going, the ones who walk away from Omelas.

BICYCLES, MUSCLES, CIGARETTES

Raymond Carver · 1973

I t had been two days since Evan Hamilton had stopped smoking, and it seemed to him everything he'd said and thought for the two days somehow suggested cigarettes. He looked at his hands under the kitchen light. He sniffed his knuckles and his fingers.

"I can smell it," he said.

"I know. It's as if it sweats out of you," Ann Hamilton said. "For three days after I stopped I could smell it on me. Even when I got out of the bath. It was disgusting." She was putting plates on the table for dinner. "I'm so sorry, dear. I know what you're going through. But, if it's any consolation, the second day is always the hardest. The third day is hard, too, of course, but from then on, if you can stay with it that long, you're over the hump. But I'm so happy you're serious about quitting, I can't tell you." She touched his arm. "Now, if you'll just call Roger, we'll eat."

Hamilton opened the front door. It was already dark. It was early in November and the days were short and cool. An older boy he had never seen before was sitting on a small, well-equipped bicycle in the driveway. The boy leaned forward just off the seat, the toes of his shoes touching the pavement and keeping him upright.

"You Mr. Hamilton?" the boy said.

"Yes, I am," Hamilton said. "What is it? Is it Roger?"

"I guess Roger is down at my house talking to my mother. Kip is there and this boy named Gary Berman. It is about my brother's bike. I don't know for sure," the boy said, twisting the handle grips, "but my mother asked me to come and get you. One of Roger's parents."

"But he's all right?" Hamilton said. "Yes, of course, I'll be right with you."

He went into the house to put his shoes on.

"Did you find him?" Ann Hamilton said.

"He's in some kind of jam," Hamilton answered. "Over a bicycle. Some boy—I didn't catch his name—is outside. He wants one of us to go back with him to his house."

"Is he all right?" Ann Hamilton said and took her apron off.

"Sure, he's all right." Hamilton looked at her and shook his head. "It sounds like it's just a childish argument, and the boy's mother is getting herself involved."

"Do you want me to go?" Ann Hamilton asked.

He thought for a minute. "Yes, I'd rather you went, but I'll go. Just hold dinner until we're back. We shouldn't be long."

"I don't like his being out after dark," Ann Hamilton said. "I don't like it."

The boy was sitting on his bicycle and working the handbrake now.

"How far?" Hamilton said as they started down the sidewalk.

"Over in Arbuckle Court," the boy answered, and when Hamilton looked at him, the boy added, "Not far. About two blocks from here."

"What seems to be the trouble?" Hamilton asked.

"I don't know for sure. I don't understand all of it. He and Kip and this Gary Berman are supposed to have used my brother's bike while we were on vacation, and I guess they wrecked it. On purpose. But I don't know. Anyway, that's what they're talking about. My brother can't find his bike and they had it last, Kip and Roger. My mom is trying to find out where it's at."

"I know Kip," Hamilton said. "Who's this other boy?"

"Gary Berman. I guess he's new in the neighborhood. His dad is coming as soon as he gets home."

They turned a corner. The boy pushed himself along, keeping just slightly ahead. Hamilton saw an orchard, and then they turned another corner onto a dead-end street. He hadn't known of the existence of this street and was sure he would not recognize any of the people who lived here. He looked around him at the unfamiliar houses and was struck with the range of his son's personal life.

The boy turned into a driveway and got off the bicycle and leaned it against the house. When the boy opened the front door, Hamilton followed him through the living room and into the kitchen, where he saw his son sitting on one side of a table along with Kip Hollister and another boy. Hamilton looked closely at Roger and then he turned to the stout, dark-haired woman at the head of the table.

"You're Roger's father?" the woman said to him.

"Yes, my name is Evan Hamilton. Good evening."

"I'm Mrs. Miller, Gilbert's mother," she said. "Sorry to ask you over here, but we have a problem."

Hamilton sat down in a chair at the other end of the table and looked around. A boy of nine or ten, the boy whose bicycle was missing, Hamilton supposed, sat next to the woman. Another boy, fourteen or so, sat on the draining board, legs dangling, and watched another boy who was talking on the telephone. Grinning slyly at something that had just been said to him over the line, the boy reached over to the sink with a cigarette. Hamilton heard the sound of the cigarette sputting out in a glass of water. The boy who had brought him leaned against the refrigerator and crossed his arms.

"Did you get one of Kip's parents?" the woman said to the boy.

"His sister said they were shopping. I went to Gary Berman's and his father will be here in a few minutes. I left the address."

"Mr. Hamilton," the woman said, "I'll tell you what happened. We were on vacation last month and Kip wanted to borrow Gilbert's bike so that Roger could help him with Kip's paper route. I guess Roger's bike had a flat tire or something. Well, as it turns out—"

"Gary was choking me, Dad," Roger said.

"What?" Hamilton said, looking at his son carefully.

"He was choking me. I got the marks." His son pulled down the collar of his T-shirt to show his neck.

"They were out in the garage," the woman continued. "I didn't know what they were doing until Curt, my oldest, went out to see."

"He started it!" Gary Berman said to Hamilton. "He called me a jerk." Gary Berman looked toward the front door.

"I think my bike cost about sixty dollars, you guys," the boy named Gilbert said. "You can pay me for it."

"You keep out of this, Gilbert," the woman said to him.

Hamilton took a breath. "Go on," he said.

"Well, as it turns out, Kip and Roger used Gilbert's bike to help Kip deliver his papers, and then the two of them, and Gary too, they say, took turns rolling it."

"What do you mean 'rolling it'?" Hamilton said.

"Rolling it," the woman said. "Sending it down the street with a push and letting it fall over. Then, mind you—and they just admitted this a few minutes ago—Kip and Roger took it up to the school and threw it against a goalpost."

"Is that true, Roger?" Hamilton said, looking at his son again.

"Part of it's true, Dad," Roger said, looking down and rubbing his finger over the table. "But we only rolled it once. Kip did it, then Gary, and then I did it."

"Once is too much," Hamilton said. "Once is one too many times, Roger. I'm surprised and disappointed in you. And you too, Kip," Hamilton said.

"But you see," the woman said, "someone's fibbing tonight or else not telling all he knows, for the fact is the bike's still missing."

The older boys in the kitchen laughed and kidded with the boy who still talked on the telephone.

"We don't know where the bike is, Mrs. Miller," the boy named Kip said. "We told you already. The last time we saw it was when me and Roger took it to my house after we had it at school. I mean, that was the next to last time. The very last time was when I took it back here the next morning and parked it behind the house." He shook his head. "We don't know where it is," the boy said.

"Sixty dollars," the boy named Gilbert said to the boy named Kip. "You can pay me off like five dollars a week."

"Gilbert, I'm warning you," the woman said. "You see, *they* claim," the woman went on, frowning now, "it disappeared from *here*, from behind the house. But how can we believe them when they haven't been all that truthful this evening?"

"We've told the truth," Roger said. "Everything."

Gilbert leaned back in his chair and shook his head at Hamilton's son.

The doorbell sounded and the boy on the draining board jumped down and went into the living room.

A stiff-shouldered man with a crew haircut and sharp gray eyes entered the kitchen without speaking. He glanced at the woman and moved over behind Gary Berman's chair.

"You must be Mr. Berman?" the woman said. "Happy to meet you. I'm Gilbert's mother, and this is Mr. Hamilton, Roger's father."

The man inclined his head at Hamilton but did not offer his hand.

"What's all this about?" Berman said to his son.

The boys at the table began to speak at once.

"Quiet down!" Berman said. "I'm talking to Gary. You'll get your turn."

The boy began his account of the affair. His father listened closely, now and then narrowing his eyes to study the other two boys.

When Gary Berman had finished, the woman said, "I'd like to get to the bottom of this. I'm not accusing any one of them, you understand, Mr. Hamilton, Mr. Berman—I'd just like to get to the bottom of this." She looked steadily at Roger and Kip, who were shaking their heads at Gary Berman.

"It's not true, Gary," Roger said.

"Dad, can I talk to you in private?" Gary Berman said.

"Let's go," the man said, and they walked into the living room.

Hamilton watched them go. He had the feeling he should stop them, this secrecy. His palms were wet, and he reached to his shirt pocket for a cigarette. Then, breathing deeply, he passed the back of his hand under his nose and said, "Roger, do you know any more about this, other than what you've already said? Do you know where Gilbert's bike is?"

"No, I don't," the boy said. "I swear it."

"When was the last time you saw the bicycle?" Hamilton said.

"When we brought it home from school and left it at Kip's house."

"Kip," Hamilton said, "do you know where Gilbert's bicycle is now?"

"I swear I don't, either," the boy answered. "I brought it back the next morning after we had it at school and I parked it behind the garage."

"I thought you said you left it behind the *house*," the woman said quickly.

"I mean the house! That's what I meant," the boy said.

"Did you come back here some other day to ride it?" she asked, leaning forward.

"No, I didn't," Kip answered.

"Kip?" she said.

"I didn't! I don't know where it is!" the boy shouted.

The woman raised her shoulders and let them drop. "How do you know who or what to believe?" she said to Hamilton. "All I know is, Gilbert's missing a bicycle."

G ary Berman and his father returned to the kitchen.

"It was Roger's idea to roll it," Gary Berman said.

"It was yours!" Roger said, coming out of his chair. "You wanted to! Then you wanted to take it to the orchard and strip it!"

"You shut up!" Berman said to Roger. "You can speak when spoken to, young man, not before. Gary, I'll handle this—dragged out at night because of a couple of roughnecks! Now if either of you," Berman said, looking first at Kip and then Roger, "know where this kid's bicycle is, I'd advise you to start talking."

"I think you're getting out of line," Hamilton said.

"What?" Berman said, his forehead darkening. "And I think you'd do better to mind your own business!"

"Let's go, Roger," Hamilton said, standing up. "Kip, you come now or stay." He turned to the woman. "I don't know what else we can do tonight. I intend to talk this over more with Roger, but if there is a question of restitution I feel since Roger did help manhandle the bike, he can pay a third if it comes to that."

"I don't know what to say," the woman replied, following Hamilton through the living room. "I'll talk to Gilbert's father—he's out of town now. We'll see. It's probably one of those things finally, but I'll talk to his father."

Hamilton moved to one side so that the boys could pass ahead of him onto the porch, and from behind him he heard Gary Berman say, "He called me a jerk, Dad."

"He did, did he?" Hamilton heard Berman say. "Well, he's the jerk. He looks like a jerk."

Hamilton turned and said, "I think you're seriously out of line here tonight, Mr. Berman. Why don't you get control of yourself?"

"And I told you I think you should keep out of it!" Berman said.

"You get home, Roger," Hamilton said, moistening his lips. "I mean it," he said, "get going!" Roger and Kip moved out to the sidewalk. Hamilton stood in the doorway and looked at Berman, who was crossing the living room with his son.

"Mr. Hamilton," the woman began nervously but did not finish.

"What do you want?" Berman said to him. "Watch out now, get out of my way!" Berman brushed Hamilton's shoulder and Hamilton stepped off the porch into some prickly cracking bushes. He couldn't believe it was happening. He moved out of the bushes and lunged at the man where he stood on the porch. They fell heavily onto the lawn. They rolled on the lawn, Hamilton wrestling Berman onto his back and coming down hard with his knees on the man's biceps. He had Berman by the collar now and began to pound his head against the lawn while the woman cried, "God almighty, someone stop them! For God's sake, someone call the police!"

Hamilton stopped.

Berman looked up at him and said, "Get off me."

"Are you all right?" the woman called to the men as they separated. "For God's sake," she said. She looked at the men, who stood a few feet apart, backs to each other, breathing hard. The older boys had crowded onto the porch to watch; now that it was over, they waited, watching the men, and then they began feinting and punching each other on the arms and ribs.

"You boys get back in the house," the woman said. "I never thought I'd see," she said and put her hand on her breast.

Hamilton was sweating and his lungs burned when he tried to take a deep breath. There was a ball of something in his throat so that he couldn't swallow for a minute. He started walking, his son and the boy named Kip at his sides. He heard car doors slam, an engine start. Headlights swept over him as he walked.

Roger sobbed once, and Hamilton put his arm around the boy's shoulders.

"I better get home," Kip said and began to cry. "My dad'll be looking for me," and the boy ran.

I'm sorry," Hamilton said. "I'm sorry you had to see something like that," Hamilton said to his son.

They kept walking and when they reached their block, Hamilton took his arm away.

"What if he'd picked up a knife, Dad? Or a club?"

"He wouldn't have done anything like that," Hamilton said.

"But what if he had?" his son said.

"It's hard to say what people will do when they're angry," Hamilton said.

They started up the walk to their door. His heart moved when Hamilton saw the lighted windows.

"Let me feel your muscle," his son said.

"Not now," Hamilton said. "You just go in now and have your dinner and hurry up to bed. Tell your mother I'm all right and I'm going to sit on the porch for a few minutes."

The boy rocked from one foot to the other and looked at his father, and then he dashed into the house and began calling, "Mom! Mom!"

He sat on the porch and leaned against the garage wall and stretched his legs. The sweat had dried on his forehead. He felt clammy under his clothes.

He had once seen his father—a pale, slow-talking man with slumped

shoulders—in something like this. It was a bad one, and both men had
been hurt. It had happened in a cafe. The other man was a farmhand.
Hamilton had loved his father and could recall many things about him.
But now he recalled his father's one fistfight as if it were all there was to
the man.

He was still sitting on the porch when his wife came out.

"Dear God," she said and took his head in her hands. "Come in and
shower and then have something to eat and tell me about it. Everything
is still warm. Roger has gone to bed."

But he heard his son calling him.

"He's still awake," she said.

"I'll be down in a minute," Hamilton said. "Then maybe we should
have a drink."

She shook her head. "I really don't believe any of this yet."

He went into the boy's room and sat down at the foot of the bed.

"It's pretty late and you're still up, so I'll say good night," Hamilton said.

"Good night," the boy said, hands behind his neck, elbows jutting.

He was in his pajamas and had a warm fresh smell about him that
Hamilton breathed deeply. He patted his son through the covers.

"You take it easy from now on. Stay away from that part of the
neighborhood, and don't let me ever hear of you damaging a bicycle or
any other personal property. Is that clear?" Hamilton said.

The boy nodded. He took his hands from behind his neck and began
picking at something on the bedspread.

"Okay, then," Hamilton said, "I'll say good night."

He moved to kiss his son, but the boy began talking.

"Dad, was Grandfather strong like you? When he was your age, I
mean, you know, and you—"

"And I was nine years old? Is that what you mean? Yes, I guess he
was," Hamilton said.

"Sometimes I can hardly remember him," the boy said. "I don't want to forget him or anything, you know? You know what I mean, Dad?"

When Hamilton did not answer at once, the boy went on. "When you were young, was it like it is with you and me? Did you love him more than me? Or just the same?" The boy said this abruptly. He moved his feet under the covers and looked away. When Hamilton still did not answer, the boy said, "Did he smoke? I think I remember a pipe or something."

"He started smoking a pipe before he died, that's true," Hamilton said. "He used to smoke cigarettes a long time ago and then he'd get depressed with something or other and quit, but later he'd change brands and start in again. Let me show you something," Hamilton said. "Smell the back of my hand."

The boy took the hand in his, sniffed it, and said, "I guess I don't smell anything, Dad. What is it?"

Hamilton sniffed the hand and then the fingers. "Now I can't smell anything, either," he said. "It was there before, but now it's gone." Maybe it was scared out of me, he thought. "I wanted to show you something. All right, it's late now. You better go to sleep," Hamilton said.

The boy rolled onto his side and watched his father walk to the door and watched him put his hand to the switch. And then the boy said, "Dad? You'll think I'm pretty crazy, but I wish I'd known you when you were little. I mean, about as old as I am right now. I don't know how to say it, but I'm lonesome about it. It's like—it's like I miss you already if I think about it now. That's pretty crazy, isn't it? Anyway, please leave the door open."

Hamilton left the door open, and then he thought better of it and closed it halfway.

THE FLOWERS

Alice Walker • 1973

It seemed to Myop as she skipped lightly from hen house to pigpen to smoke-house that the days had never been as beautiful as these. The air held a keenness that made her nose twitch. The harvesting of the corn and cot-ton, peanuts and squash, made each day a golden surprise that caused excited little tremors to run up her jaws.

Myop carried a short, knobby stick. She struck out at random at chickens she liked, and worked out the beat of a song on the fence around the pigpen. She felt light and good in the warm sun. She was ten, and nothing existed for her but her song, the stick clutched in her dark brown hand, and the tat-de-ta-ta-ta of accompaniment.

Turning her back on the rusty boards of her family's sharecropper cabin, Myop walked along the fence till it ran into the stream made by the spring. Around the spring, where the family got drinking water, silver ferns and wildflowers grew. Along the shallow banks pigs rooted. Myop watched the tiny white bubbles disrupt the thin black scale of soil and the water that si-lently rose and slid away down the stream.

She had explored the woods behind the house many times. Often, in late autumn, her mother took her to gather nuts among the fallen leaves. Today she made her own path, bouncing this way and that way, vaguely keeping an eye out for snakes. She found, in addition to various common but pretty ferns and leaves, an armful of strange blue flowers with velvety ridges and a sweetsuds bush full of the brown, fragrant buds.

By twelve o'clock, her arms laden with sprigs of her findings, she was a mile or more from home. She had often been as far before, but the strangeness of the land made it not as pleasant as her usual haunts. It seemed gloomy in the little cove in which she found herself. The air was damp, the silence close and deep.

Myop began to circle back to the house, back to the peacefulness of the morning. It was then she stepped smack into his eyes. Her heel became lodged in the broken ridge between brow and nose, and she reached down quickly, unafraid, to free herself. It was only when she saw his naked grin that she gave a little yelp of surprise.

He had been a tall man. From feet to neck covered a long space. His head lay beside him. When she pushed back the leaves and layers of earth and debris Myop saw that he'd had large white teeth, all of them cracked or broken, long fingers, and very big bones. All his clothes had rotted away except some threads of blue denim from his overalls. The buckles of the overalls had turned green.

Myop gazed around the spot with interest. Very near where she'd stepped into the head was a wild pink rose. As she picked it to add to her bundle she noticed a raised mound, a ring, around the rose's root. It was the rotted remains of a noose, a bit of shredding plowline, now blending benignly into the soil. Around an overhanging limb of a great spreading oak clung another piece. Frayed, rotted, bleached, and frazzled—barely there—but spinning restlessly in the breeze. Myop laid down her flowers.

And the summer was over.

GIRL

Jamaica Kincaid · 1978

Wash the white clothes on Monday and put them on the stone heap; wash the color clothes on Tuesday and put them on the clothesline to dry; don't walk barehead in the hot sun; cook pumpkin fritters in very hot sweet oil; soak your little cloths right after you take them off; when buying cotton to make yourself a nice blouse, be sure that it doesn't have gum on it, because that way it won't hold up well after a wash; soak salt fish overnight before you cook it; is it true that you sing benna in Sunday school?; always eat your food in such a way that it won't turn someone else's stomach; on Sundays try to walk like a lady and not like the slut you are so bent on becoming; don't sing benna in Sunday school; you mustn't speak to wharf-rat boys, not even to give directions; don't eat fruits on the street—flies will follow you; *but I don't sing benna on Sundays at all and never in Sunday school*; this is how to sew on a button; this is how to make a buttonhole for the button you have just sewed on; this is how to hem a dress when you see the hem coming down and so to prevent yourself from looking like the slut I know you are so bent on becoming; this is how you iron your father's khaki shirt so that it doesn't have a crease; this is how you iron your father's khaki pants so that they don't have a crease; this is how you grow okra—far from the house, because okra tree harbors red ants;

when you are growing dasheen, make sure it gets plenty of water or else it makes your throat itch when you are eating it; this is how you sweep a corner; this is how you sweep a whole house; this is how you sweep a yard; this is how you smile to someone you don't like too much; this is how you smile to someone you don't like at all; this is how you smile to someone you like completely; this is how you set a table for tea; this is how you set a table for dinner; this is how you set a table for dinner with an important guest; this is how you set a table for lunch; this is how you set a table for breakfast; this is how to behave in the presence of men who don't know you very well, and this way they won't recognize immediately the slut I have warned you against becoming; be sure to wash every day, even if it is with your own spit; don't squat down to play marbles—you are not a boy, you know; don't pick people's flowers—you might catch something; don't throw stones at blackbirds, because it might not be a blackbird at all; this is how to make a bread pudding; this is how to make doukona; this is how to make pepper pot; this is how to make a good medicine for a cold; this is how to make a good medicine to throw away a child before it even becomes a child; this is how to catch a fish; this is how to throw back a fish you don't like, and that way something bad won't fall on you; this is how to bully a man; this is how a man bullies you; this is how to love a man, and if this doesn't work there are other ways, and if they don't work don't feel too bad about giving up; this is how to spit up in the air if you feel like it, and this is how to move quick so that it doesn't fall on you; this is how to make ends meet; always squeeze bread to make sure it's fresh; *but what if the baker won't let me feel the bread?*; you mean to say that after all you are really going to be the kind of woman who the baker won't let near the bread?

THE RED
CONVERTIBLE

Louise Erdrich • 1981

I was the first one to drive a convertible on my reservation. And of course it was red, a red Olds. I owned that car along with my brother Stephan. We owned it together until his boots filled with water on a windy night and he bought out my share. Now Stephan owns the whole car and his younger brother Marty (that's myself) walks everywhere he goes.

How did I earn enough money to buy my share in the first place? My one talent was I could always make money. I had a touch for it, unusual in a Chippewa and especially in my family. From the first I was different that way and everyone recognized it. I was the only kid they let in the Rolla legion hall to shine shoes, for example, and one Christmas I sold spiritual bouquets for the Mission door-to-door. The nuns let me keep a percentage. Once I started, it seemed the more money I made the easier the money came. Everyone encouraged it. When I was fifteen I got a job washing dishes at the Joliet Café, and that was where my first big break came.

It wasn't long before I was promoted to busing tables, and then the short-order cook quit and I was hired to take her place. No sooner than you know it I was managing the Joliet. The rest is history. I went on managing. I soon became part-owner and of course there was no stopping me then. It wasn't long before the whole thing was mine.

After I'd owned the Joliet one year it burned down. The whole operation. I was only twenty. I had it all and I lost it quick, but before I lost it I had every one of my relatives, and their relatives, to dinner and I also bought that red Olds I mentioned, along with Stephan.

That time we first saw it! I'll tell you when we first saw it. We had gotten a ride up to Winnipeg and both of us had money. Don't ask me why because we never mentioned a car or anything, we just had all our money. Mine was cash, a big bankroll. Stephan had two checks—a week's extra pay for being laid off, and his regular check from the Jewel Bearing Plant.

We were walking down Portage anyway, seeing the sights, when we saw it. There it was, parked, large as alive. Really as *if* it was alive. I thought of the word "repose" because the car wasn't simply stopped, parked, or whatever. That car reposed, calm and gleaming, a FOR SALE sign in its left front window. Then before we had thought it over at all, the car belonged to us and our pockets were empty. We had just enough money for gas back home.

We went places in that car, me and Stephan. A little bit of insurance money came through from the fire and we took off driving all one whole summer. I can't tell you all the places we went to. We started off toward the Little Knife River and Mandaree in Fort Berthold and then we found ourselves down in Wakpala somehow and then suddenly we were over in Montana on the Rocky Boys and yet the summer was not even half over. Some people hang on to details when they travel, but we didn't let them bother us and just lived our everyday lives here to there.

I do remember there was this one place with willows, however; I laid

under those trees and it was comfortable. So comfortable. The branches
bent down all around me like a tent or a stable. And quiet, it was quiet,
even though there was a dance close enough so I could see it going on.
It was not too still, or too windy either, that day. When the dust rises up
and hangs in the air around the dancers like that I feel comfortable.
Stephan was asleep. Later on he woke up and we started driving again.
We were somewhere in Montana, or maybe on the Blood Reserve, it
could have been anywhere. Anyway, it was where we met the girl.

All her hair was in buns around her ears, that's the first thing I saw.
She was alongside the road with her arm out so we stopped. That
girl was short, so short her lumbershirt looked comical on her, like a
nightgown. She had jeans on and fancy moccasins and she carried a
little suitcase.

"Hop on in," says Stephan. So she climbs in between us.

"We'll take you home," I says, "Where do you live?"

"Chicken," she says.

"Where's that?" I ask her.

"Alaska."

"Okay," Stephan says, and we drive.

We got up there and never wanted to leave. The sun doesn't truly set
there in summer and the night is more a soft dusk. You might doze off,
sometimes, but before you know it you're up again, like an animal in
nature. You never feel like you have to sleep hard or put away the world.
And things would grow up there. One day just dirt or moss, the next
day flowers and long grass. The girl's family really took to us. They fed
us and put us up. We had our own tent to live in by their house and the
kids would be in and out of there all day and night.

One night the girl, Susy (she had another, longer name, but they
called her Susy for short), came in to visit us. We sat around in the tent
talking of this thing and that. It was getting darker by that time and the

cold was even getting just a little mean. I told Susy it was time for us to go. She stood up on a chair. "You never seen my hair," she said. That was true. She was standing on a chair, but still, when she unclipped her buns the hair reached all the way to the ground. Our eyes opened. You couldn't tell how much hair she had when it was rolled up so neatly. Then Stephan did something funny. He went up to the chair and said, "Jump on my shoulders." So she did that and her hair reached down past Stephan's waist and he started twirling, this way and that, so her hair was flung out from side to side. "I always wondered what it was like to have long pretty hair," Stephan says! Well, we laughed. It was a funny sight, the way he did it. The next morning we got up and took leave of those people.

On to greener pastures, as they say. It was down through Spokane and across Idaho then Montana, and very soon we were racing the weather right along under the Canadian border through Columbus, Des Lacs, and then we were in Bottineau County and soon home. We'd made most of the trip, that summer, without putting up the car hood at all. We got home just in time, it turned out, for the Army to remember Stephan had signed up to join it.

I don't wonder that the Army was so glad to get Stephan that they turned him into a Marine. He was built like a brick outhouse anyway. We liked to tease him that they really wanted him for his Indian nose, though. He had a nose big and sharp as a hatchet. He had a nose like the nose on Red Tomahawk, the Indian who killed Sitting Bull, whose profile is on signs all along the North Dakota highways. Stephan went off to training camp, came home once during Christmas, then the next thing you know we got an overseas letter from Stephan. It was 1968, and he was stationed in Khe Sanh. I wrote him back several times. I kept him informed all about the car. Most of the time I had it up on blocks in the yard or half taken apart because that long trip wore out so much of it although, I must say, it gave us a beautiful performance when we needed it.

It was at least two years before Stephan came home again. They didn't want him back for a while, I guess, so he stayed on after Christmas. In those two years, I'd put his car into almost perfect shape. I always thought of it as his car, while he was gone, though when he left he said, "Now it's yours," and even threw me his key. "Thanks for the extra key," I said, "I'll put it up in your drawer just in case I need it." He laughed.

When he came home, though, Stephan was very different, and I'll say this, the change was no good. You could hardly expect him to change for the better; I know this. But he was quiet, so quiet, and never comfortable sitting still anywhere but always up and moving around. I thought back to times we'd sat still for whole afternoons, never moving, just shifting our weight along the ground, talking to whoever sat with us, watching things. He'd always had a joke then, too, and now you couldn't get him to laugh, or when he did it was more the sound of a man choking, a sound that stopped up the laughter in the throats of other people around him. They got to leaving him alone most of the time and I didn't blame them. It was a fact, Stephan was jumpy and mean.

I'd bought a color TV set for my mother and the kids while Stephan was away. (Money still came very easy.) I was sorry I'd ever bought it, though, because of Stephan, and I was also sorry I'd bought color because with black-and-white the pictures seem older and farther away. But what are you going to do? He sat in front of it, watching it, and that was the only time he was completely still. But it was the kind of stillness that you see in a rabbit when it freezes and before it will bolt. He was not comfortable. He sat in his chair gripping the armrests with all his might as if the chair itself was moving at a high speed, and if he let go at all he would rocket forward and maybe crash right through the set.

Once I was in the same room and I heard his teeth click at something. I looked over and he'd bitten through his lip. Blood was going down his chin. I tell you right then I wanted to smash that tube to pieces. I went over to it but Stephan must have known what I was up to. He rushed from his chair and shoved me out of the way, against the wall. I told myself he didn't know what he was doing.

My mother came in, turned the set off real quiet, and told us she had made something for supper. So we went and sat down. There was still blood going down Stephan's chin but he didn't notice it, and no one said anything even though every time he took a bite of his bread his blood fell onto it until he was eating his own blood mixed in with the food.

We talked, while Stephan was not around, about what was going to happen to him. There were no Indian doctors on the reservation, no medicine people, and my mother was afraid if we brought him to a regular hospital they would keep him. "No way would we get him there in the first place," I said, "so let's just forget about it." Then I thought about the car. Stephan had not even looked at the car since he'd gotten home, though like I said, it was in tip-top condition and ready to drive.

One night Stephan was off somewhere. I took myself a hammer. I went out to that car and I did a number on its underside. Whacked it up. Bent the tailpipe double. Ripped the muffler loose. By the time I was done with the car it looked worse than any typical Indian car that has been driven all its life on reservation roads which they always say are like government promises—full of holes. It just about hurt me, I'll tell you that! I threw dirt in the carburetor and I ripped all the electric tape off the seats. I made it look just as beat up as I could. Then I sat back, and I waited for Stephan to find it.

Still, it took him over a month. That was all right because it was just getting warm enough, not melting but warm enough, to work outside, when he did find it.

"Marty," he says, walking in one day, "that red car looks like shit."

"Well it's old," I says. "You got to expect that."

"No way!" says Stephan. "That car's a classic! But you went and ran the piss right out of it, Marty, and you know it don't deserve that. I kept that car in A-1 shape. You don't remember. You're too young. But when I left, that car was running like a watch. Now I don't even know if I can get it to start again, let alone get it anywhere near its old condition."

"Well, you try," I said, like I was getting mad, "but I say it's a piece of junk."

Then I walked out before he could realize I knew he'd strung together more than six words at once.

After that I thought he'd freeze himself to death working on that vehicle. I mean he was out there all day and at night he rigged up a little lamp, ran a cord out the window, and had himself some light to see by while he worked. He was better than he had been before, but that's still not saying much. It was easier for him to do the things the rest of us did. He ate more slowly and didn't jump up and down during the meal to get this or that or look out the window. I put my hand in the back of the TV set, I admit, and fiddled around with it good so that it was almost impossible now to get a clear picture. He didn't look at it very often. He was always out with that car or going off to get parts for it. By the time it was really melting outside, he had it fixed.

I had been feeling down in the dumps about Stephan around this time. We had always been together before. Stephan and Marty. But he was such a loner now I didn't know how to take it. So I jumped at the chance one day when Stephan seemed friendly. It's not that he smiled or anything. He just said, "Let's take that old shitbox for a spin." But just the way he said it made me think he could be coming around.

We went out to the car. It was spring. The sun was shining very bright. My little sister Bonita came out and made us stand together for a picture. He leaned his elbow on the red car's windshield and he took his other arm and put it over my shoulder, very carefully, as though it was heavy for him to lift and he didn't want to bring the weight down all at once. "Smile," Bonita said, and he did.

That picture. I never look at it anymore. A few months ago, I don't know why, I got his picture out and tacked it on my wall. I felt good about Stephan at the time, close to him. I felt good having his picture on the wall until one night when I was looking at television. I was a little drunk and stoned. I looked up at the wall and Stephan was staring at me. I don't know what it was but his smile had changed. Or maybe it was gone. All I know is I couldn't stay in the same room with that picture. I was shaking. I had to get up, close the door, and go into the kitchen. A little later my friend Rayman came and we both went back into that room. We put the picture in a bag and folded the bag over and over and put the picture way back in a closet.

I still see that picture now, as if it tugs at me, whenever I pass that closet door. It is very clear in my mind. It was so sunny that day, Stephan had to squint against the glare. Or maybe the camera Bonita held flashed like a mirror, blinding him, before she snapped the picture. My face is right out in the sun, big and round. But he might have drawn back a little because the shadows on his face are deep as holes. There are two shadows curved like little hooks around the ends of his smile as if to frame it and try to keep it there—that one, first smile that looked like it might have hurt his face. He has his field jacket on, and the worn-in clothes he'd come back in and kept wearing ever since. After Bonita took the picture and went into the house, we got into the car. There was a full cooler in the trunk. We started off, east, toward Pembina and the Red River because Stephan said he wanted to see the high water.

· · · · ·

The trip over there was beautiful. When everything starts changing, drying up, clearing off, you feel so good it is like your whole life is starting. And Stephan felt it too. The top was down and the car hummed like a top. He'd really put it back in shape, even the tape on the seats was very carefully put down and glued back in layers. It's not that he smiled again or even joked or anything while we were driving, but his face looked to me as if it was clear, more peaceful. It looked as though he wasn't thinking of anything in particular except the blank fields and windbreaks and houses we were passing.

The river was high and full of winter trash when we got there. The sun was still out, but it was colder by the river. There were still little clumps of dirty snow here and there on the banks. The water hadn't gone over the banks yet, but it would, you could tell. It was just at its limit, hard, swollen, glossy like an old gray scar. We made ourselves a fire, and we sat down and watched the current go. As I watched it I felt something squeezing inside me and tightening and trying to let go all at the same time. I knew I was not just feeling it myself; I knew I was feeling what Stephan was going through at that moment. Except that Marty couldn't stand it, the feeling. I jumped to my feet. I took Stephan by the shoulders and I started shaking him. "Wake up," I says, "wake up, wake up, wake up!" I didn't know what had come over me. I sat down beside him again. His face was totally white, hard, like a stone. Then it broke, like stones break all of the sudden when water boils up inside them.

"I know it," he says. "I know it. I can't help it. It's no use."

We started talking. He said he knew what I'd done with the car that time. It was obvious it had been whacked out of shape and not just neglected. He said he wanted to give the car to me for good now; it was no use. He said he'd fixed it just to give back and I should take it.

"No," I says, "I don't want it."

"That's okay," he says. "You take it."

"I don't want it though," I says back to him and then to emphasize, just to emphasize you understand, I touch his shoulder. He slaps my hand off.

"Take that car," he says.

"No," I say, "make me," I say, and then he grabs my jacket and rips the arm loose. I get mad and push him backwards, off the log. He jumps up and bowls me over. We go down in a clinch and come up swinging hard, for all we're worth, with our fists. He socks my jaw so hard I feel like it swings loose. Then I'm at his rib cage and land a good one under his chin so his head snaps back. He's dazzled. He looks at me and I look at him and then his eyes are full of tears and blood and he's crying I think at first. But no, he's laughing. "Ha! Ha!" he says. "Ha! Ha! Take good care of it!"

"Okay," I says, "Okay no problem. Ha! Ha!"

I can't help it and I start laughing too. My face feels fat and strange and after a while I get a beer from the cooler in the trunk and when I hand it to Stephan he takes his shirt and wipes my germs off. "Hoof and mouth disease," he says. For some reason this cracks me up and so we're really laughing for a while then, and then we drink all the rest of the beers one by one and throw them in the river and see how far the current takes them, how fast, before they fill up and sink.

"I'm an Indian!" he shouts after a while.

"Whoo I'm on the lovepath! I'm out for loving!"

I think it's the old Stephan. He jumps up then and starts swinging his legs out from the knees like a fancydancer, then he's down doing something between a grouse dance and a bunny hop, no kind of dance I ever saw before but neither has anyone else on all this green growing earth. He's wild. He wants to pitch whoopee! He's up and at 'em and all over. All this time I'm laughing so hard, so hard my belly is getting tied up in a knot.

"Got to cool me off!" he shouts all of the sudden. Then he runs over to the river and jumps in.

There's boards and other things in the current. It's so high. No sound comes from the river after the splash he makes so I run right over. I look around. It's dark. I see he's halfway across the water already and I know he didn't swim there but the current took him. It's far. I hear his voice, though, very clearly across it.

"My boots are filling," he says.

He says this in a normal voice, like he just noticed and he doesn't know what to think of it. Then he's gone. A branch comes by. Another branch. By the time I get out of the river, off the snag I pulled myself onto, the sun is down. I walk back to the car, turn on the high beams, and drive it up the bank. I put it in first gear and then I take my foot off the clutch. I get out, close the door, and watch it plow softly into the water. The headlights reach in as they go down, searching, still lighted even after the water swirls over the back end. I wait. The wires short out. It is all finally dark. And then there's only the water, the sound of it going and running and going and running and running.

THE REENCOUNTER

Isaac Bashevis Singer • 1982

The telephone rang and Dr. Max Greitzer woke up. On the night table the clock showed fifteen minutes to eight. "Who could be calling so early?" he murmured. He picked up the phone and a woman's voice said, "Dr. Greitzer, excuse me for calling at this hour. A woman who was once dear to you has died. Liza Nestling."

"My God!"

"The funeral is today at eleven. I thought you would want to know."

"You are right. Thank you. Thank you. Liza Nestling played a major role in my life. May I ask whom I am speaking to?"

"It doesn't matter. Liza and I became friends after you two separated. The service will be in Gutgestalt's funeral parlor. You know the address?"

"Yes, thank you."

The woman hung up.

Dr. Greitzer lay still for a while. So Liza was gone. Twelve years had passed since their breaking up. She had been his great love. Their affair lasted about fifteen years—no, not fifteen; thirteen. The last two had been filled with so many misunderstandings and complications, with so much madness, that words could not describe them. The same powers that built this love destroyed it entirely. Dr. Greitzer and Liza Nestling

never met again. They never wrote to one another. From a friend of hers
he learned that she was having an affair with a would-be theater director, but that was the only word he had about her. He hadn't even known
that Liza was still in New York.

Dr. Greitzer was so distressed by the bad news that he didn't remember how he got dressed that morning or found his way to the funeral parlor. When he arrived, the clock across the street showed
twenty-five to nine. He opened the door, and the receptionist told him
that he had come too early. The service would not take place until eleven
o'clock.

"Is it possible for me to see her now?" Max Greitzer asked. "I am a
very close friend of hers, and . . ."

"Let me ask if she's ready." The girl disappeared behind a door.

Dr. Greitzer understood what she meant. The dead are elaborately
fixed up before they are shown to their families and those who attend
the funeral.

Soon the girl returned and said, "It's all right. Fourth floor, room
three."

A man in a black suit took him up in the elevator and opened the
door to room number 3. Liza lay in a coffin opened to her shoulders, her
face covered with gauze. He recognized her only because he knew it was
she. Her black hair had the dullness of dye. Her cheeks were rouged,
and the wrinkles around her closed eyes were hidden under makeup.
On her reddened lips there was a hint of a smile. How do they produce
a smile? Max Greitzer wondered. Liza had once accused him of being a
mechanical person, a robot with no emotion. The accusation was false
then, but now, strangely, it seemed to be true. He was neither dejected
nor frightened.

The door to the room opened and a woman with an uncanny resem-
blance to Liza entered. "It's her sister, Bella," Max Greitzer said to himself. Liza had often spoken about her younger sister, who lived in
California, but he had never met her. He stepped aside as the woman

approached the coffin. If she burst out crying, he would be nearby to comfort her. She showed no special emotion, and he decided to leave her with her sister, but it occurred to him that she might be afraid to stay alone with a corpse, even her own sister's.

After a few moments, she turned and said, "Yes, it's her."

"I expect you flew in from California," Max Greitzer said, just to say something.

"From California?"

"Your sister was once close to me. She often spoke about you. My name is Max Greitzer."

The woman stood silent and seemed to ponder his words. Then she said, "You're mistaken."

"Mistaken? You aren't her sister, Bella?"

"Don't you know that Max Greitzer died? There was an obituary in the newspapers."

Max Greitzer tried to smile. "Probably another Max Greitzer." The moment he uttered these words, he grasped the truth: he and Liza were both dead—the woman who spoke to him was not Bella but Liza herself. He now realized that if he were still alive he would be shaken with grief. Only someone on the other side of life could accept with such indifference the death of a person he had once loved. Was what he was experiencing the immortality of the soul, he wondered. If he were able, he would laugh now, but the illusion of body had vanished; he and Liza no longer had material substance. Yet they were both present. Without a voice he asked, "Is this possible?"

He heard Liza answer in her smart style, "If it is so, it must be possible." She added, "For your information, your body is lying here too."

"How did it happen? I went to sleep last night a healthy man."

"It wasn't last night and you were not healthy. A degree of amnesia seems to accompany this process. It happened to me a day ago and therefore—"

"I had a heart attack?"

"Perhaps."

"What happened to *you*?" he asked.

"With me, everything takes a long time. How did you hear about me, anyway?" she added.

"I thought I was lying in bed. Fifteen minutes to eight, the telephone rang and a woman told me about you. She refused to give her name."

"Fifteen minutes to eight, your body was already here. Do you want to go look at yourself? I've seen you. You are in number 5. They made a *krasavetz* out of you."

He hadn't heard anyone say *krasavetz* for years. It meant a beautiful man. Liza had been born in Russia and she often used this word.

"No. I'm not curious."

In the chapel it was quiet. A clean-shaven rabbi with curly hair and a gaudy tie made a speech about Liza. "She was an intellectual woman in the best sense of the word," he said. "When she came to America, she worked all day in a shop and at night she attended college, graduating with high honors. She had bad luck and many things in her life went awry, but she remained a lady of high integrity."

"I never met that man. How could he know about me?" Liza asked.

"Your relatives hired him and gave him the information," Greitzer said.

"I hate these professional compliments."

"Who's the fellow with the gray mustache on the first bench?" Max Greitzer asked.

Liza uttered something like a laugh. "My has-been husband."

"You were married? I heard only that you had a lover."

"I tried everything, with no success whatsoever."

"Where would you like to go?" Max Greitzer asked.

"Perhaps to your service."

"Absolutely not."

"What state of being is this?" Liza asked. "I see everything. I recognize everyone. There is my Aunt Reizl. Right behind her is my Cousin Becky. I once introduced you to her."

"Yes, true."

"The chapel is half empty. From the way I acted toward others in such circumstances, it is what I deserve. I'm sure that for you the chapel will be packed. Do you want to wait and see?"

"I haven't the slightest desire to find out."

The rabbi had finished his eulogy and a cantor recited "God Full of Mercy." His chanting was more like crying and Liza said, "My own father wouldn't have gone into such lamentations."

"Paid tears."

"I've had enough of it," Liza said. "Let's go."

They floated from the funeral parlor to the street. There, six limousines were lined up behind the hearse. One of the chauffeurs was eating a banana.

"Is this what they call death?" Liza asked. "It's the same city, the same streets, the same stores. I seem the same, too."

"Yes, but without a body."

"What am I then? A soul?"

"Really, I don't know what to tell you," Max Greitzer said. "Do you feel any hunger?"

"Hunger? No."

"Thirst?"

"No. No. What do you say to all this?"

"The unbelievable, the absurd, the most vulgar superstitions are proving to be true," Max Greitzer said.

"Perhaps we will find there is even a Hell and a Paradise."

"Anything is possible at this point."

"Perhaps we will be summoned to the Court on High after the burial and asked to account for our deeds?"

"Even this can be."

"How does it come about that we are together?"

"Please, don't ask any more questions. I know as little as you."

"Does this mean that all the philosophic works you read and wrote were one big lie?"

"Worse—they were sheer nonsense."

At that moment, four pallbearers carried out the coffin holding Liza's body. A wreath lay on top, with an inscription in gold letters: "To the unforgettable Liza in loving memory."

"Whose wreath is that?" Liza asked, and she answered herself, "For this he's not stingy."

"Would you like to go with them to the cemetery?" Max Greitzer asked.

"No—what for? That phony cantor may recite a whining Kaddish after me."

"What do you want to do?"

Liza listened to herself. She wanted nothing. What a peculiar state, not to have a single wish. In all the years she could remember, her will, her yearnings, her fears, tormented her without letting up. Her dreams were full of desperation, ecstasy, wild passions. More than any other catastrophe, she dreaded the final day, when all that has been is extinguished and the darkness of the grave begins. But here she was, remembering the past, and Max Greitzer was again with her. She said to him, "I imagined that the end would be much more dramatic."

"I don't believe this is the end," he said. "Perhaps a transition between two modes of existence."

"If so, how long will it last?"

"Since time has no validity, duration has no meaning."

"Well, you've remained the same with your puzzles and paradoxes. Come, we cannot just stay here if you want to avoid seeing your mourners," Liza said. "Where should we go?"

"You lead."

Max Greitzer took her astral arm and they began to rise without purpose, without a destination. As they might have done from an airplane, they looked down at the earth and saw cities, rivers, fields, lakes—everything but human beings.

"Did you say something?" Liza asked.

And Max Greitzer answered. "Of all my disenchantments, immortality is the greatest."

TAKING CARE

Joy Williams • 1982

Jones, the preacher, has been in love all his life. He is baffled by this because as far as he can see, it has never helped anyone, even when they have acknowledged it, which is not often. Jones's love is much too apparent and arouses neglect. He is like an animal in a traveling show who, through some aberration, wears a vital organ outside the skin, awkward and unfortunate, something that shouldn't be seen, certainly something that shouldn't be watched working. Now he sits on a bed beside his wife in the self-care unit of a hospital fifteen miles from their home. She has been committed here for tests. She is so weak, so tired. There is something wrong with her blood. Her arms are covered with bruises where they have gone into the veins. Her hip, too, is blue and swollen where they have drawn out samples of bone marrow. All of this is frightening. The doctors are severe and wise, answering Jones's questions in a way that makes him feel hopelessly deaf. They have told him that there really is no such thing as a disease of the blood, for the blood is not a living tissue but a passive vehicle for the transportation of food, oxygen and waste. They have told him that abnormalities in the blood corpuscles, which his wife seems to have, must be regarded as symptoms of disease elsewhere in the body. They have shown him, upon request, slides and charts of normal and pathological blood cells that look to Jones like canapés. They speak (for he insists) of leukocytosis, myelocytes and megaloblasts. None of this takes into account the love he has for his wife! Jones sits beside her in this dim pleasant room, wearing a gray suit and his clerical collar, for when he leaves her he must visit other parishioners who are patients here. This part of the hospital is like a motel. Patients can wear their regular clothes. The rooms have desks, rugs and colorful bedspreads. How he wishes that they were traveling and staying overnight, this night, in a motel. A nurse comes in with a tiny paper cup full of pills. There are three pills, or rather, capsules, and they are not for his wife but for her blood. The cup is the smallest of its type that Jones has ever seen. All perspective, all sense of time and scale seem abandoned in this hospital. For example, when Jones turns to kiss his wife's hair, he nicks the air instead.

Jones and his wife have one child, a daughter, who, in turn, has a single child, a girl born six months ago. Jones's daughter has fallen in with the stars and is using the heavens, as Jones would be the first to admit, more than he ever has. It has, however, brought her only grief and confusion. She has left her husband and brought the baby to Jones. She has also given him her dog. She is going to Mexico, where soon, in the mountains, she will have a nervous breakdown. Jones does not know this, but his daughter has seen it in the stars and is going out to meet it. Jones quickly agrees to care for both the baby and the dog, as this seems to be the only thing his daughter needs from him. The day of the baby's birth is secondary to the positions of the planets and the terms of houses, quadrants and gradients. Her symbol is a bareback rider. To Jones, this is a graceful thought. It signifies audacity. It also means luck. Jones slips some money in the pocket of his daughter's suitcase and drives her to the airport. The plane taxis down the runway and Jones waves, holding all their luck in his arms.

· · ·

One afternoon, Jones had come home and found his wife sitting in
the garden, weeping. She had been transplanting flowers, putting
them in pots before the first frost came. There was dirt on her forehead
and around her mouth. Her light clothes felt so heavy. Their weight
made her body ache. Each breath was a stone she had to swallow. She
cried and cried in the weak autumn sunshine. Jones could see the veins
throbbing in her neck. "I'm dying," she said. "It's going to take me
months to die." But after he had brought her inside, she insisted that she
felt better and made them both a cup of tea while Jones potted the rest
of the plants and carried them down cellar. She lay on the sofa and
Jones sat beside her. They talked quietly with each other. Indeed, they
were almost whispering, as though they were in a public place surrounded by strangers instead of in their own house with no one present
but themselves. "Let's go for a ride," Jones said. His wife agreed.

Together they ride, through the towns, for miles and miles, even into
the next state. She does not want to stop driving. They buy sandwiches
and milk shakes and eat in the car. Jones drives. They have to buy more
gasoline. His wife sits close to him, her eyes closed, her head tipped back
against the seat. He can see the veins beating on in her neck. Somewhere
there is a dreadful sound, almost audible. Jones presses her cold hand to
his lips. He thinks of some madness, running out of control, deeply in
the darkness of his wife. "Just don't make me go to the hospital," she
pleads. Of course she will go there. The moment had already occurred.

Jones is writing to his daughter. He received a brief letter from her this
morning, telling him where she could be reached. The foreign post-
mark was so large that it almost obliterated Jones's address. She did not
mention either her mother or the baby, which makes Jones feel peculiar.
His life seems as increate as his God's life, perhaps even imaginary. His
daughter told him about the town in which she lives. She does not plan

Tonight he will give one to his wife. The other he will pack in sugar water and store in the refrigerator. He can only hope that the bud will remain tight until Sunday, when he brings it into the terrible heat of the hospital. The baby rocks against the straps of her small carrier. Her lips are pursed as she intently watches the fields, the trees. She is warmly dressed and wearing a knitted orange cap that is twenty-three years old, the age of her mother. Jones found it just the other day. It has faded almost to pink on one side. At one time, it must have been stored in the sun. Jones, driving, feels almost gay. The snow is so beautiful. Everything is white. Jones is an educated man. He has read Melville, who says that white is the colorless all-color of atheism from which we shrink. Jones does not believe this. He sees a holiness in snow, a promise. He hopes that his wife will know it is snowing even though she is separated from the window by a curtain. Jones sees something moving across the snow, a part of the snow itself, running. Although he is going slowly, he takes his foot completely off the accelerator. "Look, darling, a snowshoe rabbit." At the sound of his voice, the baby stretches open her mouth and narrows her eyes in soundless glee. The hare is splendid. So fast! It flows around invisible obstructions, something out of a kind dream. It flies across the ditch, its paws like paddles, faintly yellow, the color of raw wood. "Look, sweet," cries Jones, "how big he is!" But suddenly the hare is curved and falling, round as a ball, its feet and head tucked closely against its body. It strikes the road and skids upside down for several yards. The car passes around and avoids it. Jones brakes and stops, amazed. He opens the door and trots back to the animal. The baby twists about in her seat as well as she can and peers after him. It is as though the animal had never been alive at all. Its head is broken in several places. Jones bends to touch its fur, but straightens again without doing so. A man emerges from the woods, swinging a shotgun. He nods at Jones and picks the hare up by the ears. As he walks away, the hare's legs rub across the ground. There are small crystal stains on the snow. Jones returns to the car. He wants to apologize but does not know for what. His life has been devoted to apologetics. It is his profession. He is concerned with both justification and remorse. He has always acted rightly, but nothing has ever come of it. "Oh, sweet," he says to the baby. She smiles at him, exposing her tooth. At home that night, after the baby's supper, Jones reads a story to her. She is asleep, panting in her sleep, but Jones tells her the story of al-Boraq, the milk-white steed of Mohammed who could stride out of the sight of mankind with a single step.

Jones sorts through a collection of records, none of which have been opened. They are still wrapped in cellophane. The jacket designs are subdued, epic. Names, instruments and orchestras are mentioned confidently. He would like to agree with their importance, for he knows that they have worth, but he is not familiar with the references. His daughter brought these records with her. They had been given to her by an older man, a professor she had been having an affair with. Naturally, this pains Jones. His daughter speaks about the men she has been involved with but no longer cares about. Where did these men come from? Where were they waiting and why have they gone? Jones remembers his daughter when she was a little girl, helping him rake leaves. For years, on April Fools' Day she would take tobacco out of his humidor and fill it with cornflakes. Jones is full of remorse and astonishment. When he saw his daughter only a few weeks ago, she was thin and nervous. She had plucked out almost all her eyebrows with her fingers from this nervousness. And her lashes. The lids of her eyes were swollen and white, like the bulbs of flowers. Her fingernails were crudely bitten, some bleeding below the quick. She was tough and remote, wanting only to go on a trip for which she had a ticket. What can he do? He seeks her in the face of the baby but she is not there. All is being both continued and resumed, but the dream is different. The dream cannot be revived. Jones breaks into one of the albums, blows the dust from the needle and plays a record. Outside it is dark. The parsonage is remote and the only buildings nearby are barns. The river cannot be seen. The music is Bruckner's *Te Deum*. Very nice. Dedicated to God. He plays the other side. A woman, Kathleen Ferrier, is singing in German. The music stuns him. *Kindertotenlieder*. He makes no attempt to seek the words' translation. The music is enough.

In the hospital, his wife waits to be translated, no longer a woman, the woman whom he loves, but a situation. Her blood moves as mysteriously as the constellations. She is under scrutiny and attack and she has abandoned Jones. She is a swimmer waiting to get on with the drowning. Jones is on the shore. In Mexico, his daughter walks along the beach with two men. She is acting out a play that has become her life. Jones is on the mountaintop. The baby cries and Jones takes her from the crib to change her. The dog paws the door. Jones lets him out. He settles down with the baby and listens to the record. The baby wiggles restlessly on his lap. Her eyes are a foal's eyes, navy blue. She has grown in a few weeks to expect everything from Jones. He props her on one edge of the couch and goes to her small toy box, where he keeps a bear, a few rattles and balls. He opens the door again and the dog immediately enters. His heavy coat is cold, fragrant with ice. He noses the baby and she squeals.

> *Oft denk' ich, sie sind nur ausgegangen*
> *Bald werden sie wieder nach Hause gelangen*

Jones selects a bright ball and pushes it gently in her direction.

It is Sunday morning and Jones is in the pulpit. The church is very old, the adjacent cemetery even older. It has become a historic landmark and no one has been buried there since World War I. There is a new

place, not far away, which the families now use. Plots are marked not
with stones but with small tablets, and immediately after any burial,
workmen roll grassed sod over the new graves so there is no blemish on
the grounds, not even for a little while. Present for today's service are
seventy-eight adults, eleven children and the junior choir. Jones counts
them as the offertory is received. The church rolls say that there are 350
members but as far as Jones can see, everyone is here today. This is the
day he baptizes the baby. He has made arrangements with one of the
ladies to hold her and bring her up to the font at the end of the first
hymn. The baby looks charming in a lacy white dress. Jones has combed
her fine hair carefully, slicking it in a curl with water, but now it has
dried and sticks up awkwardly like the crest of a kingfisher. Jones
bought the dress in Mammoth Mart, an enormous store that has a large
metal elephant dressed in overalls dancing on the roof. He feels foolish
at buying it there but he had gone to several stores and that is where he
saw the prettiest dress. He blesses the baby with water from the silver
bowl. He says, *We are saved not because we are worthy. We are saved because we are loved.* It is a brief ceremony. The baby, looking curiously at
Jones, is taken out to the nursery. Jones begins his sermon. He can't
remember when he wrote it, but here it is, typed, in front of him. *There
is nothing wrong in what one does but there is something wrong in what one
becomes.* He finds this questionable but goes on speaking. He has been
preaching for thirty-four years. He is gaunt with belief. But his wife has
a red cell count of only 2.3 million. It is not enough! She is not getting
enough oxygen! Jones is giving his sermon. Somewhere he has lost what
he was looking for. He must have known once, surely. The congregation
sways, like the wings of a ray in water. It is Sunday and for patients it is
a holiday. The doctors don't visit. There are no tests or diagnoses. Jones
would like to leave, to walk down the aisle and out into the winter,
where he would read his words into the ground. Why can't he remember his life! He finishes, sits down, stands up to present communion.
Tiny cubes of bread rest in a slumped pyramid. They are offered and

times she grasps the spoon, turns it around and thrusts the wrong end
into her mouth. Of course there is nothing that cannot be done incor-
rectly. Jones adores the baby. He sniffs her warm head. Her birth is a
deep error, an abstraction. Born in wedlock but out of love. He puts her
in the playpen and tends to the dog. He fills one dish with water and
another with kibbled biscuit. The dog eats with great civility. He eats a
little kibble and then takes some water, then kibble, then water. When
the dog has finished, the dishes are as clean as though they'd been washed.
Jones now thinks about his own dinner. He opens the refrigerator. The
ladies of the church have brought brownies, venison, cheese and apple-
sauce. There are turkey pies, pork chops, steak, haddock and sausage
patties. A brilliant light exposes all this food. There is so much of it. It
must be used. A crust has formed around the punctures in a can of Pet.
There is a clear bag of chicken livers stapled shut. Jones stares unhappily
at the beads of moisture on cartons and bottles, at the pearls of fat on
the cold cooked stew. He sits down. The room is full of lamps and
cords. He thinks of his wife, her breathing body deranged in tubes, and
begins to shake. All objects here are perplexed by such grief.

Now it is almost Christmas and Jones is walking down by the river,
around an abandoned house. The dog wades heavily through the
snow, biting it. There are petals of ice on the tree limbs and when Jones
lingers under them, the baby puts out her hand and her mouth starts
working because she would like to have it, the ice, the branch, everything. His wife will be coming home in a few days, in time for Christmas. Jones has already put up the tree and brought the ornaments down
from the attic. He will not trim it until she comes home. He wants very
much to make a fine occasion out of opening the boxes of old decora-
tions. The two of them have always enjoyed this greatly in the past.
Jones will doubtlessly drop and smash a bauble, for he does this every
year. He tramps through the snow with his small voyager. She dangles

in a shoulder sling, her legs wedged around his hip. They regard the rotting house seriously. Once it was a doctor's home and offices but long before Jones's time, the doctor, who was highly respected, had been driven away because a town girl accused him of fathering her child. The story goes that all the doctor said was, "Is that so?" This incensed the town and the girl's parents, who insisted that he take the child as soon as it was born. He did and he cared for the child very meticulously even though his practice was ruined and no one had anything more to do with him. A year later the girl told the truth—that the actual father was a young college boy whom she was now going to marry. They wanted the child back, and the doctor willingly returned the infant to them. Of course this is an old, important story. Jones has always appreciated it, but now he is annoyed at the man's passivity. His wife's sickness has changed everything for Jones. He will continue to accept but he will no longer surrender. Surely things are different for Jones now.

For insurance purposes, Jones's wife is brought out to the car in a wheelchair. She is thin and beautiful. Jones is grateful and confused. He has a mad wish to tip the orderly. Have so many years really passed? Is this not his wife, his love, fresh from giving birth? Isn't everything about to begin? In Mexico, his daughter wanders disinterestedly through a jewelry shop where she picks up a small silver egg. It opens on a hinge and inside are two figures, a bride and groom. Jones puts the baby in his wife's arms. At first the baby is alarmed because she cannot remember this person and she reaches for Jones, whimpering. But soon she is soothed by his wife's soft voice and falls asleep in her arms as they drive. Jones has readied everything carefully for his wife's homecoming. The house is clean and orderly. For days he has restricted himself to only one part of the house to ensure that his clutter will be minimal. Jones helps his wife up the steps to the door. Together they enter the shining rooms.

worked and he has not been alone. There is no way I can get him to reconcile any of his contradictions, and when this conversation begins to sound too much like many I had with my husband I say goodbye and hang up. I finish writing down what I started to write down even though by now it no longer seems true that anger is any great comfort.

I call him back five minutes later to tell him that I am sorry about all this arguing, and that I love him, but there is no answer. I call again five minutes later, thinking he might have walked out to his garage and walked back, but again there is no answer. I think of driving to where he lives again and looking for his garage to see if he is in there working, because he keeps his desk there and his books and that is where he goes to read and write. I am in my nightgown, it is after twelve and I have to leave the next morning at five. Even so, I get dressed and drive the mile or so to his place. I am afraid that when I get there I will see other cars by his house that I did not see earlier and that one of them will belong to his old girlfriend. When I drive down the driveway I see two cars that weren't there before, and one of them is parked as close as possible to his door, and I think that she is there. I walk around the small building to the back where his apartment is, and look in the window: the light is on, but I can't see anything clearly because of the half-closed venetian blinds and the steam on the glass. But things inside the room are not the same as they were earlier in the evening, and before there was no steam. I open the outer screen door and knock. I wait. No answer. I let the screen door fall shut and I walk away to check the row of garages. Now the door opens behind me as I am walking away and he comes out. I can't see him very well because it is dark in the narrow lane beside his door and he is wearing dark clothes and whatever light there is is behind him. He comes up to me and puts his arms around me without speaking, and I think he is not speaking not because he is feeling so much but because he is preparing what he will say. He lets go of me and walks around me and ahead of me out to where the cars are by the garage doors.

As we walk out there he says "Look," and my name, and I am waiting for him to say that she is here and also that it's all over between us. But he doesn't, and I have the feeling he did intend to say something like that, at least say that she was here, and that he then thought better of it for some reason. Instead, he says that everything that went wrong tonight was his fault and he's sorry. He stands with his back against a garage door and his face in the light and I stand in front of him with my back to the light. At one point he hugs me so suddenly that the fire of my cigarette crumbles against the garage door behind him. I know why we're out here and not in his room, but I don't ask him until everything is all right between us. Then he says, "She wasn't here when I called you. She came back later." He says the only reason she is there is that something is troubling her and he is the only one she can talk to about it. Then he says, "You don't understand, do you?"

I try to figure it out.

So they went to the movies and then came back to his place and then I called and then she left and he called back and we argued and then I called back twice but he had gone out to get a beer (he says) and then I drove over and in the meantime he had returned from buying beer and she had also come back and she was in his room so we talked by the garage doors. But what is the truth? Could he and she both really have come back in that short interval between my last phone call and my arrival at his place? Or is the truth really that during his call to me she waited outside or in his garage or in her car and that he then brought her in again, and that when the phone rang with my second and third calls he let it ring without answering, because he was fed up with me and with arguing? Or is the truth that she did leave and did come back later but that he remained and let the phone ring without answering? Or did he perhaps bring her in and then go out for the beer while she waited there and listened to the phone ring? The last is the least likely. I don't believe anyway that there was any trip out for beer.

CHINA

Charles Johnson · 1984

> If one man conquer in battle a thousand men,
> and if another conquers himself, he is the greatest
> of conquerors.
>
> —THE DHAMMAPADA

Evelyn's problems with her husband, Rudolph, began one evening in early March—a dreary winter evening in Seattle—when he complained after a heavy meal of pig's feet and mashed potatoes of shortness of breath, an allergy to something she put in his food perhaps, or brought on by the first signs of wild flowers around them. She suggested they get out of the house for the evening, go to a movie. He was fifty-four, a postman for thirty-three years now, with high blood pressure, emphysema, flat feet, and, as Evelyn told her friend Shelberdine Lewis, the lingering fear that he had cancer. Getting old, he was also getting hard to live with. He told her never to salt his dinners, to keep their Lincoln Continental at a crawl, and never run her fingers along his inner thigh when they sat in Reverend William Merrill's church, because anything, even sex, or laughing too loud—Rudolph was serious—might bring on heart failure.

So she chose for their Saturday night outing a peaceful movie, a mildly funny comedy a *Seattle Times* reviewer said was fit only for titters and nasal snorts, a low-key satire that made Rudolph's eyelids droop as he shoveled down unbuttered popcorn in the darkened, half-empty theater. Sticky fluids cemented Evelyn's feet to the floor. A man in the last row laughed at all the wrong places. She kept the popcorn on her lap, though she hated the unsalted stuff and wouldn't touch it, sighing as Rudolph pawed across her to shove his fingers inside the cup.

She followed the film as best she could, but occasionally her eyes frosted over, flashed white. She went blind like this now and then. The fibers of her eyes were failing; her retinas were tearing like soft tissue. At these times the world was a canvas with whiteout spilling from the far left corner toward the center; it was the sudden shock of an empty frame in a series of slides. Someday, she knew, the snow on her eyes would stay. Winter eternally: her eyes split like her walking stick. She groped along the fractured surface, waiting for her sight to thaw, listening to the film she couldn't see. Her only comfort was knowing that, despite her infirmity, her Rudolph was in even worse health.

He slid back and forth from sleep during the film (she elbowed him occasionally, or pinched his leg), then came full awake, sitting up suddenly when the movie ended and a "Coming Attractions" trailer began. It was some sort of gladiator movie, Evelyn thought, blinking, and it was pretty trashy stuff at that. The plot's revenge theme was a poor excuse for Chinese actors or Japanese (she couldn't tell those people apart) to flail the air with their hands and feet, take on fifty costumed extras at once, and leap twenty feet through the air in perfect defiance of gravity. Rudolph's mouth hung open.

"Can people really do that?" He did not take his eyes off the screen, but talked at her from the right side of his mouth. "Leap that high?"

"It's a *movie*," sighed Evelyn. "A *bad* movie."

He nodded, then asked again, "But can they?"

"Oh, Rudolph, for God's sake!" She stood up to leave, her seat slapping back loudly. "They're on *trampolines*! You can see them in the corner—there!—if you open your eyes!"

He did see them, once Evelyn twisted his head to the lower left corner of the screen, and it seemed to her that her husband looked disappointed—looked, in fact, the way he did the afternoon Dr. Guylee told Rudolph he'd developed an extrasystolic reaction, a faint, moaning sound from his heart whenever it relaxed. He said no more and, after the trailer finished, stood—there was chewing gum stuck to his trouser seat—dragged on his heavy coat with her help and followed Evelyn up the long, carpeted aisle, through the exit of the Coronet Theater, and to their car. He said nothing as she chattered on the way home, reminding him that he could not stay up all night puttering in his basement shop because the next evening they were to attend the church's revival meeting.

Rudolph, however, did not attend the revival. He complained after lunch of a light, dancing pain in his chest, which he had conveniently whenever Mount Zion Baptist Church held revivals, and she went alone, sitting with her friend Shelberdine, a beautician. She was forty-one; Evelyn, fifty-two. That evening Evelyn wore spotless white gloves, tan therapeutic stockings for the swelling in her ankles, and a white dress that brought out nicely the brown color of her skin, the most beautiful cedar brown, Rudolph said when they were courting thirty-five years ago in South Carolina. But then Evelyn had worn a matching checkered skirt and coat to meeting. With her jet black hair pinned behind her neck by a simple wooden comb, she looked as if she might have been Andrew Wyeth's starkly beautiful model for *Day of the Fair*. Rudolph, she remembered, wore black business suits, black ties, black wing tips, but he also wore white gloves because he was a senior usher—this was how she first noticed him. He was one of four young men dressed like deacons (or blackbirds), their left hands tucked into the hollow of their backs, their right carrying silver plates for the offering as

they marched in almost military fashion down each aisle: Christian soldiers, she'd thought, the cream of black manhood, and to get his attention she placed not her white envelope or coins in Rudolph's plate but
instead a note that said: "You have a beautiful smile." It was, for all her
innocence, a daring thing to do, according to Evelyn's mother—flirting
with a randy young man like Rudolph Lee Jackson, but he did have
nice, tigerish teeth. A killer smile, people called it, like all the boys in
the Jackson family: a killer smile and good hair that needed no more
than one stroke of his palm to bring out Quo Vadis rows pomaded
sweetly with the scent of Murray's.

And, of course, Rudolph was no dummy. Not a total dummy, at
least. He pretended nothing extraordinary had happened as the congregation left the little whitewashed church. He stood, the youngest son,
between his father and mother, and let old Deacon Adcock remark,
"Oh, how strong he's looking now," which was a lie. Rudolph was the
weakest of the Jackson boys, the pale, bookish, spiritual child born
when his parents were well past forty. His brothers played football, they
went into the navy; Rudolph lived in Scripture, was labeled 4-F, and
hoped to attend Moody Bible Institute in Chicago, if he could ever find
the money. Evelyn could tell Rudolph knew exactly where she was in
the crowd, that he could feel her as she and her sister, Debbie, waited
for their father to bring his DeSoto—the family prize—closer to the
front steps. When the crowd thinned, he shambled over in his slow,
ministerial walk, introduced himself, and unfolded her note.

"You write this?" he asked. "It's not right to play with the Lord's
money, you know."

"I like to play," she said.

"You do, huh?" He never looked directly at people. Women, she
guessed, terrified him. Or, to be exact, the powerful emotions they
caused in him terrified Rudolph. He was a pud puller, if she ever saw
one. He kept his eyes on a spot left of her face. "You're Joe Montgom-
ery's daughter, aren't you?"

"Maybe," teased Evelyn.

He trousered the note and stood marking the ground with his toe. "And just what you expect to get, Miss Playful, by fooling with people during collection time?"

She waited, let him look away, and, when the back-and-forth swing of his gaze crossed her again, said in her most melic, soft-breathing voice: "*You*."

Up front, portly Reverend Merrill concluded his sermon. Evelyn tipped her head slightly, smiling into memory; her hand reached left to pat Rudolph's leg gently; then she remembered it was Shelberdine beside her, and lifted her hand to the seat in front of her. She said a prayer for Rudolph's health, but mainly it was for herself, a hedge against her fear that their childless years had slipped by like wind, that she might return home one day and find him—as she had found her father—on the floor, bellied up, one arm twisted behind him where he fell, alone, his fingers locked against his chest. Rudolph had begun to run down, Evelyn decided, the minute he was turned down by Moody Bible Institute. They moved to Seattle in 1956—his brother Eli was stationed nearby and said Boeing was hiring black men. But they didn't hire Rudolph. He had kidney trouble on and off before he landed the job at the Post Office. Whenever he bent forward, he felt dizzy. Liver, heart, and lungs—they'd worn down gradually as his belly grew, but none of this was as bad as what he called "the Problem." His pecker shrank to no bigger than a pencil eraser each time he saw her undress. Or when Evelyn, as was her habit when talking, touched his arm. Was she the cause of this? Well, she knew she wasn't much to look at anymore. She'd seen the bottom of a few too many candy wrappers. Evelyn was nothing to make a man pant and jump her bones, pulling her fully clothed onto the davenport, as Rudolph had done years before, but wasn't sex something else you surrendered with age? It never seemed all that good to her anyway. And besides, he'd wanted oral sex, which Evelyn—if she knew nothing else—thought was a nasty, unsanitary thing to do with your mouth. She glanced up from under her spring hat past the pulpit, past the choir of black and brown faces to the agonized beauty of a bearded white carpenter impaled on a rood, and in this timeless image she felt comforted that suffering was inescapable, the loss of vitality inevitable, even a good thing maybe, and that she had to steel herself—yes—for someday opening her bedroom door and finding her Rudolph face down in his breakfast oatmeal. He would die before her, she knew that in her bones.

And so, after service, Sanka, and a slice of meat pie with Shelberdine downstairs in the brightly lit church basement, Evelyn returned home to tell her husband how lovely the Griffin girls had sung that day, that their neighbor Rod Kenner had been saved, and to listen, if necessary, to Rudolph's fear that the lump on his shoulder was an early-warning sign of something evil. As it turned out, Evelyn found that except for their cat, Mr. Miller, the little A-frame house was empty. She looked in his bedroom. No Rudolph. The unnaturally still house made Evelyn uneasy, and she took the excruciatingly painful twenty stairs into the basement to peer into a workroom littered with power tools, planks of wood, and the blueprints her husband used to make book-shelves and cabinets. No Rudolph. Frightened, Evelyn called the eight hospitals in Seattle, but no one had a Rudolph Lee Jackson on his books. After her last call the starburst clock in the living room read twelve-thirty. Putting down the wall phone, she felt a familiar pain in her abdomen. Another attack of Hershey squirts, probably from the meat pie. She hurried into the bathroom, lifted her skirt, and lowered her underwear around her ankles, but kept the door wide open, something impossible to do if Rudolph was home. Actually, it felt good not to have him underfoot, a little like he was dead already. But the last thing Evelyn wanted was that or, as she lay down against her lumpy backrest, to fall asleep, though she did, nodding off and dreaming until something shifted down her weight on the side of her bed away from the wall.

"Evelyn," said Rudolph, "look at this." She blinked back sleep and squinted at the cover of a magazine called *Inside Kung-Fu*, which Rudolph waved under her nose. On the cover a man stood bowlegged, one hand cocked under his armpit, the other corkscrewing straight at Evelyn's nose.

"Rudolph!" She batted the magazine aside, then swung her eyes toward the cluttered nightstand, focusing on the electric clock beside her water glass from McDonald's, Preparation H suppositories, and Harlequin romances. "It's morning!" Now she was mad. At least, working at it. "Where have you been?"

Her husband inhaled, a wheezing, whistlelike breath. He rolled the magazine into a cylinder and, as he spoke, struck his left palm with it. "That movie we saw advertised? You remember—it was called *The Five Fingers of Death*. I just saw that and one called *Deep Thrust*."

"Wonderful." Evelyn screwed up her lips. "I'm calling hospitals and you're at a Hong Kong double feature."

"Listen," said Rudolph. "You don't understand." He seemed at that moment as if he did not understand either. "It was a Seattle movie premiere. The Northwest is crawling with fighters. It has something to do with all the Asians out here. Before they showed the movie, four students from a kwoon in Chinatown went onstage—"

"A what?" asked Evelyn.

"A kwoon—it's a place to study fighting, a meditation hall." He looked at her but was really watching, Evelyn realized, something exciting she had missed. "They did a demonstration to drum up their membership. They broke boards and bricks, Evelyn. They went through what's called kata and kumite and . . ." He stopped again to breathe. "I've never seen anything so beautiful. The reason I'm late is because I wanted to talk with them after the movie."

Evelyn, suspicious, took a Valium and waited.

"I signed up for lessons," he said.

She gave a glacial look at Rudolph, then at his magazine, and said in the voice she used five years ago when he wanted to take a vacation to

Upper Volta or, before that, invest in a British car she knew they couldn't afford:

"You're fifty-*four* years old, Rudolph."

"I know that."

"You're no Muhammad Ali."

"I know that," he said.

"You're no Bruce Lee. Do you want to be Bruce Lee? Do you know where he is now, Rudolph? He'd dead—dead here in a Seattle cemetery and buried up on Capital Hill."

His shoulders slumped a little. Silently, Rudolph began undressing, his beefy backside turned toward her, slipping his pajama bottoms on before taking off his shirt so his scrawny lower body would not be fully exposed. He picked up his magazine, said, "I'm sorry if I worried you," and huffed upstairs to his bedroom. Evelyn clicked off the mushroom-shaped lamp on her nightstand. She lay on her side, listening to his slow footsteps strike the stairs, then heard his mattress creak above her—his bedroom was directly above hers—but she did not hear him click off his own light. From time to time she heard his shifting weight squeak the mattress springs. He was reading that foolish magazine, she guessed; then she grew tired and gave this impossible man up to God. With a copy of *The Thorn Birds* open on her lap, Evelyn fell heavily to sleep again.

At breakfast the next morning any mention of the lessons gave Rudolph lockjaw. He kissed her forehead, as always, before going to work, and simply said he might be home late. Climbing the stairs to his bedroom was painful for Evelyn, but she hauled herself up, pausing at each step to huff, then sat on his bed and looked over his copy of *Inside Kung-Fu*. There were articles on empty-hand combat, soft-focus photos of ferocious-looking men in funny suits, parables about legendary Zen masters, an interview with someone named Bernie Bernheim, who began to study karate at age fifty-seven and became a black belt at age sixty-one, and page after page of advertisements for exotic Asian weapons: nunchaku, shuriken, sai swords, tonfa, bo staffs, training bags of all sorts, a wooden dummy shaped like a man and called a Mook Jong, and weights. Rudolph had circled them all. He had torn the order form from the last page of the magazine. The total cost of the things he'd circled—Evelyn added them furiously, rounding off the figures—was $800.

Two minutes later she was on the telephone to Shelberdine.

"Let him tire of it," said her friend. "Didn't you tell me Rudolph had Lower Lombard Strain?"

Evelyn's nose clogged with tears.

"Why is he doing this? Is it me, do you think?"

"It's the Problem," said Shelberdine. "He wants his manhood back. Before he died, Arthur did the same. Someone at the plant told him he could get it back if he did twenty-yard sprints. He went into convulsions while running around the lake."

Evelyn felt something turn in her chest. "You don't think he'll hurt himself, do you?"

"Of course not."

"Do you think he'll hurt *me*?"

Her friend reassured Evelyn that Mid-Life Crisis brought out these shenanigans in men. Evelyn replied that she thought Mid-Life Crisis started around age forty, to which Shelberdine said, "Honey, I don't mean no harm, but Rudolph always was a little on the slow side," and Evelyn agreed. She would wait until he worked this thing out of his system, until Nature defeated him and he surrendered, as any right-thinking person would, to the breakdown of the body, the brutal fact of decay, which could only be blunted, it seemed to her, by decaying *with* someone, the comfort every Negro couple felt when, aging, they knew enough to let things wind down.

Her patience was rewarded in the beginning. Rudolph crawled home from his first lesson, hunched over, hardly able to stand, afraid he had permanently ruptured something. He collapsed face down on the living room sofa, his feet on the floor. She helped him change into his pajamas and fingered Ben-Gay into his back muscles. Evelyn had never seen her husband so close to tears.

"I can't *do* push-ups," he moaned. "Or sit-ups. I'm so stiff—I don't know my body." He lifted his head, looking up pitifully, his eyes pleading. "Call Dr. Guylee. Make an appointment for Thursday, okay?"

"Yes, dear." Evelyn hid her smile with one hand. "You shouldn't push yourself so hard."

At that, he sat up, bare-chested, his stomach bubbling over his pajama bottoms. "That's what it means. *Gung-fu* means 'hard work' in Chinese. Evelyn"—he lowered his voice—"I don't think I've ever really done hard work in my life. Not like this, something that asks me to give *every*thing, body and soul, spirit and flesh. I've always felt . . ." He looked down, his dark hands dangling between his thighs. "I've never been able to give *every*thing to *any*thing. The world never let me. It won't let me put all of myself into play. Do you know what I'm saying? Every job I've ever had, everything I've ever done, it only demanded part of me. It was like there was so much *more* of me that went unused after the job was over. I get that feeling in church sometimes." He lay back down, talking now into the sofa cushion. "Sometimes I get that feeling with you."

Her hand stopped on his shoulder. She wasn't sure she'd heard him right, his voice was so muffled. "That I've never used all of you?"

Rudolph nodded, rubbing his right knuckle where, at the kwoon, he'd lost a stretch of skin on a speedbag. "There's still part of me left over. You never tried to touch all of me, to take everything. Maybe you can't. Maybe no one can. But sometimes I get the feeling that the unused part—the unlived life—*spoils*, that you get cancer because it sits like fruit on the ground and rots." Rudolph shook his head; he'd said too much and knew it, perhaps had not even put it the way he felt inside. Stiffly, he got to his feet. "Don't ask me to stop training." His eyebrows spread inward. "If I stop, I'll die."

Evelyn twisted the cap back onto the Ben-Gay. She held out her hand, which Rudolph took. Veins on the back of his hand burgeoned abnormally like dough. Once when she was shopping at the Public Market she'd seen monstrous plastic gloves shaped like hands in a magic store window. His hand looked like that. It belonged on Lon Chaney. Her voice shook a little, panicky, "I'll call Dr. Guylee in the morning."

Evelyn knew—or thought she knew—his trouble. He'd never come to terms with the disagreeableness of things. Rudolph had always been too serious for some people, even in South Carolina. It was the thing, strange to say, that drew her to him, this crimped-browed tendency in Rudolph to listen with every atom of his life when their minister in Hodges, quoting Marcus Aurelius to give his sermon flash, said, "Live with the gods," or later in Seattle, the habit of working himself up over Reverend Merrill's reading from Ecclesiastes 9:10: "Whatsoever thy hand findeth to do, do it with all thy might." Now, he didn't *really* mean that, Evelyn knew. Nothing in the world could be taken that seriously; that's *why* this was the world. And, as all Mount Zion knew, Reverend Merrill had a weakness for high-yellow choir-girls and gin, and was forever complaining that his salary was too small for his family. People made compromises, nodded at spiritual commonplaces—the high seriousness of biblical verses that demanded nearly superhuman duty and self-denial—and laughed off their lapses into sloth, envy, and the other deadly sins. It was what made living so enjoyably *human*: this built-in inability of man to square his performance with perfection. People were naturally soft on themselves. But not her Rudolph.

Of course, he seldom complained. It was not in his nature to complain when, looking for "gods," he found only ruin and wreckage. What did he expect? Evelyn wondered. Man was evil—she'd told him that a thousand times—or, if not evil, hopelessly flawed. Everything failed; it was some sort of law. But at least there was laughter, and lovers clinging to one another against the cliff; there were novels—wonderful tales of how things should be—and perfection promised in the afterworld. He'd sit and listen, her Rudolph, when she put things this way, nodding because he knew that in his persistent hunger for perfection in the here and now he was, at best, in the minority. He kept his dissatisfaction to himself, but occasionally Evelyn would glimpse in his eyes that look, that distant, pained expression that asked: *Is this all?* She saw it after her first miscarriage, then her second; saw it when he stopped searching the want ads and settled on the Post Office as the fulfillment of his potential in the marketplace. It was always there, that look, after he turned forty, and no new, lavishly praised novel from the Book-of-the-Month Club, no feature-length movie, prayer meeting, or meal she fixed for him wiped it from Rudolph's eyes. He was, at least, this sort of man before he saw that martial-arts B movie. It was a dark vision, Evelyn decided, a dangerous vision, and in it she whiffed something that might destroy her. What that was, she couldn't say, but she knew her Rudolph better than he knew himself. He would see the error—the waste of time—in his new hobby, and she was sure he would mend his ways.

In the weeks, then months that followed Evelyn waited, watching her husband for a flag of surrender. There was no such sign. He became worse than before. He cooked his own meals, called her heavy soul food dishes "too acidic," lived on raw vegetables, seaweed, nuts, and fruit to make his body "more alkaline," and fasted on Sundays. He ordered books on something called Shaolin fighting and meditation from a store in California, and when his equipment arrived UPS from Dolan's Sports in New Jersey, he ordered more—in consternation, Evelyn read the list—leg stretchers, makiwara boards, air shields, hand grips, bokken, focus mitts, a full-length mirror (for heaven's sake) so he could correct his form, and protective equipment. For proper use of his headgear and gloves, however, he said he needed a sparring partner—an opponent— he said, to help him instinctively understand "combat strategy," how to "flow" and "close the Gap" between himself and an adversary, how to create by his movements a negative space in which the other would be neutralized.

"Well," crabbed Evelyn, "if you need a punching bag, don't look at *me*."

He sat across the kitchen table from her, doing dynamic-tension exercises as she read a new magazine called *Self*. "Did I ever tell you what a black belt means?" he asked.

"You told me."

"Sifu Chan doesn't use belts for ranking. They were introduced seventy years ago because Westerners were impatient, you know, needed signposts and all that."

"You told me," said Evelyn.

"Originally, all you got was a white belt. It symbolized innocence. Virginity." His face was immensely serious, like a preacher's. "As you worked, it got darker, dirtier, and turned brown. Then black. You were a master then. With even more work, the belt became frayed, the threads came loose, you see, and the belt showed white again."

"Rudolph, I've heard this before!" Evelyn picked up her magazine and took it into her bedroom. From there, with her legs drawn up under the blankets, she shouted: "I *won't* be your punching bag!"

So he brought friends from his kwoon, friends she wanted nothing to do with. There was something unsettling about them. Some were street fighters. Young. They wore tank-top shirts and motorcycle jackets. After drinking racks of Rainier beer on the front porch, they tossed their crumpled empties next door into Rod Kenner's yard. Together, two of Rudolph's new friends—Truck and Tuco—weighed a quarter of a ton. Evelyn kept a rolling pin under her pillow when they came, but she knew they could eat that along with her. But some of his new friends were students at the University of Washington. Truck, a Vietnamese only two years in America, planned to apply to the Police Academy once his training ended; and Tuco, who was Puerto Rican, had been fighting since he could make a fist; but a delicate young man named Andrea, a blue sash, was an actor in the drama department at the university. His kwoon training, he said, was less for self-defense than helping him understand his movements onstage—how, for example, to convincingly explode across a room in anger. Her husband liked them,

Evelyn realized in horror. And they liked him. They were separated by money, background, and religion, but something she could not identify made them seem, those nights on the porch after his class, like a single body. They called Rudolph "Older Brother" or, less politely, "Pop."

His sifu, a short, smooth-figured boy named Douglas Chan, who Evelyn figured couldn't be over eighteen, sat like the Dalai Lama in their tiny kitchen as if he owned it, sipping her tea, which Rudolph laced with Korean ginseng. Her husband lit Chan's cigarettes as if he were President Carter come to visit the common man. He recommended that Rudolph study T'ai Chi, "soft" fighting systems, ki, and something called Tao. He told him to study, as well, Newton's three laws of physics and apply them to his own body during kumite. What she remembered most about Chan were his wrist braces, ornamental weapons that had three straps and, along the black leather, highly polished studs like those worn by Steve Reeves in a movie she'd seen about Hercules. In a voice she thought girlish, he spoke of eye gouges and groin-tearing techniques, exercises called the Delayed Touch of Death and Dim Mak, with the casualness she and Shelberdine talked about bargains at Thriftway. And then they suited up, the boyish Sifu, who looked like Maharaj-ji's rougher brother, and her clumsy husband; they went out back, pushed aside the aluminum lawn furniture, and pommeled each other for half an hour. More precisely, her Rudolph was on the receiving end of hook kicks, spinning back fists faster than thought, and foot sweeps that left his body purpled for weeks. A sensible man would have known enough to drive to Swedish Hospital pronto. Rudolph, never known as a profound thinker, pushed on after Sifu Chan left, practicing his flying kicks by leaping to ground level from a four-foot hole he'd dug by their cyclone fence.

Evelyn, nibbling a Van de Kamp's pastry from Safeway—she was always nibbling, these days—watched from the kitchen window until twilight, then brought out the Ben-Gay, a cold beer, and rubbing alcohol on a tray. She figured he needed it. Instead, Rudolph, stretching under the far-reaching cedar in the backyard, politely refused, pushed the tray aside, and rubbed himself with Dit-Da-Jow, "iron-hitting wine," which smelled like the open door of an opium factory on a hot summer day. Yet this ancient potion not only instantly healed his wounds (said Rudolph) but prevented arthritis as well. She was tempted to see if it healed brain damage by pouring it into Rudolph's ears, but apparently he was doing something right. Dr. Guylee's examination had been glowing; he said Rudolph's muscle tone, whatever that was, was better. His cardiovascular system was healthier. His erections were outstanding—or upstanding—though lately he seemed to have no interest in sex. Evelyn, even she, saw in the crepuscular light changes in Rudolph's upper body as he stretched: Muscles like globes of light rippled along his shoulders; larval currents moved on his belly. The language of his new, developing body eluded her. He was not always like this. After a cold shower and sleep his muscles shrank back a little. It was only after his workouts, his weight lifting, that his body expanded like baking bread, filling out in a way that obliterated the soft Rudolph-body she knew. This new flesh had the contours of the silhouetted figures on medical charts: the body as it must be in the mind of God. Glistening with perspiration, his muscles took on the properties of the free weights he pumped relentlessly. They were profoundly tragic, too, because their beauty was earthbound. It would vanish with the world. You are ugly, his new muscles said to Evelyn; old and ugly. His self-punishment made her feel sick. She was afraid of his hard, cold weights. She hated them. Yet she wanted them, too. They had a certain monastic beauty. She thought: *He's doing this to hurt me.* She wondered: What was it like to be powerful? Was clever cynicism—even comedy—the by-product of bulging bellies, weak nerves, bad posture? Her only defense against the dumbbells that stood between them—she meant both his weights and his friends—was, as always, her acid southern tongue:

"They're all fairies, right?"

Rudolph looked dreamily her way. These post-workout periods made him feel, he said, as if there were no interval between himself and what he saw. His face was vacant, his eyes like smoke. In this afterglow (he said) he saw without judging. Without judgment, there were no distinctions. Without distinctions, there was no desire. Without desire . . .

He smiled sideways at her. "Who?"

"The people in your kwoon." Evelyn crossed her arms. "I read somewhere that most body builders are homosexual."

He refused to answer her.

"If they're not gay, then maybe I should take lessons. It's been good for you, right?" Her voice grew sharp. "I mean, isn't that what you're saying? That you and your friends are better'n everybody else?"

Rudolph's head dropped; he drew a long breath. Lately, his responses to her took the form of quietly clearing his lungs.

"You should do what you *have* to, Evelyn. You don't have to do what anybody else does." He stood up, touched his toes, then brought his forehead straight down against his unbent knees, which was physically impossible, Evelyn would have said—and faintly obscene.

It was a nightmare to watch him each evening after dinner. He walked around the house in his Everlast leg weights, tried push-ups on his fingertips and wrists, and, as she sat trying to watch "The Jeffersons," stood in a ready stance before the flickering screen, throwing punches each time the scene, or shot, changed to improve his timing. It took the fun out of watching TV, him doing that—she preferred him falling asleep in his chair beside her, as he used to. But what truly frightened Evelyn was his "doing nothing." Sitting in meditation, planted cross-legged in a full lotus on their front porch, with Mr. Miller blissfully curled on his lap, a Bodhisattva in the middle of houseplants she set out for the sun. Looking at him, you'd have thought he was dead. The whole thing smelled like self-hypnosis. He breathed too slowly, in Evelyn's view—only three breaths per minute, he claimed. He wore his gi, splotchy with dried blood and sweat, his calloused hands on his knees, the forefingers on each tipped against his thumbs, his eyes screwed shut.

During his eighth month at the kwoon, she stood watching him as he sat, wondering over the vivid changes in his body, the grim firmness where before there was jolly fat, the disquieting steadiness of his posture, where before Rudolph could not sit still in church for five minutes without fidgeting. Now he sat in zazen for forty-five minutes a day, fifteen when he awoke, fifteen (he said) at work in the mailroom during his lunch break, fifteen before going to bed. He called this withdrawal (how she hated his fancy language) similar to the necessary silences in music, "a stillness that prepared him for busyness and sound." He'd never breathed before, he told her. Not once. Not clear to the floor of himself. Never breathed and emptied himself as he did now, picturing himself sitting on the bottom of Lake Washington: himself, Rudolph Lee Jackson, at the center of the universe; for if the universe was infinite, any point where he stood would be at its center—it would shift and move with him. (That saying, Evelyn knew, was minted in Douglas Chan's mind. No Negro preacher worth the name would speak that way.) He told her that in zazen, at the bottom of the lake, he worked to discipline his mind and maintain one point of concentration; each thought, each feeling that overcame him he saw as a fragile bubble, which he could inspect passionlessly from all sides; then he let it float gently to the surface, and soon—as he slipped deeper into the vortices of himself, into the Void—even the image of himself on the lake floor vanished.

Evelyn stifled a scream.

Was she one of Rudolph's bubbles, something to detach himself from? On the porch, Evelyn watched him narrowly, sitting in a rain-whitened chair, her chin on her left fist. She snapped the fingers on her right hand under his nose. Nothing. She knocked her knuckles lightly on his forehead. Nothing. (Faker, she thought.) For another five minutes he sat and breathed, sat and breathed, then opened his eyes slowly as if he'd slept as long as Rip Van Winkle. "It's dark," he said, stunned. When he began, it was twilight. Evelyn realized something new: He was not living time as she was, not even that anymore. Things, she saw, were slower for him; to him she must seem like a woman stuck in fast-forward. She asked:

"What do you see when you go in there?"

Rudolph rubbed his eyes. "Nothing."

"Then *why* do you do it? The world's out here!"

He seemed unable to say, as if the question were senseless. His eyes angled up, like a child's, toward her face. "Nothing is peaceful some-times. The emptiness is full. I'm not afraid of it now."

"You empty yourself?" she asked. "Of me, too?"

"Yes."

Evelyn's hand shot up to cover her face. She let fly with a whimper. Rudolph rose instantly—he sent Mr. Miller flying—then fell back hard on his buttocks; the lotus cut off blood to his lower body—which pro-vided more to his brain, he claimed—and it always took him a few seconds before he could stand again. He reached up, pulled her hand down, and stroked it.

"What've I done?"

"That's it," sobbed Evelyn. "I don't know what you're doing." She lifted the end of her bathrobe, blew her nose, then looked at him through streaming, unseeing eyes. "And you don't either. I wish you'd never seen that movie. I'm sick of all your weights and workouts—sick of them, do you hear? Rudolph, I want you back the way you were: *sick*." No sooner than she said this Evelyn was sorry. But she'd done no harm. Rudolph, she saw, didn't want anything; everything, Evelyn included, delighted him, but as far as Rudolph was concerned, it was all shadows in a phantom history. He was humbler now, more patient, but he'd lost touch with everything she knew was normal in people: weakness, fear, guilt, self-doubt, the very things that gave the world thickness and made people do things. She *did* want him to desire her. No, she didn't. Not if it meant oral sex. Evelyn didn't know, really, what she wanted anymore. She felt, suddenly, as if she might dissolve before his eyes. "Rudolph, if you're 'empty,' like you say, you don't know who—or what—is talking to you. If you said you were praying, I'd understand. It would be God talking to you. But this way . . ." She pounded her fist four, five times on her thigh. "It could be *evil* spirits, you know! There *are* evil spirits, Rudolph. It could be the Devil."

Rudolph thought for a second. His chest lowered after another long breath. "Evelyn, this is going to sound funny, but I don't believe in the Devil."

Evelyn swallowed. It had come to that.

"Or God—unless we are gods."

She could tell he was at pains to pick his words carefully, afraid he might offend. Since joining the kwoon and studying ways to kill, he seemed particularly careful to avoid her own most effective weapon: the wry, cutting remark, the put-down, the direct, ego-deflating slash. Oh, he was becoming a real saint. At times, it made her want to hit him.

"Whatever is just *is*," he said. "That's all I know. Instead of worrying about whether it's good or bad, God or the Devil, I just want to be quiet, work on myself, and interfere with things as little as possible. Evelyn," he asked suddenly, "how can there be *two* things?" His brow wrinkled; he chewed his lip. "You think what I'm saying is evil, don't you?"

"I think it's strange! Rudolph, you didn't grow up in China," she said. "They can't breathe in China! I saw that today on the news. They burn soft coal, which gets into the air and turns into acid rain. They wear face masks over there, like the ones we bought when Mount St. Helens blew up. They all ride bicycles, for Christ's sake! They want what we have." Evelyn heard Rod Kenner step onto his screened porch, perhaps to listen from his rocker. She dropped her voice a little. "You grew up in Hodges, South Carolina, same as me, in a right and proper colored church. If you'd *been* to China, maybe I'd understand."

"I can only be what I've been?" This he asked softly, but his voice trembled. "Only what I was in Hodges?"

"You can't be Chinese."

"I don't want to be Chinese!" The thought made Rudolph smile and shake his head. Because she did not understand, and because he was tired of talking, Rudolph stepped back a few feet from her, stretching again, always stretching. "I only want to be what I *can* be, which isn't the greatest fighter in the world, only the fighter *I* can be. Lord knows, I'll probably get creamed in the tournament this Saturday." He added, before she could reply, "Doug asked me if I'd like to compete this weekend in full-contact matches with some people from the kwoon. I have to." He opened the screen door. "I will."

"You'll be killed—you know that, Rudolph." She dug her fingernails into her bathrobe, and dug this into him: "You know, you never were very strong. Six months ago you couldn't open a pickle jar for me."

He did not seem to hear her. "I bought a ticket for you." He held the screen door open, waiting for her to come inside. "I'll fight better if you're there."

She spent the better part of that week at Shelberdine's mornings and Reverend Merrill's church evenings, rinsing her mouth with prayer, sitting most often alone in the front row so she would not have to hear Rudolph talking to himself from the musty basement as he pounded out bench presses, skipped rope for thirty minutes in the backyard, or shadowboxed in preparation for a fight made inevitable by his new muscles. She had married a fool, that was clear, and if he expected her to sit on a bench at the Kingdome while some equally stupid brute spilled the rest of his brains—probably not enough left now to fill a teaspoon—then he was wrong. How could he see the world as "perfect"?—That was his claim. There was poverty, unemployment, twenty-one children dying every minute, every day, every year from hunger and malnutrition, over twenty murdered in Atlanta; there were sixty thousand nuclear weapons in the world, which was dreadful, what with Seattle so close to Boeing; there were far-right Republicans in the White House: *good* reasons, Evelyn thought, to be "negative and life-denying," as Rudolph would put it. It was almost sin to see harmony in an earthly hell, and in a fit of spleen she prayed God would dislocate his shoulder, do some minor damage to humble him, bring him home, and remind him that the body was vanity, a violation of every verse in the Bible. But Evelyn could not sustain her thoughts as long as he could. Not for more than a few seconds. Her mind never settled, never rested, and finally on Saturday morning, when she awoke on Shelberdine's sofa, it would not stay away from the image of her Rudolph dead before hundreds of indifferent spectators, paramedics pounding on his chest, bursting his rib cage in an effort to keep him alive.

From Shelberdine's house she called a taxi and, in the steady rain that northwesterners love, arrived at the Kingdome by noon. It's over already, Evelyn thought, walking the circular stairs to her seat, clamping shut her wet umbrella. She heard cheers, booing, an Asian voice with an accent over a microphone. The tournament began at ten, which was enough time for her white belt husband to be in the emergency ward at Harborview Hospital by now, but she had to see. At first, as she stepped down to her seat through the crowd, she could only hear—her mind grappled for the word, then remembered—kiais, or "spirit shouts," from the great floor of the stadium, many shouts, for contests were progressing in three rings simultaneously. It felt like a circus. It smelled like a locker room. Here two children stood toe to toe until one landed a front kick that sent the other child flying fifteen feet. There two lean-muscled female black belts were interlocked in a delicate ballet, like dance or a chess game, of continual motion. They had a kind of sense, these women—she noticed it immediately—a feel for space and their place in it. (Evelyn hated them immediately.) And in the farthest circle she saw, or rather felt, Rudolph, the oldest thing on the deck, who, sparring in the adult division, was squared off with another white belt, not a boy who might hurt him—the other man was middle-aged, graying, maybe only a few years younger than Rudolph—but they were sparring just the same.

Yet it was not truly him that Evelyn, sitting down, saw. Acoustics in the Kingdome whirlpooled the noise of the crowd, a rivering of voices that affected her, suddenly, like the pitch and roll of voices during service. It affected the way she watched Rudolph. She wondered: Who are these people? She caught her breath when, miscalculating his distance from his opponent, her husband stepped sideways into a roundhouse kick with lots of snap—she heard the cloth of his opponent's gi crack like a gunshot when he threw the technique. She leaned forward, gripping the huge purse on her lap when Rudolph recovered and retreated from the killing to the neutral zone, and then, in a wide stance, rethought strategy. This was not the man she'd slept with for twenty years. Not her hypochondriac Rudolph who had to rest and run cold water on his wrists after walking from the front stairs to the fence to pick up the *Seattle Times*. She did not know him, perhaps had never known him, and now she never would, for the man on the floor, the man splashed with sweat, rising on the ball of his rear foot for a flying kick—was he so foolish he still thought he could fly?—would outlive her; he'd stand healthy and strong and think of her in a bubble, one hand on her headstone, and it was all right, she thought, weeping uncontrollably, it was all right that Rudolph would return home after visiting her wet grave, clean out her bedroom, the pillboxes and paperback books, and throw open her windows to let her sour, rotting smell escape, then move a younger woman's things onto the floor space darkened by her color television, her porcelain chamber pot, her antique sewing machine. And then Evelyn was on her feet, unsure why, but the crowd had stood suddenly to clap, and Evelyn clapped, too, though for an instant she pounded her gloved hands together instinctively until her vision cleared, the momentary flash of retinal blindness giving way to a frame of her husband, the postman, twenty feet off the ground in a perfect flying kick that floored his opponent and made a Japanese judge who looked like Oddjob shout "ippon"—one point—and the fighting in the farthest ring, in herself, perhaps in all the world, was over.

PET MILK

Stuart Dybek • 1984

Today I've been drinking instant coffee and Pet milk, and watching it snow. It's not that I enjoy the taste especially, but I like the way Pet milk swirls in the coffee. Actually, my favorite thing about Pet milk is what the can opener does to the top of the can. The can is unmistakable—compact, seamless looking, its very shape suggesting that it could condense milk without any trouble. The can opener bites in neatly, and the thick liquid spills from the triangular gouge with a different look and viscosity than milk. Pet milk isn't *real* milk. The color's off, to start with. There's almost something of the past about it, like old ivory. My grandmother always drank it in her coffee. When friends dropped over and sat around the kitchen table, my grandma would ask, "Do you take cream and sugar?" Pet milk was the cream.

There was a yellow plastic radio on her kitchen table, usually tuned to the polka station, though sometimes she'd miss it by half a notch and get the Greek station instead, or the Spanish, or the Ukrainian. In Chicago, where we lived, all the incompatible states of Europe were pressed together down at the staticky right end of the dial. She didn't seem to notice, as long as she wasn't hearing English. The radio, turned low, played constantly. Its top was warped and turning amber on the side where the tubes were. I remember the sound of it on winter afternoons after school, as I sat by her table watching the Pet milk swirl and cloud in the steaming coffee, and noticing, outside her window, the sky doing the same thing above the railroad yard across the street.

And I remember, much later, seeing the same swirling sky in tiny liqueur glasses containing a drink called a King Alphonse: the crème de cacao rising like smoke in repeated explosions, blooming in kaleidoscopic clouds through the layer of heavy cream. This was in the Pilsen, a little Czech restaurant where my girlfriend, Kate, and I would go sometimes in the evening. It was the first year out of college for both of us, and we had astonished ourselves by finding real jobs—no more waitressing or pumping gas, the way we'd done in school. I was investigating credit references at a bank, and she was doing something slightly above the rank of typist for Hornblower & Weeks, the investment firm. My bank showed training films that emphasized the importance of suitable dress, good grooming, and personal neatness, even for employees like me, who worked at the switchboard in the basement. Her firm issued directives on appropriate attire—skirts, for instance, should cover the knees. She had lovely knees.

Kate and I would sometimes meet after work at the Pilsen, dressed in our proper business clothes and still feeling both a little self-conscious and glamorous, as if we were impostors wearing disguises. The place had small, round oak tables, and we'd sit in a corner under a painting called "The Street Musicians of Prague" and trade future plans as if they were escape routes. She talked of going to grad school in Europe; I wanted to apply to the Peace Corps. Our plans for the future made us laugh and feel close, but those same plans somehow made anything more than temporary between us seem impossible. It was the first time I'd ever had the feeling of missing someone I was still with.

The waiters in the Pilsen wore short black jackets over long white aprons. They were old men from the old country. We went there often enough to have our own special waiter, Rudi, a name he pronounced with a rolled R. Rudi boned our trout and seasoned our salads, and at the end of the meal he'd bring the bottle of crème de cacao from the bar, along with two little glasses and a small pitcher of heavy cream, and make us each a King Alphonse right at our table. We'd watch as he'd fill the glasses halfway up with the syrupy brown liqueur, then carefully attempt to float a layer of cream on top. If he failed to float the cream, we'd get that one free.

"Who was King Alphonse anyway, Rudi?" I sometimes asked, trying to break his concentration, and if that didn't work I nudged the table with my foot so the glass would jiggle imperceptibly just as he was floating the cream. We'd usually get one on the house. Rudi knew what I was doing. In fact, serving the King Alphonses had been his idea, and he had also suggested the trick of jarring the table. I think it pleased him, though he seemed concerned about the way I'd stare into the liqueur glass, watching the patterns.

"It's not a microscope," he'd say. "Drink."

He liked us, and we tipped extra. It felt good to be there and to be able to pay for a meal.

K ate and I met at the Pilsen for supper on my twenty-second birthday. It was May, and unseasonably hot. I'd opened my tie. Even before looking at the dinner menu, we ordered a bottle of Mumm's and a dozen oysters apiece. Rudi made a sly remark when he brought the oysters on platters of ice. They were freshly opened and smelled of the sea. I'd heard people joke about oysters being aphrodisiac but never considered it anything but a myth—the kind of idea they still had in the old country.

We squeezed on lemon, added dabs of horseradish, slid the oysters into our mouths, and then rinsed the shells with champagne and drank the salty, cold juice. There was a beefy-looking couple eating schnitzel at the next table, and they stared at us with the repugnance that public oyster-eaters in the Midwest often encounter. We laughed and grandly sipped it all down. I was already half tipsy from drinking too fast, and starting to feel filled with a euphoric, aching energy. Kate raised a brimming oyster shell to me in a toast: "To the Peace Corps!"

"To Europe!" I replied, and we clunked shells.

She touched her wineglass to mine and whispered, "Happy birthday," and then suddenly leaned across the table and kissed me.

When she sat down again, she was flushed. I caught the reflection of her face in the glass-covered "The Street Musicians of Prague" above our table. I always loved seeing her in mirrors and windows. The reflections of her beauty startled me. I had told her that once, and she seemed to fend off the compliment, saying, "That's because you've learned what to look for," as if it were a secret I'd stumbled upon. But, this time, seeing her reflection hovering ghostlike upon an imaginary Prague was like seeing a future from which she had vanished. I knew I'd never meet anyone more beautiful to me.

We killed the champagne and sat twining fingers across the table. I was sweating. I could feel the warmth of her through her skirt under the table and I touched her leg. We still hadn't ordered dinner. I left money on the table and we steered each other out a little unsteadily.

"Rudi will understand," I said.

The street was blindingly bright. A reddish sun angled just above the rims of the tallest buildings. I took my suit coat off and flipped it over my shoulder. We stopped in the doorway of a shoe store to kiss.

"Let's go somewhere," she said.

My roommate would already be home at my place, which was closer. Kate lived up north, in Evanston. It seemed a long way away.

We cut down a side street, past a fire station, to a small park, but its gate was locked. I pressed close to her against the tall iron fence. We could smell the lilacs from a bush just inside the fence, and when I jumped for an overhanging branch my shirt sleeve hooked on a fence spike and tore, and petals rained down on us as the sprig sprang from my hand.

We walked to the subway. The evening rush was winding down; we must have caught the last express heading toward Evanston. Once the train climbed from the tunnel to the elevated tracks, it wouldn't stop until the end of the line, on Howard. There weren't any seats together, so we stood swaying at the front of the car, beside the empty conductor's compartment. We wedged inside, and I clicked the door shut.

The train rocked and jounced, clattering north. We were kissing, trying to catch the rhythm of the ride with our bodies. The sun bronzed the windows on our side of the train. I lifted her skirt over her knees, hiked it higher so the sun shone off her thighs, and bunched it around her waist. She wouldn't stop kissing. She was moving her hips to pin us to each jolt of the train.

We were speeding past scorched brick walls, gray windows, back porches outlined in sun, roofs, and treetops—the landscape of the El I'd memorized from subway windows over a lifetime of rides: the podiatrist's foot sign past Fullerton; the bright pennants of Wrigley Field, at Addison; ancient hotels with TRANSIENTS WELCOME signs on their flaking back walls; peeling and graffiti-smudged billboards; the old cemetery just before Wilson Avenue. Even without looking, I knew almost exactly where we were. Within the compartment, the sound of our quick breathing was louder than the clatter of tracks. I was trying to slow down, to make it all last, and when she covered my mouth with her hand I turned my face to the window and looked out.

The train was braking a little from express speed, as it did each time it passed a local station. I could see blurred faces on the long wooden platform watching us pass—businessmen glancing up from folded newspapers, women clutching purses and shopping bags. I could see the expression on each face, momentarily arrested, as we flashed by. A high school kid in shirt sleeves, maybe sixteen, with books tucked under one arm and a cigarette in his mouth, caught sight of us, and in the instant before he disappeared he grinned and started to wave. Then he was gone, and I turned from the window, back to Kate, forgetting everything—the passing stations, the glowing late sky, even the sense of missing her—but that arrested wave stayed with me. It was as if I were standing on that platform, with my schoolbooks and a smoke, on one of those endlessly accumulated afternoons after school when I stood almost outside of time simply waiting for a train, and I thought how much I'd have loved seeing someone like us streaming by.

THE WAY WE LIVE NOW

Susan Sontag • 1986

A t first he was just losing weight, he felt only a little ill, Max said to Ellen, and he didn't call for an appointment with his doctor, according to Greg, because he was managing to keep on working at more or less the same rhythm, but he did stop smoking, Tanya pointed out, which suggests he was frightened, but also that he wanted, even more than he knew, to be healthy, or healthier, or maybe just to gain back a few pounds, said Orson, for he told her, Tanya went on, that he expected to be climbing the walls (isn't that what people say?) and found, to his surprise, that he didn't miss cigarettes at all and reveled in the sensation of his lungs being ache-free for the first time in years. But did he have a good doctor, Stephen wanted to know, since it would have been crazy not to go for a checkup after the pressure was off and he was back from the conference in Helsinki, even if by then he was feeling better. And he said, to Frank, that he would go, even though he was indeed frightened, as he admitted to Jan, but who wouldn't be frightened now, though, odd as that might seem, he hadn't been worrying until recently, he avowed to Quentin, it was only in the last six months that he had the metallic taste of panic in his mouth, because becoming seriously ill was something that happened to other people, a normal delusion, he observed to Paolo, if one was thirty-eight and had never had a serious illness; he wasn't, as Jan confirmed, a hypochondriac. Of course, it was hard not to worry, everyone was worried, but it wouldn't do to panic, because, as Max pointed out to Quentin, there wasn't anything one could do except wait and hope, wait and start being careful, be careful, and hope. And even if one did prove to be ill, one shouldn't give up, they had new treatments that promised an arrest of the disease's inexorable course, research was progressing. It seemed that everyone was in touch with everyone else several times a week, checking in, I've never spent so many hours at a time on the phone, Stephen said to Kate, and when I'm exhausted after the two or three calls made to me, giving me the latest, instead of switching off the phone to give myself a respite I tap out the number of another friend or acquaintance, to pass on the news. I'm not sure I can afford to think so much about it, Ellen said, and I suspect my own motives, there's something morbid I'm getting used to, getting excited by, this must be like what people felt in London during the Blitz. As far as I know, I'm not at risk, but you never know, said Aileen. This thing is totally unprecedented, said Frank. But don't you think he ought to see a doctor, Stephen insisted. Listen, said Orson, you can't force people to take care of themselves, and what makes you think the worst, he could be just run down, people still do get ordinary illnesses, awful ones, why are you assuming it has to be *that*. But all I want to be sure, said Stephen, is that he understands the options, because most people don't, that's why they won't see a doctor or have the test, they think there's nothing one can do. But is there anything one can do, he said to Tanya (according to Greg), I mean what do I gain if I go to the doctor; if I'm really ill, he's reported to have said, I'll find out soon enough.

And when he was in the hospital, his spirits seemed to lighten, according to Donny. He seemed more cheerful than he had been in the last months, Ursula said, and the bad news seemed to come almost as a relief, according to Ira, as a truly unexpected blow, according to Quentin, but you'd hardly expect him to have said the same thing to all his friends, because his relation to Ira was so different from his relation to Quentin (this according to Quentin, who was proud of their friendship), and perhaps he thought Quentin wouldn't be undone by seeing him weep, but Ira insisted that couldn't be the reason he behaved so differently with each, and that maybe he was feeling less shocked, mobilizing his strength to fight for his life, at the moment he saw Ira but overcome by feelings of hopelessness when Quentin arrived with flowers, because anyway the flowers threw him into a bad mood, as Quentin told Kate, since the hospital room was choked with flowers, you couldn't have crammed another flower into that room, but surely you're exaggerating, Kate said, smiling, everybody likes flowers. Well, who wouldn't exaggerate at a time like this, Quentin said sharply. Don't you think *this* is an exaggeration. Of course I do, said Kate gently, I was only teasing, I mean I didn't mean to tease. I know that, Quentin said, with tears in his eyes, and Kate hugged him and said well, when I go this evening I guess I won't bring flowers, what does he want, and Quentin said, according to Max, what he likes best is chocolate. Is there anything else, asked Kate, I mean like chocolate but not chocolate. Licorice, said Quentin, blowing his nose. And besides that. Aren't *you* exaggerating now, Quentin said, smiling. Right, said Kate, so if I want to bring him a whole raft of stuff, besides chocolate and licorice, what else. Jelly beans, Quentin said.

He didn't want to be alone, according to Paolo, and lots of people came in the first week, and the Jamaican nurse said there were other patients on the floor who would be glad to have the surplus flowers, and people weren't afraid to visit, it wasn't like the old days, as Kate pointed out to Aileen, they're not even segregated in the hospital any more, as Hilda observed, there's nothing on the door of his room warn-

ing visitors of the possibility of contagion, as there was a few years ago;
in fact, he's in a double room and, as he told Orson, the old guy on the
far side of the curtain (who's clearly on the way out, said Stephen)
doesn't even have the disease, so, as Kate went on, you really should go
and see him, he'd be happy to see you, he likes having people visit, you
aren't not going because you're afraid, are you. Of course not, Aileen
said, but I don't know what to say, I think I'll feel awkward, which he's
bound to notice, and that will make him feel worse, so I won't be doing
him any good, will I. But he won't notice anything, Kate said, patting
Aileen's hand, it's not like that, it's not the way you imagine, he's not
judging people or wondering about their motives, he's just happy to see
his friends. But I never was really a friend of his, Aileen said, you're a
friend, he's always liked you, you told me he talks about Nora with you,
I know he likes me, he's even attracted to me, but he respects you. But,
according to Wesley, the reason Aileen was so stingy with her visits was
that she could never have him to herself, there were always others there
already and by the time they left still others had arrived, she'd been in
love with him for years, and I can understand, said Donny, that Aileen
should feel bitter that if there could have been a woman friend he did
more than occasionally bed, a woman he really loved, and my God,
Victor said, who had known him in those years, he was crazy about
Nora, what a heartrending couple they were, two surly angels, then it
couldn't have been she.

And when some of the friends, the ones who came every day, waylaid
the doctor in the corridor, Stephen was the one who asked the
most informed questions, who'd been keeping up not just with the stories that appeared several times a week in the *Times* (which Greg confessed to have stopped reading, unable to stand it any more) but with
articles in the medical journals published here and in England and
France, and who knew socially one of the principal doctors in Paris who

was doing some much-publicized research on the disease, but his doctor said little more than that the pneumonia was not life-threatening, the fever was subsiding, of course he was still weak but he was responding well to the antibiotics, that he'd have to complete his stay in the hospital, which entailed a minimum of twenty-one days on the I.V., before she could start him on the new drug, for she was optimistic about the possibility of getting him into the protocol; and when Victor said that if he had so much trouble eating (he'd say to everyone, when they coaxed him to eat some of the hospital meals, that food didn't taste right, that he had a funny metallic taste in his mouth) it couldn't be good that friends were bringing him all that chocolate, the doctor just smiled and said that in these cases the patient's morale was also an important factor, and if chocolate made him feel better she saw no harm in it, which worried Stephen, as Stephen said later to Donny, because they wanted to believe in the promises and taboos of today's high-tech medicine but here this reassuringly curt and silver-haired specialist in the disease, someone quoted frequently in the papers, was talking like some oldfangled country G.P. who tells the family that tea with honey or chicken soup may do as much for the patient as penicillin, which might mean, as Max said, that they were just going through the motions of treating him, that they were not sure about what to do, or rather, as Xavier interjected, that they didn't know what the hell they were doing, that the truth, the real truth, as Hilda said, upping the ante, was that they didn't, the doctors, really have any hope.

Oh, no, said Lewis, I can't stand it, wait a minute, I can't believe it, are you sure, I mean are they sure, have they done all the tests, it's getting so when the phone rings I'm scared to answer because I think it will be someone telling me someone else is ill; but did Lewis really not know until yesterday, Robert said testily, I find that hard to believe, everybody is talking about it, it seems impossible that someone wouldn't have called Lewis; and perhaps Lewis did know, was for some reason pretending not to know already, because, Jan recalled, didn't Lewis say something months ago to Greg, and not only to Greg, about his not looking well, losing weight, and being worried about him and wishing he'd see a doctor, so it couldn't come as a total surprise. Well, everybody is worried about everybody now, said Betsy, that seems to be the way we live, the way we live now. And, after all, they were once very close, doesn't Lewis still have the keys to his apartment, you know the way you let someone keep the keys after you've broken up, only a little because you hope the person might just saunter in, drunk or high, late some evening, but mainly because it's wise to have a few sets of keys strewn around town, if you live alone, at the top of a former commercial building that, pretentious as it is, will never acquire a doorman or even a resident superintendent, someone whom you can call on for the keys late one night if you find you've lost yours or have locked yourself out. Who else has keys, Tanya inquired, I was thinking somebody might drop by tomorrow before coming to the hospital and bring some treasures, because the other day, Ira said, he was complaining about how dreary the hospital room was, and how it was like being locked up in a motel room, which got everybody started telling funny stories about motel rooms they'd known, and at Ursula's story, about the Luxury Budget Inn in Schenectady, there was an uproar of laughter around his bed, while he watched them in silence, eyes bright with fever, all the while, as Victor recalled, gobbling that damned chocolate. But, according to Jan, whom Lewis's keys enabled to tour the swank of his bachelor lair with an eye to bringing over some art consolation to brighten up the hospital room, the Byzantine icon wasn't on the wall over his bed, and that was a puzzle until Orson remembered that he'd recounted without seeming upset (this disputed by Greg) that the boy he'd recently gotten rid of had stolen it, along with four of the *maki-e* lacquer boxes, as if these were objects as easy to sell on the street as a TV or a stereo. But he's always been very generous, Kate said quietly, and though he loves something to reread one day, slyly staking out his claim to a future time, in which the diary would be an object, a relic, in which he might not actually reread it, because he would want to have put this ordeal behind him, but the diary would be there in the drawer of his stupendous Majorelle desk, and he could already, he did actually say to Quentin one late sunny afternoon, propped up in the hospital bed, with the stain of chocolate framing one corner of a heartbreaking smile, see himself in the penthouse, the October sun streaming through those clear windows instead of this streaked one, and the diary, the pathetic diary, safe inside the drawer.

It doesn't matter about the treatment's side effects, Stephen said (when talking to Max), I don't know why you're so worried about that, every strong treatment has some dangerous side effects, it's inevitable, you mean otherwise the treatment wouldn't be effective, Hilda interjected, and anyway, Stephen went on doggedly, just because there *are* side effects it doesn't mean he has to get them, or all of them, each one, or even some of them. That's just a list of all the possible things that could go wrong, because the doctors have to cover themselves, so they make up a worst-case scenario, but isn't what's happening to him, and to so many other people, Tanya interrupted, a worst-case scenario, a catastrophe no one could have imagined, it's too cruel, and isn't everything a side effect, quipped Ira, even *we* are all side effects, but we're not bad side effects, Frank said, he likes having his friends around, and we're helping each other, too; because his illness sticks us all in the same glue, mused Xavier, and, whatever the jealousies and grievances from the past that have made us wary and cranky with each other, when something like this happens (the sky is falling, the sky is falling!) you understand what's really important. I agree, Chicken Little, he is reported to have said. But don't you think, Quentin observed to Max, that being as close to him as we are, making time to drop by the hospital every day, is a way of our trying to define ourselves more firmly and irrevocably as the well, those who aren't ill, who aren't going to fall ill, as if what's happened to him couldn't happen to us, when in fact the chances are that before long one of us will end up where he is, which is probably what he felt when he was one of the cohort visiting Zack in the spring (you never knew Zack, did you?), and, according to Clarice, Zack's widow, he didn't come very often, he said he hated hospitals, and didn't feel he was doing Zack any good, that Zack would see on his face how uncomfortable he was. Oh, he was one of those, Aileen said. A coward. Like me.

And after he was sent home from the hospital, and Quentin had volunteered to move in and was cooking meals and taking telephone messages and keeping the mother in Mississippi informed, well, mainly keeping her from flying to New York and heaping her grief on her son and confusing the household routine with her oppressive ministrations, he was able to work an hour or two in his study, on days he didn't insist on going out, for a meal or a movie, which tired him. He seemed optimistic, Kate thought, his appetite was good, and what he said, Orson reported, was that he agreed when Stephen advised him that the main thing was to keep in shape, he was a fighter, right, he wouldn't be who he was if he weren't, and was he ready for the big fight, Stephen asked rhetorically (as Max told it to Donny), and he said you bet, and Stephen added it could be a lot worse, you could have gotten the disease two years ago, but now so many scientists are working on it, the American team and the French team, everyone bucking for that Nobel Prize a few years down the road, that all you have to do is stay healthy for another year or two and then there will be good treatment, real treatment. Yes, he said, Stephen said, my timing is good. And Betsy, who had been climbing on and rolling off macrobiotic diets for a decade, came up with a Japanese specialist she wanted him to see but thank God, Donny reported, he'd had the sense to refuse, but he did the telephone call to his doctor, he was willing to say the name of the disease, pronounce it often and easily, as if it were just another word, like boy or gallery or cigarette or money or deal, as in no big deal, Paolo interjected, because, as Stephen continued, to utter the name is a sign of health, a sign that one has accepted being who one is, mortal, vulnerable, not exempt, not an exception after all, it's a sign that one is willing, truly willing, to fight for one's life. And we must say the name, too, and often, Tanya added, we mustn't lag behind him in honesty, or let him feel that, the effort of honesty having been made, it's something done with and he can go on to other things. One is so much better prepared to help him, Wesley replied. In a way he's fortunate, said Yvonne, who had taken care of a problem at the New York store and was flying back to London this evening, sure, fortunate, said Wesley, no one is shunning him, Yvonne went on, no one's afraid to hug him or kiss him lightly on the mouth, in London we are, as usual, a few years behind you, people I know, people who would seem to be not even remotely at risk, are just terrified, but I'm impressed by how cool and rational you all are; you find us cool, asked Quentin. But I have to say, he's reported to have said, I'm terrified, I find it very hard to read (and you know how he loves to read, said Greg; yes, reading is his television, said Paolo) or to think, but I don't feel hysterical. I feel quite hysterical, Lewis said to Yvonne. But you're able to *do* something for him, that's wonderful, how I wish I could stay longer, Yvonne answered, it's rather beautiful, I can't help thinking, this utopia of friendship you've assembled around him (this pathetic utopia, said Kate), so that the disease, Yvonne concluded, is not, any more, out there. Yes, don't you think we're more at home here, with him, with the disease, said Tanya, because the imagined disease is so much worse than the reality of him, whom we all love, each in our fashion, having it. I know for me his getting it has quite demystified the disease, said Jan, I don't feel afraid, spooked, as I did before he became ill, when it was only news about remote acquaintances, whom I never saw again after they became ill. But you know you're not going to come down with the disease, Quentin said, to which Ellen replied, on her behalf, that's not the point, and possibly untrue, my gynecologist says that everyone is at risk, everyone who has a sexual life, because sexuality is a chain that links each of us to many others, unknown others, and now the great chain of being has become a chain of death as well. It's not the same for you, Quentin insisted, it's not the same for you as it is for me or Lewis or Frank or Paolo or Max, I'm more and more frightened, and I have every reason to be. I don't think about whether I'm at risk or not, said Hilda, I know that I was afraid to know someone with the disease, afraid of what I'd see, what I'd feel, and after the first day I came to the hospital I felt so relieved. I'll never feel that way, that fear, again; he doesn't seem different from me. He's not, Quentin said.

According to Lewis, he talked more often about those who visited more often, which is natural, said Betsy, I think he's even keeping a tally. And among those who came or checked in by phone every day, the inner circle as it were, those who were getting more points, there was still a further competition, which was what was getting on Betsy's nerves, she confessed to Jan; there's always that vulgar jockeying for position around the bedside of the gravely ill, and though we all feel suffused with virtue at our loyalty to him (speak for yourself, said Jan), to the extent that we're carving time out of every day, or almost every day, though some of us are dropping out, as Xavier pointed out, aren't we getting at least as much out of this as he is. Are we, said Jan. We're rivals for a sign from him of special pleasure over a visit, each stretching for the brass ring of his favor, wanting to feel the most wanted, the true nearest and dearest, which is inevitable with someone who doesn't have a spouse and children or an official in-house lover, hierarchies that no one would dare contest, Betsy went on, so we are the family he's founded, without meaning to, without official titles and ranks (we, we, snarled Quentin); and is it so clear, though some of us, Lewis and Quentin and

Tanya and Paolo, among others, are ex-lovers and all of us more or less
than friends, which one of us he prefers, Victor said (now it's us, raged
Quentin), because sometimes I think he looks forward more to seeing
Aileen, who has visited only three times, twice at the hospital and once
since he's been home, than he does you or me; but, according to Tanya,
after being very disappointed that Aileen hadn't come, now he was
angry, while, according to Xavier, he was not really hurt but touchingly
passive, accepting Aileen's absence as something he somehow deserved.
But he's happy to have people around, said Lewis; he says when he
doesn't have company he gets very sleepy, he sleeps (according to Quentin), and then perks up when someone arrives, it's important that he not
feel ever alone. But, said Victor, there's one person he hasn't heard from,
whom he'd probably like to hear from more than most of us; but she
didn't just vanish, even right after she broke away from him, and he
knows exactly where she lives now, said Kate, he told me he put in a call
to her last Christmas Eve, and she said it's nice to hear from you and
Merry Christmas, and he was shattered, according to Orson, and furious and disdainful, according to Ellen (what do you expect of her, said
Wesley, she was burned out), but Kate wondered if maybe he hadn't
phoned Nora in the middle of a sleepless night, what's the time difference, and Quentin said no, I don't think so, I think he wouldn't want
her to know.

And when he was feeling even better and had regained the pounds
he'd shed right away in the hospital, though the refrigerator started
to fill up with organic wheat germ and grapefruit and skimmed milk
(he's worried about his cholesterol count, Stephen lamented), and told
Quentin he could manage by himself now, and did, he started asking
everyone who visited how he looked, and everyone said he looked great,
so much better than a few weeks ago, which didn't jibe with what anyone had told him at that time; but then it was getting harder and harder

to know how he looked, to answer such a question honestly when among themselves they wanted to be honest, both for honesty's sake and (as Donny thought) to prepare for the worst, because he'd been looking like *this* for so long, at least it seemed so long, that it was as if he'd always been like this, how did he look before, but it was only a few months, and those words, pale and wan-looking and fragile, hadn't they always applied? And one Thursday Ellen, meeting Lewis at the door of the building, said, as they rode up together in the elevator, how is he *really*? But you see how he is, Lewis said tartly, he's fine, he's perfectly healthy, and Ellen understood that of course Lewis didn't think he was perfectly healthy but that he wasn't worse, and that was true, but wasn't it, well, almost heartless to talk like that. Seems inoffensive to me, Quentin said, but I know what you mean, I remember once talking to Frank, somebody, after all, who has volunteered to do five hours a week of office work at the Crisis Center (I know, said Ellen), and Frank was going on about this guy, diagnosed almost a year ago, and so much further along, who'd been complaining to Frank on the phone about the indifference of some doctor, and had gotten quite abusive about the doctor, and Frank was saying there was no reason to be so upset, the implication being that *he*, Frank, wouldn't behave so irrationally, and I said, barely able to control my scorn, but Frank, Frank, he has every reason to be upset, he's dying, and Frank said, said according to Quentin, oh, I don't like to think about it that way.

And it was while he was still home, recuperating, getting his weekly treatment, still not able to do much work, he complained, but, according to Quentin, up and about most of the time and turning up at the office several days a week, that bad news came about two remote acquaintances, one in Houston and one in Paris, news that was intercepted by Quentin on the ground that it could only depress him, but Stephen contended that it was wrong to lie to him, it was so important

for him to live in the truth; that had been one of his first victories, that
he was candid, that he was even willing to crack jokes about the disease,
but Ellen said it wasn't good to give him this end-of-the-world feeling,
too many people were getting ill, it was becoming such a common destiny that maybe some of the will to fight for his life would be drained
out of him if it seemed to be as natural as, well, death. Oh, Hilda said,
who didn't know personally either the one in Houston or the one in
Paris, but knew *of* the one in Paris, a pianist who specialized in
twentieth-century Czech and Polish music, I have his records, he's such
a valuable person, and, when Kate glared at her, continued defensively,
I know every life is equally sacred, but that *is* a thought, another thought,
I mean, all these valuable people who aren't going to have their normal
fourscore as it is now, these people aren't going to be replaced, and it's
such a loss to the culture. But this isn't going to go on forever, Wesley
said, it can't, they're bound to come up with something (they, they, muttered Stephen), but did you ever think, Greg said, that if some people
don't die, I mean even if they can keep them alive (they, they, muttered
Kate), they continue to be carriers, and that means, if you have a conscience, that you can never make love, make love fully, as you'd been
wont—wantonly, Ira said—to do. But it's better than dying, said Frank.
And in all his talk about the future, when he allowed himself to be
hopeful, according to Quentin, he never mentioned the prospect that
even if he didn't die, if he were so fortunate as to be among the first
generation of the disease's survivors, never mentioned, Kate confirmed,
that whatever happened it was over, the way he had lived until now, but,
according to Ira, he did think about it, the end of bravado, the end of
folly, the end of trusting life, the end of taking life for granted, and of
treating life as something that, samurai-like, he thought himself ready
to throw away lightly, impudently; and Kate recalled, sighing, a brief
exchange she'd insisted on having as long as two years ago, huddling on
a banquette covered with steel-gray industrial carpet on an upper level

of The Prophet and toking up for their next foray onto the dance floor: she'd said hesitantly, for it felt foolish asking a prince of debauchery to, well, take it easy, and she wasn't keen on playing big sister, a role, as Hilda confirmed, he inspired in many women, are you being careful, honey, you know what I mean. And he replied, Kate went on, no, I'm not, listen, I can't, I just can't, sex is too important to me, always has been (he started talking like that, according to Victor, after Nora left him), and if I get it, well, I get it. But he wouldn't talk like that now, would he, said Greg; he must feel awfully foolish now, said Betsy, like someone who went on smoking, saying I can't give up cigarettes, but when the bad X-ray is taken even the most besotted nicotine addict can stop on a dime. But sex isn't like cigarettes, is it, said Frank, and, besides, what good does it do to remember that he was reckless, said Lewis angrily, the appalling thing is that you just have to be unlucky once, and wouldn't he feel even worse if he'd stopped three years ago and had come down with it anyway, since one of the most terrifying features of the disease is that you don't know when you contracted it, it could have been ten years ago, because surely this disease has existed for years and years, long before it was recognized; that is, named. Who knows how long (I think a lot about that, said Max) and who knows (I know what you're going to say, Stephen interrupted) how many are going to get it.

I'm feeling fine, he's reported to have said whenever someone asked him how he was, which was almost always the first question anyone asked. Or: I'm feeling better, how are you? But he said other things, too. I'm playing leapfrog with myself, he is reported to have said, according to Victor. And: There must be a way to get something positive out of this situation, he's reported to have said to Kate. How American of him, said Paolo. Well, said Betsy, you know the old American adage: When you've got a lemon, make lemonade. The one thing I'm sure I couldn't take, Jan said he said to her, is becoming disfigured, but Stephen hastened to point out the disease doesn't take that form very often any more, its profile is mutating, and, in conversation with Ellen, wheeled up words like blood-brain barrier, I never thought there was a barrier *there*, said Jan. But he mustn't know about Max, Ellen said, that would really depress him, please don't tell him, he'll have to know, Quentin said grimly, and he'll be furious not to have been told. But there's time for that, when they take Max off the respirator, said Ellen; but isn't it incredible, Frank said, Max was fine, not feeling ill at all, and then to wake up with a fever of a hundred and five, unable to breathe, but that's the way it often starts, with absolutely no warning, Stephen said, the disease has so many forms. And when, after another week had gone by, he asked Quentin where Max was, he didn't question Quentin's account of a spree in the Bahamas, but then the number of people who visited regularly was thinning out, partly because the old feuds that had been put aside through the first hospitalization and the return home had resurfaced, and the flickering enmity between Lewis and Frank exploded, even though Kate did her best to mediate between them, and also because he himself had done something to loosen the bonds of love that united the friends around him, by seeming to take them all for granted, as if it were perfectly normal for so many people to carve out so much time and attention for him, visit him every few days, talk about him incessantly on the phone with each other; but, according to Paolo, it wasn't that he was less grateful, it was just something he was getting used to, the visits. It had become, with time, a more ordinary kind of situation, a kind of ongoing party, first at the hospital and now since he was home, barely on his feet again, it being clear, said Robert, that I'm on the B list; but Kate said, that's absurd, there's no list; and Victor said, but there is, only it's not he, it's Quentin who's drawing it up. He wants to see us, we're helping him, we have to do it the way he wants, he fell down yesterday on the way to the bathroom, he mustn't be told about Max (but he already knew, according to Donny), it's getting worse.

．　．　．

When I was home, he is reported to have said, I was afraid to sleep, as I was dropping off each night it felt like just that, as if I were falling down a black hole, to sleep felt like giving in to death, I slept every night with the light on; but here, in the hospital, I'm less afraid. And to Quentin he said, one morning, the fear rips through me, it tears me open; and, to Ira, it presses me together, squeezes me toward myself. Fear gives everything its hue, its high. I feel so, I don't know how to say it, exalted, he said to Quentin. Calamity is an amazing high, too. Sometimes I feel *so* well, so powerful, it's as if I could jump out of my skin. Am I going crazy, or what? Is it all this attention and coddling I'm getting from everybody, like a child's dream of being loved? Is it the drugs? I know it sounds crazy but sometimes I think this is a *fantastic* experience, he said shyly; but there was also the bad taste in the mouth, the pressure in the head and at the back of the neck, the red, bleeding gums, the painful, if pink-lobed, breathing, and his ivory pallor, color of white chocolate. Among those who wept when told over the phone that he was back in the hospital were Kate and Stephen (who'd been called by Quentin), and Ellen, Victor, Aileen, and Lewis (who were called by Kate), and Xavier and Ursula (who were called by Stephen). Among those who didn't weep were Hilda, who said that she'd just learned that her seventy-five-year-old aunt was dying of the disease, which she'd contracted from a transfusion given during her successful double bypass of five years ago, and Frank and Donny and Betsy, but this didn't mean, according to Tanya, that they weren't moved and appalled, and Quentin thought they might not be coming soon to the hospital but would send presents; the room, he was in a private room this time, was filling up with flowers, and plants, and books, and tapes. The high tide of barely suppressed acrimony of the last weeks at home subsided into the routines of hospital visiting, though more than a few resented Quentin's having charge of the visiting book (but it was Quentin who had the idea, Lewis pointed out); now, to insure a steady stream of visitors, preferably no more than two at a time (this, the rule in all hospitals, wasn't enforced here, at least on his floor; whether out of kindness or inefficiency, no one could decide), Quentin had to be called first, to get one's time slot, there was no more casual dropping by. And his mother could no longer be prevented from taking a plane and installing herself in a hotel near the hospital; but he seemed to mind her daily presence less than expected, Quentin said; said Ellen, it's we who mind, do you suppose she'll stay long. It was easier to be generous with each other visiting him here in the hospital, as Donny pointed out, than at home, where one minded never being alone with him; coming here, in our twos and twos, there's no doubt about what our role is, how we should be, collective, funny, distracting, undemanding, light, it's important to be light, for in all this dread there is gaiety, too, as the poet said, said Kate. (His eyes, his glittering eyes, said Lewis.) His eyes looked dull, extinguished, Wesley said to Xavier, but Betsy said his face, not just his eyes, looked soulful, warm; whatever is there, said Kate, I've never been so aware of his eyes; and Stephen said, I'm afraid of what my eyes show, the way I watch him, with too much intensity, or a phony kind of casualness, said Victor. And, unlike at home, he was clean-shaven each morning, at whatever hour they visited him; his curly hair was always combed; but he complained that the nurses had changed since he was here the last time, and that he didn't like the change, he wanted everyone to be the same. The room was furnished now with some of his personal effects (odd word for one's things, said Ellen), and Tanya brought drawings and a letter from her nine-year-old dyslexic son, who was writing now, since she'd purchased a computer; and Donny brought champagne and some helium balloons, which were anchored to the foot of his bed; tell me about something that's going on, he said, waking up from a nap to find Donny and Kate at the side of his bed, beaming at him; tell me a story, he said wistfully, said Donny, who couldn't think of anything to say; *you're* the story, Kate said. And Xavier brought an eighteenth-century Guatemalan wooden statue of St. Sebastian with upcast eyes and open mouth, and when Tanya said what's that, a tribute to eros past, Xavier said where I come from Sebastian is venerated as a protector against pestilence. Pestilence symbolized by arrows? Symbolized by arrows. All people remember is the body of a beautiful youth bound to a tree, pierced by arrows (of which he always seems oblivious, Tanya interjected), people forget that the story continues, Xavier continued, that when the Christian women came to bury the martyr they found him still alive and nursed him back to health. And he said, according to Stephen, I didn't know St. Sebastian didn't die. It's undeniable, isn't it, said Kate on the phone to Stephen, the fascination of the dying. It makes me ashamed. We're learning how to die, said Hilda; I'm not ready to learn, said Aileen; and Lewis, who was coming straight from the other hospital, the hospital where Max was still being kept in the I.C.U., met Tanya getting out of the elevator on the tenth floor, and as they walked together down the shiny corridor past the open doors, averting their eyes from the other patients sunk in their beds, with tubes in their noses, irradiated by the bluish light from the television sets, the thing I can't bear to think about, Tanya said to Lewis, is someone dying with the TV on.

He has that strange, unnerving detachment now, said Ellen, that's what upsets me, even though it makes it easier to be with him. Sometimes he was querulous. I can't stand them coming in here taking my blood every morning, what are they doing with all that blood, he is reported to have said; but where was his anger, Jan wondered. Mostly he was lovely to be with, always saying how are *you*, how are you feeling. He's so sweet now, said Aileen. He's so nice, said Tanya. (Nice, nice, groaned Paolo.) At first he was very ill, but he was rallying, according to Stephen's best information, there was no fear of his not recovering this time, and the doctor spoke of his being discharged from the hospital in another ten days if all went well, and the mother was persuaded to

SALVADOR LATE
OR EARLY

Sandra Cisneros • 1986

S alvador with eyes the color of caterpillar, Salvador of the crooked hair and crooked teeth, Salvador whose name the teacher cannot remember, is a boy who is no one's friend, runs along somewhere in that vague direction where homes are the color of bad weather, lives behind a raw wood doorway, shakes the sleepy brothers awake, ties their shoes, combs their hair with water, feeds them milk and corn flakes from a tin cup in the dim dark of the morning.

Salvador, late or early, sooner or later arrives with the string of younger brothers ready. Helps his mama, who is busy with the business of the baby. Tugs the arms of Cecilio, Arturito, makes them hurry, because today, like yesterday, Arturito has dropped the cigar box of crayons, has let go the hundred little fingers of red, green, yellow, blue, and nub of black sticks that tumble and spill over and beyond the asphalt puddles until the crossing-guard lady holds back the blur of traffic for Salvador to collect them again.

Salvador inside that wrinkled shirt, inside the throat that must clear itself and apologize each time it speaks, inside that forty-pound body of boy with its geography of scars, its history of hurt, limbs stuffed with feathers and rags, in what part of the eyes, in what part of the heart, in that cage of the chest where something throbs with both fists and knows only what Salvador knows, inside that body too small to contain the hundred balloons of happiness, the single guitar of grief, is a boy like any other disappearing out the door, beside the schoolyard gate, where he has told his brothers they must wait. Collects the hands of Cecilio and Arturito, scuttles off dodging the many schoolyard colors, the elbows and wrists crisscrossing, the several shoes running. Grows small and smaller to the eye, dissolves into the bright horizon, flutters in the air before disappearing like a memory of kites.

THE THINGS
THEY CARRIED

Tim O'Brien • 1986

First Lieutenant Jimmy Cross carried letters from a girl named Martha, a junior at Mount Sebastian College in New Jersey. They were not love letters, but Lieutenant Cross was hoping, so he kept them folded in plastic at the bottom of his rucksack. In the late afternoon, after a day's march, he would dig his foxhole, wash his hands under a canteen, unwrap the letters, hold them with the tips of his fingers, and spend the last hour of light pretending. He would imagine romantic camping trips into the White Mountains in New Hampshire. He would sometimes taste the envelope flaps, knowing her tongue had been there. More than anything, he wanted Martha to love him as he loved her, but the letters were mostly chatty, elusive on the matter of love. She was a virgin, he was almost sure. She was an English major at Mount Sebastian, and she wrote beautifully about her professors and roommates and midterm exams, about her respect for Chaucer and her great affection for Virginia Woolf. She often quoted lines of poetry; she never mentioned the war, except to say, Jimmy, take care of yourself. The letters weighed 4 ounces. They were signed Love, Martha, but Lieutenant Cross understood that Love was only a way of signing and did not mean what he sometimes pretended it meant. At dusk, he would carefully return the letters to his rucksack. Slowly, a bit distracted, he would get up and move among his men, checking the perimeter, then at full dark he would return to his hole and watch the night and wonder if Martha was a virgin.

The things they carried were largely determined by necessity. Among the necessities or near-necessities were P-38 can openers, pocket knives, heat tabs, wristwatches, dog tags, mosquito repellent, chewing gum, candy, cigarettes, salt tablets, packets of Kool-Aid, lighters, matches, sewing kits, Military Payment Certificates, C rations, and two or three canteens of water. Together, these items weighed between 12 and 18 pounds, depending upon a man's habits or rate of metabolism. Henry Dobbins, who was a big man, carried extra rations; he was especially fond of canned peaches in heavy syrup over pound cake. Dave Jensen, who practiced field hygiene, carried a toothbrush, dental floss, and several hotel-sized bars of soap he'd stolen on R&R in Sydney, Australia. Ted Lavender, who was scared, carried tranquilizers until he was shot in the head outside the village of Than Khe in mid-April. By necessity, and because it was SOP, they all carried steel helmets that weighed 5 pounds including the liner and camouflage cover. They carried the standard fatigue jackets and trousers. Very few carried underwear. On their feet they carried jungle boots—2.1 pounds—and Dave Jensen carried three pairs of socks and a can of Dr. Scholl's foot powder as a precaution against trench foot. Until he was shot, Ted Lavender carried 6 or 7 ounces of premium dope, which for him was a necessity. Mitchell Sanders, the RTO, carried condoms. Norman Bowker carried a diary. Rat Kiley carried comic books. Kiowa, a devout Baptist, carried an illustrated New Testament that had been presented to him by his father, who taught Sunday school in Oklahoma City, Oklahoma. As a hedge against bad times, however, Kiowa also carried his grandmother's distrust of the white man, his grandfather's old hunting hatchet. Necessity dictated. Because the land was mined and booby-trapped, it was SOP for each man to carry a steel-centered, nylon-covered flak jacket, which weighed 6.7 pounds, but which on hot days seemed much heavier. Because you could die so quickly, each man carried at least one large compress bandage, usually in the helmet band for easy access. Because the nights were cold, and because the monsoons were wet, each carried a green plastic poncho that could be used as a raincoat or groundsheet or makeshift tent. With its quilted liner, the poncho weighed almost 2 pounds, but it was worth every ounce. In April, for instance, when Ted Lavender was shot, they used his poncho to wrap him up, then to carry him across the paddy, then to lift him into the chopper that took him away.

They were called legs or grunts.

To carry something was to hump it, as when Lieutenant Jimmy Cross humped his love for Martha up the hills and through the swamps. In its intransitive form, to hump meant to walk, or to march, but it implied burdens far beyond the intransitive.

Almost everyone humped photographs. In his wallet, Lieutenant Cross carried two photographs of Martha. The first was a Kodacolor snapshot signed Love, though he knew better. She stood against a brick wall. Her eyes were gray and neutral, her lips slightly open as she stared straight-on at the camera. At night, sometimes, Lieutenant Cross wondered who had taken the picture, because he knew she had boyfriends, because he loved her so much, and because he could see the shadow of the picture-taker spreading out against the brick wall. The second photograph had been clipped from the 1968 Mount Sebastian yearbook. It was an action shot—women's volleyball—and Martha was bent horizontal to the floor, reaching, the palms of her hands in sharp focus, the tongue taut, the expression frank and competitive. There was no visible sweat. She wore white gym shorts. Her legs, he thought, were almost certainly the legs of a virgin, dry and without hair, the left knee cocked and carrying her entire weight, which was just over 117 pounds. Lieutenant Cross remembered touching that left knee. A dark theater, he remembered, and the movie was *Bonnie and Clyde*, and Martha wore a tweed skirt, and during the final scene, when he touched her knee, she turned and looked at him in a sad, sober way that made him pull his hand back, but he would always remember the feel of the tweed skirt and the knee beneath it and the sound of the gunfire that killed Bonnie and Clyde, how embarrassing it was, how slow and oppressive. He remembered kissing her good night at the dorm door. Right then, he thought, he should've done something brave. He should've carried her up the stairs to her room and tied her to the bed and touched that left knee all night long. He should've risked it. Whenever he looked at the photographs, he thought of new things he should've done.

What they carried was partly a function of rank, partly of field specialty.

As a first lieutenant and platoon leader, Jimmy Cross carried a compass, maps, code books, binoculars, and a .45-caliber pistol that weighed 2.9 pounds fully loaded. He carried a strobe light and the responsibility for the lives of his men.

As an RTO, Mitchell Sanders carried the PRC-25 radio, a killer, 26 pounds with its battery.

As a medic, Rat Kiley carried a canvas satchel filled with morphine and plasma and malaria tablets and surgical tape and comic books and all the things a medic must carry, including M&M's for especially bad wounds, for a total weight of nearly 18 pounds.

As a big man, therefore a machine gunner, Henry Dobbins carried the M-60, which weighed 23 pounds unloaded, but which was almost always loaded. In addition, Dobbins carried between 10 and 15 pounds of ammunition draped in belts across his chest and shoulders.

As PFCs or Spec 4s, most of them were common grunts and carried the standard M-16 gas-operated assault rifle. The weapon weighed 7.5 pounds unloaded, 8.2 pounds with its full 20-round magazine. Depending on numerous factors, such as topography and psychology, the riflemen carried anywhere from 12 to 20 magazines, usually in cloth bandoliers, adding on another 8.4 pounds at minimum, 14 pounds at maximum. When it was available, they also carried M-16 maintenance gear—rods and steel brushes and swabs and tubes of LSA oil—all of which weighed about a pound. Among the grunts, some carried the M-79 grenade launcher, 5.9 pounds unloaded, a reasonably light weapon except for the ammunition, which was heavy. A single round weighed 10 ounces. The typical load was 25 rounds. But Ted Lavender, who was scared, carried 34 rounds when he was shot and killed outside Than Khe, and he went down under an exceptional burden, more than 20 pounds of ammunition, plus the flak jacket and helmet and rations and water and toilet paper and tranquilizers and all the rest, plus the unweighed fear. He was dead weight. There was no twitching or flopping. Kiowa, who saw it happen, said it was like watching a rock fall, or a big sandbag or something—just boom, then down—not like the movies where the dead guy rolls around and does fancy spins and goes ass over teakettle—not like that, Kiowa said, the poor bastard just flat-fuck fell. Boom. Down. Nothing else. It was a bright morning in mid-April. Lieutenant Cross felt the pain. He blamed himself. They stripped off Lavender's canteens and ammo, all the heavy things, and Rat Kiley said the obvious, the guy's dead, and Mitchell Sanders used his radio to report one U.S. KIA and to request a chopper. Then they wrapped Lavender in his poncho. They carried him out to a dry paddy, established security, and sat smoking the dead man's dope until the chopper came. Lieutenant Cross kept to himself. He pictured Martha's smooth young face, thinking he loved her more than anything, more than his men, and now Ted Lavender was dead because he loved her so much and could not stop thinking about her. When the dustoff arrived, they carried Lavender aboard. Afterward they burned Than Khe. They marched pebble and to carry it in her breast pocket for several days, where it seemed weightless, and then to send it through the mail, by air, as a token of her truest feelings for him. Lieutenant Cross found this romantic. But he wondered what her truest feelings were, exactly, and what she meant by separate-but-together. He wondered how the tides and waves had come into play on that afternoon along the Jersey shoreline when Martha saw the pebble and bent down to rescue it from geology. He imagined bare feet. Martha was a poet, with the poet's sensibilities, and her feet would be brown and bare, the toenails unpainted, the eyes chilly and somber like the ocean in March, and though it was painful, he wondered who had been with her that afternoon. He imagined a pair of shadows moving along the strip of sand where things came together but also separated. It was phantom jealousy, he knew, but he couldn't help himself. He loved her so much. On the march, through the hot days of early April, he carried the pebble in his mouth, turning it with his tongue, tasting sea salt and moisture. His mind wandered. He had difficulty keeping his attention on the war. On occasion he would yell at his men to spread out the column, to keep their eyes open, but then he would slip away into daydreams, just pretending, walking barefoot along the Jersey shore, with Martha, carrying nothing. He would feel himself rising. Sun and waves and gentle winds, all love and lightness.

What they carried varied by mission.

When a mission took them to the mountains, they carried mosquito netting, machetes, canvas tarps, and extra bug juice.

If a mission seemed especially hazardous, or if it involved a place they knew to be bad, they carried everything they could. In certain heavily mined AOs, where the land was dense with Toe Poppers and Bouncing Betties, they took turns humping a 28-pound mine detector. With its headphones and big sensing plate, the equipment was a stress on the lower back and shoulders, awkward to handle, often useless because of the shrapnel in the earth, but they carried it anyway, partly for safety, partly for the illusion of safety.

On ambush, or other night missions, they carried peculiar little odds and ends. Kiowa always took along his New Testament and a pair of moccasins for silence. Dave Jensen carried night-sight vitamins high in carotene. Lee Strunk carried his slingshot; ammo, he claimed, would never be a problem. Rat Kiley carried brandy and M&M's candy. Until he was shot, Ted Lavender carried the starlight scope, which weighed 6.3 pounds with its aluminum carrying case. Henry Dobbins carried his girlfriend's pantyhose wrapped around his neck as a comforter. They all carried ghosts. When dark came, they would move out single file across the meadows and paddies to their ambush coordinates, where they would quietly set up the Claymores and lie down and spend the night waiting.

Other missions were more complicated and required special equipment. In mid-April, it was their mission to search out and destroy the elaborate tunnel complexes in the Than Khe area south of Chu Lai. To blow the tunnels, they carried one-pound blocks of pentrite high explosives, four blocks to a man, 68 pounds in all. They carried wiring, detonators, and battery-powered clackers. Dave Jensen carried earplugs. Most often, before blowing the tunnels, they were ordered by higher command to search them, which was considered bad news, but by and large they just shrugged and carried out orders. Because he was a big man, Henry Dobbins was excused from tunnel duty. The others would draw numbers. Before Lavender died there were 17 men in the platoon, and whoever drew the number 17 would strip off his gear and crawl in headfirst with a flashlight and Lieutenant Cross's .45-caliber pistol. The rest of them would fan out as security. They would sit down or kneel, not facing the hole, listening to the ground beneath them, imagining cobwebs and ghosts, whatever was down there—the tunnel walls squeezing in—how the flashlight seemed impossibly heavy in the hand

and how it was tunnel vision in the very strictest sense, compression in all ways, even time, and how you had to wiggle in—ass and elbows—a swallowed-up feeling—and how you found yourself worrying about odd things: Will your flashlight go dead? Do rats carry rabies? If you screamed, how far would the sound carry? Would your buddies hear it? Would they have the courage to drag you out? In some respects, though not many, the waiting was worse than the tunnel itself. Imagination was a killer.

On April 16, when Lee Strunk drew the number 17, he laughed and muttered something and went down quickly. The morning was hot and very still. Not good, Kiowa said. He looked at the tunnel opening, then out across a dry paddy toward the village of Than Khe. Nothing moved. No clouds or birds or people. As they waited, the men smoked and drank Kool-Aid, not talking much, feeling sympathy for Lee Strunk but also feeling the luck of the draw. You win some, you lose some, said Mitchell Sanders, and sometimes you settle for a rain check. It was a tired line and no one laughed.

Henry Dobbins ate a tropical chocolate bar. Ted Lavender popped a tranquilizer and went off to pee.

After five minutes, Lieutenant Jimmy Cross moved to the tunnel, leaned down, and examined the darkness. Trouble, he thought—a cave-in maybe. And then suddenly, without willing it, he was thinking about Martha. The stresses and fractures, the quick collapse, the two of them buried alive under all that weight. Dense, crushing love. Kneeling, watching the hole, he tried to concentrate on Lee Strunk and the war, all the dangers, but his love was too much for him, he felt paralyzed, he wanted to sleep inside her lungs and breathe her blood and be smothered. He wanted her to be a virgin and not a virgin, all at once. He wanted to know her. Intimate secrets: Why poetry? Why so sad? Why that grayness in her eyes? Why so alone? Not lonely, just alone— riding her bike across campus or sitting off by herself in the cafeteria— even dancing, she danced alone—and it was the aloneness that filled him with love. He remembered telling her that one evening. How she nodded and looked away. And how, later, when he kissed her, she received the kiss without returning it, her eyes wide open, not afraid, not a virgin's eyes, just flat and uninvolved.

Lieutenant Cross gazed at the tunnel. But he was not there. He was buried with Martha under the white sand at the Jersey shore. They were pressed together, and the pebble in his mouth was her tongue. He was smiling. Vaguely, he was aware of how quiet the day was, the sullen paddies, yet he could not bring himself to worry about matters of security. He was beyond that. He was just a kid at war, in love. He was twenty-four years old. He couldn't help it.

A few moments later Lee Strunk crawled out of the tunnel. He came up grinning, filthy but alive. Lieutenant Cross nodded and closed his eyes while the others clapped Strunk on the back and made jokes about rising from the dead.

Worms, Rat Kiley said. Right out of the grave. Fuckin' zombie.

The men laughed. They all felt great relief. Spook city, said Mitchell Sanders.

Lee Strunk made a funny ghost sound, a kind of moaning, yet very happy, and right then, when Strunk made that high happy moaning sound, when he went *Ahhooooo*, right then Ted Lavender was shot in the head on his way back from peeing. He lay with his mouth open. The teeth were broken. There was a swollen black bruise under his left eye. The cheekbone was gone. Oh shit, Rat Kiley said, the guy's dead. The guy's dead, he kept saying, which seemed profound—the guy's dead. I mean really.

The things they carried were determined to some extent by superstition. Lieutenant Cross carried his good-luck pebble. Dave Jensen carried a rabbit's foot. Norman Bowker, otherwise a very gentle person, carried a thumb that had been presented to him as a gift by Mitchell

Sanders. The thumb was dark brown, rubbery to the touch, and weighed 3 ounces at most. It had been cut from a VC corpse, a boy of fifteen or sixteen. They'd found him at the bottom of an irrigation ditch, badly burned, flies in his mouth and eyes. The boy wore black shorts and sandals. At the time of his death he had been carrying a pouch of rice, a rifle, and three magazines of ammunition.

You want my opinion, Mitchell Sanders said, there's a definite moral here.

He put his hand on the dead boy's wrist. He was quiet for a time, as if counting a pulse, then he patted the stomach, almost affectionately, and used Kiowa's hunting hatchet to remove the thumb.

Henry Dobbins asked what the moral was. Moral?

You know. *Moral.*

Sanders wrapped the thumb in toilet paper and handed it across to Norman Bowker. There was no blood. Smiling, he kicked the boy's head, watched the flies scatter, and said, It's like with that old TV show—Paladin. Have gun, will travel.

Henry Dobbins thought about it.

Yeah, well, he finally said. I don't see no moral.

There it *is,* man.

Fuck off.

They carried USO stationery and pencils and pens. They carried Sterno, safety pins, trip flares, signal flares, spools of wire, razor blades, chewing tobacco, liberated joss sticks and statuettes of the smiling Buddha, candles, grease pencils, *The Stars and Stripes*, fingernail clippers, Psy Ops leaflets, bush hats, bolos, and much more. Twice a week, when the resupply choppers came in, they carried hot chow in green mermite cans and large canvas bags filled with iced beer and soda pop. They carried plastic water containers, each with a 2-gallon capacity. Mitchell Sanders carried a set of starched tiger fatigues for special

occasions. Henry Dobbins carried Black Flag insecticide. Dave Jensen
carried empty sandbags that could be filled at night for added protection. Lee Strunk carried tanning lotion. Some things they carried in
common. Taking turns, they carried the big PRC-77 scrambler radio,
which weighed 30 pounds with its battery. They shared the weight of
memory. They took up what others could no longer bear. Often, they
carried each other, the wounded or weak. They carried infections. They
carried chess sets, basketballs, Vietnamese-English dictionaries, insig-
nia of rank, Bronze Stars and Purple Hearts, plastic cards imprinted
with the Code of Conduct. They carried diseases, among them malaria
and dysentery. They carried lice and ringworm and leeches and paddy
algae and various rots and molds. They carried the land itself—Vietnam,
the place, the soil—a powdery orange-red dust that covered their boots
and fatigues and faces. They carried the sky. The whole atmosphere,
they carried it, the humidity, the monsoons, the stink of fungus and
decay, all of it, they carried gravity. They moved like mules. By daylight
they took sniper fire, at night they were mortared, but it was not battle,
it was just the endless march, village to village, without purpose, nothing won or lost. They marched for the sake of the march. They plodded
along slowly, dumbly, leaning forward against the heat, unthinking, all
blood and bone, simple grunts, soldiering with their legs, toiling up the
hills and down into the paddies and across the rivers and up again and
down, just humping, one step and then the next and then another, but
no volition, no will, because it was automatic, it was anatomy, and the
war was entirely a matter of posture and carriage, the hump was everything, a kind of inertia, a kind of emptiness, a dullness of desire and
intellect and conscience and hope and human sensibility. Their princi-
ples were in their feet. Their calculations were biological. They had
no sense of strategy or mission. They searched the villages without
knowing what to look for, not caring, kicking over jars of rice, frisking
children and old men, blowing tunnels, sometimes setting fires and
sometimes not, then forming up and moving on to the next village,

then other villages, where it would always be the same. They carried their own lives. The pressures were enormous. In the heat of early afternoon, they would remove their helmets and flak jackets, walking bare, which was dangerous but which helped ease the strain. They would often discard things along the route of march. Purely for comfort, they would throw away rations, blow their Claymores and grenades, no matter, because by nightfall the resupply choppers would arrive with more of the same, then a day or two later still more, fresh watermelons and crates of ammunition and sunglasses and woolen sweaters—the resources were stunning—sparklers for the Fourth of July, colored eggs for Easter—it was the great American war chest—the fruits of science, the smokestacks, the canneries, the arsenals at Hartford, the Minnesota forests, the machine shops, the vast fields of corn and wheat—they carried like freight trains; they carried it on their backs and shoulders—and for all the ambiguities of Vietnam, all the mysteries and unknowns, there was at least the single abiding certainty that they would never be at a loss for things to carry.

After the chopper took Lavender away, Lieutenant Jimmy Cross led his men into the village of Than Khe. They burned everything. They shot chickens and dogs, they trashed the village well, they called in artillery and watched the wreckage, then they marched for several hours through the hot afternoon, and then at dusk, while Kiowa explained how Lavender died, Lieutenant Cross found himself trembling.

He tried not to cry. With his entrenching tool, which weighed 5 pounds, he began digging a hole in the earth.

He felt shame. He hated himself. He had loved Martha more than his men, and as a consequence Lavender was now dead, and this was something he would have to carry like a stone in his stomach for the rest of the war.

All he could do was dig. He used his entrenching tool like an ax,

slashing, feeling both love and hate, and then later, when it was full
dark, he sat at the bottom of his foxhole and wept. It went on for a long
while. In part, he was grieving for Ted Lavender, but mostly it was for
Martha, and for himself, because she belonged to another world, which
was not quite real, and because she was a junior at Mount Sebastian
College in New Jersey, a poet and a virgin and uninvolved, and because
he realized she did not love him and never would.

Like cement, Kiowa whispered in the dark. I swear to God—boom,
down. Not a word.

I've heard this, said Norman Bowker.

A pisser, you know? Still zipping himself up. Zapped while zipping.

All right, fine. That's enough.

Yeah, but you had to see it, the guy just—

I *heard*, man. Cement. So why not shut the fuck *up*?

Kiowa shook his head sadly and glanced over at the hole where
Lieutenant Jimmy Cross sat watching the night. The air was thick and
wet. A warm dense fog had settled over the paddies and there was the
stillness that precedes rain.

After a time Kiowa sighed.

One thing for sure, he said. The lieutenant's in some deep hurt. I
mean that crying jag—the way he was carrying on—it wasn't fake or
anything, it was real heavy-duty hurt. The man cares.

Sure, Norman Bowker said.

Say what you want, the man does care.

We all got problems.

Not Lavender.

No, I guess not, Bowker said. Do me a favor, though.

Shut up?

That's a smart Indian. Shut up.

Shrugging, Kiowa pulled off his boots. He wanted to say more, just to lighten up his sleep, but instead he opened his New Testament and arranged it beneath his head as a pillow. The fog made things seem hollow and unattached. He tried not to think about Ted Lavender, but then he was thinking how fast it was, no drama, down and dead, and how it was hard to feel anything except surprise. It seemed unchristian. He wished he could find some great sadness, or even anger, but the emotion wasn't there and he couldn't make it happen. Mostly he felt pleased to be alive. He liked the smell of the New Testament under his cheek, the leather and ink and paper and glue, whatever the chemicals were. He liked hearing the sounds of night. Even his fatigue, it felt fine, the stiff muscles and the prickly awareness of his own body, a floating feeling. He enjoyed not being dead. Lying there, Kiowa admired Lieutenant Jimmy Cross's capacity for grief. He wanted to share the man's pain, he wanted to care as Jimmy Cross cared. And yet when he closed his eyes, all he could think was Boom-down, and all he could feel was the pleasure of having his boots off and the fog curling in around him and the damp soil and the Bible smells and the plush comfort of night.

After a moment Norman Bowker sat up in the dark.

What the hell, he said. You want to talk, *talk*. Tell it to me.

Forget it.

No, man, go on. One thing I hate, it's a silent Indian.

For the most part they carried themselves with poise, a kind of dignity. Now and then, however, there were times of panic, when they squealed or wanted to squeal but couldn't, when they twitched and made moaning sounds and covered their heads and said Dear Jesus and flopped around on the earth and fired their weapons blindly and cringed and sobbed and begged for the noise to stop and went wild and made stupid promises to themselves and to God and to their mothers and fathers, hoping not to die. In different ways, it happened to all of them. Afterward, when the firing ended, they would blink and peek up. They would touch their bodies, feeling shame, then quickly hiding it. They would force themselves to stand. As if in slow motion, frame by frame, the world would take on the old logic—absolute silence, then the wind, then sunlight, then voices. It was the burden of being alive. Awkwardly, the men would reassemble themselves, first in private, then in groups, becoming soldiers again. They would repair the leaks in their eyes. They would check for casualties, call in dustoffs, light cigarettes, try to smile, clear their throats and spit and begin cleaning their weapons. After a time someone would shake his head and say, No lie, I almost shit my pants, and someone else would laugh, which meant it was bad, yes, but the guy had obviously not shit his pants, it wasn't that bad, and in any case nobody would ever do such a thing and then go ahead and talk about it. They would squint into the dense, oppressive sunlight. For a few moments, perhaps, they would fall silent, lighting a joint and tracking its passage from man to man, inhaling, holding in the humiliation. Scary stuff, one of them might say. But then someone else would grin or flick his eyebrows and say, Roger-dodger, almost cut me a new asshole, *almost*.

There were numerous such poses. Some carried themselves with a sort of wistful resignation, others with pride or stiff soldierly discipline or good humor or macho zeal. They were afraid of dying but they were even more afraid to show it.

They found jokes to tell.

They used a hard vocabulary to contain the terrible softness. *Greased* they'd say. *Offed, lit up, zapped while zipping.* It wasn't cruelty, just stage presence. They were actors. When someone died, it wasn't quite dying, because in a curious way it seemed scripted, and because they had their lines mostly memorized, irony mixed with tragedy, and because they called it by other names, as if to encyst and destroy the reality of death itself. They kicked corpses. They cut off thumbs. They talked grunt lingo. They told stories about Ted Lavender's supply of tranquilizers, how the poor guy didn't feel a thing, how incredibly tranquil he was.

There's a moral here, said Mitchell Sanders.

They were waiting for Lavender's chopper, smoking the dead man's dope.

The moral's pretty obvious, Sanders said, and winked. Stay away from drugs. No joke, they'll ruin your day every time.

Cute, said Henry Dobbins.

Mind blower, get it? Talk about wiggy. Nothing left, just blood and brains.

They made themselves laugh.

There it is, they'd say. Over and over—there it is, my friend, there it is—as if the repetition itself were an act of poise, a balance between crazy and almost crazy, knowing without going, there it is, which meant be cool, let it ride, because Oh yeah, man, you can't change what can't be changed, there it is, there it absolutely and positively and fucking well *is*.

They were tough.

They carried all the emotional baggage of men who might die. Grief, terror, love, longing—these were intangibles, but the intangibles had their own mass and specific gravity, they had tangible weight. They carried shameful memories. They carried the common secret of cowardice barely restrained, the instinct to run or freeze or hide, and in many respects this was the heaviest burden of all, for it could never be put down, it required perfect balance and perfect posture. They carried their reputations. They carried the soldier's greatest fear, which was the fear of blushing. Men killed, and died, because they were embarrassed not to. It was what had brought them to the war in the first place, nothing positive, no dreams of glory or honor, just to avoid the blush of dishonor. They died so as not to die of embarrassment. They crawled into tunnels and walked point and advanced under fire. Each morning, despite the unknowns, they made their legs move. They endured. They kept humping. They did not submit to the obvious alternative, which was simply to close the eyes and fall. So easy, really. Go limp and tumble to the ground and let the muscles unwind and not speak and not budge until your buddies picked you up and lifted you into the chopper that would roar and dip its nose and carry you off to the world. A mere matter of falling, yet no one ever fell. It was not courage, exactly; the object was not valor. Rather, they were too frightened to be cowards.

By and large they carried these things inside, maintaining the masks of composure. They sneered at sick call. They spoke bitterly about guys who had found release by shooting off their own toes or fingers. Pussies, they'd say. Candy-asses. It was fierce, mocking talk, with only a trace of envy or awe, but even so the image played itself out behind their eyes.

They imagined the muzzle against flesh. So easy: squeeze the trigger and blow away a toe. They imagined it. They imagined the quick, sweet pain, then the evacuation to Japan, then a hospital with warm beds and cute geisha nurses.

And they dreamed of freedom birds.

At night, on guard, staring into the dark, they were carried away by jumbo jets. They felt the rush of takeoff. Gone! they yelled. And then velocity—wings and engines—a smiling stewardess—but it was more than a plane, it was a real bird, a big sleek silver bird with feathers and talons and high screeching. They were flying. The weights fell off; there was nothing to bear. They laughed and held on tight, feeling the cold slap of wind and altitude, soaring, thinking *It's over, I'm gone!*—they were naked, they were light and free—it was all lightness, bright and fast and buoyant, light as light, a helium buzz in the brain, a giddy bubbling in the lungs as they were taken up over the clouds and the war, beyond duty, beyond gravity and mortification and global entanglements—*Sin loi!*, they yelled. *I'm sorry, motherfuckers, but I'm out of it, I'm goofed, I'm on a space cruise, I'm gone!*—and it was a restful, unencumbered sensation, just riding the light waves, sailing that big silver freedom bird over the mountains and oceans, over America, over the farms and great sleeping cities and cemeteries and highways and the golden arches of McDonald's, it was flight, a kind of fleeing, a kind of falling, falling higher and higher, spinning off the edge of the earth and beyond the sun and through the vast, silent vacuum where there were no burdens and where everything weighed exactly nothing—*Gone!* they screamed. *I'm sorry but I'm gone!*—and so at night, not quite dreaming, they gave themselves over to lightness, they were carried, they were purely borne.

On the morning after Ted Lavender died, First Lieutenant Jimmy Cross crouched at the bottom of his foxhole and burned Martha's letters. Then he burned the two photographs. There was a steady rain falling, which made it difficult, but he used heat tabs and Sterno to build a small fire, screening it with his body, holding the photographs over the tight blue flame with the tips of his fingers.

He realized it was only a gesture. Stupid, he thought. Sentimental, too, but mostly just stupid.

Lavender was dead. You couldn't burn the blame.

Besides, the letters were in his head. And even now, without photographs, Lieutenant Cross could see Martha playing volleyball in her white gym shorts and yellow T-shirt. He could see her moving in the rain.

When the fire died out, Lieutenant Cross pulled his poncho over his shoulders and ate breakfast from a can.

There was no great mystery, he decided.

In those burned letters Martha had never mentioned the war, except to say, Jimmy, take care of yourself. She wasn't involved. She signed the letters Love, but it wasn't love, and all the fine lines and technicalities did not matter. Virginity was no longer an issue. He hated her. Yes, he did. He hated her. Love, too, but it was a hard, hating kind of love.

The morning came up wet and blurry. Everything seemed part of everything else, the fog and Martha and the deepening rain.

He was a soldier, after all.

Half smiling, Lieutenant Jimmy Cross took out his maps. He shook his head hard, as if to clear it, then bent forward and began planning the day's march. In ten minutes, or maybe twenty, he would rouse the men and they would pack up and head west, where the maps showed the country to be green and inviting. They would do what they had always done. The rain might add some weight, but otherwise it would be one more day layered upon all the other days.

He was realistic about it. There was that new hardness in his stomach. He loved her but he hated her.

No more fantasies, he told himself.

Henceforth, when he thought about Martha, it would be only to think that she belonged elsewhere. He would shut down the daydreams. This was not Mount Sebastian, it was another world, where there were no pretty poems or midterm exams, a place where men died because of carelessness and gross stupidity. Kiowa was right. Boom-down, and you were dead, never partly dead.

Briefly, in the rain, Lieutenant Cross saw Martha's gray eyes gazing back at him.

He understood.

It was very sad, he thought. The things men carried inside. The things men did or felt they had to do.

He almost nodded at her, but didn't.

Instead he went back to his maps. He was now determined to perform his duties firmly and without negligence. It wouldn't help Lavender, he knew that, but from this point on he would comport himself as an officer. He would dispose of his good-luck pebble. Swallow it, maybe, or use Lee Strunk's slingshot, or just drop it along the trail. On the march he would impose strict field discipline. He would be careful to send out flank security, to prevent straggling or bunching up, to keep his troops moving at the proper pace and at the proper interval. He would insist on clean weapons. He would confiscate the remainder of Lavender's dope. Later in the day, perhaps, he would call the men together and speak to them plainly. He would accept the blame for what had happened to Ted Lavender. He would be a man about it. He would look them in the eyes, keeping his chin level, and he would issue the new SOPs in a calm, impersonal tone of voice, a lieutenant's voice, leaving no room for argument or discussion. Commencing immediately, he'd tell them, they would no longer abandon equipment along the route of march. They would police up their acts. They would get their shit together, and keep it together, and maintain it neatly and in good working order.

He would not tolerate laxity. He would show strength, distancing himself.

Among the men there would be grumbling, of course, and maybe worse, because their days would seem longer and their loads heavier, but Lieutenant Jimmy Cross reminded himself that his obligation was not to be loved but to lead. He would dispense with love; it was not now a factor. And if anyone quarreled or complained, he would simply tighten his lips and arrange his shoulders in the correct command posture. He might give a curt little nod. Or he might not. He might just shrug and say, Carry on, then they would saddle up and form into a column and move out toward the villages west of Than Khe.

RIVER OF NAMES

Dorothy Allison · 1988

At a picnic at my aunt's farm, the only time the whole family ever gathered, my sister Billie and I chased chickens into the barn. Billie ran right through the open doors and out again, but I stopped, caught by a shadow moving over me. My Cousin Tommy, eight years old as I was, swung in the sunlight with his face as black as his shoes—the rope around his neck pulled up into the sunlit heights of the barn, fascinating, horrible. Wasn't he running ahead of us? Someone came up behind me. Someone began to scream. My mama took my head in her hands and turned my eyes away.

Jesse and I have been lovers for a year now. She tells me stories about her childhood, about her father going off each day to the university, her mother who made all her dresses, her grandmother who always smelled of dill bread and vanilla. I listen with my mouth open, not believing but wanting, aching for the fairy tale she thinks is everyone's life.

"What did your grandmother smell like?"

I lie to her the way I always do, a lie stolen from a book. "Like lavender," stomach churning over the memory of sour sweat and snuff.

I realize I do not really know what lavender smells like, and I am for a moment afraid she will ask something else, some question that will betray me. But Jesse slides over to hug me, to press her face against my ear, to whisper, "How wonderful to be part of such a large family."

I hug her back and close my eyes. I cannot say a word.

I was born between the older cousins and the younger, born in a pause of babies and therefore outside, always watching. Once, way before Tommy died, I was pushed out on the steps while everyone stood listening to my Cousin Barbara. Her screams went up and down in the back of the house. Cousin Cora brought buckets of bloody rags out to be burned. The other cousins all ran off to catch the sparks or poke the fire with dogwood sticks. I waited on the porch making up words to the shouts around me. I did not understand what was happening. Some of the older cousins obviously did, their strange expressions broken by stranger laughs. I had seen them helping her up the stairs while the thick blood ran down her legs. After while the blood on the rags was thin, watery, almost pink. Cora threw them on the fire and stood motionless in the stinking smoke.

Randall went by and said there'd be a baby, a hatched egg to throw out with the rags, but there wasn't. I watched to see and there wasn't; nothing but the blood, thinning out desperately while the house slowed down and grew quiet, hours of cries growing soft and low, moaning under the smoke. My Aunt Raylene came out on the porch and almost fell on me, not seeing me, not seeing anything at all. She beat on the post until there were knuckle-sized dents in the peeling paint, beat on that post like it could feel, cursing it and herself and every child in the yard, singing up and down, "Goddamn, goddamn that girl . . . no sense . . . goddamn!"

I've these pictures my mama gave me—stained sepia prints of bare dirt
yards, plank porches, and step after step of children—cousins, uncles,
aunts; mysteries. The mystery is how many no one remembers. I show
them to Jesse, not saying who they are, and when she laughs at the broken teeth, torn overalls, the dirt, I set my teeth at what I do not want to
remember and cannot forget.

We were so many we were without number and, like tadpoles, if
there was one less from time to time, who counted? My maternal great-
grandmother had eleven daughters, seven sons; my grandmother, six
sons, five daughters. Each one made at least six. Some made nine.
Six times six, eleven times nine. They went on like multiplication tables. They died and were not missed. I come of an enormous family
and I cannot tell half their stories. Somehow it was always made to
seem they killed themselves: car wrecks, shotguns, dusty ropes, screaming, falling out of windows, things inside them. I am the point of a
pyramid, sliding back under the weight of the ones who came after,
and it does not matter that I am the lesbian, the one who will not have
children.

I tell the stories and it comes out funny. I drink bourbon and make
myself drawl, tell all those old funny stories. Someone always seems to
ask me, which one was that? I show the pictures and she says, "Wasn't
she the one in the story about the bridge?" I put the pictures away, drink
more, and someone always finds them, then says, "Goddamn! How
many of you were there, anyway?"

I don't answer.

Jesse used to say, "You've got such a fascination with violence. You've
got so many terrible stories."

She said it with her smooth mouth, that chin that nobody ever slapped, and I love that chin, but when Jesse said that, my hands shook and I wanted nothing so much as to tell her terrible stories.

So I made a list. I told her: that one went insane—got her little brother with a tire iron; the three of them slit their arms, not the wrists but the bigger veins up near the elbow; she, now she strangled the boy she was sleeping with and got sent away; that one drank lye and died laughing soundlessly. In one year I lost eight cousins. It was the year everybody ran away. Four disappeared and were never found. One fell in the river and was drowned. One was run down hitchhiking north. One was shot running through the woods, while Grace, the last one, tried to walk from Greenville to Greer for some reason nobody knew. She fell off the overpass a mile down from the Sears, Roebuck warehouse and lay there for hunger and heat and dying.

Later sleeping, but not sleeping, I found that my hands were up under Jesse's chin. I rolled away, but I didn't cry. I almost never let myself cry.

Almost always, we were raped, my cousins and I. That was some kind of joke, too.

"What's a South Carolina virgin?"

"'At's a ten-year-old can run fast."

It wasn't funny for me in my mama's bed with my stepfather; not for my Cousin Billie in the attic with my uncle; nor for Lucille in the woods with another cousin; for Danny with four strangers in a parking lot; or for Pammy, who made the papers. Cora read it out loud: "Repeatedly by persons unknown." They stayed unknown since Pammy never spoke again. Perforations, lacerations, contusions, and bruises. I heard all the words, big words, little words, words too terrible to understand.

DEAD BY AN ACT OF MAN. With the prick still in them, the broom handle, the tree branch, the grease gun . . . objects, things not to be
believed . . . whiskey bottles, can openers, grass shears, glass, metal,
vegetables . . . not to be believed, not to be believed.

Jesse says, "You've got a gift for words."

"Don't talk," I beg her, "don't talk." And this once, she just holds
me, blessedly silent.

I dig out the pictures, stare into the faces. Which one was I? Survivors
do hate themselves, I know, over the core of fierce self-love, never
understanding, always asking, "Why me and not her, not him?" There
is such mystery in it, and I have hated myself as much as I have loved
others, hated the simple fact of my own survival. Having survived, am
I supposed to say something, do something, be something?

I loved my Cousin Butch. He had this big old head, pale thin hair and
enormous, watery eyes. All the cousins did, though Butch's head was
the largest, his hair the palest. I was the dark-headed one. All the rest
of the family seemed pale carbons of each other in shades of blond,
though later on everybody's hair went brown or red, and I didn't stand
out so. Butch and I stood out—I because I was so dark and fast, and he
because of that big head and the crazy things he did. Butch used to
climb on the back of my Uncle Lucius's truck, open the gas tank and
hang his head over, breathe deeply, strangle, gag, vomit, and breathe
again. It went so deep, it tingled in your toes. I climbed up after him
and tried it myself but I was too young to hang on long, and I fell heavily to the ground, dizzy and giggling. Butch could hang on, put his
hand down into the tank and pull up a cupped palm of gas, breathe
deep and laugh. He would climb down roughly, swinging down from

the door handle, laughing, staggering, and stinking of gasoline. Someone caught him at it. Someone threw a match. "I'll teach you."

Just like that, gone before you understand.

I wake up in the night screaming, "No, no, I won't!" Dirty water rises
in the back of my throat, the liquid language of my own terror and
rage. "Hold me. Hold me." Jesse rolls over on me; her hands grip my
hipbones tightly.

"I love you. I love you. I'm here," she repeats.

I stare up into her dark eyes, puzzled, afraid. I draw a breath in
deeply, smile my bland smile. "Did I fool you?" I laugh, rolling away
from her. Jesse punches me playfully, and I catch her hand in the air.

"My love," she whispers, and cups her body against my hip, closes
her eyes. I bring my hand up in front of my face and watch the knuckles,
the nails as they tremble, tremble. I watch for a long time while she
sleeps, warm and still against me.

James went blind. One of the uncles got him in the face with home-
brewed alcohol.

Lucille climbed out the front window of Aunt Raylene's house and
jumped. They said she jumped. No one said why.

My Uncle Matthew used to beat my Aunt Raylene. The twins,
Mark and Luke, swore to stop him, pulled him out in the yard one
time, throwing him between them like a loose bag of grain. Uncle Matthew screamed like a pig coming up for slaughter. I got both my sisters
in the toolshed for safety, but I hung back to watch. Little Bo came
running out of the house, off the porch, feetfirst into his daddy's arms.
Uncle Matthew started swinging him like a scythe, going after the bigger boys, Bo's head thudding their shoulders, their hips. Afterward, Bo

crawled around in the dirt, the blood running out of his ears and his tongue hanging out of his mouth, while Mark and Luke got their daddy down. It was a long time before I realized that they never told anybody else what had happened to Bo.

Randall tried to teach Lucille and me to wrestle. "Put your hands up." His legs were wide apart, his torso bobbing up and down, his head moving constantly. Then his hand flashed at my face. I threw myself back into the dirt, lay still. He turned to Lucille, not noticing that I didn't get up. He punched at her, laughing. She wrapped her hands around her head, curled over so her knees were up against her throat.

"No, no!" he yelled. "Move like her." He turned to me. "Move." He kicked at me. I rocked into a ball, froze.

"No, no!" He kicked me. I grunted, didn't move. He turned to Lucille. "You." Her teeth were chattering but she held herself still, wrapped up tighter than bacon slices.

"You move!" he shouted. Lucille just hugged her head tighter and started to sob.

"Son of a bitch," Randall grumbled, "you two will never be any good."

He walked away. Very slowly we stood up, embarrassed, looked at each other. We knew.

If you fight back, they kill you.

My sister was seven. She was screaming. My stepfather picked her up by her left arm, swung her forward and back. It gave. The arm went around loosely. She just kept screaming. I didn't know you could break it like that.

I was running up the hall. He was right behind me. "Mama! Mama!" His left hand—he was left-handed—closed around my throat, pushed me against the wall, and then he lifted me that way. I kicked, but I couldn't reach him. He was yelling, but there was so much noise in my ears I couldn't hear him.

"Please, Daddy. Please, Daddy. I'll do anything, I promise. Daddy, anything you want. Please, Daddy."

I couldn't have said that. I couldn't talk around that fist at my throat, couldn't breathe. I woke up when I hit the floor. I looked up at him.

"If I live long enough, I'll fucking kill you."

He picked me up by my throat again.

W hat's wrong with her?"
"Why's she always following you around?"
Nobody really wanted answers.

A full bottle of vodka will kill you when you're nine and the bottle is a quart. It was a third cousin proved that. We learned what that and other things could do. Every year there was something new.

You're growing up. My big girl.

There was codeine in the cabinet, paregoric for the baby's teeth, whiskey, beer, and wine in the house. Jeanne brought home MDA, PCP, acid; Randall, grass, speed, and mescaline. It all worked to dull things down, to pass the time.

Stealing was a way to pass the time. Things we needed, things we didn't, for the nerve of it, the anger, the need. You're growing up, we told each other. But sooner or later, we all got caught. Then it was When Are You Going to Learn?

Caught, nightmares happened. "Razorback desperate" was the conclusion of the man down at the county farm where Mark and Luke were sent at fifteen. They both got their heads shaved, their earlobes sliced.

What's the matter, kid? Can't you take it?

Caught at sixteen, June was sent to Jessup County Girls' Home, where the baby was adopted out and she slashed her wrists on the bedsprings.

Lou got caught at seventeen and held in the station downtown, raped on the floor of the holding tank.

Are you a boy or are you a girl?

On your knees, kid, can you take it?

Caught at eighteen and sent to prison, Jack came back seven years later blank-faced, understanding nothing. He married a quiet girl from out of town, had three babies in four years. Then Jack came home one night from the textile mill, carrying one of those big handles off the high-speed spindle machine. He used it to beat them all to death and went back to work in the morning.

Cousin Melvina married at fourteen, had three kids in two and a half years, and welfare took them all away. She ran off with a carnival mechanic, had three more babies before he left her for a motorcycle acrobat. Welfare took those, too. But the next baby was hydrocephalic, a little waterhead they left with her, and the three that followed, even the one she used to hate so—the one she had after she fell off the porch and couldn't remember whose child it was.

"How many children do you have?" I asked her.

"You mean the ones I have, or the ones I had? Four," she told me, "or eleven."

My aunt, the one I was named for, tried to take off for Oklahoma. That was after she'd lost the youngest girl and they told her Bo would never be "right." She packed up biscuits, cold chicken, and Coca-Cola; a lot of loose clothes; Cora and her new baby, Cy; and the four youngest girls. They set off from Greenville in the afternoon, hoping to make Oklahoma by the weekend, but they only got as far as Augusta. The bridge there went out under them.

"An Act of God," my uncle said.

My aunt and Cora crawled out downriver, and two of the girls turned up in the weeds, screaming loud enough to be found in the dark.

But one of the girls never came up out of that dark water, and Nancy, who had been holding Cy, was found still wrapped around the baby, in the water, under the car.

"An Act of God," my aunt said. "God's got one damn sick sense of humor."

M y sister had her baby in a bad year. Before he was born we had talked about it. "Are you afraid?" I asked.

"He'll be fine," she'd replied, not understanding, speaking instead to the other fear. "Don't we have a tradition of bastards?"

He was fine, a classically ugly healthy little boy with that shock of white hair that marked so many of us. But afterward, it was that bad year with my sister down with pleurisy, then cystitis, and no work, no money, having to move back home with my cold-eyed stepfather. I would come home to see her, from the woman I could not admit I'd been with, and take my infinitely fragile nephew and hold him, rocking him, rocking myself.

One night I came home to screaming—the baby, my sister, no one else there. She was standing by the crib, bent over, screaming red-faced. "Shut up! Shut up!" With each word her fist slammed the mattress fanning the baby's ear.

"Don't!" I grabbed her, pulling her back, doing it as gently as I could so I wouldn't break the stitches from her operation. She had her other arm clamped across her abdomen and couldn't fight me at all. She just kept shrieking.

"That little bastard just screams and screams. That little bastard. I'll kill him."

Then the words seeped in and she looked at me while her son kept crying and kicking his feet. By his head the mattress still showed the impact of her fist.

"Oh no," she moaned, "I wasn't going to be like that. I always promised myself." She started to cry, holding her belly and sobbing. "We an't no different. We an't no different."

Jesse wraps her arm around my stomach, presses her belly into my back. I relax against her. "You sure you can't have children?" she asks. "I sure would like to see what your kids would turn out to be like."

I stiffen, say, "I can't have children. I've never wanted children."

"Still," she says, "you're so good with children, so gentle."

I think of all the times my hands have curled into fists, when I have just barely held on. I open my mouth, close it, can't speak. What could I say now? All the times I have not spoken before, all the things I just could not tell her, the shame, the self-hatred, the fear; all of that hangs between us now—a wall I cannot tear down.

I would like to turn around and talk to her, tell her . . . "I've got a dust river in my head, a river of names endlessly repeating. That dirty water rises in me, all those children screaming out their lives in my memory, and I become someone else, someone I have tried so hard not to be." But I don't say anything, and I know, as surely as I know I will never have a child, that by not speaking I am condemning us, that I cannot go on loving you and hating you for your fairy-tale life, for not asking about what you have no reason to imagine, for that soft-chinned innocence I love.

Jesse puts her hands behind my neck, smiles and says, "You tell the funniest stories."

I put my hands behind her back, feeling the ridges of my knuckles pulsing.

"Yeah," I tell her. "But I lie."

EMERGENCY

Denis Johnson · 1991

I'd been working in the emergency room for about three weeks, I guess. This was in 1973, before the summer ended. With nothing to do on the overnight shift but batch the insurance reports from the daytime shifts, I just started wandering around, over to the coronary-care unit, down to the cafeteria, et cetera, looking for Georgie, the orderly, a pretty good friend of mine. He often stole pills from the cabinets.

He was running over the tiled floor of the operating room with a mop. "Are you still doing that?" I said.

"Jesus, there's a lot of blood here," he complained.

"Where?" The floor looked clean enough to me.

"What the hell were they doing in here?" he asked me.

"They were performing surgery, Georgie," I told him.

"There's so much goop inside of us, man," he said, "and it all wants to get out." He leaned his mop against a cabinet.

"What are you crying for?" I didn't understand.

He stood still, raised both arms slowly behind his head, and tightened his ponytail. Then he grabbed the mop and started making broad random arcs with it, trembling and weeping and moving all around the place really fast. "What am I *crying* for?" he said. "Jesus. Wow, oh boy, perfect."

. . .

I was hanging out in the E.R. with fat, quivering Nurse. One of the Family Service doctors that nobody liked came in looking for Georgie to wipe up after him. "Where's Georgie?" this guy asked.

"Georgie's in O.R.," Nurse said.

"Again?"

"No," Nurse said. "Still."

"Still? Doing what?"

"Cleaning the floor."

"Again?"

"No," Nurse said again. "Still."

Back in O.R., Georgie dropped his mop and bent over in the posture of a child soiling its diapers. He stared down with his mouth open in terror.

He said, "What am I going to do about these fucking *shoes*, man?"

"Whatever you stole," I said, "I guess you already ate it all, right?"

"Listen to how they squish," he said, walking around carefully on his heels.

"Let me check your pockets, man."

He stood still a minute, and I found his stash. I left him two of each, whatever they were. "Shift is about half over," I told him.

"Good. Because I really, really, really need a drink," he said. "Will you please help me get this blood mopped up?"

Around 3:30 a.m. a guy with a knife in his eye came in, led by Georgie.

"I hope *you* didn't do that to him," Nurse said.

"Me?" Georgie said. "No. He was like this."

"My wife did it," the man said. The blade was buried to the hilt in the outside corner of his left eye. It was a hunting knife kind of thing.

"Who brought you in?" Nurse said.

"Nobody. I just walked down. It's only three blocks," the man said.

Nurse peered at him. "We'd better get you lying down."

"Okay, I'm certainly ready for something like that," the man said.

She peered a bit longer into his face.

"Is your other eye," she said, "a glass eye?"

"It's plastic, or something artificial like that," he said.

"And you can see out of *this* eye?" she asked, meaning the wounded one.

"I can see. But I can't make a fist out of my left hand because this knife is doing something to my brain."

"My God," Nurse said.

"I guess I'd better get the doctor," I said.

"There you go," Nurse agreed.

They got him lying down, and Georgie says to the patient, "Name?"

"Terrence Weber."

"Your face is dark. I can't see what you're saying."

"Georgie," I said.

"What are you saying, man? I can't see."

Nurse came over, and Georgie said to her, "His face is dark."

She leaned over the patient. "How long ago did this happen, Terry?" she shouted down into his face.

"Just a while ago. My wife did it. I was asleep," the patient said.

"Do you want the police?"

He thought about it and finally said, "Not unless I die."

Nurse went to the wall intercom and buzzed the doctor on duty, the Family Service person. "Got a surprise for you," she said over the intercom. He took his time getting down the hall to her, because he knew she hated Family Service and her happy tone of voice could only mean something beyond his competence and potentially humiliating.

He peeked into the trauma room and saw the situation: the clerk—
that is, me—standing next to the orderly, Georgie, both of us on drugs,
looking down at a patient with a knife sticking up out of his face.

"What seems to be the trouble?" he said.

The doctor gathered the three of us around him in the office and
said, "Here's the situation. We've got to get a team here, an entire
team. I want a good eye man. A great eye man. The best eye man. I
want a brain surgeon. And I want a really good gas man, get me a genius. I'm not touching that head. I'm just going to watch this one. I
know my limits. We'll just get him prepped and sit tight. Orderly!"

"Do you mean me?" Georgie said. "Should I get him prepped?"

"Is this a hospital?" the doctor asked. "Is this the emergency room?
Is that a patient? Are you the orderly?"

I dialled the hospital operator and told her to get me the eye man
and the brain man and the gas man.

Georgie could be heard across the hall, washing his hands and singing a Neil Young song that went "Hello, cowgirl in the sand. Is this
place at your command?"

"That person is not right, not at all, not one bit," the doctor said.

"As long as my instructions are audible to him it doesn't concern
me," Nurse insisted, spooning stuff up out of a little Dixie cup. "I've got
my own life and the protection of my family to think of."

"Well, okay, okay. Don't chew my head off," the doctor said.

The eye man was on vacation or something. While the hospital's
operator called around to find someone else just as good, the other spe-
cialists were hurrying through the night to join us. I stood around looking at charts and chewing up more of Georgie's pills. Some of them
tasted the way urine smells, some of them burned, some of them tasted
like chalk. Various nurses, and two physicians who'd been tending
somebody in I.C.U., were hanging out down here with us now.

Everybody had a different idea about exactly how to approach the problem of removing the knife from Terrence Weber's brain. But when Georgie came in from prepping the patient—from shaving the patient's eyebrow and disinfecting the area around the wound, and so on—he seemed to be holding the hunting knife in his left hand.

The talk just dropped off a cliff.

"Where," the doctor asked finally, "did you get that?"

Nobody said one thing more, not for quite a long time.

After a while, one of the I.C.U. nurses said, "Your shoelace is untied." Georgie laid the knife on a chart and bent down to fix his shoe.

There were twenty more minutes left to get through.

"How's the guy doing?" I asked.

"Who?" Georgie said.

It turned out that Terrence Weber still had excellent vision in the one good eye, and acceptable motor and reflex, despite his earlier motor complaint. "His vitals are normal," Nurse said. "There's nothing wrong with the guy. It's one of those things."

After a while you forget it's summer. You don't remember what the morning is. I'd worked two doubles with eight hours off in between, which I'd spent sleeping on a gurney in the nurse's station. Georgie's pills were making me feel like a giant helium-filled balloon, but I was wide awake. Georgie and I went out to the lot, to his orange pickup.

We lay down on a stretch of dusty plywood in the back of the truck with the daylight knocking against our eyelids and the fragrance of alfalfa thickening on our tongues.

"I want to go to church," Georgie said.

"Let's go to the county fair."

"I'd like to worship. I would."

"They have these injured hawks and eagles there. From the Humane Society," I said.

"I need a quiet chapel about now."

Georgie and I had a terrific time driving around. For a while the day was clear and peaceful. It was one of the moments you stay in, to hell with all the troubles of before and after. The sky is blue and the dead are coming back. Later in the afternoon, with sad resignation, the county fair bares its breasts. A champion of the drug LSD, a very famous guru of the love generation, is being interviewed amid a TV crew off to the left of the poultry cages. His eyeballs look like he bought them in a joke shop. It doesn't occur to me, as I pity this extraterrestrial, that in my life I've taken as much as he has.

After that, we got lost. We drove for hours, literally hours, but we couldn't find the road back to town.

Georgie started to complain. "That was the worst fair I've been to. Where were the rides?"

"They had rides," I said.

"I didn't see one ride."

A jackrabbit scurried out in front of us, and we hit it.

"There was a merry-go-round, a Ferris wheel, and a thing called the Hammer that people were bent over vomiting from after they got off," I said. "Are you completely blind?"

"What was that?"

"A rabbit."

"Something thumped."

"You hit him. *He* thumped."

Georgie stood on the brake pedal. "Rabbit stew."

He threw the truck in reverse and zigzagged back toward the rabbit. "Where's my hunting knife?" He almost ran over the poor animal a second time.

"We'll camp in the wilderness," he said. "In the morning we'll breakfast on its haunches." He was waving Terrence Weber's hunting knife around in what I was sure was a dangerous way.

In a minute he was standing at the edge of the fields, cutting the scrawny little thing up, tossing away its organs. "I should have been a doctor," he cried.

A family in a big Dodge, the only car we'd seen for a long time, slowed down and gawked out the windows as they passed by. The father said, "What is it, a snake?"

"No, it's not a snake," Georgie said. "It's a rabbit with babies inside it."

"Babies!" the mother said, and the father sped the car forward, over the protests of several little kids in the back.

Georgie came back to my side of the truck with his shirtfront stretched out in front of him as if he were carrying apples in it, or some such, but they were, in fact, slimy miniature bunnies. "No way I'm eating those things," I told him.

"Take them, take them. I gotta drive, take them," he said, dumping them in my lap and getting in on his side of the truck. He started driving along faster and faster, with a look of glory on his face. "We killed the mother and saved the children," he said.

"It's getting late," I said. "Let's get back to town."

"You bet." Sixty, seventy, eighty-five, just topping ninety.

"These rabbits better be kept warm." One at a time I slid the little things in between my shirt buttons and nestled them against my belly. "They're hardly moving," I told Georgie.

"We'll get some milk and sugar and all that, and we'll raise them up ourselves. They'll get as big as gorillas."

The road we were lost on cut straight through the middle of the world. It was still daytime, but the sun had no more power than an ornament or a sponge. In this light the truck's hood, which had been bright orange, had turned a deep blue.

Georgie let us drift to the shoulder of the road, slowly, slowly, as if he'd fallen asleep or given up trying to find his way.

"What is it?"

"We can't go on. I don't have any headlights," Georgie said.

We parked under a strange sky with a faint image of a quarter-moon superimposed on it.

There was a little woods beside us. This day had been dry and hot, the buck pines and what-all simmering patiently, but as we sat there smoking cigarettes it started to get very cold.

"The summer's over," I said.

That was the year when arctic clouds moved down over the Midwest and we had two weeks of winter in September.

"Do you realize it's going to snow?" Georgie asked me.

He was right, a gun-blue storm was shaping up. We got out and walked around idiotically. The beautiful chill! That sudden crispness, and the tang of evergreen stabbing us!

The gusts of snow twisted themselves around our heads while the night fell. I couldn't find the truck. We just kept getting more and more lost. I kept calling, "Georgie, can you see?" and he kept saying, "See what? See what?"

The only light visible was a streak of sunset flickering below the hem of the clouds. We headed that way.

We bumped softly down a hill toward an open field that seemed to be a military graveyard, filled with rows and rows of austere, identical markers over soldiers' graves. I'd never before come across this cemetery. On the farther side of the field, just beyond the curtains of snow, the sky was torn away and the angels were descending out of a brilliant blue summer, their huge faces streaked with light and full of pity. The sight of them cut through my heart and down the knuckles of my spine, and if there'd been anything in my bowels I would have messed my pants from fear.

Georgie opened his arms and cried out, "It's the drive-in, man!"

"The drive-in . . ." I wasn't sure what these words meant.

"They're showing movies in a fucking blizzard!" Georgie screamed.

"I see. I thought it was something else," I said.

We walked carefully down there and climbed through the busted fence and stood in the very back. The speakers, which I'd mistaken for grave markers, muttered in unison. Then there was tinkly music, of which I could very nearly make out the tune. Famous movie stars rode bicycles beside a river, laughing out of their gigantic, lovely mouths. If anybody had come to see this show, they'd left when the weather started. Not one car remained, not even a broken-down one from last week, or one left here because it was out of gas. In a couple of minutes, in the middle of a whirling square dance, the screen turned black, the cinematic summer ended, the snow went dark, there was nothing but my breath.

"I'm starting to get my eyes back," Georgie said in another minute.

A general greyness was giving birth to various shapes, it was true. "But which ones are close and which ones are far off?" I begged him to tell me.

By trial and error, with a lot of walking back and forth in wet shoes, we found the truck and sat inside it shivering.

"Let's get out of here," I said.

"We can't go anywhere without headlights."

"We've gotta get back. We're a long way from home."

"No, we're not."

"We must have come three hundred miles."

"We're right outside town, Fuckhead. We've just been driving around and around."

"This is no place to camp. I hear the Interstate over there."

"We'll just stay here till it gets late. We can drive home late. We'll be invisible."

We listened to the big rigs going from San Francisco to Pennsylvania along the Interstate, like shudders down a long hacksaw blade, while the snow buried us.

Eventually Georgie said, "We better get some milk for those bunnies."

"We don't have *milk*," I said.

"We'll mix sugar up with it."

"Will you forget about this milk all of a sudden?"

"They're mammals, man."

"Forget about those rabbits."

"Where are they, anyway?"

"You're not listening to me. I said, 'Forget the rabbits.'"

"Where are they?"

The truth was I'd forgotten all about them, and they were dead.

"They slid around behind me and got squashed," I said tearfully.

"They slid around *behind*?"

He watched while I pried them out from behind my back.

I picked them out one at a time and held them in my hands and we looked at them. There were eight. They weren't any bigger than my fingers, but everything was there.

Little feet! Eyelids! Even whiskers! "Deceased," I said.

Georgie asked, "Does everything you touch turn to shit? Does this happen to you every time?"

"No wonder they call me Fuckhead."

"It's a name that's going to stick."

"I realize that."

"'Fuckhead' is gonna ride you to your grave."

"I just said so. I agreed with you in advance," I said.

Or maybe that wasn't the time it snowed. Maybe it was the time we slept in the truck and I rolled over on the bunnies and flattened them. It doesn't matter. What's important for me to remember now is that early the next morning the snow was melted off the windshield and the daylight woke me up. A mist covered everything and, with the sunshine, was beginning to grow sharp and strange. The bunnies weren't a problem yet, or they'd already been a problem and were already forgotten, and there was nothing on my mind. I felt the beauty of the morning. I could understand how a drowning man might suddenly feel a deep thirst being quenched. Or how the slave might become a friend to his master. Georgie slept with his face right on the steering wheel.

I saw bits of snow resembling an abundance of blossoms on the stems of the drive-in speakers—no, revealing the blossoms that were always there. A bull elk stood still in the pasture beyond the fence, giving off an air of authority and stupidity. And a coyote jogged across the pasture and faded away among the saplings.

That afternoon we got back to work in time to resume everything as if it had never stopped happening and we'd never been anywhere else.

"The Lord," the intercom said, "is my shepherd." It did that each evening because this was a Catholic hospital. "Our Father, who art in Heaven," and so on.

"Yeah, yeah," Nurse said.

The man with the knife in his head, Terrence Weber, was released around suppertime. They'd kept him overnight and given him an eyepatch—all for no reason, really.

He stopped off at E.R. to say goodbye. "Well, those pills they gave me make everything taste terrible," he said.

"It could have been worse," Nurse said.

"Even my tongue."

"It's just a miracle you didn't end up sightless or at least dead," she reminded him.

The patient recognized me. He acknowledged me with a smile. "I was peeping on the lady next door while she was out there sunbathing," he said. "My wife decided to blind me."

He shook Georgie's hand. Georgie didn't know him. "Who are you supposed to be?" he asked Terrence Weber.

Some hours before that, Georgie had said something that had suddenly and completely explained the difference between us. We'd been driving back toward town, along the Old Highway, through the flatness. We picked up a hitchhiker, a boy I knew. We stopped the truck and the boy climbed slowly up out of the fields as out of the mouth of a volcano. His name was Hardee. He looked even worse than we probably did.

"We got messed up and slept in the truck all night," I told Hardee.

"I had a feeling," Hardee said. "Either that or, you know, driving a thousand miles."

"That too," I said.

"Or you're sick or diseased or something."

"Who's this guy?" Georgie asked.

"This is Hardee. He lived with me last summer. I found him on the doorstep. What happened to your dog?" I asked Hardee.

"He's still down there."

"Yeah, I heard you went to Texas."

"I was working on a bee farm," Hardee said.

"Wow. Do those things sting you?"

"Not like you'd think," Hardee said. "You're part of their daily drill. It's all part of a harmony."

Outside, the same identical stretch of ground repeatedly rolled past our faces. The day was cloudless, blinding. But Georgie said, "Look at that," pointing straight ahead of us.

One star was so hot it showed, bright and blue, in the empty sky.

"I recognized you right away," I told Hardee. "But what happened to your hair? Who chopped it off?"

"I hate to say."

"Don't tell me."

"They drafted me."

"Oh no."

"Oh yeah. I'm AWOL. I'm bad AWOL. I got to get to Canada."

"Oh, that's terrible," I said to Hardee.

"Don't worry," Georgie said. "We'll get you there."

"How?"

"Somehow. I think I know some people. Don't worry. You're on your way to Canada."

That world! These days it's all been erased and they've rolled it up like a scroll and put it away somewhere. Yes, I can touch it with my fingers. But where is it?

After a while Hardee asked Georgie, "What do you do for a job," and Georgie said, "I save lives."

STICKS

George Saunders • 1994

Every year Thanksgiving night we flocked out behind Dad as he dragged the Santa suit to the road and draped it over a kind of crucifix he'd built out of metal pole in the yard. Super Bowl week the pole was dressed in a jersey and Rod's helmet and Rod had to clear it with Dad if he wanted to take the helmet off. On the Fourth of July the pole was Uncle Sam, on Veteran's Day a soldier, on Halloween a ghost. The pole was Dad's only concession to glee. We were allowed a single Crayola from the box at a time. One Christmas Eve he shrieked at Kimmie for wasting an apple slice. He hovered over us as we poured ketchup saying: good enough good enough good enough. Birthday parties consisted of cupcakes, no ice cream. The first time I brought a date over she said: what's with your dad and that pole? and I sat there blinking.

We left home, married, had children of our own, found the seeds of meanness blooming also within us. Dad began dressing the pole with more complexity and less discernible logic. He draped some kind of fur over it on Groundhog Day and lugged out a floodlight to ensure a shadow. When an earthquake struck Chile he lay the pole on its side and spray painted a rift in the earth. Mom died and he dressed the pole as Death and hung from the crossbar photos of Mom as a baby. We'd stop by and find odd talismans from his youth arranged around the base: army medals, theater tickets, old sweatshirts, tubes of Mom's makeup. One autumn he painted the pole bright yellow. He covered it with cotton swabs that winter for warmth and provided offspring by hammering in six crossed sticks around the yard. He ran lengths of string between the pole and the sticks, and taped to the string letters of apology, admissions of error, pleas for understanding, all written in a frantic hand on index cards. He painted a sign saying LOVE and hung it from the pole and another that said FORGIVE? and then he died in the hall with the radio on and we sold the house to a young couple who yanked out the pole and the sticks and left them by the road on garbage day.

FIESTA, 1980

Junot Díaz · 1996

Mami's youngest sister—my tía Yrma—finally made it to the United States that year. She and tío Miguel got themselves an apartment in the Bronx, off the Grand Concourse and everybody decided that we should have a party. Actually, my pops decided, but everybody—meaning Mami, tía Yrma, tío Miguel and their neighbors—thought it a dope idea. On the afternoon of the party Papi came back from work around six. Right on time. We were all dressed by then, which was a smart move on our part. If Papi had walked in and caught us lounging around in our underwear, he would have kicked our asses something serious.

He didn't say nothing to nobody, not even my moms. He just pushed past her, held up his hand when she tried to talk to him and headed right into the shower. Rafa gave me the look and I gave it back to him; we both knew Papi had been with that Puerto Rican woman he was seeing and wanted to wash off the evidence quick.

Mami looked really nice that day. The United States had finally put some meat on her; she was no longer the same flaca who had arrived here three years before. She had cut her hair short and was wearing tons of cheap-ass jewelry which on her didn't look too lousy. She smelled like herself, like the wind through a tree. She always waited until the last possible minute to put on her perfume because she said it was a waste to spray it on early and then have to spray it on again once you got to the party.

We—meaning me, my brother, my little sister and Mami—waited for Papi to finish his shower. Mami seemed anxious, in her usual dispassionate way. Her hands adjusted the buckle of her belt over and over again. That morning, when she had gotten us up for school, Mami told us that she wanted to have a good time at the party. I want to dance, she said, but now, with the sun sliding out of the sky like spit off a wall, she seemed ready just to get this over with.

Rafa didn't much want to go to no party either, and me, I never wanted to go anywhere with my family. There was a baseball game in the parking lot outside and we could hear our friends, yelling, Hey, and, Cabrón, to one another. We heard the pop of a ball as it sailed over the cars, the clatter of an aluminum bat dropping to the concrete. Not that me or Rafa loved baseball; we just liked playing with the local kids, thrashing them at anything they were doing. By the sounds of the shouting, we both knew the game was close, either of us could have made a difference. Rafa frowned and when I frowned back, he put up his fist. Don't you mirror me, he said.

Don't you mirror me, I said.

He punched me—I would have hit him back but Papi marched into the living room with his towel around his waist, looking a lot smaller than he did when he was dressed. He had a few strands of hair around his nipples and a surly closed-mouth expression, like maybe he'd scalded his tongue or something.

Have they eaten? he asked Mami.

She nodded. I made you something.

You didn't let him eat, did you?

Ay, Dios mío, she said, letting her arms fall to her side.

Ay, Dios mío is right, Papi said.

I was never supposed to eat before our car trips, but earlier, when she had put out our dinner of rice, beans and sweet platanos, guess who had been the first one to clean his plate? You couldn't blame Mami really, she had been busy—cooking, getting ready, dressing my sister Madai. I should have reminded her not to feed me but I wasn't that sort of son.

Papi turned to me. Coño, muchacho, why did you eat?

Rafa had already started inching away from me. I'd once told him I considered him a low-down chickenshit for moving out of the way every time Papi was going to smack me.

Collateral damage, Rafa had said. Ever heard of it?

No.

Look it up.

Chickenshit or not, I didn't dare glance at him. Papi was old-fashioned; he expected your undivided attention when you were getting your ass whupped. You couldn't look him in the eye either—that wasn't allowed. Better to stare at his belly button, which was perfectly round and immaculate. Papi pulled me to my feet by my ear.

If you throw up—

I won't, I cried, tears in my eyes, more out of reflex than pain.

Ya, Ramón, ya. It's not his fault, Mami said.

They've known about this party forever. How did they think we were going to get there? Fly?

He finally let go of my ear and I sat back down. Madai was too scared to open her eyes. Being around Papi all her life had turned her into a major-league wuss. Anytime Papi raised his voice her lip would start trembling, like some specialized tuning fork. Rafa pretended that he had knuckles to crack and when I shoved him, he gave me a *Don't start* look. But even that little bit of recognition made me feel better.

I was the one who was always in trouble with my dad. It was like my God-given duty to piss him off, to do everything the way he hated. Our fights didn't bother me too much. I still wanted him to love me, something that never seemed strange or contradictory until years later, when he was out of our lives.

By the time my ear stopped stinging Papi was dressed and Mami was crossing each one of us, solemnly, like we were heading off to war. We said, in turn, Bendición, Mami, and she poked us in our five cardinal spots while saying, Que Dios te bendiga.

This was how all our trips began, the words that followed me every time I left the house.

None of us spoke until we were inside Papi's Volkswagen van. Brand-new, lime-green and bought to impress. Oh, we were impressed, but me, every time I was in that VW and Papi went above twenty miles an hour, I vomited. I'd never had trouble with cars before—that van was like my curse. Mami suspected it was the upholstery. In her mind, American things—appliances, mouthwash, funny-looking upholstery— all seemed to have an intrinsic badness about them. Papi was careful about taking me anywhere in the VW, but when he had to, I rode up front in Mami's usual seat so I could throw up out a window.

¿Cómo te sientes? Mami asked over my shoulder when Papi pulled onto the turnpike. She had her hand on the base of my neck. One thing about Mami, her palms never sweated.

I'm OK, I said, keeping my eyes straight ahead. I definitely didn't want to trade glances with Papi. He had this one look, furious and sharp, that always left me feeling bruised.

Toma. Mami handed me four mentas. She had thrown three out her window at the beginning of our trip, an offering to Eshú; the rest were for me.

I took one and sucked it slowly, my tongue knocking it up against my teeth. We passed Newark Airport without any incident. If Madai had been awake she would have cried because the planes flew so close to the cars.

How's he feeling? Papi asked.

Fine, I said. I glanced back at Rafa and he pretended like he didn't see me. That was the way he was, at school and at home. When I was in trouble, he didn't know me. Madai was solidly asleep, but even with

her face all wrinkled up and drooling she looked cute, her hair all separated into twists.

I turned around and concentrated on the candy. Papi even started to
joke that we might not have to scrub the van out tonight. He was beginning to loosen up, not checking his watch too much. Maybe he was
thinking about that Puerto Rican woman or maybe he was just happy
that we were all together. I could never tell. At the toll, he was feeling
positive enough to actually get out of the van and search around under
the basket for dropped coins. It was something he had once done to
amuse Madai, but now it was habit. Cars behind us honked their horns
and I slid down in my seat. Rafa didn't care; he grinned back at the
other cars and waved. His actual job was to make sure no cops were
coming. Mami shook Madai awake and as soon as she saw Papi stooping for a couple of quarters she let out this screech of delight that almost
took off the top of my head.

That was the end of the good times. Just outside the Washington
Bridge, I started feeling woozy. The smell of the upholstery got all up
inside my head and I found myself with a mouthful of saliva. Mami's
hand tensed on my shoulder and when I caught Papi's eye, he was like,
No way. Don't do it.

The first time I got sick in the van Papi was taking me to the library.
Rafa was with us and he couldn't believe I threw up. I was famous
for my steel-lined stomach. A third-world childhood could give you
that. Papi was worried enough that just as quick as Rafa could drop off
the books we were on our way home. Mami fixed me one of her honey-
and-onion concoctions and that made my stomach feel better. A week
later we tried the library again and on this go-around I couldn't get the
window open in time. When Papi got me home, he went and cleaned
out the van himself, an expression of askho on his face. This was a big

deal, since Papi almost never cleaned anything himself. He came back inside and found me sitting on the couch feeling like hell.

It's the car, he said to Mami. It's making him sick.

This time the damage was pretty minimal, nothing Papi couldn't wash off the door with a blast of the hose. He was pissed, though; he jammed his finger into my cheek, a nice solid thrust. That was the way he was with his punishments: imaginative. Earlier that year I'd written an essay in school called "My Father the Torturer," but the teacher made me write a new one. She thought I was kidding.

We drove the rest of the way to the Bronx in silence. We only stopped once, so I could brush my teeth. Mami had brought along my toothbrush and a tube of toothpaste and while every car known to man sped by us she stood outside with me so I wouldn't feel alone.

Tío Miguel was about seven feet tall and had his hair combed up and out, into a demi-fro. He gave me and Rafa big spleen-crushing hugs and then kissed Mami and finally ended up with Madai on his shoulder. The last time I'd seen Tío was at the airport, his first day in the United States. I remembered how he hadn't seemed all that troubled to be in another country.

He looked down at me. Carajo, Yunior, you look horrible!

He threw up, my brother explained.

I pushed Rafa. Thanks a lot, ass-face.

Hey, he said. Tío asked.

Tío clapped a bricklayer's hand on my shoulder. Everybody gets sick sometimes, he said. You should have seen me on the plane over here. Dios mio! He rolled his Asian-looking eyes for emphasis. I thought we were all going to die.

Everybody could tell he was lying. I smiled like he was making me feel better.

Do you want me to get you a drink? Tío asked. We got beer and rum.

Miguel, Mami said. He's young.

Young? Back in Santo Domingo, he'd be getting laid by now.

Mami thinned her lips, which took some doing.

Well, it's true, Tío said.

So, Mami, I said. When do I get to go visit the D.R.?

That's enough, Yunior.

It's the only pussy you'll ever get, Rafa said to me in English.

Not counting your girlfriend, of course.

Rafa smiled. He had to give me that one.

Papi came in from parking the van. He and Miguel gave each other the sort of handshakes that would have turned my fingers into Wonder bread.

Coño, compa'i, ¿cómo va todo? they said to each other.

Tía came out then, with an apron on and maybe the longest Lee Press-On Nails I've ever seen in my life. There was this one guru motherfucker in the *Guinness Book of World Records* who had longer nails, but I tell you, it was close. She gave everybody kisses, told me and Rafa how guapo we were—Rafa, of course, believed her—told Madai how bella she was, but when she got to Papi, she froze a little, like maybe she'd seen a wasp on the tip of his nose, but then kissed him all the same.

Mami told us to join the other kids in the living room. Tío said, Wait a minute, I want to show you the apartment. I was glad Tía said, Hold on, because from what I'd seen so far, the place had been furnished in Contemporary Dominican Tacky. The less I saw, the better. I mean, I liked plastic sofa covers but damn, Tío and Tía had taken it to another level. They had a disco ball hanging in the living room and the type of stucco ceilings that looked like stalactite heaven. The sofas all had golden tassels dangling from their edges. Tía came out of the kitchen with some people I didn't know and by the time she got done introducing everybody, only Papi and Mami were given the guided tour of the four-room third-floor apartment. Me and Rafa joined the kids in the living room. They'd already started eating. We were hungry, one of the girls explained, a pastelito in hand. The boy was about three years younger than me but the girl who'd spoken, Leti, was my age. She and another girl were on the sofa together and they were cute as hell.

Leti introduced them: the boy was her brother Wilquins and the other girl was her neighbor Mari. Leti had some serious tetas and I could tell that my brother was going to gun for her. His taste in girls was predictable. He sat down right between Leti and Mari and by the way they were smiling at him I knew he'd do fine. Neither of the girls gave me more than a cursory one-two, which didn't bother me. Sure, I liked girls but I was always too terrified to speak to them unless we were arguing or I was calling them stupidos, which was one of my favorite words that year. I turned to Wilquins and asked him what there was to do around here. Mari, who had the lowest voice I'd ever heard, said, He can't speak.

What does that mean?

He's mute.

I looked at Wilquins incredulously. He smiled and nodded, as if he'd won a prize or something.

Does he understand? I asked.

Of course he understands, Rafa said. He's not dumb.

I could tell Rafa had said that just to score points with the girls. Both of them nodded. Low-voice Mari said, He's the best student in his grade.

I thought, Not bad for a mute. I sat next to Wilquins. After about two seconds of TV Wilquins whipped out a bag of dominos and motioned to me. Did I want to play? Sure. Me and him played Rafa and Leti and we whupped their collective asses twice, which put Rafa in a real bad mood. He looked at me like maybe he wanted to take a swing, just one to make him feel better. Leti kept whispering into Rafa's ear, telling him it was OK.

In the kitchen I could hear my parents slipping into their usual modes. Papi's voice was loud and argumentative; you didn't have to be anywhere near him to catch his drift. And Mami, you had to put cups to your ears to hear hers. I went into the kitchen a few times—once so the tíos could show off how much bullshit I'd been able to cram in my head the last few years; another time for a bucket-sized cup of soda. Mami and Tía were frying tostones and the last of the pastelitos. She appeared happier now and the way her hands worked on our dinner you would think she had a life somewhere else making rare and precious things. She nudged Tía every now and then, shit they must have been doing all their lives. As soon as Mami saw me though, she gave me the eye. Don't stay long, that eye said. Don't piss your old man off.

Papi was too busy arguing about Elvis to notice me. Then somebody mentioned María Montez and Papi barked, María Montez? Let me tell you about María Montez, compa'i.

Maybe I was used to him. His voice—louder than most adults'—didn't bother me none, though the other kids shifted uneasily in their seats. Wilquins was about to raise the volume on the TV, but Rafa said, I wouldn't do that. Muteboy had balls, though. He did it anyway and then sat down. Wilquins's pop came into the living room a second later, a bottle of Presidente in hand. That dude must have had Spider-senses or something. Did you raise that? he asked Wilquins and Wilquins nodded.

Is this your house? his pops asked. He looked ready to beat Wilquins silly but he lowered the volume instead.

See, Rafa said. You nearly got your ass *kicked*.

I met the Puerto Rican woman right after Papi had gotten the van. He was taking me on short trips, trying to cure me of my vomiting. It wasn't really working but I looked forward to our trips, even though at the end of each one I'd be sick. These were the only times me and Papi did anything together. When we were alone he treated me much better, like maybe I was his son or something.

Before each drive Mami would cross me.

Bendición, Mami, I'd say.

She'd kiss my forehead. Que Dios te bendiga. And then she would give me a handful of mentas because she wanted me to be OK. Mami didn't think these excursions would cure anything, but the one time she had brought it up to Papi he had told her to shut up, what did she know about anything anyway?

Me and Papi didn't talk much. We just drove around our neighborhood. Occasionally he'd ask, How is it?

And I'd nod, no matter how I felt.

One day I was sick outside of Perth Amboy. Instead of taking me home he went the other way on Industrial Avenue, stopping a few minutes later in front of a light blue house I didn't recognize. It reminded me of the Easter eggs we colored at school, the ones we threw out the bus windows at other cars.

The Puerto Rican woman was there and she helped me clean up. She had dry papery hands and when she rubbed the towel on my chest, she did it hard, like I was a bumper she was waxing. She was very thin and had a cloud of brown hair rising above her narrow face and the sharpest blackest eyes you've ever seen.

He's cute, she said to Papi.

Not when he's throwing up, Papi said.

What's your name? she asked me. Are you Rafa?

I shook my head.

Then it's Yunior, right?

I nodded.

You're the smart one, she said, suddenly happy with herself. Maybe you want to see my books?

They weren't hers. I recognized them as ones my father must have left in her house. Papi was a voracious reader, couldn't even go cheating without a paperback in his pocket.

Why don't you go watch TV? Papi suggested. He was looking at her like she was the last piece of chicken on earth.

We got plenty of channels, she said. Use the remote if you want.

The two of them went upstairs and I was too scared of what was happening to poke around. I just sat there, ashamed, expecting something big and fiery to crash down on our heads. I watched a whole hour of the news before Papi came downstairs and said, Let's go.

About two hours later the women laid out the food and like always nobody but the kids thanked them. It must be some Dominican tradition or something. There was everything I liked—chicharrones, fried chicken, tostones, sancocho, rice, fried cheese, yuca, avocado, potato salad, a meteor-sized hunk of pernil, even a tossed salad which I could do without—but when I joined the other kids around the serving table, Papi said, Oh no you don't, and took the paper plate out of my hand. His fingers weren't gentle.

What's wrong now? Tía asked, handing me another plate.

He ain't eating, Papi said. Mami pretended to help Rafa with the pernil.

Why can't he eat?

Because I said so.

The adults who didn't know us made like they hadn't heard a thing and Tío just smiled sheepishly and told everybody to go ahead and eat. All the kids—about ten of them now—trooped back into the living room with their plates a-heaping and all the adults ducked into the kitchen and the dining room, where the radio was playing loud-ass bachatas. I was the only one without a plate. Papi stopped me before I could get away from him. He kept his voice nice and low so nobody else could hear him.

If you eat anything, I'm going to beat you. ¿Entiendes?

I nodded.

And if your brother gives you any food, I'll beat him too. Right here in front of everybody. ¿Entiendes?

I nodded again. I wanted to kill him and he must have sensed it because he gave my head a little shove.

All the kids watched me come in and sit down in front of the TV.

What's wrong with your dad? Leti asked.

He's a dick, I said.

Rafa shook his head. Don't say that shit in front of people.

Easy for you to be nice when you're eating, I said.

Hey, if I was a pukey little baby, I wouldn't get no food either.

I almost said something back but I concentrated on the TV. I wasn't going to start it. No fucking way. So I watched Bruce Lee beat Chuck Norris into the floor of the Colosseum and tried to pretend that there was no food anywhere in the house. It was Tía who finally saved me. She came into the living room and said, Since you ain't eating, Yunior, you can at least help me get some ice.

I didn't want to, but she mistook my reluctance for something else.

I already asked your father.

She held my hand while we walked; Tía didn't have any kids but I could tell she wanted them. She was the sort of relative who always remembered your birthday but who you only went to visit because you had to. We didn't get past the first-floor landing before she opened her pocketbook and handed me the first of three pastelitos she had smuggled out of the apartment.

Go ahead, she said. And as soon as you get inside make sure you brush your teeth.

Thanks a lot, Tía, I said.

Those pastelitos didn't stand a chance.

She sat next to me on the stairs and smoked her cigarette. All the way down on the first floor and we could still hear the music and the adults and the television. Tía looked a ton like Mami; the two of them were both short and light-skinned. Tía smiled a lot and that was what set them apart the most.

How is it at home, Yunior?

What do you mean?

How's it going in the apartment? Are you kids OK?

I knew an interrogation when I heard one, no matter how sugar-coated it was. I didn't say anything. Don't get me wrong, I loved my tía, but something told me to keep my mouth shut. Maybe it was family loyalty, maybe I just wanted to protect Mami or I was afraid that Papi would find out—it could have been anything really.

Is your mom all right?

I shrugged.

Have there been lots of fights?

None, I said. Too many shrugs would have been just as bad as an answer. Papi's at work too much.

Work, Tía said, like it was somebody's name she didn't like.

Me and Rafa, we didn't talk much about the Puerto Rican woman. When we ate dinner at her house, the few times Papi had taken us over there, we still acted like nothing was out of the ordinary. Pass the ketchup, man. No sweat, bro. The affair was like a hole in our living room floor, one we'd gotten so used to circumnavigating that we sometimes forgot it was there.

By midnight all the adults were crazy dancing. I was sitting outside Tía's bedroom—where Madai was sleeping—trying not to attract attention. Rafa had me guarding the door; he and Leti were in there too, with some of the other kids, getting busy no doubt. Wilquins had gone across the hall to bed so I had me and the roaches to mess around with.

Whenever I peered into the main room I saw about twenty moms and dads dancing and drinking beers. Every now and then somebody yelled, ¡Quisqueya! And then everybody else would yell and stomp their feet. From what I could see my parents seemed to be enjoying themselves.

Mami and Tía spent a lot of time side by side, whispering, and I kept expecting something to come of this, a brawl maybe. I'd never once been out with my family when it hadn't turned to shit. We weren't even theatrical or straight crazy like other families. We fought like sixth-graders, without any real dignity. I guess the whole night I'd been waiting for a blowup, something between Papi and Mami. This was how I always figured Papi would be exposed, out in public, where everybody would know.

You're a cheater!

But everything was calmer than usual. And Mami didn't look like she was about to say anything to Papi. The two of them danced every now and then but they never lasted more than a song before Mami joined Tía again in whatever conversation they were having.

I tried to imagine Mami before Papi. Maybe I was tired, or just sad, thinking about the way my family was. Maybe I already knew how it would all end up in a few years, Mami without Papi, and that was why I did it. Picturing her alone wasn't easy. It seemed like Papi had always been with her, even when we were waiting in Santo Domingo for him to send for us.

The only photograph our family had of Mami as a young woman, before she married Papi, was the one that somebody took of her at an election party that I found one day while rummaging for money to go to the arcade. Mami had it tucked into her immigration papers. In the photo, she's surrounded by laughing cousins I will never meet, who are all shiny from dancing, whose clothes are rumpled and loose. You can tell it's night and hot and that the mosquitos have been biting. She sits straight and even in a crowd she stands out, smiling quietly like maybe she's the one everybody's celebrating. You can't see her hands but I imagined they're knotting a straw or a bit of thread. This was the woman my father met a year later on the Malecón, the woman Mami thought she'd always be.

Mami must have caught me studying her because she stopped what she was doing and gave me a smile, maybe her first one of the night. Suddenly I wanted to go over and hug her, for no other reason than I loved her, but there were about eleven fat jiggling bodies between us. So I sat down on the tiled floor and waited.

I must have fallen asleep because the next thing I knew Rafa was kicking me and saying, Let's go. He looked like he'd been hitting those girls off; he was all smiles. I got to my feet in time to kiss Tía and Tío good-bye. Mami was holding the serving dish she had brought with her.

Where's Papi? I asked.

He's downstairs, bringing the van around. Mami leaned down to kiss me.

You were good today, she said.

And then Papi burst in and told us to get the hell downstairs before some pendejo cop gave him a ticket. More kisses, more handshakes and then we were gone.

I don't remember being out of sorts after I met the Puerto Rican woman, but I must have been because Mami only asked me questions when she thought something was wrong in my life. It took her about ten passes but finally she cornered me one afternoon when we were alone in the apartment. Our upstairs neighbors were beating the crap out of their kids, and me and her had been listening to it all afternoon. She put her hand on mine and said, Is everything OK, Yunior? Have you been fighting with your brother?

Me and Rafa had already talked. We'd been in the basement, where our parents couldn't hear us. He told me that yeah, he knew about her.

Papi's taken me there twice now, he said.

Why didn't you tell me? I asked.

What the hell was I going to say? *Hey, Yunior, guess what happened yesterday? I met Papi's sucia!*

I didn't say anything to Mami either. She watched me, very very closely. Later I would think, maybe if I had told her, she would have confronted him, would have done something, but who can know these things? I said I'd been having trouble in school and like that everything was back to normal between us. She put her hand on my shoulder and squeezed and that was that.

We were on the turnpike, just past Exit 11, when I started feeling it again. I sat up from leaning against Rafa. His fingers smelled and he'd gone to sleep almost as soon as he got into the van. Madai was out too but at least she wasn't snoring.

In the darkness, I saw that Papi had a hand on Mami's knee and that the two of them were quiet and still. They weren't slumped back or anything; they were both wide awake, bolted into their seats. I couldn't see either of their faces and no matter how hard I tried I could not imagine their expressions. Neither of them moved. Every now and then the van was filled with the bright rush of somebody else's headlights. Finally I said, Mami, and they both looked back, already knowing what was happening.

SILENCE

Lucia Berlin • 1998

I started out quiet, living in mountain mining towns, moving too often to make a friend. I'd find me a tree or a room in an old deserted mill, to sit in silence.

My mother was usually reading or sleeping so I spoke mostly with my father. As soon as he got in the door or when he took me up into the mountains or down dark into the mines, I was talking nonstop.

Then he went overseas and we were in El Paso, Texas, where I went to Vilas school. In third grade I read well but I didn't even know addition. Heavy brace on my crooked back. I was tall but still childlike. A changeling in this city, as if I'd been reared in the woods by mountain goats. I kept peeing in my pants, splashing until I refused to go to school or even speak to the principal.

My mother's old high school teacher got me in as a scholarship student at the exclusive Radford School for Girls, two bus rides across El Paso. I still had all of the above problems but now I was also dressed like a ragamuffin. I lived in the slums and there was something particularly unacceptable about my hair.

I haven't talked much about this school. I don't mind telling people awful things if I can make them funny. It was never funny. Once at recess I took a drink from a garden hose and the teacher grabbed it from me, told me I was common.

But the library. Every day we got to spend an hour in it, free to look at any book, at every book, to sit down and read, or go through the card catalogue. When there were fifteen minutes left the librarian let us know, so we could check out a book. The librarian was so, don't laugh, soft-spoken. Not just quiet but nice. She'd tell you, "This is where biographies are," and then explain what a biography was.

"Here are reference books. If there is ever anything you want to know, you just ask me and we'll find the answer in a book."

This was a wonderful thing to hear and I believed her.

Then Miss Brick's purse got stolen from beneath her desk. She said that it must have been me who took it. I was sent to Lucinda de Leftwitch Templin's office. Lucinda de said she knew I didn't come from a privileged home like most of her girls, and that this might be difficult for me sometimes. She understood, she said, but really she was saying, "Where's the purse?"

I left. Didn't even go back to get the bus money or lunch in my cubby. Took off across town, all the long way, all the long day. My mother met me on the porch with a switch. They had called to say I had stolen the purse and then run away. She didn't even ask me if I stole it. "Little thief, humiliating me," whack, "brat, ungrateful," whack. Lucinda de called her the next day to tell her a janitor had stolen the purse but my mother didn't even apologize to me. She just said, "Bitch," after she hung up.

That's how I ended up in St. Joseph's, which I loved. But those kids hated me too, for all of the above reasons but now worse for new reasons, one being that Sister Cecilia always called on me and I got stars and Saint pictures and was the pet! pet! until I stopped raising my hand.

Uncle John took off for Nacogdoches, which left me alone with my mother and Grandpa. Uncle John always used to eat with me, or drink while I ate. He talked to me while I helped him repair furniture, took me to movies and let me hold his slimy glass eye. It was terrible when he was gone. Grandpa and Mamie (my grandma) were at his dentist office all day and then when they got home Mamie kept my little sister safe away in the kitchen or in Mamie's room. My mother was out, being a gray lady at the army hospital or playing bridge. Grandpa was out at the Elks or who knows. The house was scary and empty without John and I'd have to hide from Grandpa and Mama when either of them was drunk. Home was bad and school was bad.

I decided not to talk. I just sort of gave it up. It lasted so long Sister Cecilia tried to pray with me in the cloakroom. She meant well and was just touching me in sympathy, praying. I got scared and pushed her and she fell down and I got expelled.

That's when I met Hope.

School was almost over so I would stay home and go back to Vilas in the fall. I still wasn't talking, even when my mother poured a whole pitcher of iced tea over my head or twisted as she pinched me so the pinches looked like stars, the Big Dipper, Little Dipper, the Lyre up and down my arms.

I played jacks on the concrete above the steps, wishing that the Syrian kid next door would ask me over. She played on their concrete porch. She was small and thin but seemed old. Not grown-up or mature but like an old woman-child. Long shiny black hair with bangs hanging down over her eyes. In order to see she had to tip her head back. She looked like a baby baboon. In a nice way, I mean. A little face and huge black eyes. All of the six Haddad kids looked emaciated but the adults were huge, two or three hundred pounds.

I knew she noticed me too because if I was doing cherries in the basket so was she. Or shooting stars, except she didn't ever drop a jack, even with twelves. For weeks our balls and jacks made a nice bop bop crash bop bop crash rhythm until finally she did come over to the fence. She must have heard my mother yelling at me because she said,

"You talk yet?"

I shook my head.

"Good. Talking to me won't count."

I hopped the fence. That night I was so happy I had a friend that when I went to bed I called out, "Good night!"

We had played jacks for hours that day and then she taught me mumblety-peg. Dangerous games with a knife. Triple flips into the grass, and the scariest was one hand flat on the ground, stabbing between each finger. Faster faster faster blood. I don't think we spoke at all. We rarely did, all summer long. All I remember are her first and last words.

I have never had a friend again like Hope, my onliest true friend. I gradually became a part of the Haddad family. I believe that if this had not happened I would have grown up to be not just neurotic, alcoholic, and insecure, but seriously disturbed. Wacko.

The six children and the father spoke English. The mother, grandma, and five or six other old women spoke only Arabic. Looking back, it seems like I went through sort of an orientation. The children watched as I learned to run, really run, to vault the fence, not climb it. I became expert with the knife, tops, and marbles. I learned cusswords and gestures in English, Spanish, and Arabic. For the grandma I washed dishes, watered, raked the sand in the backyard, beat rugs with a woven-cane beater, helped the old women roll out bread on the Ping-Pong tables in the basement. Lazy afternoons washing bloody menstrual rags in a tub in the backyard with Hope and Shahala, her older sister. This seemed not disgusting but magic, like a mysterious rite. In the mornings I stood in line with the other girls to get my ears washed and my hair braided, to get kibbe on fresh hot bread. The women hollered at me, "*Hjaddadinah!*" Kissed me and slapped me as if I belonged there. Mr. Haddad let me and Hope sit on couches and drive around town in the bed of his Haddad's Beautiful Furniture truck.

I learned to steal. Pomegranates and figs from blind old Guca's yard,

Blue Waltz perfume, Tangee lipstick from Kress's, licorice and sodas from the Sunshine Grocery. Stores delivered then, and one day the Sunshine delivery boy was bringing groceries to both our houses just as Hope and I were getting home, eating banana Popsicles. Our mothers were both outside.

"Your kids stole them Popsicles!" he said.

My mother slapped me whack whack. "Get inside, you criminal lying cheating brat!" But Mrs. Haddad said, "You lousy liar! *Hjaddadinah! Tlajhama!* Don't you talk bad about my kids! I'm not going to your store no more!"

And she never did, taking a bus all the way to Mesa to shop, knowing full well that Hope had stolen the Popsicle. This made sense to me. I didn't just want my mother to believe me when I was innocent, which she never did, but to stand up for me when I was guilty.

When we got skates Hope and I covered El Paso, skated over the whole town. We went to movies, letting the other in by the fire exit door. *The Spanish Main, Till the End of Time.* Chopin bleeding all over the piano keys. We saw *Mildred Pierce* six times and *The Beast with Five Fingers* ten.

The best time we had was the cards. Anytime we could, we hung out around her brother Sammy, who was seventeen. He and his friends were handsome and tough and wild. I have told you about Sammy and the cards. We sold chances for musical vanity boxes. We brought him the money and he gave us a cut. That's how we got the skates.

We sold chances everywhere. Hotels and the train station, the USO, Juárez. But even neighborhoods were magic. You walk down a street, past houses and yards, and sometimes in the evening you can see people eating or sitting around and it's a lovely glimpse of how people live. Hope and I went inside hundreds of houses. Seven years old, both funny-looking in different ways, people liked us and were kind to us. "Come in. Have some lemonade." We saw four Siamese cats who used the real toilet and even flushed it. We saw parrots and one five-hundred-pound person who had not been out of the house for twenty years. But even more we liked all the pretty things: paintings and china shepherdesses, mirrors, cuckoo clocks and grandfather clocks, quilts and rugs of many colors. We liked sitting in Mexican kitchens full of canaries, drinking real orange juice and eating pan dulce. Hope was so smart, she learned Spanish just from listening around the neighborhood, so she could talk to the old women.

We glowed when Sammy praised us, hugged us. He made us bologna sandwiches and let us sit near them on the grass. We told them all about the people we met. Rich ones, poor ones, Chinese ones, black ones until the conductor made us leave the colored waiting room at the station. Only one bad person, the man with the dogs. He didn't do anything or say anything bad, just scared us to death with his pale smirky face.

When Sammy bought the old car, Hope figured it out right away. That nobody was going to get any vanity box.

She leaped in a fury over the fence into my yard, howling, hair flying like an Indian warrior in the movies. She opened her knife and made big gashes in our index fingers, held them dripping together.

"I will never ever speak to Sammy again," she said. "Say it!"

"I will never ever speak to Sammy again," I said.

I exaggerate a lot and I get fiction and reality mixed up, but I don't actually ever lie. I wasn't lying when I made that vow. I knew he had used us, lied to us, and cheated all those people. I was never going to speak to him.

A few weeks later I was climbing the hill up Upson, near the hospital. Hot. (See, I'm trying to justify what happened. It was always hot.) Sammy pulled up in the old blue open car, the car Hope and I had worked to pay for. It is true too that coming from mountain towns and except for some taxis I had rarely been in a car.

"Come for a ride."

Some words drive me crazy. Lately every newspaper article has a

benchmark or a watershed or an icon in it. At least one of these applies
to that moment in my life.

I was a little girl; I don't believe it was an actual sexual attraction.
But I was awed by his physical beauty, his magnetism. Whatever the
excuse . . . Well, so okay, there is no excuse for what I did. I spoke to
him. I got into the car.

It was wonderful, riding in the open car. The wind cooled us off as
we sped around the Plaza, past the Wigwam theater, the Del Norte, the
Popular Dry Goods Company, then up Mesa toward Upson. I was going
to ask him to let me out a few blocks before home just as I saw Hope in
a fig tree on the vacant lot where Upson and Randolph came together.

Hope screamed. Sat up in the tree shaking her fist at me, cursing in
Syrian. Maybe everything that has happened to me since was a result of
this curse. Makes sense.

I got out of the car, sick at heart, shaking, climbed the stairs to our
house like an old person, fell onto the porch swing.

I knew that it was the end of my friendship and I knew I was wrong.

Each day was endless. Hope walked past me as if I were invisible,
played on the other side of the fence as if our yard did not exist. She and
her sisters spoke only Syrian now. Loud if they were outside. I understood a lot of the bad things they said. Hope played jacks alone on the
porch for hours, wailing Arabic songs, beautiful; her harsh plaintive
voice made me weep for missing her.

Except for Sammy, none of the Haddads would speak to me. Her
mother spat at me and shook her fist. Sammy would call to me from the
car, away from our house. Tell me he was sorry. He tried to be nice,
saying he knew that she was really still my friend and please don't
be sad. That he understood why I couldn't talk to him, to please forgive
him. I turned away so I couldn't see him when he spoke.

I have never been so lonely in my life. Benchmark lonely. The days
were endless, the sound of her ball relentless hour after hour on the
concrete, the swish of her knife into the grass, glint of the blade.

There weren't any other children in our neighborhood. For weeks we played alone. She perfected knife tricks on their grass. I colored and read, lying on the porch swing.

She left for good just before school started. Sammy and her father carried her bed and bed table and a chair down to the huge furniture truck. Hope climbed in back, sat up in the bed so she could see out. She didn't look at me. She looked tiny in the huge truck. I watched until she disappeared. Sammy called to me from the fence, told me that she had gone to Odessa, Texas, to live with some relatives. I say Odessa, Texas, because once someone said, "This is Olga; she's from Odessa." And I thought, so? Turned out it was in the Ukraine. I thought the only Odessa was where Hope went.

School started and it wasn't so bad. I didn't care about being always alone or laughed at. My back brace was getting too small and my back hurt. Good, I thought, it's what I deserve.

Uncle John came back. Five minutes in the door he said to my mother, "Her brace is too small!"

I was so glad to see him. He fixed me a bowl of puffed wheat with milk, about six spoons of sugar, and at least three tablespoons of vanilla. He sat across from me at the kitchen table, drinking bourbon while I ate. I told him about my friend Hope, about everything. I even told him about the school troubles. I had almost forgotten them. He grunted or said, "Hot damn!" while I talked and he understood everything, especially about Hope.

He never said things like "Don't worry, it will all work out." In fact, once Mamie said, "Things could be worse."

"Worse?" he said. "Things could be a heckuva lot better!" He was an alcoholic too, but drink just made him sweeter, not like them. Or he'd take off, to Mexico or Nacogdoches or Carlsbad, to jail sometimes, I realize now.

He was handsome, dark like Grandpa, with only one blue eye since Grandpa shot out the other one. His glass eye was green. I know that it is true that Grandpa shot him, but how it happened has about ten different versions. When Uncle John was home he slept in the shed out back, near where he had made my room on the back porch.

Uncle John wore a cowboy hat and boots and was like a brave movie cowboy part of the time, at others just a pitiful crying bum.

"Sick again," Mamie would sigh about them.

"Drunk, Mamie," I'd say.

I tried to hide when Grandpa was drunk because he would catch me and rock me. He was doing it once in the big rocker, holding me tight, the chair bouncing off the ground inches from the red-hot stove, his thing jabbing jabbing my behind. He was singing, "Old Tin Pan with a Hole in the Bottom." Loud. Panting and grunting. Only a few feet away Mamie sat, reading the Bible while I screamed, "Mamie! Help me!" Uncle John showed up, drunk and dusty. He grabbed me away from Grandpa, pulled the old man up by his shirt. He said he'd kill him with his bare hands next time. Then he slammed shut Mamie's Bible.

"Read it over, Ma. You got it wrong, the part about turning the other cheek. That don't mean when somebody hurts a child."

She was crying, said he'd like to break her heart.

While I was finishing the cereal he asked me if Grandpa had been bothering me. I said no. I told him that he had done it to Sally, once, that I saw.

"Little Sally? What did you do?"

"Nothing." I had done nothing. I had watched with a mixture of feelings: fear, sex, jealousy, anger. John came around, pulled up a chair and shook me, hard. He was furious.

"That was rotten! You hear me? Where was Mamie?"

"Watering. Sally had been asleep, but she woke up."

"When I'm gone you're the only one here with any sense. You have to protect her. Do you hear me?"

I nodded, ashamed. But I was more ashamed of how I had felt when it happened. He figured it out somehow. He always understood all the things you didn't even get straight in your head, much less say.

"You think Sally has it pretty good. You're jealous of her because Mamie pays her so much attention. So even if this was a bad thing he was doing at least it used to be your bad thing, right? Honey, sure you're jealous of her. She's treated swell. But remember how mad you got at Mamie? How you begged her to help you? Answer me!"

"I remember."

"Well, you were as bad as Mamie. Worse! Silence can be wicked, plumb wicked. Anything else you done wrong, 'sides from betraying your sister and a friend?"

"I stole. Candy and . . ."

"I mean hurting people."

"No."

He said he was going to stick around awhile, get me straightened out, get his Antique Repair Shop going before winter.

I worked for him weekends and after school in the shed and the backyard. Sanding, sanding or rubbing wood with a rag soaked in linseed oil and turpentine. His friends Tino and Sam came sometimes to help him with caning, reupholstering, refinishing. If my mother or Grandpa came home they left the back way, because Tino was Mexican and Sam was colored. Mamie liked them, though, and always brought out brownies or oatmeal cookies if she was there.

Once Tino brought a Mexican woman, Mecha, almost a girl, really pretty, with rings and earrings, painted eyelids and long nails, a shiny green dress. She didn't speak English but pantomimed could she help me paint a kitchen stool. I nodded, sure. Uncle John told me to hurry up, paint fast before the paint ran out, and I guess Tino told Mecha the same thing in Spanish. We were furiously slapping the brushes around the rungs and up the legs, fast as we could while the three men held their sides, laughing at us. The two of us figured it out at about the same time, and we both began laughing too. Mamie came out to see what the fuss was. She called Uncle John over to her. She was really mad about the woman, said it was wicked to have her here. John nodded and scratched his head. When Mamie went in, he came over and after a while said, "Well, let's call it a day."

While we cleaned the brushes, he explained that the woman was a whore, that Mamie figured that out by the way she was dressed and painted. He ended up explaining a lot of things that had bothered me. I understood more about my parents and Grandpa and movies and dogs. He forgot to tell me that whores charged money, so I was still confused about whores.

"Mecha was nice. I hate Mamie," I said.

"Don't say that word! Anyhow you don't hate her. You're mad because she doesn't like you. She sees you out wandering the streets, hanging out with Syrians and Uncle John. She figures you're a lost cause, a born Moynihan. You want her to love you, that's all. Anytime you think you hate somebody, what you do is pray for them. Try it, you'll see. And while you're busy praying for her, you might try helping her once in a while. Give her some kinda reason to like a surly brat like you."

On weekends sometimes he'd take me to the dog track in Juárez, or to gambling games around town. I loved the races and was good at picking winners. The only time I liked going to card games was when he played with railroad men, in a caboose at the train yards. I climbed the ladder to the roof and watched all the trains coming in and going out, switching, coupling. It got to be that most of the card games were in the back of Chinese laundries. I'd sit in the front reading for hours while somewhere in back he played poker. The heat and the smell of cleaning solvent mixed with singed wool and sweat was nauseating. A few times he left out the back way and forgot me, so that only when the laundryman came to close up did he find me asleep in the chair. I'd have to go home, far, in the dark, and most of the time nobody would

be there. Mamie took Sally to choir practice and to the Eastern Star and
to make bandages for servicemen.

About once a month we'd go to a barbershop. A different one each
time. He'd ask for a shave and a haircut. I'd sit on a chair reading *Argosy*
while the barber cut his hair, just waiting for the shave part. Uncle John
would be tilted way back in the chair and just as the barber was finishing the shave he'd ask, "Say, do you happen to have any eyedrops?"
which they always did. The barber would stand over him and put drops
in his eyes. The green glass eye would start spinning around and the
barber would scream bloody murder. Then everybody'd laugh.

If only I had understood him half as much as he always understood
me, I could have found out how he hurt, why he worked so hard to get
laughs. He did make everybody laugh. We ate in cafés all over Juárez
and El Paso that were like people's houses. Just a lot of tables in one
room of a regular house, with good food. Everybody knew him and the
waitresses always laughed when he asked if it was warmed-over coffee.

"Oh, no!"

"Well, how'd you get it so hot?"

I could usually tell just how drunk he was, and if it was a lot I'd
make some excuse and walk or ride the trolley home. One day though,
I had been sleeping in the cab of the truck, woke after he got in and
started off. We were on Rim Road going faster faster. He had a bottle
between his thighs, was driving with his elbows as he counted the
money he held in a fan over the steering wheel.

"Slow down!"

"I'm in the money, honey!"

"Slow down! Hold on to the wheel!"

The truck thumped, shuddered high up and then thumped down.
Money flew all over the cab. I looked out the back window. A little boy
was standing in the street, his arm bleeding. A collie was lying next to
him, really bloody, trying to get up.

"Stop. Stop the truck. We have to go back. Uncle John!"

"I can't!"

"Slow down. You have to turn around!" I was sobbing hysterically.

At home he reached across and opened my door. "You go on in."

I don't know if I stopped speaking to him. He never came home. Not that night, not for days, weeks, months. I prayed for him.

The war ended and my father came home. We moved to South America.

Uncle John ended up on skid row in Los Angeles, a really hopeless wino. Then he met Dora, who played trumpet in the Salvation Army band. She had him go into the shelter and have some soup and she talked to him. She said later that he made her laugh. They fell in love and were married and he never drank again. When I was older I went to visit them in Los Angeles. She was working as a riveter at Lockheed and he had an antique repair shop in his garage. They were maybe the sweetest two people I ever knew, sweet together, I mean. We went to Forest Lawn and the La Brea tar pits and the Grotto restaurant. Mostly I helped Uncle John in the shop, sanding furniture, polishing with the turpentine and linseed oil rag. We talked about life, told jokes. Neither of us ever mentioned El Paso. Of course by this time I had realized all the reasons why he couldn't stop the truck, because by this time I was an alcoholic.

THE TWENTY-SEVENTH MAN

Nathan Englander · 1998

The orders were given from Stalin's country house at Kuntsevo. He relayed them to the agent in charge with no greater emotion than for the killing of kulaks or clergy or the outspoken wives of very dear friends. The accused were to be apprehended the same day, arrive at the prison gates at the same moment, and—with a gasp and simultaneous final breath—be sent off to their damnation in a single rattling burst of gunfire.

It was not an issue of hatred, only one of allegiance. For Stalin knew there could be loyalty to only one nation. What he did not know so well were the authors' names on his list. When presented to him the next morning he signed the warrant anyway, though there were now twenty-seven, and yesterday there had been twenty-six.

No matter, except maybe to the twenty-seventh.

The orders left little room for variation, and none for tardiness. They were to be carried out in secrecy and—the only point that was reiterated—simultaneously. But how were the agents to get the men from Moscow and Gorky, Smolensk and Penza, Shuya and Podolsk, to the prison near the village of X at the very same time?

The agent in charge felt his strength was in leadership and gave up the role of strategist to the inside of his hat. He cut the list into strips and sprinkled them into the freshly blocked crown, mixing carefully so as not to disturb its shape. Most of these writers were in Moscow. The handful who were in their native villages, taking the waters somewhere, or locked in a cabin trying to finish that seminal work would surely receive a stiff cuffing when a pair of agents, aggravated by the trek, stepped through the door.

After the lottery, those agents who had drawn a name warranting a long journey accepted the good-natured insults and mockery of friends. Most would have it easy, nothing more to worry about than hurrying some old rebel to a car, or getting their shirts wrinkled in a heel-dragging, hair-pulling rural scene that could be as messy as necessary in front of a pack of superstitious peasants.

Then there were those who had it hard. Such as the two agents assigned to Vasily Korinsky, who, seeing no way out, was prepared to exit his bedroom quietly but whose wife, Paulina, struck the shorter of the two officers with an Oriental-style brass vase. There was a scuffle, Paulina was subdued, the short officer taken out unconscious, and a precious hour lost on their estimated time.

There was the pair assigned to Moishe Bretzky, a true lover of vodka and its country of origin. One would not have pegged him as one of history's most sensitive Yiddish poets. He was huge, slovenly, and smelly as a horse. Once a year, during the Ten Days of Penitence, he would take notice of his sinful ways and sober up for Yom Kippur. After the fast, he would grab pen and pad and write furiously for weeks in his sister's ventless kitchen—the shroud of atonement still draped over his splitting head. The finished work was toasted with a brimming shot of vodka. Then Bretzky's thirst would begin to rage and off he would go for another year. His sister's husband would have put an end to this annual practice if it weren't for the rubles he received for the sweat-curled pages Bretzky abandoned.

It took the whole of the night for the two agents to locate Bretzky. They tracked him down in one of the whorehouses that did not exist, and if they did, government agents surely did not frequent them. Nonetheless, having escaped notice, they slipped into the room. Bretzky was passed out on his stomach with a smiling trollop pinned under each arm. The time-consuming process of freeing the whores, getting Bretzky upright, and moving him into the hallway reduced the younger man to tears.

The senior agent left his partner in charge of the body while he went to chat with the senior woman of the house. Introducing himself numerous times, as if they had never met, he explained his predicament and enlisted the help of a dozen women.

Twelve of the house's strongest companions—in an array of pink and red robes, froufrou slippers, and painted toenails—carried the giant bear to the waiting car amid a roar of giggles. It was a sight Bretzky would have enjoyed tremendously had he been conscious.

The least troubling of the troublesome abductions was that of Y. Zunser, oldest of the group and a target of the first serious verbal attacks on the cosmopolitans back in '49. In the February 19 edition of *Literaturnaya Gazeta* he had been criticized as an obsolete author, accused of being anti-Soviet, and chided for using a pen name to hide his Jewish roots. In that same edition they printed his real name, Melman, stripping him of the privacy he had so enjoyed.

Three years later they came for him. The two agents were not enthusiastic about the task. They had shared a Jewish literature instructor in high school, whom they admired despite his ethnicity and who even coerced them into writing a poem or two. Both were rather decent fellows, and capturing an eighty-one-year-old man did not exactly jibe with their vision of bravely serving the party. They were simply following instructions. But somewhere amid their justifications lay a deep fear of punishment.

It was not yet dawn and Zunser was already dressed, sitting with a cup of tea. The agents begged him to stand up on his own, one of them trying the name Zunser and the other pleading with Melman. He refused.

"I will neither resist nor help. The responsibility must rest fully upon your conscience."

"We have orders," they said.

"I did not say you were without orders. I said that you have to bear responsibility."

They first tried lifting him by his arms, but Zunser was too delicate for the maneuver. Then one grabbed his ankles while the other clasped his chest. Zunser's head lolled back. The agents were afraid of killing him, an option they had been warned against. They put him on the floor and the larger of the two scooped him up, cradling the old man like a child.

Zunser begged a moment's pause as they passed a portrait of his deceased wife. He fancied the picture had a new moroseness to it, as if the sepia-toned eyes might well up and shed a tear. He spoke aloud. "No matter, Katya. Life ended for me on the day of your death; everything since has been but nostalgia." The agent shifted the weight of the romantic in his arms and headed out the door.

The solitary complicated abduction that took place out of Moscow was the one that should have been the easiest of the twenty-seven. It was the simple task of removing Pinchas Pelovits from the inn on the road that ran to X and the prison beyond.

Pinchas Pelovits had constructed his own world with a compassionate God and a diverse group of worshipers. In it, he tested these people with moral dilemmas and tragedies—testing them sometimes more with joy and good fortune. He recorded the trials and events of this world in his notebooks in the form of stories and novels, essays, poems, songs, anthems, tales, jokes, and extensive histories that led up to the era in which he dwelled.

His parents never knew what label to give their son, who wrote all day but did not publish, who laughed and cried over his novels but was gratingly logical in his contact with the everyday world. What they did know was that Pinchas wasn't going to take over the inn.

When they became too old to run the business, the only viable option was to sell out at a ridiculously low price—provided the new owners would leave the boy his room and feed him when he was hungry. Even when the business became the property of the state, Pinchas, in the dreamer's room, was left in peace: *Why bother, he's harmless, sort of a good-luck charm for the inn, no one even knows he's here, maybe he's writing a history of the place, and we'll all be made famous.* He wasn't. But who knows, maybe he would have, had his name—mumbled on the lips of travelers—not found its way onto Stalin's list.

The two agents assigned Pinchas arrived at the inn driving a beat-up droshky and posing as the sons of now poor landowners, a touch they thought might tickle their superiors. One carried a Luger (a trinket he brought home from the war), and the other kept a billy club stashed in his boot. They found the narrow hallway with Pinchas's room and knocked lightly on his door. "Not hungry" was the response. The agent with the Luger gave the door a hip check; it didn't budge. "Try the handle," said the voice. The agent did, swinging it open.

"You're coming with us," said the one with the club in his boot.

"Absolutely not," Pinchas stated matter-of-factly. The agent wondered if his "You're coming with us" had sounded as bold.

"Put the book down on the pile, put your shoes on, and let's go." The agent with the Luger spoke slowly. "You're under arrest for anti-Soviet activity."

Pinchas was baffled by the charge. He meditated for a moment and came to the conclusion that there was only one moral outrage he'd been involved in, though it seemed to him a bit excessive to be incarcerated for it.

"Well, you can have them, but they're not really mine. They were in a copy of a Zunser book that a guest forgot and I didn't know where to return them. Regardless, I studied them thoroughly. You may take me away." He proceeded to hand the agents five postcards. Three were intricate pen-and-ink drawings of a geisha in various positions with her legs spread wide. The other two were identical photographs of a sturdy Russian maiden in front of a painted tropical background wearing a hula skirt and making a vain attempt to cover her breasts. Pinchas began stacking his notebooks while the agents divvied the cards. He was sad that he had not resisted temptation. He would miss taking his walks and also the desk upon whose mottled surface he had written.

"May I bring my desk?"

The agent with the Luger was getting fidgety. "You won't be needing anything, just put on your shoes."

"I'd much prefer my books to shoes," Pinchas said. "In the summer I sometimes take walks without shoes but never without a novel. If you would have a seat while I organize my notes—" and Pinchas fell to the floor, struck in the head with the pistol grip. He was carried from the inn rolled in a blanket, his feet poking forth, bare.

Pinchas awoke, his head throbbing from the blow and the exceedingly tight blindfold. This was aggravated by the sound of ice cracking under the droshky wheels, as happens along the river route west of X. "The bridge is out on this road," he told them. "You'd best cut through the old Bunakov place. Everybody does it in winter."

The billy club was drawn from the agent's boot, and Pinchas was struck on the head once again. The idea of arriving only to have their prisoner blurt out the name of the secret prison was mortifying. In an attempt to confound him, they turned off on a clearly unused road.

There are reasons that unused roads are not used. It wasn't half a kilometer before they had broken a wheel and it was off to a nearby pig farm on foot. The agent with the gun commandeered a donkey-drawn cart, leaving a furious pig farmer cursing and kicking the side of his barn.

The trio were all a bit relieved upon arrival: Pinchas because he started to get the idea that this business had to do with something more than his minor infraction, and the agents because three other cars had shown up only minutes before they had—all inexcusably late.

By the time the latecomers had been delivered, the initial terror of the other twenty-three had subsided. The situation was tense and grave, but also unique. An eminent selection of Europe's surviving Yiddish literary community was being held within the confines of an oversized closet. Had they known they were going to die, it might have been different. Since they didn't, I. J. Manger wasn't about to let Mani Zaretsky see him cry for rachmones. He didn't have time to anyway. Pyotr Kolyazin, the famed atheist, had already dragged him into a heated discussion about the ramifications of using God's will to drastically alter the outcome of previously "logical" plots. Manger took this to be an attack on his work and asked Kolyazin if he labeled everything he didn't understand "illogical." There was also the present situation to discuss, as well as old rivalries, new poems, disputed reviews, journals that just aren't the same, up-and-coming editors, and, of course, the gossip, for hadn't they heard that Lev had used his latest manuscript for kindling?

When the noise got too great, a guard opened the peephole in the door to find that a symposium had broken loose. As a result, by the time numbers twenty-four through twenty-seven arrived, the others had already been separated into smaller cells.

Each cell was meant to house four prisoners and contained three rotting mats to sleep on. In a corner was a bucket. There were crude holes in the wood-plank walls, and it was hard to tell if the captors had punched them as a form of ventilation or if the previous prisoners had painstakingly scratched them through to confirm the existence of a world outside.

The four latecomers had lain down immediately, Pinchas on the floor. He was dazed and shivering, stifling his moans so the others might rest. His companions did not even think of sleep: Vasily Korinsky because of worry about what might be the outcome for his wife; Y. Zunser because he was trying to adapt to the change (the only alteration he had planned for in his daily routine was death, and that in his sleep); Bretzky because he hadn't really awakened.

Excepting Pinchas, none had an inkling of how long they'd traveled, whether from morning until night or into the next day. Pinchas tried to use his journey as an anchor, but in the dark he soon lost his notion of time gone by. He listened for the others' breathing, making sure they were alive.

The lightbulb hanging from a frayed wire in the ceiling went on. This was a relief; not only an end to the darkness but a separation, a seam in the seeming endlessness.

They stared unblinking into the dim glow of the bulb and worried about its abandoning them. All except Bretzky, whose huge form already ached for a vodka and who dared not crack an eye.

Zunser was the first to speak. "With morning there is hope."

"For what?" asked Korinsky out of the side of his mouth. His eye was pressed up against a hole in the back wall.

"A way out," Zunser said. He watched the bulb, wondering how much electricity there was in the wire, how he would reach it, and how many of them it would serve.

Korinsky misunderstood the statement to be an optimistic one. "Feh on your way out and feh on your morning. It's pitch dark outside. Either it's night or we're in a place with no sun. I'm freezing to death."

The others were a bit shocked when Bretzky spoke: "Past the fact that you are not one of the whores I paid for and this is not the bed we fell into, I'm uncertain. Whatever the situation, I shall endure it, but without your whining about being cold in front of an old man in shirt-sleeves and this skinny one with no shoes." His powers of observation were already returning and Yom Kippur still months away.

"I'm fine," said Pinchas. "I'd much rather have a book than shoes."

They all knitted their brows and studied the man; even Bretzky propped himself up on an elbow.

Zunser laughed, and then the other three started in. Yes, it would be much better to have a book. Whose book? Surely not the pamphlet by that fool Horiansky—this being a well-publicized and recent failure. They laughed some more. Korinsky stopped, worrying that one of the other men in the room might be Horiansky. Horiansky, thankfully, was on the other end of the hall and was spared that final degradation before his death.

No one said another word until the lightbulb went off again, and then they remained silent because it was supposed to be night. However, it was not. Korinsky could see light seeping through the holes and chinks in the boards. He would tell them so when the bulb came back on, if it did.

Pinchas could have laughed indefinitely, or at least until the time of his execution. His mind was not trained, never taught any restraint or punished for its reckless abandon. He had written because it was all that interested him, aside from his walks, and the pictures at which he had peeked. Not since childhood had he skipped a day of writing.

Composing without pen and paper, he decided on something short, something he could hone, add a little bit to every day until his release.

Zunser felt the coldness of the floor seeping into his bones, turning them brittle. It was time anyway. He had lived a long life, enjoyed recognition for something he loved doing. All the others who had reached his level of fame had gone to the ovens or were in America. How much more meaningless was success with the competition gone? Why write at all when your readers have been turned to ash? Never outlive your language. Zunser rolled onto his side.

Bretzky sweated the alcohol out of his blood. He tried to convince himself that it was a vision of drink, a clearer vision because he was getting older, but a hallucination nonetheless. How many times had he turned, after hearing his name called, to find no one? He fumbled for a breast, a soft pink cheek, a swatch of satin, and fell asleep.

Before closing his eyes only to find more darkness, Pinchas recited the first paragraph a final time:

> The morning that Mendel Muskatev awoke to find his desk was gone, his room was gone, and the sun was gone, he assumed he had died. This worried him, so he said the prayer for the dead, keeping himself in mind. Then he wondered if one was allowed to do such a thing, and worried instead that the first thing he had done upon being dead was sin.

When the light came on, Korinsky stirred noticeably, as if to break the ice, as if they were bound by the dictates of civilized society. "You know it isn't morning, it's about nine o'clock or ten, midnight at the latest."

Pinchas was reciting his paragraph quietly, playing with the words, making changes, wishing he had a piece of slate.

Korinsky waited for an answer, staring at the other three. It was hard to believe they were writers. He figured he too must be disheveled, but at least there was some style left in him. These others, a drunk, an incontinent old curmudgeon, and an idiot, could not be of his caliber. Even the deficient Horiansky would be appreciated now. "I said, it's not morning. They're trying to fool us, mess up our internal clocks."

"Then go back to sleep and leave us to be fooled." Bretzky had already warned this sot yesterday. He didn't need murder added to his list of trumped-up charges.

"You shouldn't be so snide with me. I'm only trying to see if we can maintain a little dignity while they're holding us here."

Zunser had set himself up against a wall. He had folded his mat and used it like a chair, cushioning himself from the splinters. "You say 'holding' as if this is temporary and in the next stage we will find ourselves someplace more to our liking."

Korinsky looked at Zunser, surveying him boldly. He did not like being goaded, especially by some old coot who had no idea to whom he was talking.

"Comrade," he addressed Zunser in a most acerbic tone, "I am quite sure my incarceration is due to bureaucratic confusion of some sort. I've no idea what you wrote that landed you here, but I have an impeccable record. I was a principal member of the Anti-Fascist Committee, and my ode, *Stalin of Silver; Stalin of Gold*, happens to be a national favorite."

"'We spilled out blood in revolution, only to choke on Stalin's pollution.'" Bretzky quoted a bastardization of Korinsky's ballad.

"How dare you mock me!"

"I've not had the pleasure of hearing the original," Zunser said, "but I must say the mockery is quite entertaining."

"'Our hearts cheered as one for revolution, now we bask in the glory of great Stalin's solution.'" All three heads turned to Pinchas, Korinsky's the quickest.

"Perfect." Korinsky sneered at the other two men. "I must say it is nice to be in the presence of at least one fan."

Among the many social interactions Pinchas had never before been involved in, this was one. He did not know when adulation was being requested.

"Oh, I'm no fan, sir. You're a master of the Yiddish language, but the core of all your work is flawed by a heavy-handed party message that has nothing to do with the people about whom you write." This with an eloquence which to Korinsky sounded like the fool was condescending.

"The characters are only vehicles, fictions!" He was shouting at

Pinchas. Then he caught himself shouting at an idiot, while the other two men convulsed with laughter.

"They are very real," said Pinchas before returning to his rocking and mumbling.

"What are you two fops making fun of? At least I have a body of work that is read."

Bretzky was angry again. "Speak to me as you like. If it begins to bother me too much, I'll pinch your head off from your neck." He made a pinching motion with his massive fingers. "But I must warn you against speaking to your elders with disrespect. Furthermore, I have a most cloudy feeling that the face on the old man also belongs to the legendary Zunser, whose accomplishments far exceed those of any of the writers, Yiddish or otherwise, alive in Russia today."

"Zunser?" said Korinsky.

"Y. Zunser!" screamed Pinchas. He could not imagine being confined with such a singular mind. Pinchas had never even considered that Zunser was an actual person. My God, he had seen the great seer pee into a bucket. "Zunser," he said to the man. He stood and banged his fist against the door, screaming "Zunser" over and over again, like it was a password his keepers would understand and know the game was finished.

A guard came down the hall and beat Pinchas to the floor. He left them a bowl of water and a few crusts of black bread. The three ate quickly. Bretzky held up the casualty while Zunser poured some water into his mouth, made him swallow.

"The man is crazy, he is going to get us all killed." Korinsky sat with his eye against a knothole, peering into the darkness of their day.

"Maybe us, but who would dare to kill the poet laureate of the Communist empire?" Bretzky's tone was biting, though his outward appearance did not reflect it. He cradled Pinchas's limp form while Zunser mopped the boy's brow with his sleeve.

"This is no time for joking. I was going to arrange for a meeting with the warden, but that lunatic's screaming fouled it up. Swooning like a young girl. Has he never before met a man he admired?" Korinsky hooked a finger through one of the larger holes, as if he were trying to feel the texture of the darkness outside. "Who knows when that guard will return?"

"I would not rush to get out," said Zunser. "I can assure you there is only one way to exit."

"Your talk gets us nowhere." Korinsky stood and leaned a shoulder against a cold board.

"And what has gotten you somewhere?" said Zunser. "Your love ballads to the regime? There are no hoofbeats to be heard in the distance. Stalin doesn't spur his horse, racing to your rescue."

"He doesn't know. He wouldn't let them do this to me."

"Maybe not to you, but to the Jew that has your name and lives in your house and lies next to your wife, yes." Zunser massaged a stiffening knee.

"It's not my life. It's my culture, my language. No more."

"Only your language?" Zunser waved him away. "Who are we without Yiddish?"

"The four sons of the Passover seder, at best." Korinsky sounded bitter.

"This is more than tradition, Korinsky. It's blood." Bretzky spat into the pail. "I used to drink with Kapler, shot for shot."

"And?" Korinsky kept his eye to a hole but listened closely.

"And have you seen a movie directed by Kapler lately? He made a friendship with the exalted comrade's daughter. Now he is in a labor camp—if he's alive. Stalin did not take too well to Jewish hands on his daughter's pure white skin."

"You two wizards can turn a Stalin to a Hitler."

Bretzky reached over and gave Korinsky a pat on the leg. "We don't need the Nazis, my friend."

"Feh, you're a paranoid, like all drunks."

Zunser shook his head. He was tiring of the Communist and worried about the boy. "He's got a fever. And he's lucky if there isn't a crack in that head." The old man took off his shoes and put his socks on Pinchas.

"Let me," said Bretzky.

"No," Zunser said. "You give him the shoes, mine won't fit him." Pinchas's feet slipped easily into Bretzky's scuffed and cracking shoes.

"Here, take it." Korinsky gave them his mat. "Believe me, it's not for the mitzvah. I just couldn't stand to spend another second trapped with your righteous stares."

"The eyes you feel are not ours," said Zunser.

Korinsky glowered at the wall.

Pinchas Pelovits was not unconscious. He had only lost his way. He heard the conversations, but paid them little heed. The weight of his body lay on him like a corpse. He worked on his story, saying it aloud to himself, hoping the others would hear and follow it and bring him back.

Mendel figured he'd best consult the local rabbi, who might be able to direct him in such matters. It was Mendel's first time visiting the rabbi in his study—not having previously concerned himself with the nuances of worship. Mendel was much surprised to find that the rabbi's study was of the exact dimensions of his missing room. In fact, it appeared that the tractate the man was poring over rested on the missing desk.

The bulb glowed. And with light came relief. What if they had been left in the darkness? They hated the bulb for its control, such a flimsy thing.

They had left a little water for the morning. Again, Bretzky held Pinchas while Zunser tipped the bowl against the boy's lips. Korinsky watched, wanting to tell them to be careful not to spill, to make sure they saved some for him.

Pinchas sputtered, then said, "Fine, that's fine." He spoke loudly for someone in such apparent ill health. Zunser passed the bowl to Korinsky before taking his own sip.

"Very good to have you with us," said Zunser, trying to catch the boy's eyes with his own. "I wanted to ask you, why is my presence so unsettling? We are all writers here, if I understand the situation correctly."

Zunser used Bretzky to belabor the point. "Come on, tell the boy who you are."

"Moishe Bretzky. They call me The Glutton in the gossip columns."

Zunser smiled at the boy. "You see. A big name. A legend for his poetry, as much for his antics. Now, tell us. Who are you?"

"Pinchas Pelovits."

None had heard the name. Zunser's curiosity was piqued. Bretzky didn't care either way. Korinsky was only further pained at having to put up with a madman who wasn't even famous.

"I am the one who doesn't belong here," Pinchas said. "Though if I could, I'd take the place of any of you."

"But you are not here in place of us, you are here as one of us. Do you write?"

"Oh, yes, that's all I do. That's all I've ever done, except for reading and my walks."

"If it makes any difference, we welcome you as an equal." Zunser surveyed the cubicle. "I'd much rather be saying this to you in my home."

"Are you sure I'm here for being a writer?" Pinchas looked at the three men.

"Not just for being a writer, my friend." Bretzky clapped him lightly on the back. "You are here as a subversive writer. An enemy of the state! Quite a feat for an unknown."

The door opened and all four were dragged from the cell and taken by a guard to private interrogation chambers—Bretzky escorted by three guards of his own. There they were beaten, degraded, made to confess to

numerous crimes, and to sign confessions that they had knowingly dis-
tributed Zionist propaganda aimed at toppling the Soviet government.

Zunser and Pinchas had been in adjoining chambers and heard each
other's screams. Bretzky and Korinsky also shared a common wall,
though there was silence after each blow. Korinsky's sense of repute was
so strong that he stifled his screaming. Bretzky did not call out. Instead
he cried and cried. His abusers mocked him for it, jeering at the over-
grown baby. His tears did not fall from the pain, however. They came
out of the sober realization of man's cruelty and the picture of the suffering being dealt to his peers, especially Zunser.

Afterward, they were given a fair amount of water, a hunk of bread,
and some cold potato-and-radish soup. They were returned to the same
cell in the darkness. Zunser and Pinchas needed to be carried.

Pinchas had focused on his story, his screams sounding as if they
were coming from afar. With every stripe he received, he added a phrase,
the impact reaching his mind like the dull rap of a windowpane settling
in its sash:

> "Rabbi, have you noticed we are without a sun today?" Mendel
> asked by way of an introduction.
> "My shutters are closed against the noise."
> "Did no one else mention it at morning prayers?"
> "No one else arrived," said the rabbi, continuing to study.
> "Well, don't you think that strange?"
> "I had. I had until you told me about this sun. Now I understand—
> no sensible man would get up to greet a dawn that never came."

They were all awake when the bulb went on. Zunser was making
peace with himself, preparing for certain death. The fingers of his left
hand were twisted and split. Only his thumb had a nail.

Pinchas had a question for Zunser. "All your work treats fate as if it
were a mosquito to be shooed away. All your characters struggle for

survival and yet you play the victim. You had to have known they would come."

"You have a point," Zunser said, "a fair question. And I answer it with another: Why should I always be the one to survive? I watched Europe's Jews go up the chimneys. I buried a wife and a child. I do believe one can elude the fates. But why assume the goal is to live?" Zunser slid the mangled hand onto his stomach. "How many more tragedies do I want to survive? Let someone take witness of mine."

Bretzky disagreed. "We've lost our universe, this is true. Still, a man can't condemn himself to death for the sin of living. We can't cower in the shadows of the camps forever."

"I would give anything to escape," said Korinsky.

Zunser turned his gaze toward the bulb. "That is the single rule I have maintained in every story I ever wrote. The desperate are never given the choice."

"Then," asked Pinchas, and to him there was no one else but his mentor in the room, "you don't believe there is any reason I was brought here to be with you? It isn't part of anything larger, some cosmic balance, a great joke of the heavens?"

"I think that somewhere a clerk made a mistake."

"That," Pinchas said, "I cannot bear."

All the talking had strained Zunser and he coughed up a bit of blood. Pinchas attempted to help Zunser but couldn't stand up. Bretzky and Korinsky started to their feet. "Sit, sit," Zunser said. They did, but watched him closely as he tried to clear his lungs.

Pinchas Pelovits spent the rest of that day on the last lines of his story. When the light went out, he had already finished.

They hadn't been in darkness long when they were awakened by the noise and the gleam from the bulb. Korinsky immediately put his eye to the wall.

"They are lining up everyone outside. There are machine guns. It is morning, and everyone is blinking as if they were newly born."

Pinchas interrupted. "I have something I would like to recite. It's a story I wrote while we've been staying here."

"Go ahead," said Zunser.

"Let's hear it," said Bretzky.

Korinsky pulled the hair from his head. "What difference can it make now?"

"For whom?" asked Pinchas, and then proceeded to recite his little tale:

The morning that Mendel Muskatev awoke to find his desk was gone, his room was gone, and the sun was gone, he assumed he had died. This worried him, so he said the prayer for the dead, keeping himself in mind. Then he wondered if one was allowed to do such a thing, and worried instead that the first thing he had done upon being dead was sin.

Mendel figured he'd best consult the local rabbi, who might be able to direct him in such matters. It was Mendel's first time visiting the rabbi in his study—not having previously concerned himself with the nuances of worship. Mendel was much surprised to find that the rabbi's study was of the exact dimensions of his missing room. In fact, it appeared that the tractate the man was poring over rested on the missing desk.

"Rabbi, have you noticed we are without a sun today?" Mendel asked by way of an introduction.

"My shutters are closed against the noise."

"Did no one else mention it at morning prayers?"

"No one else arrived," said the rabbi, continuing to study.

"Well, don't you think that strange?"

"I had. I had until you told me about this sun. Now I

understand—no sensible man would get up to greet a dawn that never came."

"This is all very startling, Rabbi. But I think we—at some point in the night—have died."

The rabbi stood up, grinning. "And here I am with an eternity's worth of Talmud to study."

Mendel took in the volumes lining the walls.

"I've a desk and a chair, and a shtender in the corner should I want to stand," said the rabbi. "Yes, it would seem I'm in heaven." He patted Mendel on the shoulder. "I must thank you for rushing over to tell me." The rabbi shook Mendel's hand and nodded good-naturedly, already searching for his place in the text. "Did you come for some other reason?"

"I did," said Mendel, trying to find a space between the books where once there was a door. "I wanted to know"—and here his voice began to quiver—"which one of us is to say the prayer?"

Bretzky stood. "Bravo," he said, clapping his hands. "It's like a shooting star. A tale to be extinguished along with the teller." He stepped forward to meet the agent in charge at the door. "No, the meaning, it was not lost on me."

Korinsky pulled his knees into his chest, hugged them. "No," he admitted, "it was not lost."

Pinchas did not blush or bow his head. He stared at Zunser, wondered what the noble Zunser was thinking, as they were driven from the cell.

Outside all the others were being assembled. There were Horiansky and Lubovitch, Lev and Soltzky. All those great voices with the greatest stories of their lives to tell, and forced to take them to the grave. Pinchas, having increased his readership threefold, had a smile on his face.

Pinchas Pelovits was the twenty-seventh, or the fourteenth from

either end, if you wanted to count his place in line. Bretzky supported
Pinchas by holding up his right side, for his equilibrium had not returned. Zunser supported him on the left, but was in bad shape himself.

"Did you like it?" Pinchas asked.

"Very much," Zunser said. "You're a talented boy."

Pinchas smiled again, then fell, his head landing on the stockingless
calves of Zunser. One of his borrowed shoes flew forward, though his
feet slid backward in the dirt. Bretzky fell atop the other two. He was
shot five or six times, but being such a big man and such a strong man,
he lived long enough to recognize the crack of the guns and know that
he was dead.

BULLET IN
THE BRAIN

Tobias Wolff · 1998

Anders couldn't get to the bank until just before it closed, so of course the line was endless and he got stuck behind two women whose loud, stupid conversation put him in a murderous temper. He was never in the best of tempers anyway, Anders—a book critic known for the weary, elegant savagery with which he dispatched almost everything he reviewed.

With the line still doubled around the rope, one of the tellers stuck a "POSITION CLOSED" sign in her window and walked to the back of the bank, where she leaned against a desk and began to pass the time with a man shuffling papers. The women in front of Anders broke off their conversation and watched the teller with hatred. "Oh, that's nice," one of them said. She turned to Anders and added, confident of his accord, "One of those little human touches that keep us coming back for more."

Anders had conceived his own towering hatred of the teller, but he immediately turned it on the presumptuous crybaby in front of him. "Damned unfair," he said. "Tragic, really. If they're not chopping off the wrong leg, or bombing your ancestral village, they're closing their positions."

She stood her ground. "I didn't say it was tragic," she said. "I just think it's a pretty lousy way to treat your customers."

"Unforgivable," Anders said. "Heaven will take note."

She sucked in her cheeks but stared past him and said nothing. Anders saw that the other woman, her friend, was looking in the same direction. And then the tellers stopped what they were doing, and the customers slowly turned, and silence came over the bank. Two men wearing black ski masks and blue business suits were standing to the side of the door. One of them had a pistol pressed against the guard's neck. The guard's eyes were closed, and his lips were moving. The other man had a sawed-off shotgun. "Keep your big mouth shut!" the man with the pistol said, though no one had spoken a word. "One of you tellers hits the alarm, you're all dead meat. Got it?"

The tellers nodded.

"Oh, bravo," Anders said. "*Dead meat.*" He turned to the woman in front of him. "Great script, eh? The stern, brass-knuckled poetry of the dangerous classes."

She looked at him with drowning eyes.

The man with the shotgun pushed the guard to his knees. He handed the shotgun to his partner and yanked the guard's wrists up behind his back and locked them together with a pair of handcuffs. He toppled him onto the floor with a kick between the shoulder blades. Then he took his shotgun back and went over to the security gate at the end of the counter. He was short and heavy and moved with peculiar slowness, even torpor. "Buzz him in," his partner said. The man with the shotgun opened the gate and sauntered along the line of tellers, handing each of them a Hefty bag. When he came to the empty position he looked over at the man with the pistol, who said, "Whose slot is that?"

Anders watched the teller. She put her hand to her throat and turned to the man she'd been talking to. He nodded. "Mine," she said.

"Then get your ugly ass in gear and fill that bag."

"There you go," Anders said to the woman in front of him. "Justice is done."

"Hey! Bright boy! Did I tell you to talk?"

"No," Anders said.

"Then shut your trap."

"Did you hear that?" Anders said. "'Bright boy.' Right out of 'The Killers.'"

"Please be quiet," the woman said.

"Hey, you deaf or what?" The man with the pistol walked over to Anders. He poked the weapon into Anders' gut. "You think I'm playing games?"

"No," Anders said, but the barrel tickled like a stiff finger and he had to fight back the titters. He did this by making himself stare into the man's eyes, which were clearly visible behind the holes in the mask: pale blue and rawly red-rimmed. The man's left eyelid kept twitching. He breathed out a piercing, ammoniac smell that shocked Anders more than anything that had happened, and he was beginning to develop a sense of unease when the man prodded him again with the pistol.

"You like me, bright boy?" he said. "You want to suck my dick?"

"No," Anders said.

"Then stop looking at me."

Anders fixed his gaze on the man's shiny wing-tip shoes.

"Not down there. Up there." He stuck the pistol under Anders' chin and pushed it upward until Anders was looking at the ceiling.

Anders had never paid much attention to that part of the bank, a pompous old building with marble floors and counters and pillars, and gilt scrollwork over the tellers' cages. The domed ceiling had been decorated with mythological figures whose fleshy, toga-draped ugliness Anders had taken in at a glance many years earlier and afterward declined to notice. Now he had no choice but to scrutinize the painter's work. It was even worse than he remembered, and all of it executed with the utmost gravity. The artist had a few tricks up his sleeve and used them again and again—a certain rosy blush on the underside of the clouds, a coy backward glance on the faces of the cupids and fauns. The ceiling was crowded with various dramas, but the one that caught Anders' eye was Zeus and Europa—portrayed, in this rendition, as a bull ogling a cow from behind a haystack. To make the cow sexy, the painter had canted her hips suggestively and given her long, droopy eyelashes through which she gazed back at the bull with sultry welcome. The bull wore a smirk and his eyebrows were arched. If there'd been a bubble coming out of his mouth, it would have said, "Hubba hubba."

"What's so funny, bright boy?"

"Nothing."

"You think I'm comical? You think I'm some kind of clown?"

"No."

"You think you can fuck with me?"

"No."

"Fuck with me again, you're history. *Capiche?*"

Anders burst out laughing. He covered his mouth with both hands and said, "I'm sorry, I'm sorry," then snorted helplessly through his fingers and said, "*Capiche*—oh, God, *capiche*," and at that the man with the pistol raised the pistol and shot Anders right in the head.

The bullet smashed Anders' skull and ploughed through his brain and exited behind his right ear, scattering shards of bone into the cerebral cortex, the corpus callosum, back toward the basal ganglia, and down into the thalamus. But before all this occurred, the first appearance of the bullet in the cerebrum set off a crackling chain of ion transports and neuro-transmissions. Because of their peculiar origin these traced a peculiar pattern, flukishly calling to life a summer afternoon some forty years past, and long since lost to memory. After striking the cranium the bullet was moving at 900 feet per second, a pathetically sluggish, glacial pace compared to the synaptic lightning that flashed around it. Once in the brain, that is, the bullet came under the mediation of brain time, which gave Anders plenty of leisure to contemplate the scene that, in a phrase he would have abhorred, "passed before his eyes."

It is worth noting what Anders did not remember, given what he did remember. He did not remember his first lover, Sherry, or what he had most madly loved about her, before it came to irritate him—her unembarrassed carnality, and especially the cordial way she had with his unit, which she called Mr. Mole, as in, "Uh-oh, looks like Mr. Mole wants to play," and, "Let's hide Mr. Mole!" Anders did not remember his wife, whom he had also loved before she exhausted him with her predictability, or his daughter, now a sullen professor of economics at Dartmouth. He did not remember standing just outside his daughter's door as she lectured her bear about his naughtiness and described the truly appalling punishments Paws would receive unless he changed his ways. He did not remember a single line of the hundreds of poems he had committed to memory in his youth so that he could give himself the shivers at will—not "Silent, upon a peak in Darien," or "My God, I heard this day," or "All my pretty ones? Did you say all? O hell-kite! All?" None of these did he remember; not one. Anders did not remember his dying mother saying of his father, "I should have stabbed him in his sleep."

He did not remember Professor Josephs telling his class how Athenian prisoners in Sicily had been released if they could recite Aeschylus, and then reciting Aeschylus himself, right there, in the Greek. Anders did not remember how his eyes had burned at those sounds. He did not remember the surprise of seeing a college classmate's name on the jacket of a novel not long after they graduated, or the respect he had felt after reading the book. He did not remember the pleasure of giving respect.

Nor did Anders remember seeing a woman leap to her death from the building opposite his own just days after his daughter was born. He did not remember shouting, "Lord have mercy!" He did not remember deliberately crashing his father's car into a tree, or having his ribs kicked in by three policemen at an anti-war rally, or waking himself up with laughter. He did not remember when he began to regard the heap of books on his desk with boredom and dread, or when he grew angry at writers for writing them. He did not remember when everything began to remind him of something else.

This is what he remembered. Heat. A baseball field. Yellow grass, the whirr of insects, himself leaning against a tree as the boys of the neighborhood gather for a pickup game. He looks on as the others argue the relative genius of Mantle and Mays. They have been worrying this subject all summer, and it has become tedious to Anders: an oppression, like the heat.

Then the last two boys arrive, Coyle and a cousin of his from Mississippi. Anders has never met Coyle's cousin before and will never see him again. He says hi with the rest but takes no further notice of him until they've chosen sides and someone asks the cousin what position he wants to play. "Shortstop," the boy says. "Short's the best position they is." Anders turns and looks at him. He wants to hear Coyle's cousin repeat what he's just said, but he knows better than to ask. The others will think he's being a jerk, ragging the kid for his grammar. But that isn't it, not at all—it's that Anders is strangely roused, elated, by those final two words, their pure unexpectedness and their music. He takes the field in a trance, repeating them to himself.

The bullet is already in the brain; it won't be outrun forever, or charmed to a halt. In the end it will do its work and leave the troubled skull behind, dragging its comet's tail of memory and hope and talent and love into the marble hall of commerce. That can't be helped. But for now Anders can still make time. Time for the shadows to lengthen on the grass, time for the tethered dog to bark at the flying ball, time for the boy in right field to smack his sweat-blackened mitt and softly chant, *They is, they is, they is.*

THE HERMIT'S STORY

Rick Bass • 1998

An ice storm, following seven days of snow; the vast fields and drifts of snow turning to sheets of glazed ice that shine and shimmer blue in the moonlight, as if the color is being fabricated not by the bending and absorption of light but by some chemical reaction within the glossy ice; as if the source of all blueness lies somewhere up here in the north—the core of it beneath one of those frozen fields; as if blue is a thing that emerges, in some parts of the world, from the soil itself, after the sun goes down.

Blue creeping up fissures and cracks from depths of several hundred feet; blue working its way up through the gleaming ribs of Ann's buried dogs; blue trailing like smoke from the dogs' empty eye sockets and nostrils—blue rising as if from deep-dug chimneys until it reaches the surface and spreads laterally and becomes entombed, or trapped—but still alive, and drifting—within those moonstruck fields of ice.

Blue like a scent trapped in the ice, waiting for some soft release, some thawing, so that it can continue spreading.

It's Thanksgiving. Susan and I are over at Ann and Roger's house for dinner. The storm has knocked out all the power down in town—it's a clear, cold, starry night, and if you were to climb one of the mountains on snowshoes and look forty miles south toward where town lies, instead of seeing the usual small scatterings of light—like fallen stars, stars sunken to the bottom of a lake, but still glowing—you would see nothing but darkness—a bowl of silence and darkness in balance for once with the mountains up here, rather than opposing or complementing our darkness, our peace.

As it is, we do not climb up on snowshoes to look down at the dark town—the power lines dragged down by the clutches of ice—but can tell instead just by the way there is no faint glow over the mountains to the south that the power is out; that this Thanksgiving, life for those in town is the same as it always is for us in the mountains, and it is a good feeling, a familial one, coming on the holiday as it does—though doubtless too the townspeople are feeling less snug and cozy about it than we are.

We've got our lanterns and candles burning. A fire's going in the stove, as it will all winter long and into the spring. Ann's dogs are asleep in their straw nests, breathing in that same blue light that is being exhaled from the skeletons of their ancestors just beneath and all around them. There is the faint smell of cold-storage meat—slabs and slabs of it—coming from down in the basement, and we have just finished off an entire chocolate pie and three bottles of wine. Roger, who does not know how to read, is examining the empty bottles, trying to read some of the words on the labels. He recognizes the words *the* and *in* and *USA*. It may be that he will never learn to read—that he will be unable to—but we are in no rush; he has all of his life to accomplish this. I for one believe that he will learn.

Ann has a story for us. It's about a fellow named Gray Owl, up in Canada, who owned half a dozen speckled German shorthaired pointers and who hired Ann to train them all at once. It was twenty years ago, she says—her last good job.

She worked the dogs all summer and into the autumn, and finally had them ready for field trials. She took them back up to Gray Owl—way up in Saskatchewan—driving all day and night in her old truck, which was old even then, with dogs piled up on top of one another, sleeping and snoring: dogs on her lap, dogs on the seat, dogs on the floorboard.

Ann was taking the dogs up there to show Gray Owl how to work them: how to take advantage of their newfound talents. She could be a sculptor or some other kind of artist; she speaks of her work as if the dogs are rough blocks of stone whose internal form exists already and is waiting only to be chiseled free and then released by her, beautiful, into the world.

Basically, in six months the dogs had been transformed from gangling, bouncing puppies into six wonderful hunters, and she needed to show their owner which characteristics to nurture, which ones to discourage. With all dogs, Ann said, there was a tendency, upon their leaving her tutelage, for a kind of chitinous encrustation to set in, a sort of oxidation, upon the dogs leaving her hands and being returned to someone less knowledgeable and passionate, less committed than she. It was as if there were a tendency for the dogs' greatness to disappear back into the stone.

So she went up there to give both the dogs and Gray Owl a checkout session. She drove with the heater on and the windows down; the cold Canadian air was invigorating, cleaner. She could smell the scent of the damp alder and cottonwood leaves beneath the many feet of snow. We laughed at her when she said it, but she told us that up in Canada she could taste the fish in the water as she drove alongside creeks and rivers.

She got to Gray Owl's around midnight. He had a little guest cabin but had not heated it for her, uncertain as to the day of her arrival, so she and the six dogs slept together on a cold mattress beneath mounds of elk hides: their last night together. She had brought a box of quail with which to work the dogs, and she built a small fire in the stove and set the box of quail next to it.

The quail muttered and cheeped all night and the stove popped and hissed and Ann and the dogs slept for twelve hours straight, as if submerged in another time, or as if everyone else in the world were submerged in time—and as if she and the dogs were pioneers, or survivors of some kind: upright and exploring the present, alive in the world, free of that strange chitin.

She spent a week up there, showing Gray Owl how his dogs worked. She said he scarcely recognized them afield, and that it took a few days just for him to get over his amazement. They worked the dogs both individually and, as Gray Owl came to understand and appreciate what Ann had crafted, in groups. They traveled across snowy hills on snowshoes, the sky the color of snow, so that often it was like moving through a dream, and, except for the rasp of the snowshoes beneath them and the pull of gravity, they might have believed they had ascended into some sky-place where all the world was snow.

They worked into the wind—north—whenever they could. Ann would carry birds in a pouch over her shoulder and from time to time would fling a startled bird out into that dreary, icy snowscape. The quail would fly off with great haste, a dark-feathered buzz bomb disappearing quickly into the teeth of cold, and then Gray Owl and Ann and the dog, or dogs, would go find it, following it by scent only, as always.

Snot icicles would be hanging from the dogs' nostrils. They would always find the bird. The dogs would point it, Gray Owl or Ann would step forward and flush it, and the beleaguered bird would leap into the sky again, and once more they would push on after it, pursuing that bird toward the horizon as if driving it with a whip. Whenever the bird wheeled and flew downwind, they'd quarter away from it, then get a mile or so downwind from it and push it back north.

When the quail finally became too exhausted to fly, Ann would pick it up from beneath the dogs' noses as they held point staunchly, put the tired bird in her game bag, and replace it with a fresh one, and off they'd go again. They carried their lunch in Gray Owl's daypack, as well as emergency supplies—a tent and some dry clothes—in case they should become lost, and around noon each day (they could rarely see the sun, only an ice-white haze, so that they relied instead only on their internal rhythms) they would stop and make a pot of tea on the sputtering little gas stove. Sometimes one or two of the quail would die from exposure, and they would cook that on the stove and eat it out there in the tundra, tossing the feathers up into the wind as if to launch one more flight, and feeding the head, guts, and feet to the dogs.

Seen from above, their tracks might have seemed aimless and wandering rather than with the purpose, the focus that was burning hot in both their and the dogs' hearts. Perhaps someone viewing the tracks could have discerned the pattern, or perhaps not, but it did not matter, for their tracks—the patterns, direction, and tracing of them—were obscured by the drifting snow, sometimes within minutes after they were laid down.

Toward the end of the week, Ann said, they were finally running all six dogs at once, like a herd of silent wild horses through all that snow, and as she would be going home the next day there was no need to conserve any of the birds she had brought, and she was turning them loose several at a time: birds flying in all directions, and the dogs, as ever, tracking them to the ends of the earth.

It was almost a whiteout that last day, and it was hard to keep track of all the dogs. Ann was sweating from the exertion as well as the tension of trying to keep an eye on, and evaluate, each dog, and the sweat was freezing on her, an ice skin. She jokingly told Gray Owl that next time she was going to try to find a client who lived in Arizona, or even South America. Gray Owl smiled and then told her that they were lost, but no matter, the storm would clear in a day or two.

They knew it was getting near dusk—there was a faint dulling to the sheer whiteness, a kind of increasing heaviness in the air, a new density to the faint light around them—and the dogs slipped in and out of sight, working just at the edges of their vision.

The temperature was dropping as the north wind increased—"No question about which way south is," Gray Owl said, "so we'll turn around and walk south for three hours, and if we don't find a road, we'll make camp"—and now the dogs were coming back with frozen quail held gingerly in their mouths, for once the birds were dead, the dogs were allowed to retrieve them, though the dogs must have been puzzled that there had been no shots. Ann said she fired a few rounds of the cap pistol into the air to make the dogs think she had hit those birds. Surely they believed she was a goddess.

They turned and headed south—Ann with a bag of frozen birds over her shoulder, and the dogs, knowing that the hunt was over now, once again like a team of horses in harness, though wild and prancy.

After an hour of increasing discomfort—Ann's and Gray Owl's hands and feet numb, and ice beginning to form on the dogs' paws, so that the dogs were having to high-step—they came in day's last light to the edge of a wide clearing: a terrain that was remarkable and soothing for its lack of hills. It was a frozen lake, which meant—said Gray Owl— they had drifted west (or perhaps east) by as much as ten miles.

Ann said that Gray Owl looked tired and old and guilty, as would any host who had caused his guest some unasked-for inconvenience. They knelt and began massaging the dogs' paws and then lit the little stove and held each dog's foot, one at a time, over the tiny blue flame to help it thaw out.

Gray Owl walked to the edge of the lake ice and kicked at it with his foot, hoping to find fresh water beneath for the dogs; if they ate too much snow, especially after working so hard, they'd get violent diarrhea and might then become too weak to continue home the next day, or the next, or whenever the storm quit.

Ann said that she had barely been able to see Gray Owl's outline through the swirling snow, even though he was less than twenty yards away. He kicked once at the sheet of ice, the vast plate of it, with his heel, then disappeared below the ice.

Ann wanted to believe that she had blinked and lost sight of him, or that a gust of snow had swept past and hidden him, but it had been too fast, too total: she knew that the lake had swallowed him. She was sorry for Gray Owl, she said, and worried for his dogs—afraid they would try to follow his scent down into the icy lake and be lost as well—but what she had been most upset about, she said—to be perfectly honest—was that Gray Owl had been wearing the little daypack with the tent and emergency rations. She had it in her mind to try to save Gray Owl, and to try to keep the dogs from going through the ice, but if he drowned, she was going to have to figure out how to try to get that daypack off of the drowned man and set up the wet tent in the blizzard on the snowy prairie and then crawl inside and survive. She would have to go into the water naked, so that when she came back out—if she came back out—she would have dry clothes to put on.

The dogs came galloping up, seeming as large as deer or elk in that dim landscape against which there was nothing else to give the viewer a perspective, and Ann whoaed them right at the lake's edge, where they stopped immediately, as if they had suddenly been cast with a sheet of ice.

Ann knew the dogs would stay there forever, or until she released them, and it troubled her to think that if she drowned, they too would die—that they would stand there motionless, as she had commanded them, for as long as they could, until at some point—days later, perhaps—they would lie down, trembling with exhaustion—they might lick at some snow, for moisture—but that then the snows would cover them, and still they would remain there, chins resting on their front paws, staring straight ahead and unseeing into the storm, wondering where the scent of her had gone.

Ann eased out onto the ice. She followed the tracks until she came to the jagged hole in the ice through which Gray Owl had plunged. She was almost half again lighter than he, but she could feel the ice crackling beneath her own feet. It sounded different, too, in a way she could not place—it did not have the squeaky, percussive resonance of the lake-ice back home—and she wondered if Canadian ice froze differently or just sounded different.

She got down on all fours and crept closer to the hole. It was right at dusk. She peered down into the hole and dimly saw Gray Owl standing down there, waving his arms at her. He did not appear to be swimming. Slowly, she took one glove off and eased her bare hand into the hole. She could find no water, and, tentatively, she reached deeper.

Gray Owl's hand found hers and he pulled her down in. Ice broke as she fell, but he caught her in his arms. She could smell the wood smoke in his jacket from the alder he burned in his cabin. There was no water at all, and it was warm beneath the ice.

"This happens a lot more than people realize," he said. "It's not really a phenomenon; it's just what happens. A cold snap comes in October, freezes a skin of ice over the lake—it's got to be a shallow one, almost a marsh. Then a snowfall comes, insulating the ice. The lake drains in fall and winter—percolates down through the soil"—he stamped the spongy ground beneath them—"but the ice up top remains. And nobody ever knows any different. People look out at the surface and think, *Aha, a frozen lake.*" Gray Owl laughed.

"Did you know it would be like this?" Ann asked.

"No," he said. "I was looking for water. I just got lucky."

Ann walked back to shore beneath the ice to fetch her stove and to release the dogs from their whoa command. The dry lake was only about eight feet deep, but it grew shallow quickly closer to shore, so that Ann had to crouch to keep from bumping her head on the overhead ice, and then crawl; and then there was only space to wriggle, and to emerge she had to break the ice above her by bumping and then battering it with her head and elbows, struggling like some embryonic hatchling; and when she stood up, waist-deep amid sparkling shards of ice—it was nighttime now—the dogs barked ferociously at her, but they remained where she had ordered them. She was surprised at how far off course she was when she climbed out; she had traveled only twenty feet, but already the dogs were twice that far away from her. She knew humans had a poorly evolved, almost nonexistent sense of direction, but this error—over such a short distance—shocked her. It was as if there were in us a thing—an impulse, a catalyst—that denies our ever going straight to another thing. Like dogs working left and right into the wind, she thought, before converging on the scent.

Except that the dogs would not get lost, while she could easily imagine herself and Gray Owl getting lost beneath the lake, walking in circles forever, unable to find even the simplest of things: the shore.

She gathered the stove and dogs. She was tempted to try to go back in the way she had come out—it seemed so easy—but she considered the consequences of getting lost in the other direction, and instead followed her original tracks out to where Gray Owl had first dropped through the ice. It was true night now, and the blizzard was still blowing hard, plastering snow and ice around her face like a mask. The dogs did not want to go down into the hole, so she lowered them to Gray Owl and then climbed gratefully back down into the warmth herself.

The air was a thing of its own—recognizable as air, and breathable as such, but with a taste and odor, an essence, unlike any other air they'd ever breathed. It had a different density to it, so that smaller, shallower breaths were required; there was very much the feeling that if they breathed in too much of the strange, dense air, they would drown.

They wanted to explore the lake, and were thirsty, but it felt like a victory simply to be warm—or rather, not cold—and they were so exhausted that instead they made pallets out of the dead marsh grass that rustled around their ankles, and they slept curled up on the tiniest of hammocks, to keep from getting damp in the pockets and puddles of water that still lingered here and there.

All eight of them slept as if in a nest, heads and arms draped across other ribs and hips; and it was, said Ann, the best and deepest sleep she'd ever had—the sleep of hounds, the sleep of childhood. How long

they slept, she never knew, for she wasn't sure, later, how much of their
subsequent time they spent wandering beneath the lake, and then up on
the prairie, homeward again, but when they awoke, it was still night, or
night once more, and clearing, with bright stars visible through the
porthole, their point of embarkation; and even from beneath the ice, in
certain places where, for whatever reasons—temperature, oxygen content, wind scour—the ice was clear rather than glazed, they could see
the spangling of stars, though more dimly; and strangely, rather than
seeming to distance them from the stars, this phenomenon seemed to
pull them closer, as if they were up in the stars, traveling the Milky
Way, or as if the stars were embedded in the ice.

It was very cold outside—up above—and there was a steady stream,
a current like a river, of the night's colder, heavier air plunging down
through their porthole—as if trying to fill the empty lake with that
frozen air—but there was also the hot muck of the earth's massive res-
pirations breathing out warmth and being trapped and protected beneath that ice, so that there were warm currents doing battle with the
lone cold current.

The result was that it was breezy down there, and the dogs' noses
twitched in their sleep as the images brought by these scents painted
themselves across their sleeping brains in the language we call dreams
but which, for the dogs, was reality: the scent of an owl *real*, not a
dream; the scent of bear, cattail, willow, loon, *real*, even though they
were sleeping, and even though those things were not visible, only over
the next horizon.

The ice was contracting, groaning and cracking and squeaking up
tighter, shrinking beneath the great cold—a concussive, grinding sound,
as if giants were walking across the ice above—and it was this sound
that awakened them. They snuggled in warmer among the rattly dried
yellowing grasses and listened to the tremendous clashings, as if they
were safe beneath the sea and were watching waves of starlight sweep-

ing across their hiding place; or as if they were in some place, some
position, where they could watch mountains being born.

After a while the moon came up and washed out the stars. The light
was blue and silver and seemed, Ann said, to be like a living thing. It
filled the sheet of ice just above their heads with a shimmering cobalt
light, which again rippled as if the ice were moving, rather than the
earth itself, with the moon tracking it—and like deer drawn by gravity
getting up in the night to feed for an hour or so before settling back in,
Gray Owl and Ann and the dogs rose from their nests of straw and
began to travel.

They walked a long way. The air was damp down there, and whenever they'd get chilled, they'd stop and make a little fire out of a bundle
of dry cattails. There were pockets and puddles of swamp gas pooled in
place, and sometimes a spark from the cattails would ignite one of those,
and the pockets of gas would light up like when you toss gas on a fire—
explosions of brilliance, like flashbulbs, marsh patches igniting like
falling dominoes, or like children playing hopscotch—until a large
enough flash-pocket was reached—sometimes thirty or forty yards
away—that the puff of flame would blow a chimney-hole through the
ice, venting the other gas pockets, and the fires would crackle out, the
scent of grass smoke sweet in their lungs, and they could feel gusts of
warmth from the little flickering fires, and currents of the colder,
heavier air sliding down through the new ventholes and pooling around
their ankles. The moonlight would strafe down through those rents in
the ice, and shards of moon-ice would be glittering and spinning like
diamond-motes in those newly vented columns of moonlight; and they
pushed on, still lost, but so alive.

The small explosions were fun, but they frightened the dogs, so Ann
and Gray Owl lit twisted bundles of cattails and used them for torches
to light their way, rather than building warming fires, though occasionally they would still pass through an invisible patch of methane and a

stray ember would fall from their torches, and the whole chain of
fire and light would begin again, culminating once more with a vent-
hole being blown open and shards of glittering ice tumbling down into
their lair.

What would it have looked like, seen from above—the orange blur-
rings of their wandering trail beneath the ice; and what would the sheet
of lake-ice itself have looked like that night—throbbing with ice-bound,
subterranean blue and orange light of moon and fire? But again, there
was no one to view the spectacle: only the travelers themselves, and they
had no perspective, no vantage from which to view or judge themselves.
They were simply pushing on from one fire to the next, carrying their
tiny torches.

They knew they were getting near a shore—the southern shore,
they hoped, as they followed the glazed moon's lure above—when the
dogs began to encounter shore birds that had somehow found their way
beneath the ice through fissures and rifts and were taking refuge in the
cattails. Small winter birds—juncos, nuthatches, chickadees—skittered
away from the smoky approach of their torches; only a few late-migrating
(or winter-trapped) snipe held tight and steadfast; and the dogs began
to race ahead of Gray Owl and Ann, working these familiar scents: blue
and silver ghost-shadows of dog muscle weaving ahead through slants
of moonlight.

The dogs emitted the odor of adrenaline when they worked, Ann
said—a scent like damp, fresh-cut green hay—and with nowhere to
vent, the odor was dense and thick around them, so that Ann wondered
if it too might be flammable, like the methane; if in the dogs' passions
they might literally immolate themselves.

They followed the dogs closely with their torches. The ceiling was
low, about eight feet, so that the tips of their torches' flames seared the
ice above them, leaving a drip behind them and transforming the milky,
almost opaque cobalt and orange ice behind them, wherever they passed,
into wandering ribbons of clear ice, translucent to the sky—a script of

flame, or buried flame, ice-bound flame—and they hurried to keep up with the dogs.

Now the dogs had the snipe surrounded, as Ann told it, and one by one the dogs went on point, each dog freezing as it pointed to the birds' hiding places, and Gray Owl moved in to flush the birds, which launched themselves with vigor against the roof of the ice above, fluttering like bats; but the snipe were too small, not powerful enough to break through those frozen four inches of water (though they could fly four thousand miles to South America each year and then back to Canada six months later—is freedom a lateral component, or a vertical one?), and as Gray Owl kicked at the clumps of frost-bent cattails where the snipe were hiding and they burst into flight, only to hit their heads on the ice above them, they came tumbling back down, raining limp and unconscious back to their soft grassy nests.

The dogs began retrieving them, carrying them gingerly, delicately—not caring for the taste of snipe, which ate only earthworms—and Ann and Gray Owl gathered the tiny birds from the dogs, placed them in their pockets, and continued on to the shore, chasing that moon, the ceiling lowering to six feet, then four, then to a crawlspace, and after they had bashed their way out and stepped back out into the frigid air, they tucked the still-unconscious snipe into little crooks in branches, up against the trunks of trees and off the ground, out of harm's way, and passed on, south—as if late in their own migration—while the snipe rested, warm and terrified and heart-fluttering, but saved, for now, against the trunks of those trees.

Long after Ann and Gray Owl and the pack of dogs had passed through, the birds would awaken, their bright, dark eyes luminous in the moonlight, and the first sight they would see would be the frozen marsh before them, with its chain of still-steaming vent-holes stretching back across all the way to the other shore. Perhaps these were birds that had been unable to migrate owing to injuries, or some genetic absence. Perhaps they had tried to migrate in the past but had found either their winter habitat destroyed or the path so fragmented and fraught with danger that it made more sense—to these few birds—to ignore the tuggings of the stars and seasons and instead to try to carve out new lives, new ways of being, even in such a stark and severe landscape: or rather, in a stark and severe period—knowing that lushness and bounty were still retained with that landscape; that it was only a phase, that better days would come. That in fact (the snipe knowing these things with their blood, ten million years in the world) the austere times were the very thing, the very imbalance, that would summon the resurrection of that frozen richness within the soil—if indeed that richness, that magic, that hope, did yet exist beneath the ice and snow. Spring would come like its own green fire, if only the injured ones could hold on.

And what would the snipe think or remember, upon reawakening and finding themselves still in that desolate position, desolate place and time, but still alive, and with hope?

Would it seem to them that a thing like grace had passed through, as they slept—that a slender winding river of it had passed through and rewarded them for their faith and endurance?

Believing, stubbornly, that that green land beneath them would blossom once more. Maybe not soon; but again.

If the snipe survived, they would be among the first to see it. Perhaps they believed that the pack of dogs, and Gray Owl's and Ann's advancing torches, had only been one of winter's dreams. Even with the proof—the scribings—of grace's passage before them—the vent-holes still steaming—perhaps they believed it was a dream. Gray Owl, Ann, and the dogs headed south for half a day until they reached the snow-packed, wind-scoured road on which they'd parked. The road looked different, Ann said, buried beneath snowdrifts, and they didn't know whether to turn east or west. The dogs chose west, and Gray Owl and Ann followed them. Two hours later they were back at their truck, and that night they were back at Gray Owl's cabin; by the next night Ann was home again.

She says that even now she sometimes has dreams about being beneath the ice—about living beneath the ice—and that it seems to her as
if she was down there for much longer than a day and a night; that instead she might have been gone for years.

It was twenty years ago, when it happened. Gray Owl has since
died, and all those dogs are dead now, too. She is the only one who still
carries—in the flesh, at any rate—the memory of that passage.

Ann would never discuss such a thing, but I suspect that it, that one
day and night, helped give her a model for what things were like for her
dogs when they were hunting and when they went on point: how the
world must have appeared to them when they were in that trance, that
blue zone, where the odors of things wrote their images across the dogs'
hot brainpans. A zone where sight, and the appearance of things—
surfaces—disappeared, and where instead their essence—the heat mole-
cules of scent—was revealed, illuminated, circumscribed, possessed.

I suspect that she holds that knowledge—the memory of that one
day and night—especially since she is now the sole possessor—as tightly,
and securely, as one might clench some bright small gem in one's fist:
not a gem given to one by some favored or beloved individual but, even
more valuable, some gem found while out on a walk—perhaps by hap-
penstance, or perhaps by some unavoidable rhythm of fate—and hence
containing great magic, great strength.

Such is the nature of the kinds of people living, scattered here and
there, in this valley.

A TEMPORARY MATTER

Jhumpa Lahiri · 1998

The notice informed them that it was a temporary matter: for five days their electricity would be cut off for one hour, beginning at eight P.M. A line had gone down in the last snowstorm, and the repairmen were going to take advantage of the milder evenings to set it right. The work would affect only the houses on the quiet tree-lined street, within walking distance of a row of brick-faced stores and a trolley stop, where Shoba and Shukumar had lived for three years.

"It's good of them to warn us," Shoba conceded after reading the notice aloud, more for her own benefit than Shukumar's. She let the strap of her leather satchel, plump with files, slip from her shoulders, and left it in the hallway as she walked into the kitchen. She wore a navy blue poplin raincoat over gray sweatpants and white sneakers, looking, at thirty-three, like the type of woman she'd once claimed she would never resemble.

She'd come from the gym. Her cranberry lipstick was visible only on the outer reaches of her mouth, and her eyeliner had left charcoal patches beneath her lower lashes. She used to look this way sometimes, Shukumar thought, on mornings after a party or a night at a bar, when she'd been too lazy to wash her face, too eager to collapse into his arms.

She dropped a sheaf of mail on the table without a glance. Her eyes were still fixed on the notice in her other hand. "But they should do this sort of thing during the day."

"When I'm here, you mean," Shukumar said. He put a glass lid on a pot of lamb, adjusting it so only the slightest bit of steam could escape. Since January he'd been working at home, trying to complete the final chapters of his dissertation on agrarian revolts in India. "When do the repairs start?"

"It says March nineteenth. Is today the nineteenth?" Shoba walked over to the framed corkboard that hung on the wall by the fridge, bare except for a calendar of William Morris wallpaper patterns. She looked at it as if for the first time, studying the wallpaper pattern carefully on the top half before allowing her eyes to fall to the numbered grid on the bottom. A friend had sent the calendar in the mail as a Christmas gift, even though Shoba and Shukumar hadn't celebrated Christmas that year.

"Today then," Shoba announced. "You have a dentist appointment next Friday, by the way."

He ran his tongue over the tops of his teeth; he'd forgotten to brush them that morning. It wasn't the first time. He hadn't left the house at all that day, or the day before. The more Shoba stayed out, the more she began putting in extra hours at work and taking on additional projects, the more he wanted to stay in, not even leaving to get the mail, or to buy fruit or wine at the stores by the trolley stop.

Six months ago, in September, Shukumar was at an academic conference in Baltimore when Shoba went into labor, three weeks before her due date. He hadn't wanted to go to the conference, but she had insisted; it was important to make contacts, and he would be entering the job market next year. She told him that she had his number at the hotel, and a copy of his schedule and flight numbers, and she had arranged with her friend Gillian for a ride to the hospital in the event of an emergency. When the cab pulled away that morning for the airport,

Shoba stood waving good-bye in her robe, with one arm resting on the mound of her belly as if it were a perfectly natural part of her body.

Each time he thought of that moment, the last moment he saw Shoba pregnant, it was the cab he remembered most, a station wagon, painted red with blue lettering. It was cavernous compared to their own car. Although Shukumar was six feet tall, with hands too big ever to rest comfortably in the pockets of his jeans, he felt dwarfed in the back seat. As the cab sped down Beacon Street, he imagined a day when he and Shoba might need to buy a station wagon of their own, to cart their children back and forth from music lessons and dentist appointments. He imagined himself gripping the wheel, as Shoba turned around to hand the children juice boxes. Once, these images of parenthood had troubled Shukumar, adding to his anxiety that he was still a student at thirty-five. But that early autumn morning, the trees still heavy with bronze leaves, he welcomed the image for the first time.

A member of the staff had found him somehow among the identical convention rooms and handed him a stiff square of stationery. It was only a telephone number, but Shukumar knew it was the hospital. When he returned to Boston it was over. The baby had been born dead. Shoba was lying on a bed, asleep, in a private room so small there was barely enough space to stand beside her, in a wing of the hospital they hadn't been to on the tour for expectant parents. Her placenta had weakened and she'd had a cesarean, though not quickly enough. The doctor explained that these things happen. He smiled in the kindest way it was possible to smile at people known only professionally. Shoba would be back on her feet in a few weeks. There was nothing to indicate that she would not be able to have children in the future.

These days Shoba was always gone by the time Shukumar woke up. He would open his eyes and see the long black hairs she shed on her pillow and think of her, dressed, sipping her third cup of coffee already, in her office downtown, where she searched for typographical errors in textbooks and marked them, in a code she had once explained to him, with an assortment of colored pencils. She would do the same for his dissertation, she promised, when it was ready. He envied her the specificity of her task, so unlike the elusive nature of his. He was a mediocre student who had a facility for absorbing details without curiosity. Until September he had been diligent if not dedicated, summarizing chapters, outlining arguments on pads of yellow lined paper. But now he would lie in their bed until he grew bored, gazing at his side of the closet which Shoba always left partly open, at the row of the tweed jackets and corduroy trousers he would not have to choose from to teach his classes that semester. After the baby died it was too late to withdraw from his teaching duties. But his adviser had arranged things so that he had the spring semester to himself. Shukumar was in his sixth year of graduate school. "That and the summer should give you a good push," his adviser had said. "You should be able to wrap things up by next September."

But nothing was pushing Shukumar. Instead he thought of how he and Shoba had become experts at avoiding each other in their three-bedroom house, spending as much time on separate floors as possible. He thought of how he no longer looked forward to weekends, when she sat for hours on the sofa with her colored pencils and her files, so that he feared that putting on a record in his own house might be rude. He thought of how long it had been since she looked into his eyes and smiled, or whispered his name on those rare occasions they still reached for each other's bodies before sleeping.

In the beginning he had believed that it would pass, that he and Shoba would get through it all somehow. She was only thirty-three. She was strong, on her feet again. But it wasn't a consolation. It was often nearly lunchtime when Shukumar would finally pull himself out of bed and head downstairs to the coffeepot, pouring out the extra bit Shoba left for him, along with an empty mug, on the countertop.

Shukumar gathered onion skins in his hands and let them drop into the garbage pail, on top of the ribbons of fat he'd trimmed from the lamb. He ran the water in the sink, soaking the knife and the cutting board, and rubbed a lemon half along his fingertips to get rid of the garlic smell, a trick he'd learned from Shoba. It was seven-thirty. Through the window he saw the sky, like soft black pitch. Uneven banks of snow still lined the sidewalks, though it was warm enough for people to walk about without hats or gloves. Nearly three feet had fallen in the last storm, so that for a week people had to walk single file, in narrow trenches. For a week that was Shukumar's excuse for not leaving the house. But now the trenches were widening, and water drained steadily into grates in the pavement.

"The lamb won't be done by eight," Shukumar said. "We may have to eat in the dark."

"We can light candles," Shoba suggested. She unclipped her hair, coiled neatly at her nape during the days, and pried the sneakers from her feet without untying them. "I'm going to shower before the lights go," she said, heading for the staircase. "I'll be down."

Shukumar moved her satchel and her sneakers to the side of the fridge. She wasn't this way before. She used to put her coat on a hanger, her sneakers in the closet, and she paid bills as soon as they came. But now she treated the house as if it were a hotel. The fact that the yellow chintz armchair in the living room clashed with the blue-and-maroon Turkish carpet no longer bothered her. On the enclosed porch at the back of the house, a crisp white bag still sat on the wicker chaise, filled with lace she had once planned to turn into curtains.

While Shoba showered, Shukumar went into the downstairs bathroom and found a new toothbrush in its box beneath the sink. The cheap, stiff bristles hurt his gums, and he spit some blood into the basin. The spare brush was one of many stored in a metal basket. Shoba had bought them once when they were on sale, in the event that a visitor decided, at the last minute, to spend the night.

It was typical of her. She was the type to prepare for surprises, good and bad. If she found a skirt or a purse she liked she bought two. She kept the bonuses from her job in a separate bank account in her name. It hadn't bothered him. His own mother had fallen to pieces when his father died, abandoning the house he grew up in and moving back to Calcutta, leaving Shukumar to settle it all. He liked that Shoba was different. It astonished him, her capacity to think ahead. When she used to do the shopping, the pantry was always stocked with extra bottles of olive and corn oil, depending on whether they were cooking Italian or Indian. There were endless boxes of pasta in all shapes and colors, zippered sacks of basmati rice, whole sides of lambs and goats from the Muslim butchers at Haymarket, chopped up and frozen in endless plastic bags. Every other Saturday they wound through the maze of stalls Shukumar eventually knew by heart. He watched in disbelief as she bought more food, trailing behind her with canvas bags as she pushed through the crowd, arguing under the morning sun with boys too young to shave but already missing teeth, who twisted up brown paper bags of artichokes, plums, gingerroot, and yams, and dropped them on their scales, and tossed them to Shoba one by one. She didn't mind being jostled, even when she was pregnant. She was tall, and broad-shouldered, with hips that her obstetrician assured her were made for childbearing. During the drive back home, as the car curved along the Charles, they invariably marveled at how much food they'd bought.

It never went to waste. When friends dropped by, Shoba would throw together meals that appeared to have taken half a day to prepare, from things she had frozen and bottled, not cheap things in tins but peppers she had marinated herself with rosemary, and chutneys that she cooked on Sundays, stirring boiling pots of tomatoes and prunes. Her labeled mason jars lined the shelves of the kitchen, in endless sealed pyramids, enough, they'd agreed, to last for their grandchildren to taste. They'd eaten it all by now. Shukumar had been going through their supplies steadily, preparing meals for the two of them, measuring out

cupfuls of rice, defrosting bags of meat day after day. He combed
through her cookbooks every afternoon, following her penciled instructions to use two teaspoons of ground coriander seeds instead of one, or
red lentils instead of yellow. Each of the recipes was dated, telling the
first time they had eaten the dish together. April 2, cauliflower with
fennel. January 14, chicken with almonds and sultanas. He had no
memory of eating those meals, and yet there they were, recorded in her
neat proofreader's hand. Shukumar enjoyed cooking now. It was the one
thing that made him feel productive. If it weren't for him, he knew,
Shoba would eat a bowl of cereal for her dinner.

Tonight, with no lights, they would have to eat together. For months
now they'd served themselves from the stove, and he'd taken his plate
into his study, letting the meal grow cold on his desk before shoving
it into his mouth without pause, while Shoba took her plate to the living
room and watched game shows, or proofread files with her arsenal of
colored pencils at hand.

At some point in the evening she visited him. When he heard her
approach he would put away his novel and begin typing sentences. She
would rest her hands on his shoulders and stare with him into the blue
glow of the computer screen. "Don't work too hard," she would say after
a minute or two, and head off to bed. It was the one time in the day she
sought him out, and yet he'd come to dread it. He knew it was something she forced herself to do. She would look around the walls of the
room, which they had decorated together last summer with a border of
marching ducks and rabbits playing trumpets and drums. By the end of
August there was a cherry crib under the window, a white changing
table with mint-green knobs, and a rocking chair with checkered cush-
ions. Shukumar had disassembled it all before bringing Shoba back
from the hospital, scraping off the rabbits and ducks with a spatula. For
some reason the room did not haunt him the way it haunted Shoba. In
January, when he stopped working at his carrel in the library, he set up

his desk there deliberately, partly because the room soothed him, and partly because it was a place Shoba avoided.

Shukumar returned to the kitchen and began to open drawers. He tried to locate a candle among the scissors, the eggbeaters and whisks, the mortar and pestle she'd bought in a bazaar in Calcutta, and used to pound garlic cloves and cardamom pods, back when she used to cook. He found a flashlight, but no batteries, and a half-empty box of birthday candles. Shoba had thrown him a surprise birthday party last May. One hundred and twenty people had crammed into the house—all the friends and the friends of friends they now systematically avoided. Bottles of vinho verde had nested in a bed of ice in the bathtub. Shoba was in her fifth month, drinking ginger ale from a martini glass. She had made a vanilla cream cake with custard and spun sugar. All night she kept Shukumar's long fingers linked with hers as they walked among the guests at the party.

Since September their only guest had been Shoba's mother. She came from Arizona and stayed with them for two months after Shoba returned from the hospital. She cooked dinner every night, drove herself to the supermarket, washed their clothes, put them away. She was a religious woman. She set up a small shrine, a framed picture of a lavender-faced goddess and a plate of marigold petals, on the bedside table in the guest room, and prayed twice a day for healthy grandchildren in the future. She was polite to Shukumar without being friendly. She folded his sweaters with an expertise she had learned from her job in a department store. She replaced a missing button on his winter coat and knit him a beige and brown scarf, presenting it to him without the least bit of ceremony, as if he had only dropped it and hadn't noticed. She never talked to him about Shoba; once, when he mentioned the baby's death, she looked up from her knitting, and said, "But you weren't even there."

It struck him as odd that there were no real candles in the house. That Shoba hadn't prepared for such an ordinary emergency. He looked now for something to put the birthday candles in and settled on the soil of a potted ivy that normally sat on the windowsill over the sink. Even though the plant was inches from the tap, the soil was so dry that he had to water it first before the candles would stand straight. He pushed aside the things on the kitchen table, the piles of mail, the unread library books. He remembered their first meals there, when they were so thrilled to be married, to be living together in the same house at last, that they would just reach for each other foolishly, more eager to make love than to eat. He put down two embroidered place mats, a wedding gift from an uncle in Lucknow, and set out the plates and wineglasses they usually saved for guests. He put the ivy in the middle, the white-edged, star-shaped leaves girded by ten little candles. He switched on the digital clock radio and tuned it to a jazz station.

"What's all this?" Shoba said when she came downstairs. Her hair was wrapped in a thick white towel. She undid the towel and draped it over a chair, allowing her hair, damp and dark, to fall across her back. As she walked absently toward the stove she took out a few tangles with her fingers. She wore a clean pair of sweatpants, a T-shirt, an old flannel robe. Her stomach was flat again, her waist narrow before the flare of her hips, the belt of the robe tied in a floppy knot.

It was nearly eight. Shukumar put the rice on the table and the lentils from the night before into the microwave oven, punching the numbers on the timer.

"You made *rogan josh*," Shoba observed, looking through the glass lid at the bright paprika stew.

Shukumar took out a piece of lamb, pinching it quickly between his fingers so as not to scald himself. He prodded a larger piece with a serving spoon to make sure the meat slipped easily from the bone. "It's ready," he announced.

The microwave had just beeped when the lights went out, and the music disappeared.

"Perfect timing," Shoba said.

"All I could find were birthday candles." He lit up the ivy, keeping the rest of the candles and a book of matches by his plate.

"It doesn't matter," she said, running a finger along the stem of her wineglass. "It looks lovely."

In the dimness, he knew how she sat, a bit forward in her chair, ankles crossed against the lowest rung, left elbow on the table. During his search for the candles, Shukumar had found a bottle of wine in a crate he had thought was empty. He clamped the bottle between his knees while he turned in the corkscrew. He worried about spilling, and so he picked up the glasses and held them close to his lap while he filled them. They served themselves, stirring the rice with their forks, squinting as they extracted bay leaves and cloves from the stew. Every few minutes Shukumar lit a few more birthday candles and drove them into the soil of the pot.

"It's like India," Shoba said, watching him tend his makeshift candelabra. "Sometimes the current disappears for hours at a stretch. I once had to attend an entire rice ceremony in the dark. The baby just cried and cried. It must have been so hot."

Their baby had never cried, Shukumar considered. Their baby would never have a rice ceremony, even though Shoba had already made the guest list, and decided on which of her three brothers she was going to ask to feed the child its first taste of solid food, at six months if it was a boy, seven if it was a girl.

"Are you hot?" he asked her. He pushed the blazing ivy pot to the other end of the table, closer to the piles of books and mail, making it even more difficult for them to see each other. He was suddenly irritated that he couldn't go upstairs and sit in front of the computer.

"No. It's delicious," she said, tapping her plate with her fork. "It really is."

He refilled the wine in her glass. She thanked him.

They weren't like this before. Now he had to struggle to say something that interested her, something that made her look up from her plate, or from her proofreading files. Eventually he gave up trying to amuse her. He learned not to mind the silences.

"I remember during power failures at my grandmother's house, we all had to say something," Shoba continued. He could barely see her face, but from her tone he knew her eyes were narrowed, as if trying to focus on a distant object. It was a habit of hers.

"Like what?"

"I don't know. A little poem. A joke. A fact about the world. For some reason my relatives always wanted me to tell them the names of my friends in America. I don't know why the information was so interesting to them. The last time I saw my aunt she asked after four girls I went to elementary school with in Tucson. I barely remember them now."

Shukumar hadn't spent as much time in India as Shoba had. His parents, who settled in New Hampshire, used to go back without him. The first time he'd gone as an infant he'd nearly died of amoebic dysentery. His father, a nervous type, was afraid to take him again, in case something were to happen, and left him with his aunt and uncle in Concord. As a teenager he preferred sailing camp or scooping ice cream during the summers to going to Calcutta. It wasn't until after his father died, in his last year of college, that the country began to interest him, and he studied its history from course books as if it were any other subject. He wished now that he had his own childhood story of India.

"Let's do that," she said suddenly.

"Do what?"

"Say something to each other in the dark."

"Like what? I don't know any jokes."

"No, no jokes." She thought for a minute. "How about telling each other something we've never told before."

"I used to play this game in high school," Shukumar recalled. "When I got drunk."

"You're thinking of truth or dare. This is different. Okay, I'll start." She took a sip of wine. "The first time I was alone in your apartment, I looked in your address book to see if you'd written me in. I think we'd known each other two weeks."

"Where was I?"

"You went to answer the telephone in the other room. It was your mother, and I figured it would be a long call. I wanted to know if you'd promoted me from the margins of your newspaper."

"Had I?"

"No. But I didn't give up on you. Now it's your turn."

He couldn't think of anything, but Shoba was waiting for him to speak. She hadn't appeared so determined in months. What was there left to say to her? He thought back to their first meeting, four years earlier at a lecture hall in Cambridge, where a group of Bengali poets were giving a recital. They'd ended up side by side, on folding wooden chairs. Shukumar was soon bored; he was unable to decipher the literary diction, and couldn't join the rest of the audience as they sighed and nodded solemnly after certain phrases. Peering at the newspaper folded in his lap, he studied the temperatures of cities around the world. Ninety-one degrees in Singapore yesterday, fifty-one in Stockholm. When he turned his head to the left, he saw a woman next to him making a grocery list on the back of a folder, and was startled to find that she was beautiful.

"Okay," he said, remembering. "The first time we went out to dinner, to the Portuguese place, I forgot to tip the waiter. I went back the next morning, found out his name, left money with the manager."

"You went all the way back to Somerville just to tip a waiter?"

"I took a cab."

"Why did you forget to tip the waiter?"

The birthday candles had burned out, but he pictured her face clearly in the dark, the wide tilting eyes, the full grape-toned lips, the fall at age two from her high chair still visible as a comma on her chin. Each day, Shukumar noticed, her beauty, which had once overwhelmed him, seemed to fade. The cosmetics that had seemed superfluous were necessary now, not to improve her but to define her somehow.

"By the end of the meal I had a funny feeling that I might marry you," he said, admitting it to himself as well as to her for the first time. "It must have distracted me."

The next night Shoba came home earlier than usual. There was lamb left over from the evening before, and Shukumar heated it up so that they were able to eat by seven. He'd gone out that day, through the melting snow, and bought a packet of taper candles from the corner store, and batteries to fit the flashlight. He had the candles ready on the countertop, standing in brass holders shaped like lotuses, but they ate under the glow of the copper-shaded ceiling lamp that hung over the table.

When they had finished eating, Shukumar was surprised to see that Shoba was stacking her plate on top of his, and then carrying them over to the sink. He had assumed she would retreat to the living room, behind her barricade of files.

"Don't worry about the dishes," he said, taking them from her hands.

"It seems silly not to," she replied, pouring a drop of detergent onto a sponge. "It's nearly eight o'clock."

His heart quickened. All day Shukumar had looked forward to the lights going out. He thought about what Shoba had said the night before, about looking in his address book. It felt good to remember her as she was then, how bold yet nervous she'd been when they first met, how hopeful. They stood side by side at the sink, their reflections fitting together in the frame of the window. It made him shy, the way he felt the first time they stood together in a mirror. He couldn't recall the last time they'd been photographed. They had stopped attending parties, went nowhere together. The film in his camera still contained pictures of Shoba, in the yard, when she was pregnant.

After finishing the dishes, they leaned against the counter, drying their hands on either end of a towel. At eight o'clock the house went black. Shukumar lit the wicks of the candles, impressed by their long, steady flames.

"Let's sit outside," Shoba said. "I think it's warm still."

They each took a candle and sat down on the steps. It seemed strange to be sitting outside with patches of snow still on the ground. But everyone was out of their houses tonight, the air fresh enough to make people restless. Screen doors opened and closed. A small parade of neighbors passed by with flashlights.

"We're going to the bookstore to browse," a silver-haired man called out. He was walking with his wife, a thin woman in a windbreaker, and holding a dog on a leash. They were the Bradfords, and they had tucked a sympathy card into Shoba and Shukumar's mailbox back in September. "I hear they've got their power."

"They'd better," Shukumar said. "Or you'll be browsing in the dark."

The woman laughed, slipping her arm through the crook of her husband's elbow. "Want to join us?"

"No thanks," Shoba and Shukumar called out together. It surprised Shukumar that his words matched hers.

He wondered what Shoba would tell him in the dark. The worst possibilities had already run through his head. That she'd had an affair. That she didn't respect him for being thirty-five and still a student. That she blamed him for being in Baltimore the way her mother did. But he knew those things weren't true. She'd been faithful, as had he. She believed in him. It was she who had insisted he go to Baltimore. What didn't they know about each other? He knew she curled her fingers tightly when she slept, that her body twitched during bad dreams. He knew it was honeydew she favored over cantaloupe. He knew that when they returned from the hospital the first thing she did when she walked into the house was pick out objects of theirs and toss them into a pile in the hallway: books from the shelves, plants from the windowsills, paintings from walls, photos from tables, pots and pans that hung from the hooks over the stove. Shukumar had stepped out of her way, watching as she moved methodically from room to room. When she was satisfied, she stood there staring at the pile she'd made, her lips drawn back in such distaste that Shukumar had thought she would spit. Then she'd started to cry.

He began to feel cold as he sat there on the steps. He felt that he needed her to talk first, in order to reciprocate.

"That time when your mother came to visit us," she said finally. "When I said one night that I had to stay late at work, I went out with Gillian and had a martini."

He looked at her profile, the slender nose, the slightly masculine set of her jaw. He remembered that night well; eating with his mother, tired from teaching two classes back to back, wishing Shoba were there to say more of the right things because he came up with only the wrong ones. It had been twelve years since his father had died, and his mother had come to spend two weeks with him and Shoba, so they could honor his father's memory together. Each night his mother cooked something his father had liked, but she was too upset to eat the dishes herself, and her eyes would well up as Shoba stroked her hand. "It's so touching," Shoba had said to him at the time. Now he pictured Shoba with Gillian, in a bar with striped velvet sofas, the one they used to go to after the movies, making sure she got her extra olive, asking Gillian for a cigarette. He imagined her complaining, and Gillian sympathizing about visits from in-laws. It was Gillian who had driven Shoba to the hospital.

"Your turn," she said, stopping his thoughts.

At the end of their street Shukumar heard sounds of a drill and the electricians shouting over it. He looked at the darkened facades of the houses lining the street. Candles glowed in the windows of one. In spite of the warmth, smoke rose from the chimney.

"I cheated on my Oriental Civilization exam in college," he said. "It was my last semester, my last set of exams. My father had died a few months before. I could see the blue book of the guy next to me. He was an American guy, a maniac. He knew Urdu and Sanskrit. I couldn't remember if the verse we had to identify was an example of a *ghazal* or not. I looked at his answer and copied it down."

It had happened over fifteen years ago. He felt relief now, having told her.

She turned to him, looking not at his face, but at his shoes—old moccasins he wore as if they were slippers, the leather at the back permanently flattened. He wondered if it bothered her, what he'd said. She took his hand and pressed it. "You didn't have to tell me why you did it," she said, moving closer to him.

They sat together until nine o'clock, when the lights came on. They heard some people across the street clapping from their porch, and televisions being turned on. The Bradfords walked back down the street, eating ice-cream cones and waving. Shoba and Shukumar waved back. Then they stood up, his hand still in hers, and went inside.

Somehow, without saying anything, it had turned into this. Into an exchange of confessions—the little ways they'd hurt or disappointed each other, and themselves. The following day Shukumar thought for hours about what to say to her. He was torn between admitting that he once ripped out a photo of a woman in one of the fashion magazines she used to subscribe to and carried it in his books for a week, or saying that he really hadn't lost the sweater-vest she bought him for their third wedding anniversary but had exchanged it for cash at Filene's, and that he had gotten drunk alone in the middle of the day at a hotel bar. For their first anniversary, Shoba had cooked a ten-course dinner just for him. The vest depressed him. "My wife gave me a sweater-vest for our anniversary," he complained to the bartender, his head heavy with cognac. "What do you expect?" the bartender had replied. "You're married."

As for the picture of the woman, he didn't know why he'd ripped it out. She wasn't as pretty as Shoba. She wore a white sequined dress, and had a sullen face and lean, mannish legs. Her bare arms were raised, her fists around her head, as if she were about to punch herself in the ears. It was an advertisement for stockings. Shoba had been pregnant at the time, her stomach suddenly immense, to the point where Shukumar no longer wanted to touch her. The first time he saw the picture he was lying in bed next to her, watching her as she read. When he noticed the magazine in the recycling pile he found the woman and tore out the page as carefully as he could. For about a week he allowed himself a glimpse each day. He felt an intense desire for the woman, but it was a desire that turned to disgust after a minute or two. It was the closest he'd come to infidelity.

He told Shoba about the sweater on the third night, the picture on the fourth. She said nothing as he spoke, expressed no protest or reproach. She simply listened, and then she took his hand, pressing it as she had before. On the third night, she told him that once after a lecture they'd attended, she let him speak to the chairman of his department without telling him that he had a dab of pâté on his chin. She'd been irritated with him for some reason, and so she'd let him go on and on, about securing his fellowship for the following semester, without putting a finger to her own chin as a signal. The fourth night, she said that she never liked the one poem he'd ever published in his life, in a literary magazine in Utah. He'd written the poem after meeting Shoba. She added that she found the poem sentimental.

Something happened when the house was dark. They were able to talk to each other again. The third night after supper they'd sat together on the sofa, and once it was dark he began kissing her awkwardly on her forehead and her face, and though it was dark he closed his eyes, and knew that she did, too. The fourth night they walked carefully upstairs, to bed, feeling together for the final step with their feet before the landing, and making love with a desperation they had forgotten. She wept without sound, and whispered his name, and traced his eyebrows with her finger in the dark. As he made love to her he wondered what he would say to her the next night, and what she would say, the thought of it exciting him. "Hold me," he said, "hold me in your arms." By the time the lights came back on downstairs, they'd fallen asleep.

The morning of the fifth night Shukumar found another notice from the electric company in the mailbox. The line had been repaired ahead of schedule, it said. He was disappointed. He had planned on making shrimp *malai* for Shoba, but when he arrived at the store he didn't feel like cooking anymore. It wasn't the same, he thought, knowing that the lights wouldn't go out. In the store the shrimp looked gray and thin. The coconut milk tin was dusty and overpriced. Still, he bought them, along with a beeswax candle and two bottles of wine.

She came home at seven-thirty. "I suppose this is the end of our game," he said when he saw her reading the notice.

She looked at him. "You can still light candles if you want." She hadn't been to the gym tonight. She wore a suit beneath the raincoat. Her makeup had been retouched recently.

When she went upstairs to change, Shukumar poured himself some wine and put on a record, a Thelonius Monk album he knew she liked.

When she came downstairs they ate together. She didn't thank him or compliment him. They simply ate in a darkened room, in the glow of a beeswax candle. They had survived a difficult time. They finished off the shrimp. They finished off the first bottle of wine and moved on to the second. They sat together until the candle had nearly burned away.

She shifted in her chair, and Shukumar thought that she was about to say something. But instead she blew out the candle, stood up, turned on the light switch, and sat down again.

"Shouldn't we keep the lights off?" Shukumar asked. She set her plate aside and clasped her hands on the table. "I want you to see my face when I tell you this," she said gently.

His heart began to pound. The day she told him she was pregnant, she had used the very same words, saying them in the same gentle way, turning off the basketball game he'd been watching on television. He hadn't been prepared then. Now he was.

Only he didn't want her to be pregnant again. He didn't want to have to pretend to be happy.

"I've been looking for an apartment and I've found one," she said, narrowing her eyes on something, it seemed, behind his left shoulder. It was nobody's fault, she continued. They'd been through enough. She needed some time alone. She had money saved up for a security deposit. The apartment was on Beacon Hill, so she could walk to work. She had signed the lease that night before coming home.

She wouldn't look at him, but he stared at her. It was obvious that she'd rehearsed the lines. All this time she'd been looking for an apartment, testing the water pressure, asking a Realtor if heat and hot water were included in the rent. It sickened Shukumar, knowing that she had spent these past evenings preparing for a life without him. He was relieved and yet he was sickened. This was what she'd been trying to tell him for the past four evenings. This was the point of her game.

Now it was his turn to speak. There was something he'd sworn he would never tell her, and for six months he had done his best to block it from his mind. Before the ultrasound she had asked the doctor not to tell her the sex of their child, and Shukumar had agreed. She had wanted it to be a surprise.

Later, those few times they talked about what had happened, she said at least they'd been spared that knowledge. In a way she almost took pride in her decision, for it enabled her to seek refuge in a mystery. He knew that she assumed it was a mystery for him, too. He'd arrived too late from Baltimore—when it was all over and she was lying on the hospital bed. But he hadn't. He'd arrived early enough to see their baby, and to hold him before they cremated him. At first he had recoiled at the suggestion, but the doctor said holding the baby might help him with the process of grieving. Shoba was asleep. The baby had been cleaned off, his bulbous lids shut tight to the world.

"Our baby was a boy," he said. "His skin was more red than brown. He had black hair on his head. He weighed almost five pounds. His fingers were curled shut, just like yours in the night."

Shoba looked at him now, her face contorted with sorrow. He had cheated on a college exam, ripped a picture of a woman out of a magazine. He had returned a sweater and got drunk in the middle of the day instead. These were the things he had told her. He had held his son, who had known life only within her, against his chest in a darkened room in an unknown wing of the hospital. He had held him until a nurse knocked and took him away, and he promised himself that day that he would never tell Shoba, because he still loved her then, and it was the one thing in her life that she had wanted to be a surprise.

Shukumar stood up and stacked his plate on top of hers. He carried the plates to the sink, but instead of running the tap he looked out the window. Outside the evening was still warm, and the Bradfords were walking arm in arm. As he watched the couple the room went dark, and he spun around. Shoba had turned the lights off. She came back to the table and sat down, and after a moment Shukumar joined her. They wept together, for the things they now knew.

THE PENTHOUSE

Andrew Holleran · 1999

The first time I saw Ashley Moore he was floating over Central Park in a balloon—in an advertisement in the *New York Times* for Saks Fifth Avenue. He had just won the Coty Award at the age of twenty-six and they were featuring his line of clothes in their stores that year. Even though Ashley Moore was not his real name, or even the first he'd attached to a label, he had, by creating a designer dress that secretaries could afford, become successful—after a series of flops—at a very young age. In the photograph he is wearing a tuxedo and a smile as he tips a bottle of champagne into the glass held by one of the models wearing his dresses (a pair of twins he used to go dancing with at the Twelfth Floor)—so handsome he looks like a thirties movie star; he and the Chrysler Building, someone said at the time, were the two most beautiful things in New York.

And, the day I saw that advertisement in the paper, he was rich and famous, too—too famous to go to the places I did, though one night at the Everard Baths that same year I heard a ruckus, turned a corner, and saw Ashley standing in the hallway, saying to a very handsome, dark-haired man with a thin mustache, who was lying on a bunk in a room with the door opened: "What is this? I can't even get you on the phone, and here you are reading the *Post* stark naked for everyone with the price of a locker to *shtup*." That was the first time I heard Ashley's un-nerving voice; as hard and flat as a frying pan he had just used to hit you over the head. ("Next to Ashley," someone said, "Thelma Ritter sang bel canto.") The man in the room was the Prince, I learned later—Ashley's soon-to-be-ex-boyfriend, a beautiful Jew who indeed used to read the newspaper at the baths while waiting for someone to stop in, and who eventually, after opening up a sandwich shop in Soho, met an accountant and moved to a suburb in New Jersey—as far from Ashley as he could get. Ashley would never have gone to the baths for any other reason; at least I never saw him there again. He was living at the time with a famous decorator in a part of town on the Upper East Side a friend used to call "the Land of Ormolu," and his social life was fairly private. Even when they came to Fire Island, for instance, they vanished moments after walking ashore from the seaplane; nor did Ashley ever dance at the Sandpiper, or stroll the beach—he remained all weekend inside a vast oceanfront compound people called "the House of Pain" (because meals there were as formal as state dinners) in a harem of one, completely invisible to the outside world.

The world that he worked in, however, was becoming increasingly visible in the late seventies, which is when I saw it for the first time after a friend got a few of us invitations to a fashion show Michaele Voll-bracht was having on a covered pier on the Hudson River, where we sat down a few rows from the elevated runway. The place was mobbed. The lights dimmed. Rows of gaunt, grave people leaned forward with ex-pectant faces. The music began. The models walked out in sequined clothes with a circus motif, turned, walked back again. There were lights, music, a sense of drama, and a well-dressed, attentive audience. "But no script," said my friend when it was over, echoing my thoughts. "It was everything you get in the theater except the play. They had nothing but the clothes on their backs."

"That's fashion," said the publicist who had brought us.

"I think it's mostly about evening," a woman was saying to a TV reporter in the aisle to our right. "I think it's a very American collection, rooted, of course, in couture, but still very much of New York of today. I think it's about the past *and* a new way to be modern."

"Oh please. This show isn't about anything," the publicist muttered to us as we filed past her, "but selling rags. At least Ashley never pretends that it's anything else."

He knew Ashley, and his was the next show he took us to: Ashley's last, as it turned out, in a large room at the Fashion Institute of Technology. He had just sued his backers for a large sum of money, and whether or not he knew the outcome of his lawsuit that night, you could tell he was mocking the whole milieu. Not only was there no music, drama, production values, or theme—the audience arrived on what, once you walked past a curtain, turned out to be the runway itself, so that you found yourself suddenly being stared at by everyone down below; a reversal of roles that was by no means a pleasant surprise for everyone—though Ashley, when I glanced down at him, seemed to be getting a kick out of the momentary shock on the arriving faces. Down on the floor, out of the glare, one walked among the dresses on mannequins as if in an atelier—dummies people ignored as they drank white wine and gossiped. It was Ashley's way of saying: no more spectacle, no more va-va-voom. These are the dresses, on dummies, inspect them if you like. The lawsuit against his backers had already been filed; when it was settled a month later he had no real reason to produce another line of clothes—financial, that is.

When asked if he missed his old life—it's rare for someone to retire at the age of thirty-two—he said: "You know? I *did* it, and I don't miss it." For a few months I don't think he even noticed its loss; like some star that sends light out far into the galaxy long after it has collapsed, his face was still in all six windows of I. Magnin's in San Francisco, and May Cohen's in Jacksonville, Florida—where, like an actor taking his show on the road, he went, the winter after his last fashion show, to emcee a charity auction, and to decorate a house in the annual tour of designer homes, and, in Huntsville, to chair a fashion show for a diabetes foundation. In Denver he went to the gay rodeo, in Milwaukee he appeared on a talk show, and then one day, after that gave out, he returned to Manhattan, to find that his career was not even talked about. ("I *used* to be famous," he always told his tricks.) And so, just when his colleague Halston went on to introduce Ultrasuede and make appearances with Liza Minnelli, Elsa Peretti, and Victor Hugo at Studio, Ashley moved downtown and retired to a penthouse.

The penthouse he rented commands the north side of Abingdon Square, like some fortress castle, overlooking what was the heart of gay life in 1980, the Village. The previous owner had been a drug dealer named Norman Pearl—a man who would flood the terrace in winter and hold ice-skating parties where all the guests, on LSD, went whirling around to Donna Summer. The building had a canopy, a mirrored lobby, and a doorman, and the triangular park across the street gave it a sort of Upper East Side elegance; while only a few blocks away were things the Upper East Side did not have—the abandoned piers along the river where sex could be had at all hours of the day and night, and, a few blocks in other directions, back-room bars like the Toilet and the Strap. Ten stories up, on the terrace of the penthouse, however, one felt above it all.

And you were: The penthouse itself was not large, but the terrace, five times its size, had views of the river and harbor. On a summer night, sitting inside while the wind buffeted the canvas awnings, people felt, surrounded by its white candlelit walls, as if they were in a house on the coast of Turkey; or, gazing down at Wall Street's lighted towers from the terrace outside, as if it weren't a cottage at all but a ship that had been anchored off a steep, volcanic island just east of the World Trade Center, an island you might swim to on the right drug. In other words, the place was enchanting; the reason people went when he asked them—the penthouse.

He had them come over, I suspect now, the way a decorator furnishes a library with books that the owners will never read but which are an essential element of the decor. It's not that Ashley was unread—he could quote by heart Somerset Maugham—but he must have felt some desire for an intellectual life (if only the ambience) when, the first night he had twenty of us to dinner, he looked up, seated on a pillow underneath the spot-lighted Hurrell photograph of Joan Crawford that hung above the mantelpiece, and said: "This is what I like. I want my table surrounded with writers and drag queens and hustlers and professors. You know? Berlin in the thirties. Paris in the twenties. I want the *mix*." Some mix! Louis, who worked the door at Studio 54 two nights a week and was so obsessed with fashion models he had constructed a little altar in his bedroom to a Bruce Weber discovery he was stalking named Jeff Aquilon; his roommate, a limousine driver equally obsessed with Jackie Onassis; a novelist who'd not published a thing since his first book eight years ago; a professor from Rutgers writing a book on Edith Wharton; a drag queen named Honeypot Larue whose boyfriend was a bouncer at Xenon; a drug dealer named Doctor Love who'd burned down a town house on Bank Street after the landlord caught him manufacturing angel dust there and kicked him out; a young decorator who spent most of that summer recuperating from a chin implant that kept shifting; two even younger graduates of FIT who, after a year spent selling clothes at Macy's, decided it would be easier to work as hustlers; Victor, the author of a book on Hollywood's treatment of homosexuals, whose lectures in local bookstores Ashley attended dressed like a beatnik at Deux Magots, with a black beret and scarf round his neck, until Ashley started having people over to see the slide show in his penthouse—the only person Ashley deferred to on the subject of the movies (though that had its limitations: "I never sleep with people who know more about the movies than I do," Ashley always said when someone asked if he and Victor were lovers).

The penthouse was perfect for such an evening—even if Ashley had not invited the people who came there. ("You know," he said to Victor after hosting his thirty-eighth birthday party, "your friends are nicer than my friends.") It was nearly devoid of furniture—some potted jade plants, a mirrored wall against which eight gilt ballroom chairs guarded a low, black-lacquered table, and big white canvas pillows guests sat on when they ate—and therefore easy to use for lectures and soirees. "The seventies were about lounging," Ashley explained to us in that hard, flat voice our first night there, just days after that decade's expiration. "It was about banquettes and Quaaludes. The eighties will be about conversation. That's why I got these chairs where you have to sit up straight, and sparkle. I expect everyone to sparkle," he said to his visitors, striking them dumb with fears of inadequacy instead. As for the chairs themselves, or the rent on the penthouse, there was one rule: One asked no questions. When someone gasped, "Where did you *get* these chairs?" he was ignored. ("Why should I tell him where I got the chairs?" he said in that steely voice. "He can't afford them. What's the point?") You learned very quickly: His cat didn't like being touched, and Ashley didn't like being queried on any subject. This introduced a certain tension. When that same evening the decorator asked Ashley, over dinner, why Gloria Vanderbilt had been turned down by the co-op board of River House, Ashley put down his chopsticks, glanced at the cat, pointed to the man, and said: "Kill, Doris. Kill!" Then he droned, over our nervous laughter: "Some people want to know how the Incas built those incredible walls in Cuzco, or why fog forms, or how the stars still emit light even after they've died—George wants to know why River House told Gloria to take a hike." And George started to choke so badly on his noodles he had to go to the bathroom and throw up.

We were invited that first night to Ashley's to watch the opening episode of a series on PBS called *I, Claudius*, broadcast that winter, though as the novelist muttered to me when we passed each other in the hall: "This is the closest any of us will ever come to the court of Caligula, and I don't mean what's on TV."

"You got that right," an emphatic voice said; we looked and saw Honeypot Larue powdering his nose in front of a mirror in Ashley's bedroom. "He always makes you wonder—who's next?"

"It's not that," said the professor in a low voice as he joined us, "it's that he doesn't bother to pretend—it's rather refreshing, almost exhilarating, in a way, the refusal to observe the niceties. He has simply stripped away the genteel *politesse*."

"I agree," said the novelist. "No doubt because he's operated in the business world, a world where politeness has no function, where money is money. That's why he's ended up sounding like—" He stopped, then said: "I'm not sure what it is he sounds like. He sounds like—"

"A gangster," said Honeypot Larue, still fluffing before the mirror. The novelist and the professor stared at him.

"Look," said Honeypot, "I don't know why you're bothering to figure him out—it's very simple. He's mean! He's a mean queen and that's all there is to it!"

"What do you mean?" said the professor.

"I mean, she's mean," he said. "Look. Here's an example. I ran into him last night on Christopher Street on my way home from the Strap. He said, 'Hi, you!'" He paused, powder puff in hand, and looked over at us. "You know, of course, he doesn't know any of our names—that's why when you see him out somewhere, he always yells, 'Hi, you.' He asked what I was doing. I said I'd just been at the Strap. He said: 'A pretty thing like you wasting your seed there!' And I thought: That's the first nice thing he's ever said to me."

"Nice?" said the novelist.

"That I was a pretty thing," he said. "Hang around, you'll see. You can't enjoy yourself here because you never know what he's going to say next. I think I prefer a slightly more romantic approach," said Honeypot Larue.

"But you see," said Louis breathlessly at our backs, "that's Ashley.

Ashley isn't romantic. He has no illusions. Ashley is very direct," he said in a hushed, worshipful tone.

Ashley was very direct. When the professor from Rutgers asked him another question later that evening over dessert, we all went mute. We were sitting on the pillows eating blanc mange when the professor noticed the floor-to-ceiling bookcase behind Ashley filled entirely with bound volumes of *Vogue* magazines stretching back to the twenties, and he said, in the ecstatic voice of someone who has just seen an unexpected explanation for the universe: "Do you mean you do *re*search the way I do for an article? You mean you look at old copies of *Vogue* for ideas, you actually study them?" And Ashley, putting down his champagne, gave him that look which only a basilisk has and—after a beat, and a raised eyebrow—replied: "How many ways do you think there are to make *shmatte*?" That was all Ashley ever said about his profession.

His profession actually was increasingly academic. He still spoke of going uptown occasionally to a party at Halston's or Giorgio Sant'Angelo's, or to dinner with Fabrice, but he was no longer working, in a city that does little else during the day. He spoke on the phone with the people who'd helped him during his career—the backers who still wanted to introduce something with his name on it (anything, apparently), the magazine editors, columnists, models, and publicists with whom he'd partied when he was showing a line twice a year. But that was all he did, and when he hung up the phone, he found himself with people who were much more fascinated than he was with fashion and excited to be in the company of one of its names. Our fantasy was Ashley—even if we were all afraid of his turning his attention on us, and could not understand what he was doing with us in the first place, so far from the Land of Ormolu. Then one afternoon it occurred to me. I was riding my bike down the old West Side Highway, eye level with the upper story of the rotting piers that bordered it, when I stopped to watch a man silhouetted in the broken windows of a pier waiting for someone to approach him, and then I looked over at Ashley's pent-house, its green-and-white-striped awnings shining in the sun, like a cruise ship that was indeed anchored off some island to let its passengers go ashore. It was the only tall building over there; there was nothing between it and the river to impede its view of the Hudson and the piers; it seemed to both snub, and preside over, the black roofs beneath it—part of the Village but not quite. And I realized why Ashley was there—for the same reason we were, though I never actually saw him at the piers, or in the bars (one could not imagine Ashley standing in the Ramrod like everyone else, waiting), and never asked him, when I arrived at the penthouse, God forbid, what he had done that day with his wealth, good looks, and freedom . . . even when he complained one afternoon, "The only people who cruise me are middle-aged Chinese businessmen and nine-foot-tall Puerto Rican transvestites," since this obviously was a joke. Ashley was very handsome—a square-jawed, all-American, masculine-appearing, corn-fed blond—though you never knew, when the door to the penthouse opened, whether this masculine-looking all-American would be standing there bare-chested in camouflage fatigues, dog tags, and paratrooper boots, or in a Titian-blue ball gown by Charles James, looking like a debutante on the Cunard line in 1933. Sometimes it was both. ("The trouble with you," we overheard him tell a young art critic that evening, "is that you're afraid to let the *woman* in you out! Haven't you ever been running down the boardwalk in the Pines and felt your tits bobbing? Forget this article you're trying to finish on Matisse—do one on Dovima!")

Nevertheless, whatever he wore you never commented on it—Ashley trusted a compliment no more than he liked a question. You let him lead you without a word into the penthouse in his fireman's boots, gold lamé jockstrap, and diamond earrings to a terrace full of people who were equally speechless and thus looked even more, when they turned toward you, like the cover for an album by the Village People. (The penthouse was often crowded with men who dressed not as what they

were but what they were hoping to attract; as if the object of their sexual
fantasy was only looking for a mirror image of himself. The FIT graduate who could talk for an hour about what to look for in a moisturizer
dressed like a pipe fitter on an offshore oil rig; the novelist like a Puerto
Rican boxer on the skids, the drug dealer like an investment banker at
Morgan Guaranty, the Edith Wharton scholar like a Hell's Angel from
upstate New York.) Then there was the core group—the ever present
scattering of men with dark mustaches and dark eyes, as perfectly
matched as a necklace of black pearls: Ashley's type, or rather attempt
to replace the Prince (home before the TV with his hubby in suburban
New Jersey). "Where does he *get* these people?" the novelist asked one
evening.

"He gets them in those Chinese-Cuban restaurants on Eighth Avenue," Louis said. "He walks right in when he sees a cute one, when
they're eating alone, and invites them down. I was with him today when
he did it! He found one in the elevator in Mario Buatta's building, he
finds 'em everywhere, he could find one in the Arctic Circle!" he said
with a whoop. "His type is very definite. He found one in Georgia last
week! We were returning from Thomasville, through all these white,
WASP towns, and when we got to Atlanta, Ashley got out of the taxi,
took one look at the men waiting for cabs, and said, 'Mmm, Jews.' You
have to look like the Prince to get in bed with *him*."

The bed was in a room you saw when you went to use the bathroom;
in the corner, with black sheets and pillowcases, surrounded by a weight
bench and bar bells, and high heels scattered on the floor, and curtains
stirring at the windows whose light made it a luminous and shadowed
lair that made you think of a spider, a spider that devoured its mate,
since his consort was never around for very long. Each Sunday that
winter when we went over to watch the latest episode of *I, Claudius*, and
eat Chinese takeout, we would find the previous boyfriend gone, or
looking abashed; few of them lasted any longer than an emperor's sister
on the BBC. Those trips down to earth produced a constantly changing

cast of characters who paradoxically all looked alike—strangers who were brought up to the penthouse and then dropped just as quickly. None was conventionally handsome, at least compared to the perfection of the Prince. I remember a slightly overweight statistician from Staten Island, a shoe salesman from Bayonne, an orthodontist from the Five Towns, and a Cuban who was famous on Fire Island for his deep voice and donkey dick. But none of them, not even the last, endured. ("He asked me if we were having an affair," I overheard Ashley say one night as he came into the kitchen. "I told him, 'We're having a sexual encounter.'") The only way to keep going to the penthouse, it seemed, was not to become a trick, or even a favorite; I knew people were doomed when Ashley went up to them and showed them a photograph he'd ripped out of a French fashion magazine and said: "I saw this and thought of you." (Fatal words!) No one survived this sentence; he tasted and moved on; it was unnerving even to be walked to the door, much less have him wait for you in the doorway while the elevator came up—staring at you as he stood there with one arm on his hip and the other on top of the door, like Elizabeth Taylor in the poster for *Cat on a Hot Tin Roof.* The minute the doors closed on the elevator, people let out sighs of relief.

Sometimes Ashley walked out with us when we left the building—wearing Thierry Mugler or Kansai, and a little black leather jacket from Gaultier he'd brought back from Paris that looked confusingly like something sold on the rack in a New Jersey mall. "Whadda ya think? Am I overdressed for evening?" he would ask, not expecting a reply. We didn't know what he expected, especially when he decided to stay with us and prowl the town. (When out with Ashley, we were told to call him "Clem," unless there was a line at the door, whereupon he used his real name and we all got in immediately.) "I know two new wave queens on Fourteenth Street who are having a party," Louis said as we walked out one night. "We could go there. But I hate new wave. I hate the clothes, the music, the look." After a beat, Ashley said: "It has aspects." An hour later, we were there. Of course, the rest of the week he had other, better places to go, one felt: the life we read about in the *Post*. The dinner for Karl Lagerfeld, the party at Lutèce. Whatever was on Page Six. Ashley talked to two women every day—his mother, and Claudia Cohen. What minor gossip the entourage brought back every Sunday night when we assembled to watch *I, Claudius* Ashley listened to with a stone face and expressionless eye. There wasn't much he didn't know. The only person he seemed curious about—and listened to—was the novelist, and he brought no gossip whatsoever, because he'd spent all day sitting home trying to think of something to write, and didn't even try to provide what everyone thought Ashley wanted.

Nobody could. I was happiest in the kitchen, rinsing dishes after dinner before *I, Claudius* began, while Louis loaded the dishwasher beside me; out of range of whatever it was that made being at the penthouse so nerve-racking. (The novelist dubbed the place "The House of Good Taste and Bad Manners," two things often in conjunction, he said, in New York and Los Angeles. But that didn't explain it.) It was as if Ashley had gone to all that effort to create this beautiful space—the bleached floors and striped awnings, the lilies in a spotlight—like some insect that waits at the bottom of a flower only to devour anything foolish enough to be beguiled by its beauty; as if the beauty was the object, and our appreciation of it a minor detail. He was one of those people who put a great effort into hospitality and then, once the guest has arrived, begins to extract a price for it all. At least that's what it felt like even in the relative safety of the kitchen, while the party went on in the candlelit living room, where Ashley sat surrounded by a circle of men with mustaches and dark good looks.

The Prince was still Ashley's main topic when we met him. "Real men don't move their hands and arms around when they talk," Ashley said to someone one night. "They sit entirely still. Have you ever seen the Prince? He hardly moves a muscle. He's like Mount Rushmore. It makes me crazy." "I saw the Prince," said the bouncer. "In Soho." "People go by his shop just to see him through the window," said Ashley.

"He makes sandwiches. He makes cakes. He's a big success. He won't take my calls." One day, lying in the sun on the terrace, he said to the novelist, "I think the Prince was it. I don't think I'll ever have another boyfriend." "Why not?" said the novelist. "Because I'll never find anyone like him. And even if I could—I'd drive him away, the way I lost the Prince. I've got money, looks, fame, and a big cock. Who can have sex with me?" he said, turning to the novelist, his forehead beaded with sweat, his eyes invisible beneath two slices of cucumber, his head covered in a towel wrapped as a turban. "It's not that," said the novelist. "It's not what you are. It's what you're not that's your problem."

"What am I not?" said Ashley.

Everyone held his breath; but the novelist, without even looking at Ashley, said: "You're not—vulnerable. The problem with you, Ashley, is that you haven't got any problems. You're too successful. You have no depth."

"So what should I do?" said Ashley. "Invest unwisely? Dress like Iggy Pop?"

"No," said the novelist, "but—"

"But what?" said Ashley, putting on more Bain de Soleil.

"You need some problems," he said.

"I've had my problems," said Ashley. "I've had my ups and downs."

"You have?" said the novelist.

"I've had lawsuits," said Ashley, "dresses that bombed, friends burning to death on foam-rubber mattresses, hair loss, bankruptcy, boyfriends who wouldn't commit, lovers who ripped my head off when I set the table wrong. I lived for eight years in the House of Pain."

"Well," said the novelist, "you seem to have survived it all with no permanent sadness."

"What's that?" said Ashley. "A bad Tony?"

"It's Lucretius," said the novelist. "Tears are in the nature of things. Which is why this is so hard to take," he said, waving an arm at the terrace. "It has no tragic vision."

"Please," said Ashley. "You get up and you throw some flowers in a vase, or, if you're Jeanne Moreau, in the salad," he said, referring to a movie we'd seen the night before, "you put Chanel Number Nine on your tush, and call a boyfriend for lunch. What's so difficult? The one thing I've never understood is the desire to suffer. Life's bad enough. Just yesterday I had a tragic vision—when I ran into Julio Ramirez. It was a horrible shock."

"Cancer?" said the decorator, leaning forward.

"What cancer?" said Ashley. "He shaved his mustache off."

"*No!*" gasped the decorator.

"They're all doing it," said Ashley. "Armando shaved his off last month. Now his whole set has done it and it's starting to spread. You watch. All it leaves are these thin, wounded little mouths. These prim lips. What people refuse to accept is that they look best one way, and when they find that, like Perry Ellis, they should stick to it—no matter what—till the day they die. It's called 'classic.' But no, people think it's time for something new. So we're going to see thousands of thin, wounded little mouths in the coming months! *Brace* yourself. Have you been to the Boy Bar?"

"No," said the novelist.

"They would die before they grew a mustache," said Ashley. "Everything about them is thin and wounded. Not just the lips."

"There's a new bar on Second Avenue," said the decorator, "that's even worse! It looks like an art gallery—all white, with blinding lights. I walked by it last night. I felt like a vampire!"

"That's how you're supposed to feel," said Ashley. "They don't want to look at you. They want to look at each other. So they turn up the lights. They make every moment last call. Because they know that makes you feel like Bela Lugosi."

"But why?" said the decorator. "It's so mean!"

"Of course it's mean," said Ashley. "They want our apartments. I see them sitting in cafes on St. Marks Place, all in black. They look like a

Jules Feiffer cartoon. You want to go up to them and say: 'Are you aware this has been done?' But you don't, because it would be a waste of time. They don't know Feiffer. All they know is *Gilligan's Island*. They've spent their whole childhoods watching TV. It's made them ironic. And thin and wounded. Not just the lips."

"Some of them are cute," said Louis.

"Some of them could sit on my face and I'd be a very happy woman," said Ashley. "But very few. Because there's one problem."

"And that is—" said the professor.

"They would die before they'd grow a mustache. Which is unfortunate for those of us who like them. If women had mustaches, I'd be straight. My idea of a man—forgive me if I'm narrow-minded—involves a mustache."

"But you don't have a mustache," said the decorator.

"Exactly," said Ashley. "Some of these kids are shaving their bodies, too. They've got hair on their head, and hair on their balls, and nothing in between. They're into retro and Nair. Victor runs around with them now. They love Victor. They get to talk about movies *and* be political. I watched his demonstration on West Street yesterday through my binoculars. They were yelling at cops on horses—like Streisand in *The Way We Were*."

"I wouldn't get near a cop on a horse," barked the gay postcard tycoon. "The horse could kick, and ruin your hair plugs."

"Victor goes right up to the nag," said Ashley. "He lives for these confrontations. He loves these kids. He brings them by before the demonstrations. I serve them lunch."

"But what do they *make* of all this?" said the decorator.

"They walk right out and stare at the view," said Ashley. "They don't even see the rest. They couldn't care less about the bleached floors, or the chinoiserie, or the Coromandel. They don't get the references to Chanel. They're like Ninotchka—little Communists. They wear black, Levi's cutoffs, and shoes that would crack a fire hydrant. They look like

ICBMs. They're out to kick ass. Something I've never wanted to do, personally. There's other things you can do with ass. So tell me about Proust," he said, turning to the novelist, who had promised to give Ashley a reading list. "What's his *shtik*?"

"His *shtik*?" said the novelist, raising his eyebrows.

"In twenty-five words or less," said Ashley.

"Well . . . ," said the novelist. "Proust is a man who went to a party— and then went home and wrote a book about what was wrong with it. Which is essentially what all novelists do," he said. "We go to a party and then tell why it was awful."

"Like Victor and the movies."

"Yes," said the novelist. "Victor sees movies morally—in terms of homophobia."

"Oh please," said Ashley impatiently. "So what if Franklin Pangborn's a little nelly in *Flying Down to Rio*? Who cares what straight people think about us? I don't care if they understand what I do in bed. *I* don't even understand what I do in bed, I could care less what *they* think about it. Straight people's opinions don't interest me, and the only reason what we do interests them," he said, wiping the lenses of his little dark glasses with white frames, "is because they're so deeply bored. I think you're bored," he said, turning to the novelist.

"I am," said the novelist, sitting up and blushing, as if he'd been found out. "Something is over. I feel I've stayed too long at a party, only I don't know where to go next. So I stay. But something is over."

"So find what's starting," said Ashley.

"Not this new wave stuff!" said the novelist, sitting forward. "I refuse to go to the Mudd Club and wear safety pins in my ears, or go to Roxy and roller-skate to what's left of disco. I think it *all* sucks!"

"Don't be so picky," said Ashley. "So hard to please. It's like the pier. If I see something I like, I take my bike, go downstairs, and race over— he may be gone, or taken, or had a sex change by the time I get there, but I made the effort, and there'll be someone else. It's like fashion. Of the moment. Though I'm working harder at the pier than I ever did on Seventh Avenue. It's difficult to have sex when you can have it any hour of the day or night. That's why I don't live in San Francisco. As it is, I'm spending too much time on the pier. The pier is not for people with short attention spans. I won't even wait for a table at Mortimer's. What am I doing at the piers? I'll tell you what I'm doing at the piers. I'm looking for the Prince. Who doesn't go to the piers. Who's living in New Jersey. While I'm meeting schmucks."

"I'm not meeting anyone," said the decorator.

"Wait till your chin settles," said Ashley.

"Is that all it takes?" said the professor. "Because I'm not meeting anyone either!"

"Because you have a brain," said Ashley. "You're better off. Listen," he said. "If you end up the same way after sleeping with them that you were *before* you slept with them, why sleep with them? It just means you have to change the sheets."

"But sleeping with them is heaven," said the novelist.

"Whose heaven?" said Ashley. "Heaven is going around the world this fall on the *QE2*. Did I tell you Louis and I are going around the world on the *QE2*? This fall. He'll be my escort. God knows I've got the dresses for a cruise."

No one said a word—torn between their registration of this addition to Ashley's glamour, and the realization that, come autumn, all this would be ending. Then Ashley put the binoculars down and said, "What do you think about salad?" and looked at the entourage.

"What do *you* think about salad?" the professor said, with the beatific smile of a baby, so happy to be at Ashley's penthouse about to have lunch that he had forgotten the cardinal rule.

"What do *I* think about salad?" said Ashley in a dark voice. "I know what *I* think about salad. I want to know what *you* think about salad. I could care less if I ever saw lettuce again in my life."

There was a silence in which all the hospitality had collapsed, like a soufflé, and even the professor's smile curdled on his face; but then the doorbell rang, and Ashley left the terrace. "Oh, *cooool!*" we heard the new arrival say in a deep voice, "A real penthouse! I've never seen a penthouse! You really live here?" and Ashley reply in his flat monotone: "You could say so. But it's a constant effort. People think you have a penthouse the way you have a T-shirt. But you don't. It's work all day long." And then onto the terrace came Ashley, Victor, and the new face—a big, hairy young man wearing a black T-shirt that said VENCER-EMOS, and a yarmulke; the latest object of Ashley's eyes.

Someone who refused to come to the penthouse (and claimed our host was a "disgrace to his profession!") said that Ashley Moore surrounded himself with people he could dominate—that we were all losers—but this seemed slightly reductive. The new arrival, whose father ran a yeshiva, was quite bright; even if all we discussed that day was Crawford's performance in *Mildred Pierce*. No one, at Ashley's, ever discussed serious subjects. Nobody there wanted to. The staffer at the UN didn't want to talk about famine relief in Africa, for instance, or the city attorney about problems facing New York, or Ashley about fashion; they all wanted to listen to the hustlers talk about their johns, or Honeypot Larue tell us why the big, beefy bouncers from Brooklyn wanted to go home with him and not a real woman. The two FIT graduates who had quit Macy's to hustle ("We're still in retail!") but now spent the day sitting at home waiting for the phone to ring; the novelist, who spent the day staring at the walls of his tiny apartment on West Street waiting for an idea; even Victor, and his disciple, the young gay militant, spent that afternoon in a deep discussion of whether this winter's coat for gay men would be the green nylon bomber with the orange lining.

"I remember car coats," said Ashley at one point. "Car coats on men walking their dogs on Fifty-third Street while the dogs peed. With bombers, you can see the butt and basket. With car coats, you were always guessing." I could not imagine Ashley guessing. The most unsettling thing about Ashley, someone said, was that he knew exactly what he wanted in a world where most of us do not.

The latter category, he said, included the people who came to the penthouse; we were like dancers between songs who slow down and even stop while trying to decide if the new theme being introduced is worth dancing to. The novelist was right. The year we went to Ashley's was a strange time: Something was ending, but nothing had replaced it, and Ashley's penthouse seemed like an oasis. Outside, the city seemed increasingly cold—the bigger the dance club, the colder it was. Bond's— as big as an airplane hangar—featured, the night Ashley took us to the opening, not only a row of dancing fountains, but so much fake fog the guests refused to evacuate when a real fire started because they thought it was an effect. At the Gilded Grape we danced beneath ten Puerto Ricans in gilded G-strings on trapezes. At Le Club we ran into people like Ashley's former business partner, now a cable TV hostess, writhing on the floor between the legs of a Turkish wrestler covered in olive oil. ("Listen," said Ashley before the decorator could speak, "don't complain. It keeps her off the street and off the phone.") At Twelve West I walked in one night to find Ashley and Patti LaBelle judging the Mister Blueboy Contest. After the winner (a sobbing bartender from Ohio) was announced, people started dancing to a medley from *My Fair Lady* set to a disco beat. At Roxy they were roller-skating to the music. Even the fashion shows—the novelist said—were empty and meaningless. ("There was a woman weeping," said the novelist when we got to the penthouse one night. "*Weeping.*" "She weeps at all of them," Ashley said. "Except Stephen Sprouse. They had a fight.") Our visits to the penthouse, after all, took up only a small portion of our lives—Sunday nights, the occasional afternoon; the rest of the time we were out in the city, and the city in 1980 was changing.

Sometimes, on a weeknight, I would see the professor—whose chief activity, now that he was on sabbatical, seemed to be avoiding his book—at a bar like Ty's or the Eagle. It was odd seeing another member of the entourage in these places. We hadn't much in common with each other—only that we went to Ashley's—and since what we had in common could be viewed from so many angles, even remarks about our host were tentative and brief. There was no way of knowing, after all, if the other person admired, or despised, Ashley—found him the acme of glamour or vulgarity. Ashley himself was a hybrid. Raised by a dancer at the Copacabana whose husband—a cowboy she had met on his way to Germany during World War Two—had died before Ashley was born; raised to be, in essence, a showgirl, I wonder if Ashley himself knew what he was. "I'm sorry we didn't have more time to get to know each other," a playwright who'd been Ashley's neighbor on Fire Island one summer said when I overheard them talking on the terrace. "It's just as well," said Ashley. "If we'd spent time together, you'd have seen right through me, and then you'd have hated me."

We were all confused that year—the professor in the window of Ty's, ignoring the room as he stared at the empty street outside, wasn't just a man looking out the window of a bar on a slow night; he was all of us, waiting for something new. Christopher Street was deserted on weeknights now. The young queens preferred the East Village, where, on St. Marks Place, a group called Fags Against Facial Hair had stenciled on the sidewalk the words clones, go home. Even at the Cockring, the last of the small dance clubs, whose floor was the size of Ashley's bedroom, they were starting to play music that brought the dancers to a halt, like hunters in a ballet some witch has cast a spell upon; songs so raw, barbed, snotty we would hang our heads and walk off the floor— leaving a single, scrawny youth in baggy clothes bouncing around like a corpse being given electric shocks to bring it back to life. His movements took up a lot of space. The dance looked childish and affected— a spoiled brat's tantrum—as if he resented, not enjoyed, being in New York. Even Louis, who loved every new thing, hung around the penthouse after Studio, unless Ashley wanted to go out. Eventually the penthouse became for us what an embassy must be for frightened

travelers in a country undergoing a revolution, a place where it was re-
assuring, no matter what was going on outside, to hear Ashley tell new-
comers as he led them through the room, "There are only two looks
now, Chinese and modern. This is a little bit of both." Occasionally he
tried to help the people who seemed most stuck. After watching Louis,
for instance, who could not live on what he earned two nights at Studio,
walk up the beach at Fire Island one day telling friends on blankets that
he needed a job, Ashley said when he got back, "The trouble with you
is that you know five thousand queens from the Pines and Studio, but
what you need to know are five people who can actually give you a job."
(Of course no one knew quite what Louis did; the little business card he
had printed said merely "Consulting.") Finally Ashley hired Louis himself as an assistant—though all that seemed to entail was hailing cabs
when they went out. But the decorator he got a client. The hustlers he
recommended to a madam in the East Fifties. The drug dealer he sent
to Minneapolis to dry out. The limo driver he found work for with a
woman who lived in the apartment beneath Jackie O. And Victor—who
still lived in an apartment with a tub in the kitchen—he got a new
shower and bathroom, designed by the decorator, though not without
demanding a strict accounting of costs before reimbursing him. ("She's
the cheapest white woman on the planet!" the decorator fumed. "Those
ballroom chairs he has? They're rented from a catering firm! She lives
in perpetual terror that she's going to be taken advantage of! She never
leaves the apartment unless it's free! I'm writing a book—called *Deco-
rating for Jews!*" "Ashley isn't Jewish," said the novelist. "Who cares?"
said the decorator, and stomped out of the room.) The shower and bathroom were the exception—most of what he did was, very astutely, tell
people what they should do to get on with their lives.

Even the novelist—whom he respected in a way he did not the others, because, someone said, Ashley wanted to be a writer (and the novelist wanted to be a designer)—needed, in Ashley's eyes, a fundamental
change. "For instance, let's start with basics. Where do you live?"

"At West Street and Bank," he said.

"In Bob Ritter's building?"

"Yes."

"The police call that building 'Love, American Style,'" said Ashley as he fastened a small faux pearl clip earring to his ear. "Because it's filled with hookers and fags and freaks."

"That's what I am," said the novelist.

"No, you're not," said Ashley. "You're a Princeton graduate. You're a nice Ivy League boy living *la vie bohème*. You want to live in a place your parents can never visit. Well, you got it. The hallways in that building stink of piss. They're so narrow, you can't even go down them in a hat. You have to exit that building sideways in drag. I lived there in 1969. The apartments are tiny and someone is always throwing up in the mailbox. I have a proposition."

"Which is?" said the novelist.

"I may have to leave town at any moment," said Ashley. "Because I'm in a pyramid."

"What's a pyramid?" asked the young yeshiva graduate.

"It's a Ponzi scheme," said Victor, intervening before Ashley could even consider telling the cat to kill him. "You put in five hundred or a thousand bucks, and you get your money back only when you bring somebody new into it. It's a way to double your money."

"The money's the least of it," said Ashley in his hard, flat tone, cutting back into the conversation like a buzz saw. "It's a reason to be social. It's for ladies who lunch. They get to dress up, go out, show off their Bill Blass, and dish. It's the latest version of mah-jongg. But it's illegal. Because the city doesn't want anyone making money unless it gets a cut. You can't go out at night in Thierry Mugler without getting beaten up, and they're upset about pyramids. Go figure. Anyway, they're going to raid one. In fact, they're going to raid ours, because we've got names that will make better copy for Page Six. The district attorney isn't stupid. He knows what makes the news. I've been advised to go

away—till Morgenthau cools his chops. I've been asked to design Myra
Blanchard's wedding in Montecito. I'm going to do *A Midsummer
Night's Dream*. On a hilltop above Santa Barbara. And I want you to
move in here. With Doris. I've got her food in the pantry. She's no problem. She doesn't even like to be touched."

"I can't," said the novelist.

"Why not?" said Ashley.

"I'd have to readjust to new surroundings," he said. "Besides, I use
the people in my building as characters. I could never give them up."

"So what about you?" said Ashley, turning to Victor.

"I'd feel guilty," said Victor, squirming on his mat.

"Why?" said Ashley.

"I couldn't walk past the doorman," Victor said.

"Because?"

"He's a doorman," said Victor.

"What's wrong with that?" said Ashley.

"No one should be a doorman," said Victor. "I would never know
what to say when I walked by him."

"Hello will do," said Ashley. "You don't have to discuss Marx."

"But he's older than I am," said Victor. "He shouldn't be a doorman."

"This is a free country," said Ashley. "Anyone who wants to can be
a doorman. And he makes a lot more money than you two do."

"Money isn't important to me," said the novelist.

"What is?" said Ashley.

"Beauty," said the novelist.

"Beauty!" Ashley barked.

"Creating art," said the novelist. "Or . . . trying to," he said, blushing.

"Forget art," said Ashley. "You need a book that will sell. Then
worry about art. Nobody makes art thinking they're making art. It's the
wrong way to go about it. The dresses Charles James made that are in
the Brooklyn Museum he used to pin up on Puerto Ricans in the Chel-
sea Hotel. Because he loved to make dresses. First you have to make a

dress, then *maybe* the dress is art. With a book, first you have to enter-tain." He raised his head and looked over at the novelist through the little white-rimmed sunglasses he was wearing beneath a lime green towel he'd wrapped around his head as a turban. "I could write a best-seller in a year," he said. "I would analyze what the current best-sellers have, sit down, and write one. That's what you should do. If you're going to write, write a blockbuster, like Jacqueline Susann. I can see you writing a blockbuster on this terrace. Take my advice—your apartment is holding you back. It's like heroin, rent control. You think you're a success because your rent's a hundred and twenty dollars a month. Don't let me be the first to tell you—this is not enough. You do not put on your tombstone: 'My apartment was rent-controlled.' You have to *do* something with your life."

"I just want a husband," said Honeypot Larue.

"That's all very nice, but don't hold your breath. You don't want a husband for a living. You do something else, and maybe a husband comes along," droned Ashley. "Do something while you're waiting. Do something new!"

"There is nothing new," said the novelist. "That's why you have all those back issues of *Vogue*. There is nothing new."

"There's slightly new," said Ashley. "There's new because they've forgotten what's old. There's new because Aaron just moved into Man-hattan, and he wasn't here before." And he looked over at the new face, sweating in his yarmulke under the blazing sun.

The novelist lay there, as immobile as a stone. Then he said: "Why do the police call my building 'Love, American Style'?"

"Because no one even remotely straight lives in it," said Ashley.

"It's going co-op," said Victor.

"If the women's house of detention were standing," said Ashley, "it would be going co-op. And it would be a lot nicer than Love, American Style. You're supposed to look back on your days of struggle as basically a happy time. I don't. I hated every day I woke up in that apartment. I was poor. I hated being poor," he said. "I still can't decide which would be worse in life—to be poor or to have a small cock," he said.

And with that sally the terrace fell silent, while I stared at the source of this philosophy—our host, streaming with sweat like a golden idol, his eyes covered with cucumber slices. Victor closed his eyes and sighed. The novelist and the professor looked at one another. And then I saw the novelist look at Ashley—with a faint grimace I attributed to the brilliant light, but which may have been more than that. A siren was heading downtown in the street below; a tug was pushing a barge up the river; the sky itself was dead white; it was one of those moments of sudden stillness when you realize everything you have been saying, and doing, is a waste of time, and you want to leave immediately. But no one did, till four o'clock anyway, when Ashley had to get ready for the people in his pyramid, scheduled to arrive at six. It was a big surprise when I opened the *Post* two days later and saw the headline: Ashley vanished, it turned out, the way he appeared—in the pages of a newspaper. Only this time it was an article about his indictment by the district attorney.

That was the end of the penthouse—or the seventies, if you prefer. That was the last I saw of Ashley, at any rate. He spent two nights on Riker's Island and the rest of the summer in Santa Barbara. The person he sublet the penthouse to—a tall, angelic-looking man whose chief claim to fame was having produced the Sleaze Ball—alienated Ashley from the landlord somehow, and when Ashley returned to Manhattan in the fall, the penthouse had new locks. Walking past the building the following winter it was obvious someone else had moved in; there were tiny white lights strung along the terrace, and a blue glow under the eaves—a note that might have made sense at some party in the Pines but looked tacky in the city.

Of course, anyone who leaves a city as I did expects to find everything just as he left it when he returns. But though I went back to New

York the following decade—sometimes just to buy a pair of shoes I was sure I could find nowhere else—I inevitably learned that Hudson's, on Fourth Avenue, no longer carried them; and the big, dusty room where old Jewish men had shuffled about, telling young Puerto Ricans to climb the ladders and get the shoe I wanted to try on (the one that went with plaid shirts), was now a brand-new gutted space with polished blond floors, white walls, ficus trees in pots, and piped-in disco music. Everything was being upscaled. The same thing happened to Paragon on Broadway; and Unique Clothing. The final straw came the day I returned to Canal Jeans and was told they no longer carried painter's pants; in the strange way we personalize the discontinuation of products in a consumer culture, I felt someone had told me *I* was obsolete. This is a tale about fashion, after all.

The rest of the entourage gradually peeled away from the city during the decade that followed, I learned on my intermittent visits; the hustlers went to California, after trying Seattle—the perfect antidote to New York, they decided; one ended up in San Francisco and the other in Los Angeles. The man who stole the penthouse from Ashley eventually ran out of people to con and left New York for Minneapolis, where he ran a hair salon with Doctor Love. The decorator got a loft, redid it, but was then kicked out by the building's new owner because he had never obtained a proper lease. Ashley moved to a new apartment in one of the turrets of the Ansonia; then to an apartment with a roommate in midtown, where he began making dresses again, though nothing apparently came of that.

Other things happened, of course—a certain look (jeans, black leather jacket) remained a constant on men downtown, but the draining of energy from the West to the East Village continued. The city decided to renovate parks that had been drug bazaars for most of the seventies. The Zeckendorf Towers went up on Union Square, obliterating one of my favorite views of the city: the cluster of spires, floodlit at night, that made one think, looking north from Astor Place, of Dresden. The line of people waiting to get into the Boy Bar got longer and longer. On St. Marks Place, and along Second Avenue, unlicensed merchants began selling old magazines, records, clothes, and books on bedspreads they laid out on the sidewalk, so that walking to the St. Marks Baths you had to pick your way through what seemed to be the scattered contents of a hundred children's closets. Then the St. Marks Baths closed, its two slender black doors vanishing beneath a thick paste of fliers for new wave bands, and people who had gone there started going to the Jewel, a movie house up the street, instead. And then the restaurant mania began— when everyone went out to dinner, since the theater was not worth going to, and they couldn't have sex anymore. And it seemed as if that was all there was to do in New York: eat in public.

Years passed. Then one day, last spring, I ran into the novelist in one of the big, new bookstores that have sprouted all over lower Manhattan, though it took me a few moments to recognize him. Standing at the magazine rack, he looked like a little old man, silver-haired, eyebrows entirely gray, shoulders hunched as he read a copy of *Face*, his mustache gone, revealing, as Ashley predicted of us all, a thin, wounded mouth. Walking out we passed a table on which Victor's book on Hollywood homophobia, just reissued, was displayed. "When was the last time you saw him?" I said when we were on the street. "At one of his lectures at the center," he said. "He asked half the people in the audience to stand up, and when they did, he said: 'This is how many of you will be dead in five years.' He and Ashley had a big fight about Act Up, and they never spoke again."

"And when was the last time you saw Ashley?" I said.

"In the Ansonia," he said. "He had this round room he got some guy to marbleize—and he invited a bunch of people over for drinks, hoping he could get it published in a magazine. I didn't stay very long," he said. "I didn't know anyone there except Ashley. He'd decided to become a decorator, he said. He had the personality of a decorator, I always thought. The eye, the taste, the desire to arrange things. Ashley loved to arrange things. You know how he tried to arrange *us*. Ashley was a control queen," he said as we strolled up Greenwich Avenue toward Eleventh Street. "Then he ran into something he couldn't control."

"When did he get sick?" I said.

"Just after Victor," said the novelist, "and Louis."

"And when did you last see Louis?"

"At Studio. He was wearing an overcoat. He looked ninety-five."

"And what happened to the professor?"

"Never wrote the book on Edith Wharton. Died five years ago in Key West."

"And the guy Louis lived with?"

"Became Jackie O's driver!" he said.

"You see," I said, "there are happy endings sometimes. People's dreams can come true."

"But then Jackie O died," he said.

"Well," I said. "How's the decorator?"

"Lives in a tiny place on Tenth Street," he said. "Never goes out."

"And Honeypot Larue?"

"Works for Merrill Lynch. Vice president," he said. "House on the Island, boyfriend, very muscular, three-piece suits and a beard."

"Honeypot with a beard!"

"Facial hair is coming back," said the novelist. "It had to. There's nothing else you can do."

"And what about you? Do you still go to fashion shows?" I said.

"Oh no," he said as we turned into Abingdon Square. "Fashion seems so tacky now. All these transparent tops. I think it's cruel to the models—some breasts shouldn't be exposed! But people are so desperate to be hip—they'll do anything. All anybody wants now is to push their product. This city has become very bourgeois. Haven't you noticed? It's incredibly boring. This younger generation is the worst of all. They're utterly materialistic. They all want a penthouse," he said as we stopped in front of Ashley's old building.

"Who's in Ashley's now?" I said.

"Some Korean businessman," he said. "I asked the doorman. I went in the other day just for old time's sake. But I couldn't wait to get out."

"Why?"

"Because it brought back all those afternoons sun-bathing with Ashley!" he said. "That awful time! Those lectures about writing like Jacqueline Susann. It all reminded me of how much time I wasted hanging around that place. How much time I've wasted, period. It's a time of life I'm rather ashamed of," he said. "That's why I was so relieved when I finally brought it to an end."

"Brought it to an end?" I said.

"Yes," he said, squinting up at the penthouse. "By turning Ashley in. The professor and I were the ones who called the cops and told them where the pyramid was meeting that day. We had to," he said. "We couldn't stand the vulgarity anymore. It really was all so very vulgar!" he said, with a frown, and then he shook his head and said good-bye.

For a city that counts fashion as one of its leading industries, the people and streets I'd been walking looked remarkably the same—besides the shaved heads and muscles, tattoos and earrings. The West Village itself was even more peculiar in that respect; watching the novelist walking up Hudson Street, it looked like a kind of ghost town, a stage set in an empty theater. The streets I took on my way to the river were utterly familiar—more restful, dignified, if possible, than before—the houses with their vine-covered grilles and high windows, exactly what had been here before gay men moved in, and then left for a new neighborhood to the north. The West Side Highway, from which I used to gaze at Ashley's penthouse, had long since been dismantled, and with it the piers and rotting warehouses—where now people walked upon the one remaining dock in the open air, the brilliant April sunshine, like figures in some painting by Seurat, on promenade. The whole side of the island was being redone—like a hotel room being made up for a new customer. West Street was torn up, and one had to walk that day

along a narrow strip of wooden planks between a ditch and the door-
ways of the bars. Eventually, if newspaper reports were accurate, there
would be some sort of park. At the moment it was still in transition,
however, although to make this park the entire infrastructure of the
world Ashley had come downtown to dip into had vanished; only the
penthouse, still grandly surveying the roofs beneath it, remained, its
gray granite shining in the sun, a vessel for another generation's dreams.

THE FIX

Percival Everett • 1999

Douglas Langley owned a little sandwich shop at the intersection of Fourteenth and T streets in the District. Beside his shop was a seldom-used alley and above his shop lived a man by the name of Sherman Olney, whom Douglas had seen beaten to near extinction one night by a couple of silky-looking men who seemed to know Sherman and wanted something in particular from him. Douglas had been drawn outside from cleaning up the storeroom by a rhythmic thumping sound, like someone dropping a telephone book onto a table over and over. He stepped out into the November chill and discovered that the sound was actually that of the larger man's fists finding again and again the belly of Sherman Olney, who was being kept on his feet by the second assailant. Douglas ran back inside and grabbed the pistol he kept in the rolltop desk in his business office. He returned to the scene with the powerful flashlight his son had given him and shone the light into the faces of the two villains.

The men were not overly impressed by the light, the bigger one saying, "Hey, man, you better get that light out of my face!"

They did however show proper respect for the discharging of the .32 by running away. Sherman Olney crumpled to the ground, moaning and clutching at his middle, saying he didn't have it anymore.

"Are you all right?" Douglas asked, realizing how stupid the question was before it was fully out.

But Sherman's response was equally insipid as he said, "Yes."

"Come, let's get you inside." Douglas helped the man to his feet and into the shop. He locked the glass door behind them, then took Sherman over to the counter and helped him onto a stool.

"Thanks," Sherman said.

"You want me to call the cops?" Douglas asked.

Sherman Olney shook his head. "They're long gone by now."

"I'll make you a sandwich," Douglas said as he stepped behind the counter.

"Really, that's not necessary."

"You'll like it. I don't know first aid, but I can make a sandwich." Douglas made the man a pastrami and Muenster on rye sandwich and poured him a glass of barely cold milk, then took him to sit in one of the three booths in the shop. Douglas sat across the table from the man, watched him take a bite of the sandwich.

"What did they want?" Douglas put to him.

"To hurt me," Sherman said, his mouth working on the tough bread. He picked a seed from his teeth and put it on his plate. "They wanted to hurt me."

"My name is Douglas Langley."

"Sherman Olney."

"What were they after, Sherman?" Douglas asked, but he didn't get an answer.

As they sat there, the quiet of the room was disturbed by the loud refrigerator motor kicking on. Douglas felt the vibration of it through the soles of his shoes.

"Your compressor is a little shot," Sherman said.

Douglas looked at him, not knowing what he was talking about.

"Your fridge. The compressor is bad."

"Oh, yes," Douglas said. "It's loud."

"I can fix it."

Douglas just looked at him.

"You want me to fix it?"

Douglas didn't know what to say. Certainly he wanted the machine fixed, but what if this man just liked to take things apart? What if he made it worse? Douglas imagined the kitchen floor strewn with refrigerator parts. But he said, "Sure."

With that, Sherman got up and walked back into the kitchen, Douglas on his heels. The skinny man removed the plate from the bottom of the big and embarrassingly old machine and looked around. "Do you have any chewing gum?" Sherman asked.

As it turned out, Douglas had, in his pocket, the last stick of a pack of Juicy Fruit, which he promptly handed over. Sherman unwrapped the stick, folded it into his mouth, then lay there on the floor chewing.

"What are you doing?" Douglas asked.

Sherman paused him with a finger, then, as if feeling the texture of the gum with his tongue, he took it from his mouth and stuck it into the workings of the refrigerator. And just like that the machine ran with a quiet steady hum, just like it had when it was new.

"How'd you do that?" Douglas asked.

Sherman, now on his feet, shrugged.

"Thank you, this is terrific. All you used was chewing gum. Can you fix other things?"

Sherman nodded.

"What are you? Are you a repairman or an electrician?" Douglas asked.

"I can fix things."

"Would you like another sandwich?"

Sherman shook his head again and said. "I should be going. Thanks for the food and all your help."

"Those men might be waiting for you," Douglas said. He suddenly remembered his pistol. He could feel the weight of it in his pocket. "Just sit in here awhile." Douglas felt a great deal of sympathy for the under-fed man who had just repaired his refrigerator. "Where do you live? I could drive you."

"Actually, I don't have a place to live." Sherman stared down at the floor.

"Come over here." Douglas led the man to the big metal sink across the kitchen. He turned the ancient lever and the pipes started with a thin whistle and then screeched as the water came out. "Tell me, can you fix that?"

"Do you want me to?"

"Yes." Douglas turned off the water.

"Do you have a wrench?"

Douglas stepped away and into his business office, where he dug his way through a pile of sweaters and newspapers until he found a twelve-inch crescent wrench and a pipe wrench. He took them back to Sher-man. "Will these do?"

"Yes." Sherman took the wrench and got down under the sink.

Douglas bent low to try and see what the man was doing, but before he could figure anything out, Sherman was getting up.

"There you go," Sherman said.

Incredulous, Douglas reached over to the faucet and turned on the water. The water came out smoothly and quietly. He turned it off, then tried it again. "You did it."

"It's nothing. An easy repair."

"You know, I could really use somebody like you around here," Douglas said. "Do you need a job? I mean, do you want a job? I can't pay much. Just minimum wage, but I can let you stay in the apartment up-stairs. Actually, it's just a room. Are you interested?"

"You don't even know me," Sherman said.

Douglas stopped. Of course the man was right. He didn't know anything about him. But he had a strong feeling that Sherman Olney was an honest man. An honest man who could fix things. "You're right," Douglas admitted. "But I'm a good judge of character."

"I don't know," Sherman said.

"You said you don't have a place to go. You can live here and work until you find another place or another job." Douglas was unsure why he was pleading so with the stranger and, in fact, had a terribly uneasy feeling about the whole business, but, for some reason, he really wanted him to stay.

"Okay," Sherman said.

Douglas took the man up the back stairs and showed him the little room. The single bulb hung from a cord in the middle of the ceiling and its dim light revealed the single bed made up with a yellow chenille spread. Douglas had taken many naps there.

"This is it," Douglas said.

"It's perfect." Sherman stepped fully into the room and looked around.

"The bathroom is down the hall. There's a narrow shower stall in it."

"I'm sure I'll be comfortable."

"There's food downstairs. Help yourself."

"Thank you."

Douglas stood in awkward silence for a while wondering what else there was to say. Then he said, "Well, I guess I should go on home to my wife."

"And I should get some sleep."

Douglas nodded and left the shop.

Douglas's wife said, "Are you crazy?"

Douglas sat at the kitchen table and held his face in his hands. He could smell the ham, salami, turkey, Muenster, cheddar, and Swiss from his day's work. He peeked through his fingers and watched his short, plump wife reach over and turn down the volume of the television on the counter. The muted mouths of the news anchors were still moving.

"I asked you a question," she said.

"It sounded more like an assertion." He looked at her eyes, which were narrowed and burning into him. "He's a fine fellow. Just a little down on his luck, Sheila."

Sheila laughed, then stopped cold. "And he's in the shop all alone." She shook her head, her lips tightening across her teeth. "You have lost your mind. Now, you go right back down there and you get rid of that guy."

"I don't feel like driving," Douglas said.

"I'll drive you."

He sighed. Sheila was obviously right. Even he hadn't understood his impulse to offer the man a job and invite him to use the room above the shop. So, he would let her drive him back down there and he'd tell Sherman Olney he'd have to go.

They got into the old, forest green Buick LeSabre, Sheila behind the wheel and Douglas sunk down into the passenger seat that Sheila's concentrated weight had through the years mashed so flat. He usually hated when she drove, but especially right at that moment, as she was angry and with a mission. She took their corner at Underwood on two wheels and sped through the city and moderately heavy traffic back toward the shop.

"You really should slow down," Douglas said. He watched a man in a blue suit toss his briefcase between two parked cars and dive after it out of the way.

"You're one to give advice. You? An old fool who takes in a stray human being and leaves him alone in your place of business is giving advice? He's probably cleaned us out already."

Douglas considered the situation and felt incredibly stupid. He could not, in fact, assure Sheila that she was wrong. Sherman might be halfway to Philadelphia with twelve pounds of Genoa salami. For all he knew Sherman Olney had turned on the gas of the oven, grilled his dinner, and blown the restaurant to smithereens. He rolled down his window just a crack and listened for sirens.

"If anything bad has happened, I'm having you committed," Sheila said. She let out a brief scream and rattled the steering wheel. "Then I'll sell what little we have left and spend the rest of my life in Bermuda. That's what I'll do."

When Sheila made marks on the street braking to a stop, the store was still there and not ablaze. All the lights were off and the only people on the street were a couple of hookers on the far corner. Douglas unlocked and opened the front door of the shop, then followed Sheila inside. They walked past the tables and counter and into the kitchen where Douglas switched on the bright overhead lights. The fluorescent tubes flickered, then filled the place with a steady buzz.

"Go check the safe," Sheila said.

"There was no money in it," Douglas said. "There never is." She knew that. He had taken the money home and was going to drop it at the bank on his way to work the next day. He always did that.

"Check it anyway."

He walked into his business office and switched on the standing lamp by the door. He looked across the room to see that the safe was still closed and that the stack of newspapers was still in front of it. "Hasn't been touched," he said.

"What's his name?" Sheila asked.

"Sherman."

"Sherman!" she called up the stairs. "Sherman!"

In short order, Sherman came walking down the stairs in his trousers and sleeveless undershirt. He was rubbing his eyes, trying to adjust to the bright light.

"Sherman," Douglas said, "it's me, Douglas."

"Douglas? What are you doing back?" He stood in front of them in his stocking feet. "By the way, I fixed the toilet and also that funny massager thing."

"You mean, my foot massager?" Sheila asked.

"If you say so."

"I told you, Sherman can fix things," Douglas said to Sheila. "That's why I hired him." Sheila had purchased the foot massager from a fancy store in Georgetown. On the days when she worked in the shop she used to disappear every couple of hours for about fifteen minutes and then return happy and refreshed. She would be upstairs in the bathroom, sitting on the closed toilet with her feet stationed on her machine. Then the thing stopped working. Sheila loved that machine.

"The man at the store said my foot massager couldn't be repaired," Sheila said.

Sherman shrugged. "Well, it works now."

"I'll be right back," Sheila said and she walked away from the men and up the stairs.

Sherman watched her, then turned to Douglas. "Why did you come back?"

"Well, you see, Sheila doesn't think it's a good idea that you stay here. You know, alone and everything. Since we don't know you or anything about you." Douglas blew out a long slow breath. "I'm really sorry."

Upstairs, Sheila screamed, then came running back to the top of the stairs. "It works! It works! He did fix it." She came down, smiling at Sherman. "Thank you so much."

"You're welcome," Sherman said.

"I was just telling Sherman that we're sorry but he's going to have to leave."

"Don't be silly," Sheila said.

Douglas stared at her and rubbed a hand over his face. He gave Sheila a baffled look.

"No, no, it's certainly all right if Sherman sleeps here. And tomorrow, he can get to work." She grabbed Sherman's arm and turned him toward the stairs. "Now, you get on back up there and get some rest."

Sherman said nothing, but followed her directions. Douglas and Sheila watched him disappear upstairs.

Douglas looked at his wife. "What happened to you?"

"He fixed my foot rubber."

"So, that makes him a good guy? Just like that?"

"I don't know," she said, uncertainly. She seemed to reconsider for a second. "I guess. Come on, let's go home."

Two weeks later, Sherman had said nothing more about himself, responding only to trivial questions put to him. He did however repair or make better every machine in the restaurant. He had fixed the toaster oven, the gas lines of the big griddle, the dishwasher, the phone, the neon OPEN sign, the electric-eye buzzer on the front door, the meat slicer, the coffee machine, the manual mustard dispenser, and the cash register. Douglas found the man's skills invaluable and wondered how he had ever managed without him. Still, his presence was disconcerting as he never spoke of his past or family or friends and he never went out, not even to the store, his food being already there, and so Douglas began to worry that he might be a fugitive from the law.

He never leaves the shop," Sheila complained. She was sitting in the passenger seat while Douglas drove them to the movie theater.

"That's where he lives," Douglas said. "All the food he needs is right there. I'm hardly paying him anything."

"You pay him plenty. He doesn't have to pay rent and he doesn't have to buy food."

"I don't see what the trouble is," he said. "After all, he's fixed your massage thingamajig. And he fixed your curling iron and your VCR and your watch and he even got the squeak out of your shoes."

"I know. I know." Sheila sighed. "Still, just what do we know about this man?"

"He's honest, I know that. He never even glances at the till. I've never seen anyone who cares less about money." Douglas turned right onto Connecticut.

"That's exactly how a crook wants to come across."

"Well, Sherman's no crook. Why, I'd trust the man with my life. There are very few people I can say that about."

Sheila laughed softly and disbelievingly. "Well, don't you sound melodramatic."

Douglas really couldn't argue with her. Everything she had said was correct and he was at a loss to explain his tenacious defense of a man who was, after all, a relative stranger. He pulled the car into a parallel space and killed the engine.

"The car didn't do that thing," Sheila said. She was referring to the way the car usually refused to shut off, the stubborn engine firing a couple of extra times.

Douglas glanced over at her.

"Sherman," she said.

"This morning. He opened the hood, grabbed this and jiggled that and then slammed it shut."

The fact of the matter was finally that Sherman hadn't stolen anything and hadn't come across in any way threatening and so Douglas kept his fears and suspicions in check and counted his savings. No more electricians. No more plumbers. No more repairmen of any kind. Sherman's handiness, however, did not remain a secret, in spite of Douglas's best efforts.

It began when Sherman offered and then repaired a small radio-controlled automobile owned by a fat boy.

The fat boy, who wore his hair in braids, came into the shop with two of his skinny friends. They sat at the counter and ordered a large soda to split.

"This thing is a piece of crap," the fat boy said. His name was Loomis Rump.

"I told you not to spend your money on that thing," one of the skinny kids said.

"Shut up," said Loomis.

"Timmy's right, Loomis," the third boy said. He sucked the last of the soda through the straw. "That's a cheap one. The good remote controls aren't made of that thin plastic."

"What do you know?" Loomis said. Loomis pushed his toy another few inches away from him across the counter, toward Sherman. Sherman looked at it, then picked it up.

Douglas was watching from the register. He observed as Sherman held the car up to the light and seemed to smile.

"Just stopped working, eh?" Sherman said to the boys.

"It's a piece of crap," Loomis said.

"Would you like me to fix it?" Sherman asked.

Douglas stepped closer, thinking this time he might see how the repair was done. Loomis handed the remote to Sherman. Douglas stared intently at the man's hands. Sherman took out his pocketknife and used the small blade to undo the Phillips-head screws in order to remove the back panel from the remote control. Then it was all a blur. Douglas saw nothing and then Sherman was replacing the panel.

"There you go," Sherman said and gave the car and controller back to Loomis.

Loomis Rump laughed. "You didn't even do nothing," he said.

"Anything," Sherman corrected him.

Loomis put the car on the floor and switched on the remote. The car rolled away, nearly tripping a postal worker, and crashed to a stop at the door. It capsized, but its wheels kept spinning.

"Hey, hey," the skinny boys shouted.

"Thanks, mister," Loomis said.

The boys left.

Fat Loomis Rump and his skinny pals told their friends and they brought in their broken toys. Sherman fixed them. The fat boy's friends told their parents and Douglas found his shop increasingly crowded with customers and their small appliances.

"The Rump boy told me that you fixed his toy car and the Johnson woman told me that you repaired her radio," the short man who wore the waterworks uniform said.

Sherman was wiping down the counter.

"Is that true?"

Sherman nodded.

"Well, you see these cuts on my face?"

Douglas could see the cuts under the man's three-day growth of stubble from the door to the kitchen. Sherman leaned forward and studied the wounds.

"They seem to be healing nicely," Sherman said.

"It's this damn razor," the man said and he pulled the small unit from his trousers pocket. "It cuts me bad every time I try to shave."

"You'd like me to fix your razor?"

"If you wouldn't mind. But I don't have any money."

"That's okay." Sherman took the razor and began taking it apart. Douglas, as always, moved closer and tried to see. He smiled at the waterworks man who smiled back. Other people gathered around and watched Sherman's hands. Then they watched him hand the reassembled little machine back to the waterworks man. The man turned on the shaver and put it to his face.

"Hey," he said. "This is wonderful. It works just like it did when it was new. This is wonderful. Thank you. Can I bring you some money tomorrow?"

"Not necessary," Sherman said.

"This is wonderful."

Everyone in the restaurant oohed and aahed.

"Look," the waterworks man said. "I'm not bleeding."

Sherman sat quietly at the end of the counter and fixed whatever was put in front of him. He repaired hair dryers and calculators and watches and cellular phones and carburetors. And while people waited for the repairs, they ate sandwiches and this appealed to Douglas, though he didn't like his handyman's time so consumed. But the fact of the matter was that there was little more to fix in the shop.

One day a woman who believed her husband was having an affair came in and complained over a turkey and provolone on wheat. Sherman sat next to her at the counter and listened as she finished, ". . . and then he comes home hours after he's gotten off from work, smelling of beer and perfume and he doesn't want to talk or anything and says he has a sinus headache and I'm wondering if I ought to follow him or check the mileage on his car before he leaves in the morning. What should I do?"

"Tell him it's his turn to cook and that you'll be late and don't tell him where you're going," Sherman said.

Everyone in the shop nodded, more in shared confusion than in agreement.

"Where should I go?" the woman asked.

"Go to the library and read about the praying mantis," Sherman said.

Douglas came up to Sherman after the woman had left and asked, "Do you think that was a good idea?"

Sherman shrugged.

The woman came in the next week, her face full with a smile and announced that her home life was now perfect.

"Everything at home is perfect now," she said. "Thanks to Sherman."

Customers slapped Sherman on the back.

So began a new dimension of fixing in the shop as people came in, along with their electric pencil sharpeners, pacemakers, and microwaves, their relationship woes, and their tax problems. Sherman saved the man who owned the automotive-supply business across the street twelve thousand dollars and got him some fifty-seven dollars in refund.

One night after the shop was closed, Douglas and Sherman sat at the counter and ate the stale leftover doughnuts and drank coffee. Douglas looked at his handyman and shook his head. "That was really something the way you straightened the Rhinehart boy's teeth."

"Physics," Sherman said.

Douglas washed down a dry bite and set his cup on the counter. "I know I've asked you before, but we've known each other longer now. How did you learn to fix things?"

"Fixing things is easy. You just have to know how things work."

"That's it," Douglas said more than asked.

Sherman nodded.

"Doesn't it make you happy to do it?"

Sherman looked at Douglas, questioning.

"I ask because you never smile."

"Oh," Sherman said and took another bite of doughnut.

The next day Sherman fixed a chain saw and a laptop computer and thirty-two parking tickets. Sherman, who had always been quiet, became increasingly more so. He would listen, nod, and fix the problem. That evening, a few minutes before closing, just after Sherman had solved the Morado woman's sexual-identity problem, two paramedics came in with a patient on a stretcher.

"This is my wife," the more distressed of the ambulance men said of the supine woman. "She's been hit by a car and she died in our rig on the way to the hospital," he cried.

Sherman looked at the woman, pulling back the blanket.

"She had massive internal—"

Sherman stopped the man with a raised hand, pulled the blanket off and then threw it over himself and the dead woman. Douglas stepped over to stand with the paramedics.

Sherman worked under the blanket, moving this way and that way, and then he and the woman emerged, alive and well. The paramedic hugged her.

"You're alive," the man said to his wife.

The other paramedic shook Sherman's hand. Douglas just stared at his handyman.

"Thank you, thank you," the husband said, crying.

The woman was confused, but she, too, offered Sherman thanks.

Sherman nodded and walked quietly away, disappearing into the kitchen.

The paramedics and the restored woman left. Douglas locked the shop and walked into the kitchen where he found Sherman sitting on the floor with his back against the refrigerator.

"I don't know what to say," Douglas said. His head was swimming. "You just brought that woman back to life."

Sherman's face looked lifeless. He seemed drained of all energy. He lifted his sad face up to look at Douglas.

"How did you do that?" Douglas asked.

Sherman shrugged.

"You just brought a woman back to life and you give me a shrug?" Douglas could hear the fear in his voice. "Who are you? What are you? Are you from outer space or something?"

"No," Sherman said.

"Then what's going on?"

"I can fix things."

"That wasn't a thing," Douglas pointed out. "That was a human being."

"Yeah, I know."

Douglas ran a hand over his face and just stared down at Sherman. "I wonder what Sheila will say."

"Please don't tell anyone about this," Sherman said.

Douglas snorted out a laugh. "Don't tell anyone. I don't have to tell anyone. Everyone probably knows by now. What do you think those paramedics are out doing right now? They're telling anybody and everybody that there's some freak in Langley's Sandwich Shop who can revive the dead."

Sherman held his face in his hands.

"Who are you?"

News spread. Television-news trucks and teams camped outside the front door of the sandwich shop. They were waiting with cameras ready when Douglas showed up to open for business the day following the resurrection.

"Yes, this is my shop," he said. "No, I don't know how it was done," he said. "No, you can't come in just yet," he said.

Sherman was sitting at the counter waiting, his face long, his eyes red as if from crying.

"This is crazy," Douglas said.

Sherman nodded.

"They want to talk to you." Douglas looked closely at Sherman. "Are you all right?"

But Sherman was looking past Douglas and through the front window where the crowd was growing ever larger.

"Are you going to talk to them?" Douglas asked.

Sherman shook his sad face. "I have to run away," he said. "Everyone knows where I am now."

Douglas at first thought Sherman was making cryptic reference to the men who had been beating him that night long ago, but then realized that Sherman meant simply *everyone*.

Sherman stood and walked into the back of the shop. Douglas followed him, not knowing why, unable to stop himself. He followed the man out of the store and down the alley, away from the shop and the horde of people.

Sherman watched the change come over Douglas and said, "Of course not."

"But you—" The rest of Douglas's sentence didn't have a chance to find air as he was once again repeating Sherman's steps.

They ran up this street and across that avenue, crossed bridges and scurried through tunnels and no matter how far away from the shop they seemed to get, the chanting remained, however faint. Douglas finally asked where they were going and confessed that he was afraid. They were sitting on a bench in the park and it was by now just after sundown.

"You don't have to come with me," Sherman said. "I only need to get away from all of them." He shook his head and said, more to himself, "I knew this would happen."

"If you knew this would happen, why did you fix all of those things?"

"Because I can. Because I was asked."

Douglas gave nervous glances this way and that across the park. "This has something to do with why the men were beating you that night, doesn't it?"

"They were from the government or some businesses, I'm not completely sure," Sherman said. "They wanted me to fix a bunch of things and I said no."

"But they asked you," Douglas said. "You just told me—"

"You have to be careful about what you fix. If you fix the valves in an engine, but the bearings are shot, you'll get more compression, but the engine will still burn up." Sherman looked at Douglas's puzzled face. "If you irrigate a desert, you might empty a sea. It's a complicated business, fixing things."

Douglas said, "So, what do we do now?"

Sherman was now weeping, tears streaming down his face and curving just under his chin before falling to the open collar of his light blue shirt. Douglas watched him, not believing that he was seeing the same man who had fixed so many machines and so many relationships and so many businesses and concerns and even fixed a dead woman.

Sherman raised his tear-filled eyes to Douglas. "I am the empty sea," he said.

The chanting became louder and Douglas turned to see the night dotted with yellow-orange torches. The quality of the chanting had become strained and there was an urgency in the intonation that did not sound affable.

The two men ran, Douglas pushing Sherman, as he was now so engaged in sobbing that he had trouble keeping on his feet. They made it to the big bridge that crossed the bay and stopped in the middle, discovering that at either end thousands of people waited. They sang their dirge into the dark sky, their flames winking.

"Fix us!" they shouted. "Fix us! Fix us!"

Sherman looked down at the peaceful water below. It was a long drop that no one could hope to survive. He looked at Douglas.

Douglas nodded.

The masses of people pressed in from either side.

Sherman stepped over the railing and stood on the brink, the toes of his shoes pushed well over the edge.

"Don't!" they all screamed. "Fix us! Fix us!"

WATER CHILD

Edwidge Danticat · 2000

The letter came on the first of the month, as usual. It was written, as most of them were, in near-calligraphic style, in blue ink, on see-through airmail paper.

Ma chère Nadine,
We are so happy to have this occasion to put pen to
paper to write to you. How are you? All is well with us,
grace à Dieu, except your father whose health is,
as always, unreliable. Today it is his knees. Tomorrow
it will be something else. You know how it is when you
are old. He and I both thank you for the money you
sent last month. We know it is difficult for you,
but we are very grateful. This month your father
hopes to see yet another doctor. We have not heard
your voice in a while and our ears long for it.
Please telephone us.

It was signed, "Your mother and father who embrace you very tightly."

· · ·

Three weeks had gone by since the letter arrived, and Nadine still hadn't called. She had raided her savings to wire double the usual amount but hadn't called. Instead she took the letter out each day as she ate a tuna melt for lunch in the hospital cafeteria, where each first Friday for the last three years she had added a brownie to her meal for scheduled variety.

Every time she read the letter, she tried to find something else between the lines, a note of sympathy, commiseration, condolence. But it simply wasn't there. The more time went by, the more brittle and fragile the letter became. Each time she held the paper between her fingers she wondered how her mother had not torn it with the pen she'd used to compose each carefully inscribed word. How had the postal workers in both Port-au-Prince and Brooklyn not lacerated the thin page and envelope? And how had the letter not turned to dust in her purse during her bus ride to and from work? Or while rubbing against the inner lining of the left pocket of her nursing uniform, where she kept it all day long?

She carefully folded the letter once again and replaced it in her pocket as one of her colleagues approached the corner table by the window that she occupied in solitude for a whole hour each working day. Josette kissed her on both cheeks while fumbling in her own pocket for lunch money. As Nadine's lunch hour was winding down, Josette's was just beginning.

Nadine smiled to herself at this ability of Josette's to make an ordinary encounter feel so intimate, then turned her face to the view outside, to the brown buildings and their barred windows. She let her eyes linger on the nursing station of the Psych ward across the alley and entertained a vision she often had of seeing a patient dive out of one of the windows.

"Ms. Hinds is back from ICU," Josette was saying. "She's so upset and sezi that Doctor Vega had to give her a sedative."

Nadine and Josette worked different ends of Ear, Nose, and Throat and saw many post-op patients wake up bewildered to discover that their total laryngectomies meant they would no longer be able to talk. No matter how the doctors, nurses, and counselors prepared them, it was still a shock.

Josette always gave Nadine a report on the patients whenever she came to take over the table. She was one of the younger Haitian RNs, one of those who had come to Brooklyn in early childhood and spoke English with no accent at all, but she liked to throw in a Creole word here and there in conversation to flaunt her origins. Aside from the brief lunch encounters, and times when one or the other needed a bit of extra help with a patient, they barely spoke at all.

"I am going now," Nadine said, rising from her seat. "My throne is yours."

When she returned to her one-bedroom condo in Canarsie that evening, Nadine was greeted by voices from the large television set that she kept on twenty-four hours a day. Along with the uneven piles of newspapers and magazines scattered between the fold-out couch and the floor-to-ceiling bookshelves in her living room, the television was her way of bringing voices into her life that required neither reaction nor response. At thirty, she'd tried other hobbies—African dance and drawing classes, Internet surfing—but these tasks had demanded either too much effort or too much superficial interaction with other people.

She took off the white sneakers that she wore at work and remained standing to watch the last ten minutes of a news broadcast. It wasn't until a game show began that she pressed the playback button on her blinking answering machine.

Her one message was from Eric, her former beau, suitor, lover, the near father of her nearly born child.

"Alo, allo, hello," he stammered, creating his own odd pauses between Creole, French, and English, like the electively mute, newly arrived

immigrant children whose worried parents brought them to the ward
for consultations, even though there was nothing wrong with their
vocal cords.

"Just saying hello to you." He chose heavily accented English. Long
pause. "Okay. Bye."

Whenever he called her now, which was about once a month since
their breakup, she removed the microcassette from the answering machine and placed it on the altar she had erected on top of the dresser in her
bedroom. It wasn't anything too elaborate. There was a framed drawing
that she had made of a cocoa-brown, dewy-eyed baby that could as easily
have been a boy as a girl, the plump, fleshy cheeks resembling hers and
the high forehead resembling his. Next to the plain wooden frame were a
dozen now dried red roses that Eric had bought her as they'd left the
clinic after the procedure. She had once read about a shrine to unborn
children in Japan, where water was poured over altars of stone to honor
them, so she had filled her favorite drinking glass with water and a pebble
and had added that to her own shrine, along with a total of now seven
microcassettes with messages from Eric, messages she had never returned.

That night, as the apartment seemed oddly quiet in spite of the TV
voices, she took out her mother's letter for its second reading of the day,
ran her fingers down the delicate page, and reached for the phone to
dial her parents' number. She'd almost called many times in the last
three months, but had lost her nerve, thinking her voice might betray
all that she could not say. She nearly dialed the whole thing this time.
There were only a few numbers left when she put the phone down, tore
the letter into two, then four, then eight, then countless pieces, collapsed among her old magazines and newspapers, and wept.

Another letter arrived at Nadine's house a week later. It was on the
same kind of airmail paper, but this time the words were meticulously typed. The *a*s and *o*s, which had been struck over many times,

created underlayers, shadows, and small holes within the vowels' perimeters.

> *Ma chère Nadine,*
> *Your father and I thank you very much for the extra*
> *money. Your father used it to see a doctor, not about his*
> *knees, but his prostate that the doctor says is inflamed. Not*
> *to worry, he was given some medications and it seems as if*
> *he will be fine for a while. All the tests brought us short for*
> *the monthly expenses, but we will manage. We would like*
> *so much to talk to you. We wait every Sunday afternoon,*
> *hoping you will return to our beautiful routine. We pray*
> *that we have not abused your generosity, but you are our*
> *only child and we only ask for what we need. You know*
> *how it is when you are old. We have tried to telephone*
> *you, but we are always greeted by your répondeur,*
> *which will not accept collect calls. In any case, we*
> *wait to hear from you.*
> *Your mother and father who embrace you*
> *very tightly.*

The next day, Nadine ignored her tuna melt altogether to read the letter over many times. She did not even notice the lunch hour pass. Josette arrived sooner than she expected. Josette, like all the other nurses, knew not to ask any questions about Nadine's past, present, future, or her international-looking mail. Word circulated quickly from old employees to new arrivals that Nadine Osnac was not a friendly woman. Anyone who had sought detailed conversations with her, or who had shown interest in sharing the table while she was sitting there, had met only with cold silence and a blank stare out to the Psych ward. Josette, however, still occasionally ventured a social invitation, since they were both from the same country and all.

"Some of the girls are going to the city after work," Josette was saying. "A little banbòch to celebrate Ms. Hinds' discharge tomorrow."

"No thanks," Nadine said, departing from the table a bit more abruptly than usual.

That same afternoon, Ms. Hinds began throwing things across her small private room, one of the few in the ward. Nadine nearly took a flower vase in the face as she rushed in to help. Unlike most of the patients in the ward, who were middle-aged or older, Ms. Hinds was a twenty-five-year-old nonsmoker.

When Nadine arrived, Ms. Hinds was thrashing about so much that the nurses, worried that she would yank out the metal tube inserted in her neck and suffocate, were trying to pin her down to put restraints on her arms and legs. Nadine quickly joined in the struggle, assigning herself Ms. Hinds' right arm, pockmarked from weeks of IVs in hard-to-conquer veins.

"Where's Doctor Vega?" Josette shouted as she caught one of Ms. Hinds' random kicks in her chest. Nadine lost her grip on the IV arm. She was looking closely at Ms. Hinds' face, her eyes tightly shut beneath where her eyebrows used to be, her thinner lower lip protruding defiantly past her upper one as though she were preparing to spit long distance in a contest, her whole body hairless under the cerulean-blue hospital gown, which came with neither a bonnet nor a hat to protect her now completely bald head.

"The doctor's on his way," one of the male nurses said. He had a firm hold of Ms. Hinds' left leg, but couldn't pin it down to the bed long enough to restrain it.

"Leave her alone," Nadine shouted to the others.

One by one, the nurses each took a few steps back, releasing Ms. Hinds' extremities. With her need to struggle suddenly gone, Ms. Hinds curled into a fetal position and sank into the middle of the bed.

"Let me be alone with her," Nadine said in a much softer voice.

The others lingered a while, as if not wanting to leave, but they had other patients to see to, so, one at a time, they backed out the door.

Nadine lowered the bed rail to give Ms. Hinds a sense of freedom, even if limited.

"Ms. Hinds, is there something you want?" she asked.

Ms. Hinds opened her mouth wide, trying to force air past her lips, but all that came out was the hiss of oxygen and mucus filtering through the tube in her neck.

Nadine looked over at the night table, where there should have been a pad and pen, but Ms. Hinds had knocked them onto the floor with the magazines her parents had brought for her. She walked over and picked up the pad and pen and pushed them toward Ms. Hinds, who was still lying in a ball in the middle of the bed.

Looking puzzled, Ms. Hinds turned her face toward Nadine, slowly unwrapping her body from around itself.

"I'm here, Ms. Hinds," Nadine said, now holding the pad within a few inches of Ms. Hinds' face. "Go ahead."

Ms. Hinds held out the gaunt fingers of her right hand. The fingers came apart slowly; then Ms. Hinds extended the whole hand, grabbing the pad. She had to force herself to sit up in order to write and she grimaced as she did so, trying to maintain her grip on the pad and slide up against the pillow Nadine propped behind her back.

Ms. Hinds scribbled down a few quick words, then held up the pad for Nadine to read. At first Nadine could not understand the handwriting. It was unsteady and hurried and the words ran together, but Nadine sounded them out, one letter at a time, with some encouragement from Ms. Hinds, who slowly moved her head up and down when Nadine guessed correctly.

"I can't speak," Nadine made out.

"That's right," Nadine said. "You can't."

Looking even more perplexed at Nadine's unsympathetic reaction,

Ms. Hinds grabbed the pad from Nadine's hand and scribbled, "I'm a teacher."

"I know," Nadine said.

"WHY SEND ME HOME LIKE THIS?" Ms. Hinds scribbled next.

"Because we have done all we can for you here," Nadine said. "Now you must work with a speech therapist. You can get an artificial larynx, a voice box. The speech therapist will help you."

"Feel like a basenji," Ms. Hinds wrote, her face sinking closer to her chest.

"What's a b-a-s-e-n-j-i?" Nadine asked, spelling out the word.

"A dog," Ms. Hinds wrote. "Doesn't bark."

"A dog that doesn't bark?" Nadine asked. "What kind of dog is that?"

"Exists," Ms. Hinds wrote, as she bit down hard on her quivering lower lip.

That night at home, Nadine found herself more exhausted than usual. With the television news as white noise, she dialed Eric's home phone number, hoping she was finally ready to hear his voice for more than the twenty-five seconds her answering machine allowed. He should be home resting now, she thought, preparing to start his second job as a night janitor at Medgar Evers College.

Her mind was suddenly blank. What would she say? She was trying to think of something frivolous, a line of small talk, when she heard the message that his number had been changed to one that was unlisted.

She quickly hung up and redialed, only to get the same message. After dialing a few more times, she decided to call her parents instead.

Ten years ago her parents had sold everything they owned and moved from what passed for a lower-middle-class neighborhood to one on the edge of a slum, in order to send her to nursing school abroad. Ten years ago she'd dreamed of seeing the world, of making her own way in it. These were the intangibles she'd proposed to her mother, the kindergarten teacher, and her father, the camion driver, in the guise of a nursing career. This was what they'd sacrificed everything for. But she always knew that she would repay them. And she had, with half her salary every month, and sometimes more. In return, what she got was the chance to parent them rather than have them parent her. Calling them, however, on the rare occasions that she actually called rather than received their calls, always made her wish to be the one guarded, rather than the guardian, to be reassured now and then that some wounds could heal, that some decisions would not haunt her forever.

"Manman," her voice immediately dropped to a whisper when her mother's came over the phone line, squealing with happiness.

For every decibel Nadine's voice dropped, her mother's rose. "My love, we were so worried about you. How are you? We have not heard your voice in so long."

"I'm fine, Manman," she said.

"You sound low. You sound down. We have to start planning again when you can come or when we can come see you, as soon as Papa can travel."

"How is Papa?" she asked.

"He's right here. Let me put him on. He'll be very glad to hear you."

Suddenly her father was on the phone, his tone calmer but excited in his own way. "We were waiting so long for this call, chérie."

"I know, Papa. I've been working really hard."

They never spoke of difficult things during these phone calls, of money or illnesses or doctors' visits. Papa always downplayed his aches and pains, which her mother would highlight in the letters. Events were relayed briefly, a list of accomplishments, no discussion of failures or losses, which could spoil moods for days, weeks, and months, until the next phone call.

"Do you have a boyfriend?" Her mother took back the phone. Nadine could imagine her skipping around their living room like a child's ball bouncing. "Is there anyone in your life?"

"No, Manman," she said.

"Don't wait too long," her mother said. "You don't want to be old alone."

"All right, Manman."

"Papa and I saw a kolibri today." Her mother liked moving from one subject to another. Her parents loved birds, especially hummingbirds, and never failed to report a sighting to her. Since every schoolboy made it his mission to slingshot hummingbirds to death, she was amazed that there were any left in Port-au-Prince, especially in her parents' neighborhood.

"It was just a little one," her mother was saying. "Very small."

She could hear her father add, "It's very clever. I think it's going to last. It loves our new hibiscus."

"You have hibiscus?" Nadine asked.

"Just a hedge," her mother said. "It's just starting to blossom. It brings us bees too, but I wouldn't say we have a hive."

"That's nice, Manman," she said. "I have to go now."

"So soon?"

"Please say good night to Papa."

"Okay, my heart."

"I promise I'll call again."

The next morning, Nadine watched as Ms. Hinds packed her things and changed into a bright-yellow oversized sweatsuit and matching cap while waiting for the doctor to come and sign her discharge papers.

"My mother bought me this hideous outfit," Ms. Hinds wrote on the pad, which was now half filled with words: commands to the nurses, updates to her parents from the previous evening's visit.

"Is someone coming for you?" Nadine asked.

"My parents," Ms. Hinds wrote. Handing Nadine the pad, she reached up and stroked the raised tip of the metal tube in her neck, as if she were worried about her parents seeing it again.

"Good," Nadine said. "The doctor will be here soon." Nadine was tempted to warn Ms. Hinds that whatever form of relief she must be feeling now would only last for a while, the dread of being voiceless hitting her anew each day as though it had just happened, when she would awake from dreams in which she'd spoken to find that she had no voice, or when she would see something alarming and realize that she couldn't scream for help, or even when she would realize that she herself was slowly forgetting, without the help of old audio or videocassettes or answering-machine greetings, what her own voice used to sound like. She didn't say anything, however. Like all her other patients, Ms. Hinds would soon find all this out herself.

Nadine spent half her lunch hour staring at the barred windows on the brown building across the alley, watching the Psych nurses scribbling in charts and filing them, rushing to answer sudden calls from the ward.

Josette walked up to the table much earlier than usual, obviously looking for her.

"What is it?" Nadine asked.

"Se Ms. Hinds," Josette said. "She'd like to say good-bye to you."

She thought of asking Josette to tell Ms. Hinds that she couldn't be found, but fearing that this would create some type of conspirational camaraderie between her and Josette, she decided against it.

Ms. Hinds and her parents were waiting by the elevator bank in the ward. Ms. Hinds was sitting in a wheelchair with her discharge papers and a clear plastic bag full of odds and ends on her lap. Her father, a strapping man, was clutching the back of the wheelchair with moist, nervous hands, which gripped the chair more tightly for fear of losing hold. The mother, thin and short like Ms. Hinds, looked as though she was fighting back cries, tears, a tempest of anger, barters with God.

Instead she fussed, trying to wrench the discharge papers and the bag from her daughter, irritating Ms. Hinds, who raised her pad from beneath the bag and scribbled quickly, "Nurse Osnac, my parents, Nicole and Justin Hinds."

Nadine shook each parent's hand in turn.

"Glad to make your acquaintance," said the father.

The mother said nothing.

"Thank you for everything," said the father. "Please share our thanks with the doctors, the other nurses, everyone."

The elevator doors suddenly opened and they found themselves staring at the bodies that filled it to capacity, the doctors and nurses traveling between floors, the visitors. The Hindses let the doors close, and the others departed without them.

Ms. Hinds turned to an empty page toward the back of her pad and wrote, "Bye, Nurse Osnac."

"Good luck," Nadine said.

Another elevator opened. There were fewer people in this one and enough room for the Hindses. The father pushed the wheelchair, which jerked forward, nearly dumping Ms. Hinds facefirst into the elevator.

The elevator doors closed behind them sharply, leaving Nadine alone, facing a distorted reflection of herself in the wide, shiny metal surface. Had she carried to full term, her child, aborted two months after his or her conception, would likely have been born today, or yesterday, or tomorrow, probably sometime this week, but this month for certain.

She thought of this for only a moment, then of her parents, of Eric, of the pebble in the water glass in her bedroom at home, all of them belonging to the widened, unrecognizable woman staring back at her from the closed elevator doors.

THE AMERICAN
EMBASSY

Chimamanda Ngozi Adichie • 2003

She stood in line outside the American embassy in Lagos, staring straight ahead, barely moving, a blue plastic file of documents tucked under her arm. She was the forty-eighth person in the line of about two hundred that trailed from the closed gates of the American embassy all the way past the smaller, vine-encrusted gates of the Czech embassy. She did not notice the newspaper vendors who blew whistles and pushed *The Guardian*, *Thenews*, and *The Vanguard* in her face. Or the beggars who walked up and down holding out enamel plates. Or the ice-cream bicycles that honked. She did not fan herself with a magazine or swipe at the tiny fly hovering near her ear. When the man standing behind her tapped her on the back and asked, "Do you have change, *abeg*, two tens for twenty naira?" she stared at him for a while, to focus, to remember where she was, before she shook her head and said, "No."

The air hung heavy with moist heat. It weighed on her head, made it even more difficult to keep her mind blank, which Dr. Balogun had said yesterday was what she would have to do. He had refused to give her any more tranquilizers because she needed to be alert for the visa interview. It was easy enough for him to say that, as though she knew how to go about keeping her mind blank, as though it was in her power, as though she invited those images of her son Ugonna's small, plump body crumpling before her, the splash on his chest so red she wanted to scold him about playing with the palm oil in the kitchen. Not that he could even reach up to the shelf where she kept oils and spices, not that he could unscrew the cap on the plastic bottle of palm oil. He was only four years old.

The man behind her tapped her again. She jerked around and nearly screamed from the sharp pain that ran down her back. Twisted muscle, Dr. Balogun had said, his expression awed that she had sustained nothing more serious after jumping down from the balcony.

"See what that useless soldier is doing there," the man behind her said.

She turned to look across the street, moving her neck slowly. A small crowd had gathered. A soldier was flogging a bespectacled man with a long whip that curled in the air before it landed on the man's face, or his neck, she wasn't sure because the man's hands were raised as if to ward off the whip. She saw the man's glasses slip off and fall. She saw the heel of the soldier's boot squash the black frames, the tinted lenses.

"See how the people are pleading with the soldier," the man behind her said. "Our people have become too used to pleading with soldiers."

She said nothing. He was persistent with his friendliness, unlike the woman in front of her who had said earlier, "I have been talking to you and you just look at me like a moo-moo!" and now ignored her. Perhaps he was wondering why she did not share in the familiarity that had developed among the others in the line. Because they had all woken up early—those who had slept at all—to get to the American embassy before dawn; because they had all struggled for the visa line, dodging the soldiers' swinging whips as they were herded back and forth before the line was finally formed; because they were all afraid that the American embassy might decide not to open its gates today, and they would have to do it all over again the day after tomorrow since the embassy did not open on Wednesdays, they had formed friendships. Buttoned-up men and women exchanged newspapers and denunciations of General Abacha's government, while young people in jeans, bristling with savoir faire, shared tips on ways to answer questions for the American student visa.

"Look at his face, all that bleeding. The whip cut his face," the man behind her said.

She did not look, because she knew the blood would be red, like fresh palm oil. Instead she looked up Eleke Crescent, a winding street of embassies with vast lawns, and at the crowds of people on the sides of the street. A breathing sidewalk. A market that sprung up during the American embassy hours and disappeared when the embassy closed. There was the chair-rental outfit where the stacks of white plastic chairs that cost one hundred naira per hour decreased fast. There were the wooden boards propped on cement blocks, colorfully displaying sweets and mangoes and oranges. There were the young people who cushioned cigarette-filled trays on their heads with rolls of cloth. There were the blind beggars led by children, singing blessings in English, Yoruba, pidgin, Igbo, Hausa when somebody put money in their plates. And there was, of course, the makeshift photo studio. A tall man standing beside a tripod, holding up a chalk-written sign that read EXCELLENT ONE-HOUR PHOTOS, CORRECT AMERICAN VISA SPECIFICATIONS. She had had her passport photo taken there, sitting on a rickety stool, and she was not surprised that it came out grainy, with her face much lighter-skinned. But then, she had no choice, she couldn't have taken the photo earlier.

Two days ago she had buried her child in a grave near a vegetable patch in their ancestral hometown of Umunnachi, surrounded by well-wishers she did not remember now. The day before, she had driven her husband in the boot of their Toyota to the home of a friend, who smuggled him out of the country. And the day before that, she hadn't needed to take a passport photo; her life was normal and she had taken Ugonna to school, had bought him a sausage roll at Mr. Biggs, had sung along with Majek Fashek on her car radio. If a fortune-teller had told her that she, in the space of a few days, would no longer recognize her life, she would have laughed. Perhaps even given the fortune-teller ten naira extra for having a wild imagination.

"Sometimes I wonder if the American embassy people look out of their window and enjoy watching the soldiers flogging people," the man behind her was saying. She wished he would shut up. It was his talking that made it harder to keep her mind blank, free of Ugonna. She looked across the street again; the soldier was walking away now, and even from this distance she could see the glower on his face. The glower of a grown man who could flog another grown man if he wanted to, when he wanted to. His swagger was as flamboyant as that of the men who four nights ago broke her back door open and barged in.

Where is your husband? Where is he? They had torn open the wardrobes in the two rooms, even the drawers. She could have told them that her husband was over six feet tall, that he could not possibly hide in a drawer. Three men in black trousers. They had smelled of alcohol and pepper soup, and much later, as she held Ugonna's still body, she knew that she would never eat pepper soup again.

Where has your husband gone? Where? They pressed a gun to her head, and she said, "I don't know, he just left yesterday," standing still even though the warm urine trickled down her legs.

One of them, the one wearing a black hooded shirt who smelled the most like alcohol, had eyes that were startlingly bloodshot, so red they looked painful. He shouted the most, kicked at the TV set. *You know about the story your husband wrote in the newspaper? You know he is a liar? You know people like him should be in jail because they cause trouble, because they don't want Nigeria to move forward?*

He sat down on the sofa, where her husband always sat to watch the nightly news on NTA, and yanked at her so that she landed awkwardly on his lap. His gun poked her waist. *Fine woman, why you marry a troublemaker?* She felt his sickening hardness, smelled the fermentation on his breath.

Leave her alone, the other one said. The one with the bald head that gleamed, as though coated in Vaseline. *Let's go.*

She pried herself free and got up from the sofa, and the man in the hooded shirt, still seated, slapped her behind. It was then that Ugonna started to cry, to run to her. The man in the hooded shirt was laughing, saying how soft her body was, waving his gun. Ugonna was screaming now; he never screamed when he cried, he was not that kind of child. Then the gun went off and the palm oil splash appeared on Ugonna's chest.

"See oranges here," the man in line behind her said, offering her a plastic bag of six peeled oranges. She had not noticed him buy them.

She shook her head. "Thank you."

"Take one. I noticed that you have not eaten anything since morning."

She looked at him properly then, for the first time. A nondescript face with a dark complexion unusually smooth for a man. There was something aspirational about his crisp-ironed shirt and blue tie, about the careful way he spoke English as though he feared he would make a mistake. Perhaps he worked for one of the new-generation banks and was making a much better living than he had ever imagined possible.

"No, thank you," she said. The woman in front turned to glance at her and then went back to talking to some people about a special church service called the AmericanVisa Miracle Ministry.

"You should eat, oh," the man behind her said, although he no longer held out the bag of oranges.

She shook her head again; the pain was still there, somewhere between her eyes. It was as if jumping from the balcony had dislodged some bits and pieces inside her head so that they now clattered painfully. Jumping had not been her only choice, she could have climbed onto the mango tree whose branch reached across the balcony, she could have dashed down the stairs. The men had been arguing, so loudly that they blocked out reality, and she believed for a moment that maybe that popping sound had not been a gun, maybe it was the kind of sneaky thunder that came at the beginning of harmattan, maybe the red splash really was palm oil, and Ugonna had gotten to the bottle somehow and was now playing a fainting game even though it was not a game he had ever played. Then their words pulled her back. *You think she will tell people it was an accident? Is this what Oga asked us to do? A small child! We have to hit the mother. No, that is double trouble. Yes. No, let's go, my friend!*

She had dashed out to the balcony then, climbed over the railing, jumped down without thinking of the two storeys, and crawled into the dustbin by the gate. After she heard the roar of their car driving away, she went back to her flat, smelling of the rotten plantain peels in the dustbin. She held Ugonna's body, placed her cheek to his quiet chest, and realized that she had never felt so ashamed. She had failed him.

"You are anxious about the visa interview, *abi*?" the man behind her asked.

She shrugged, gently, so as not to hurt her back, and forced a vacant smile.

"Just make sure that you look the interviewer straight in the eye as you answer the questions. Even if you make a mistake, don't correct yourself, because they will assume you are lying. I have many friends they have refused, for small-small reasons. Me, I am applying for a visitor's visa. My brother lives in Texas and I want to go for a holiday."

He sounded like the voices that had been around her, people who had helped with her husband's escape and with Ugonna's funeral, who had brought her to the embassy. Don't falter as you answer the questions, the voices had said. Tell them all about Ugonna, what he was like, but don't overdo it, because every day people lie to them to get asylum visas, about dead relatives that were never even born. Make Ugonna real. Cry, but don't cry too much.

"They don't give our people immigrant visas anymore, unless the person is rich by American standards. But I hear people from European countries have no problems getting visas. Are you applying for an immigrant visa or a visitor's?" the man asked.

"Asylum." She did not look at his face; rather, she felt his surprise.

"Asylum? That will be very difficult to prove."

She wondered if he read *The New Nigeria*, if he knew about her husband. He probably did. Everyone supportive of the pro-democracy press knew about her husband, especially because he was the first journalist to publicly call the coup plot a sham, to write a story accusing General Abacha of inventing a coup so that he could kill and jail his opponents. Soldiers had come to the newspaper office and carted away large numbers of that edition in a black truck; still, photocopies got out and circulated throughout Lagos—a neighbor had seen a copy pasted on the wall of a bridge next to posters announcing church crusades and new films. The soldiers had detained her husband for two weeks and broken the skin on his forehead, leaving a scar the shape of an L. Friends had gingerly touched the scar when they gathered at their flat to celebrate his release, bringing bottles of whiskey. She remembered somebody saying to him, *Nigeria will be well because of you*, and she remembered her husband's expression, that look of the excited messiah, as he talked about the soldier who had given him a cigarette after beating him, all the while stammering in the way he did when he was in high spirits. She had found that stammer endearing years ago; she no longer did.

"Many people apply for asylum visa and don't get it," the man behind her said. Loudly. Perhaps he had been talking all the while.

"Do you read *The New Nigeria*?" she asked. She did not turn to face the man, instead she watched a couple ahead in the line buy packets of biscuits; the packets crackled as they opened them.

"Yes. Do you want it? The vendors may still have some copies."

"No. I was just asking."

"Very good paper. Those two editors, they are the kind of people Nigeria needs. They risk their lives to tell us the truth. Truly brave men. If only we had more people with that kind of courage."

It was not courage, it was simply an exaggerated selfishness. A month ago, when her husband forgot about his cousin's wedding even

over, blowing his whistle. She could not see *The New Nigeria* among the papers balanced on his arm. Perhaps it had sold out. Her husband's latest story, "The Abacha Years So Far: 1993 to 1997," had not worried her at first, because he had written nothing new, only compiled killings and failed contracts and missing money. It was not as if Nigerians did not already know these things. She had not expected much trouble, or much attention, but only a day after the paper came out, BBC radio carried the story on the news and interviewed an exiled Nigerian professor of politics who said her husband deserved a Human Rights Award. *He fights repression with the pen, he gives a voice to the voiceless, he makes the world know.*

Her husband had tried to hide his nervousness from her. Then, after someone called him anonymously—he got anonymous calls all the time, he was that kind of journalist, the kind who cultivated friendships along the way—to say that the head of state was personally furious, he no longer hid his fear; he let her see his shaking hands. Soldiers were on their way to arrest him, the caller said. The word was, it would be his last arrest, he would never come back. He climbed into the boot of the car minutes after the call, so that if the soldiers asked, the gateman could honestly claim not to know when her husband had left. She took Ugonna down to a neighbor's flat and then quickly sprinkled water in the boot, even though her husband told her to hurry, because she felt somehow that a wet boot would be cooler, that he would breathe better. She drove him to his coeditor's house. The next day, he called her from Benin Republic; the coeditor had contacts who had sneaked him over the border. His visa to America, the one he got when he went for a training course in Atlanta, was still valid, and he would apply for asylum when he arrived in New York. She told him not to worry, she and Ugonna would be fine, she would apply for a visa at the end of the school term and they would join him in America. That night, Ugonna was restless and she let him stay up and play with his toy car while she read a book. When she saw the three men burst in through the kitchen door, she hated herself for not insisting that Ugonna go to bed. If only—

"Ah, this sun is not gentle at all. These American embassy people should at least build a shade for us. They can use some of the money they collect for visa fee," the man behind her said.

Somebody behind him said the Americans were collecting the money for their own use. Another person said it was intentional to keep applicants waiting in the sun. Yet another laughed. She motioned to the blind begging couple and fumbled in her bag for a twenty-naira note. When she put it in the bowl, they chanted, "God bless you, you will have money, you will have good husband, you will have good job," in Pidgin English and then in Igbo and Yoruba. She watched them walk away. They had not told her, "You will have many good children." She had heard them tell that to the woman in front of her.

The embassy gates swung open and a man in a brown uniform shouted, "First fifty on the line, come in and fill out the forms. All the rest, come back another day. The embassy can attend to only fifty today."

"We are lucky, *abi*?" the man behind her said.

She watched the visa interviewer behind the glass screen, the way her limp auburn hair grazed the folded neck, the way green eyes peered at her papers above silver frames as though the glasses were unnecessary.

"Can you go through your story again, ma'am? You haven't given me any details," the visa interviewer said with an encouraging smile. This, she knew, was her opportunity to talk about Ugonna.

She looked at the next window for a moment, at a man in a dark suit who was leaning close to the screen, reverently, as though praying to the visa interviewer behind. And she realized that she would die gladly at the hands of the man in the black hooded shirt or the one with the shiny bald head before she said a word about Ugonna to this interviewer, or to anybody at the American embassy. Before she hawked Ugonna for a visa to safety.

Her son had been killed, that was all she would say. Killed. Nothing about how his laughter started somehow above his head, high and tin-kly. How he called sweets and biscuits "breadie-breadie." How he grasped her neck tight when she held him. How her husband said that he would be an artist because he didn't try to build with his LEGO blocks but instead he arranged them, side by side, alternating colors. They did not deserve to know.

"Ma'am? You say it was the government?" the visa interviewer asked.

"Government" was such a big label, it was freeing, it gave people room to maneuver and excuse and re-blame. Three men. Three men like her husband or her brother or the man behind her on the visa line. Three men.

"Yes. They were government agents," she said.

"Can you prove it? Do you have any evidence to show that?"

"Yes. But I buried it yesterday. My son's body."

"Ma'am, I am sorry about your son," the visa interviewer said. "But I need some evidence that you know it was the government. There is fighting going on between ethnic groups, there are private assassina-tions. I need some evidence of the government's involvement and I need some evidence that you will be in danger if you stay on in Nigeria."

She looked at the faded pink lips, moving to show tiny teeth. Faded pink lips in a freckled, insulated face. She had the urge to ask the visa interviewer if the stories in *The New Nigeria* were worth the life of a child. But she didn't. She doubted that the visa interviewer knew about pro-democracy newspapers or about the long, tired lines outside the embassy gates in cordoned-off areas with no shade where the furious sun caused friendships and headaches and despair.

"Ma'am? The United States offers a new life to victims of political persecution but there needs to be proof . . ."

A new life. It was Ugonna who had given her a new life, surprised her by how quickly she took to the new identity he gave her, the new person he made her. "I'm Ugonna's mother," she would say at his nursery school, to teachers, to parents of other children. At his funeral in Umunnachi, because her friends and family had been wearing dresses in the same Ankara print, somebody had asked, "Which one is the mother?" and she had looked up, alert for a moment, and said, "I'm Ugonna's mother." She wanted to go back to their ancestral hometown and plant ixora flowers, the kind whose needle-thin stalks she had sucked as a child. One plant would do, his plot was so small. When it bloomed, and the flowers welcomed bees, she wanted to pluck and suck at them while squatting in the dirt. And afterwards, she wanted to arrange the sucked flowers side by side, like Ugonna had done with his LEGO blocks. That, she realized, was the new life she wanted.

At the next window, the American visa interviewer was speaking too loudly into his microphone, "I'm not going to accept your lies, sir!"

The Nigerian visa applicant in the dark suit began to shout and to gesture, waving his see-through plastic file that bulged with documents. "This is wrong! How can you treat people like this? I will take this to Washington!" until a security guard came and led him away.

"Ma'am? Ma'am?"

Was she imagining it, or was the sympathy draining from the visa interviewer's face? She saw the swift way the woman pushed her reddish-gold hair back even though it did not disturb her, it stayed quiet on her neck, framing a pale face. Her future rested on that face. The face of a person who did not understand her, who probably did not cook with palm oil, or know that palm oil when fresh was a bright, bright red and when not fresh, congealed to a lumpy orange.

She turned slowly and headed for the exit.

"Ma'am?" she heard the interviewer's voice behind her.

She didn't turn. She walked out of the American embassy, past the beggars who still made their rounds with enamel bowls held outstretched, and got into her car.

THE CONDUCTOR

Aleksandar Hemon • 2005

In the 1989 *Anthology of Contemporary Bosnian Poetry*, Muhamed D. was represented with four poems. My copy of the anthology disappeared during the war, and I cannot recall the titles, but I do remember the subjects: one of them was about all the minarets of Sarajevo lighting up simultaneously at sunset on a Ramadan day; another was about the deaf Beethoven conducting his Ninth Symphony, unaware of the audience's ovations until the contralto touched his shoulder and turned him around. I was in my early twenties when the book came out, and compulsively writing poetry every day. I bought the anthology to see where I would fit into the pleiad of Bosnian poets. I thought that Muhamed D.'s poems were silly and fake; his use of Beethoven struck me as pretentious, and his mysticism as alien to my own rock 'n' roll affectations. But in one of the few reviews the anthology received, the critic raved, in syntax tortured on the rack of platitudes, about the range of Muhamed D.'s poetic skills and the courage he had shown in shedding the primitive Bosnian tradition for more modern forms. "Not only is Muhamed D. the greatest living Bosnian poet," the reviewer said, "he is the only one who is truly alive."

I had not managed to get any of my poetry published—nor would I ever manage—but I considered myself a far better, more soulful poet than Muhamed D. I had written about a thousand poems in less than two years, and occasionally I shored those fragments into a book manuscript that I sent to various contests. I can confess, now that I've long since stopped writing poetry, that I never really understood what I wrote. I didn't know what my poems were about, but I believed in them. I liked their titles ("Peter Pan and the Lesbians," "Love and Obstacles," et cetera), and I felt that they attained a realm of human innocence and experience that was unknowable, even by me. I delayed showing them to anyone else; I was waiting for readers to evolve, I suppose, to the point where they could grasp the vast spaces of my ego.

I met Muhamed D. for the first time in 1991, at a café called Dom pisaca, or Writers' Club, adjacent to the offices of the Bosnian Writers' Association. He was short and stocky, suddenly balding in his mid-forties, his expression frozen in an ugly permanent frown. I shook his hand limply, barely concealing my contempt. He spoke with the clear, provincial inflections of Travnik, his hometown, and was misclad in a dun shirt, brown pants, and an inflammable-green tie. I was a cool-dressed city boy, all denim and T-shirts, born and bred in the purest concrete, skipping vowels and slurring my consonants in a way that cannot even be imitated by anyone who did not grow up inhaling Sarajevo smog. He offered me a seat at his table, and I joined him, along with several of the other anthology veterans, who all wore the suffering faces of the sublime, as though they were forever imprisoned in the lofty dominion of poetry.

For some demented reason, Muhamed D. introduced me to them as a philharmonic orchestra conductor. My objections were drowned out as the other poets started howling the "Ode to Joy" while making conducting gestures, and I was instantly nicknamed "Dirigent"—Conductor—thereby becoming safely and permanently marked as a nonpoet. I stopped trying to correct the mistake as soon as I realized that it didn't matter: it was my role to be only an audience for their drunken, anthological greatness.

Muhamed D. sat at the head of the Table, governing confidently as they babbled, ranted, sang heartbreaking songs, and went about their bohemian business, guzzling ambrosial beer. I occupied the corner chair, witnessing and waiting, dreaming up put-downs that I would never utter, building up my arrogance while craving their acceptance. Later that night, Muhamed D. demanded that I explain musical notation. "How do you read those dots and flags?" he asked. "And what do you really do with the stick?" Although I had no idea, I tried to come up with some reasonable explanations, if only to expose his ignorance, but he just shook his head in discouragement. Almost every night I spent at the Table, there was a point where I failed to enlighten the poets as to how music was written, thereby confirming their initial assumption that I was a lousy conductor, but a funny guy. I wondered how Muhamed D. could write a poem about Beethoven while being entirely oblivious of the way the damn notation system worked.

But the poets liked me, and I hoped that some of the pretty literature students who frequently served as their muses would like me too. I particularly fancied three of them: Aida, Selma, and Ljilja, all of whom pronounced soft consonants while pouting their moist lips, emitting energy that caused instant erections. I kept trying to get at least one of them away from the Table, so that I could impress her with a recitation of "Love and Obstacles." Not infrequently, I got sufficiently inebriated to find myself loudly singing a *sevdalinka*, sending significant glances toward the three muses, and emulating conducting moves for their enjoyment, while a brain-freezing vision of laying all three of them simultaneously twinkled on my horizon. But it never worked out: I couldn't sing, my conducting was ludicrous, I never recited any of my poems, I wasn't even published, and instead I had to listen to Muhamed D. singing his *sevdalinka* with a trembling voice that opened the worlds of permanent dusk, where sorrow reigned and the mere sight of a woman's neck caused maddening bouts of desire. The eyes of the literature muses would fill with tears, and he could pick whichever volunteer he chose to amuse him for the rest of the night. I'd totter home alone, composing a poem that would show them all that Muhamed D. had nothing on me, that would make Aida, Selma, and Ljilja regret never having let me touch them. I celebrated and sang myself on empty Sarajevo streets, and by the time I had unlocked the door and sneaked into my bed without waking up my poetry-free parents, I would have a masterpiece, so formidable and memorable that I would not bother to write it down. The next morning, I would wake up with my skin oozing a sticky alcoholic sweat and the sappy masterpiece gone forever from my mind. Then I would embark upon a furious series of un-rhymed, anarchic poems, ridiculing Muhamed D. and the Table and the muses in impenetrably coded words, envisioning the devoted scholar who, one day, after decades of exploring my notes and papers, would decode the lines and recognize how tragically misunderstood and unappreciated I was. After writing all day, I'd head off to the Writers' Club and start the whole process again.

One night, Muhamed D. recited a new poem called "Sarajevo," which had two boys (*wisely chewing gum, / swallowing peppermint words*) walking the streets with a soccer ball (*They throw the ball through the snow, across Mis Irbina Street / as if lobbing a hand grenade across Lethe*). They accidentally drop the ball into the Miljacka, and the ball floats until it is caught in a whirlpool. They try to retrieve it with a device I had used once upon a time on my own lost ball: a crate is strung on a rope that stretches from bank to bank, and boys on either bank hold the ends of the rope, manipulating it until the ball is caught. Muhamed D. watches them from a bridge:

> *Whichever way I go, now, I'll reach the other shore.*
> *Old, I no longer know what they know: how to regain*
> *what is meant to be lost. On the river surface*
> *snowflake after snowflake perishes.*

He began his recitation in a susurrous voice, riding a tide of iambic throttles and weighted caesuras up to thunderous orgasmic heights, from where he returned to a whisper and then ceased altogether, his head bowed, his eyes closed. He seemed to have fallen asleep. The Table was silent, the muses entranced. So I said, "Fuck, that's old. What are you now—a hundred?" Uncomfortable with the silence, doubtless as jealous as I was, the rest of the Table burst out laughing, slapping their knees. I sensed the solidarity in mocking Muhamed, and for the first time I thought I would be remembered for something other than conducting—I would be remembered for having made Muhamed old. He smiled at me benevolently, already forgiving. But that very night, everybody at the Table started calling him "Dedo"—Old Man.

This took place just before the war, in the relatively rosy times when we were euphoric with the imminence of disaster—we drank and laughed and experimented with poetic forms into the late hours. We tried to keep the war away from the Table, but now and then a budding Serbian patriot would start ranting about the suppression of his people's culture, whereupon Dedo, with his newly acquired elder status, would indeed suppress him with a sequence of carefully arranged insults and curses. Inevitably, the nationalist would declare Dedo an Islamofascist and storm off, never to return, while we, the fools, laughed uproariously. We knew—but we didn't want to know—what was going to happen, the sky descending upon our heads like the shadow of a falling piano in a cartoon.

Around that time I found a way to come to the United States for a little while. In the weeks before I left, I roamed the city, haunting the territories of my past: here was a place where I had once stumbled and broken both of my index fingers; I was sitting on this bench when I first wedged my hand into Azra's tight brassiere; there was the kiosk where I had bought my first pack of cigarettes (Chesterfields); that was the fence that had torn a scar into my thigh as I was jumping it; in that library I had checked out a copy of *The Dwarf from a Forgotten Country* for the first time; on this bridge Dedo had stood, watching the boys recover the ball, and one of those boys could have been me.

Finally, I selected, reluctantly, some of my poems to show to Dedo. I met him at the Table early one afternoon, before everyone else arrived. I gave him the poems, and he read them, while I smoked and watched slush splash against the windows, then slide slowly down.

"You should stick to conducting," he said finally, and lit his cigarette. His eyebrows looked like hirsute little comets. The clarity of his gaze was what hurt me. These poems were told in the voice of postmodern Old Testament prophets, they were the cries of tormented individuals whose very souls were being depleted by the plague of relentless modernity. Was it possible, my poems asked, to maintain the reality of a person's self in this cruelly unreal world? The very inadequacy of poetry was a testimony to the disintegration of humanity, et cetera. But of course, I explained none of that. I stared at him with watery eyes, pleading for compassion, while he berated my sloppy prosody and the cold self-centeredness that was exactly the opposite of soul. "A poet is one with everything," he said. "You are everywhere, so you are never alone." Everywhere, my ass—the water dried in my eyes, and with an air of triumphant rationalism I tore my poetry out of his hands and left him in the dust of his neo-Romantic ontology. But outside—outside I dumped those prophetic poems, the founding documents of my life, into a gaping garbage container. I never went back to the Table, I never wrote poetry again, and a few days later I left Sarajevo for good.

My story is boring: I was not in Sarajevo when the war began; I felt helplessness and guilt as I watched the destruction of my hometown on TV; I lived in America. Dedo, of course, stayed for the siege— if you are the greatest living Bosnian poet, if you write a poem called "Sarajevo," then it is your duty to stay. I contemplated going back to Sarajevo early in the war, but realized that I was not and never would be needed there. So I struggled to make a living, while Dedo struggled to stay alive. For a long time, I didn't hear anything about him, and to tell the truth, I didn't really investigate—I had many other people to worry about, starting with myself. But news of him reached me occasionally: he signed some petitions; for one reason or another, he wrote an open letter to the pope; to an audience of annoyed Western diplomats he recited Herbert's "Report from the Besieged City" (*Too old to carry arms and fight like the others—/ they graciously gave me the inferior role of chronicler*). Once I heard that he had been killed; a hasty paper even published an obituary. But it turned out that he had only been wounded—he had come back from the other side of Lethe with a bullet in his thigh— and he wrote a poem about it. The paper that published the obituary published the poem too. Predictably, it was called "Resurrection." In it, he walks the city as a ghost, after the siege, but nobody remembers him, and he says to them:

> *Can't you recall me? I am the one*
> *Who carried upstairs your bloodied canisters,*
> *Who slipped his slimy hand under the widow's skirt.*
> *Who wailed the songs of sorrow,*
> *Who kept himself alive when fools were willing to die.*

Then he meets himself after the siege, *older than old*, and says to himself, alluding to Dante, *I did not know death hath undone so much*. It was a soul-rending poem, and I found myself hating him for it: he had written it practically on his deathbed, with no apparent effort, as his thigh wound throbbed with pus. I tried to translate it, but neither my Bosnian nor my English was good enough.

And he kept writing like a maniac, as though his resurrected life was to be entirely given over to poetry. Poems, mimeographed on coarse paper, bound in a frail booklet, were sent to me by long-unheard-from friends, carrying the smell (and microorganisms) of the many hands

that had touched them on their way out of besieged Sarajevo. There
were, naturally, images of death and destruction: dogs tearing at one
another's throats; a boy rolling the body of a sniper-shot man up
the street, much like Sisyphus; a surgeon putting together his wife's face
after it has been blown apart by shrapnel, a piece of her cheek missing,
the exact spot where he liked to plant his good-night kiss; clusters of
amputated limbs burning in a hospital oven, the poet facing the toy hell.
But there were also poems that were different, and I cannot quite define
the difference: A boy kicks a soccer ball up so that it lands on the nape
of his neck, and he balances it there; a young woman inhales cigarette
smoke and holds it in as she smiles, everything stopping at that moment: *No tracing bullets lighting up the sky, / no pain in my riven thigh / no
sounds*; a foreign conductor hangs on a rope, like a deft spider, over his
orchestra playing the *Eroica* in a burnt-out building. I must confess that
I believed for a moment that I was the conductor, that I was part of
Dedo's world, that something of me remained in Sarajevo.

Still, living displaces false sentiments. I had to go on with my American life, keeping Dedo out of it, busying myself with local survival, getting jobs, getting into graduate school, getting laid. Every once in a while
I unleashed the power of his words upon a sensitive American woman.
The first one was Cheryl, the idle wife of a Barrington lawyer, whom I
met at a Bosnian benefit dinner that she was kind enough to organize. At
least one Bosnian was required to benefit from her benefit dinner, so she
tracked me down through a friend, an expert in disability studies with
whom I had read a paper at a regional MLA conference. Cheryl was
generous beyond the dinner; before she went back to Barrington, I took
her to my tiny studio—a monument to the struggles of immigration,
with its sagging mattress, rotting shower curtain, and insomniac drum-
mer next door. I recited Dedo's poems to her, pretending they were my
own. She particularly liked the one about the man walking, during a lull
in shelling, with his rooster on a leash, *a soul fastened to a dying animal.*
Then I removed the permed tresses from her forehead so that I could kiss

it and slowly undressed her. Cheryl writhed in my embrace, kissed me with clammy passion, hoisted her hips, and moaned with pleasure, as though the intensity of her orgasm would directly succor the Bosnian resistance. I could not help thinking, in the end, that she was fucking Dedo, for it was his words that had seduced her. But I took what was given and then rolled off into the darkness of my actual life.

After the charitable Cheryl, I was somewhat ashamed and for a while I could not stand to look at Dedo's poetry. I finished graduate school; I sold my stories; I was an author now. And somewhere along the way the war ended. On my book tour, I traveled around the country, reading to minuscule audiences, talking about Bosnia to a mixture of international relations and South Slavic languages students, simplifying the incomprehensible, and fretting all along that an enraged reader would stand up and expose me as a fraud, as someone who had no talent—and therefore no right—to talk about the suffering of others. It never happened: I was Bosnian, I looked and conducted myself like a Bosnian, and everyone was content to think that I was in constant, un-interrupted communication with the tormented soul of my homeland.

At one of those readings, I met Bill T., a professor of Slavic lan-guages. He seemed to speak all of them, Bosnian included, and he was translating Dedo's latest book. With his red face, long, curly beard, and squat, sinewy body, Bill looked like a Viking. His ferocity was frighten-ing, so I immediately flattered him by saying how immeasurably im-portant it was to have Dedo's poetry translated into English. We went out drinking, and Bill T. drank like a true Viking too, while detailing the saga of his adventures in Slavic lands: a month with shepherds in the mountains of Macedonia; a year of teaching English in Siberia; his interviews with Solidarnosz veterans; the Slovenian carnival songs he had recorded. He had also spent some years, just for the hell of it, in Guatemala, Honduras, and Marrakech. The man had been everywhere, had done everything, and the drunker I got, the greater he was, and the more of nothing I had to say.

This was in Iowa City, I believe. I woke up the next morning on Bill T.'s sofa. My pants were laid out on the coffee table. Along the walls were dusty stacks of books. In the light fixture above me I could see the silhouettes of dead flies. A ruddy-faced boy with a gossamer mustache sat on the floor next to the sofa and watched me with enormous eyes.

"What are you doing here?" the boy asked calmly.

"I don't really know," I said, and sat up, exposing my naked thighs. "Where is Bill?"

"He stepped out."

"Where is your mom?"

"She's busy at the moment."

"What is your name?"

"Ethan."

"Nice to meet you, Ethan."

"Likewise," Ethan said. Then he grabbed my pants and threw them at me.

It was while I was slouching down the linden-lined street, where people nodded at me from sunny porches and able-bodied squirrels raced up and down the trees—it was then that the story Bill had told me the night before about Dedo fully hit me and I had to sit down on the curb to deal with it.

Dedo had come to Iowa City, Bill said, to be in the International Writing Program for twelve weeks. Bill had arranged it all, and volunteered to put Dedo up in the room above his garage. Dedo arrived with a small duffel bag, emaciated and exhausted, with the English he picked up while translating Yeats and a half-gallon of Jack Daniel's he picked up in a duty-free shop. The first week, he locked himself in above the garage and drank without pause. Every day, Bill knocked on the door, imploring him to come out, to meet the dean and the faculty, to mingle. Dedo refused to open the door and eventually stopped responding altogether. Finally, Bill broke the door down, and the room was an unreal mess: Dedo had not slept in the bed at all, and it was inexplicably wet;

there were monstrous, bloody footprints everywhere, because Dedo had apparently broken the Jack Daniel's bottle, then walked all over it. A box of cookies had been torn open and the cookies were crushed but not eaten. In the trash can were dozens of Podravka liver pâté cans, cleaned out and then filled with cigarette butts. Dedo was sleeping on the floor in the corner farthest from the window, facing the wall.

They subjected him to repeated cold showers; they cleaned him up and aired out the room; they practically force-fed him. For another week he wouldn't stick his nose out of the room. And then, Bill said, he began writing. He did not sleep for a week, delivering poems first thing in the morning, demanding translations by the afternoon. "American poets used to be like that," Bill said wistfully. "Now all they do is teach and complain and fuck their students on the sly."

Bill canceled his classes and set out to translate Dedo's poems. It was like entering the eye of a storm every day. In one poem, Bill said, a bee lands on a sniper's hand, and he waits for the bee to sting him. In another one, Dedo sees an orange for the first time since the siege began, and he is not sure what is inside it—whether oranges have changed during his time away from the world; when he finally peels it, the smell inhales him. In another, Dedo is running down Sniper Alley and a woman is telling him that his shoe is untied, and with a perfect clarity of purpose, with the ultimate respect for death, he stoops to tie it, and the shooting ceases, for even the killers appreciate an orderly world. "I could not believe," Bill said, "that such things could come out of that pandemonium."

At the end of the third week Dedo gave a reading. With a mug of Jack at hand he barked and hissed his verses at the audience, waving a shaky finger. After he had read, Bill came out and read the translations slowly and serenely in his deep Viking voice. But the audience was confused by Dedo's hostility. They clapped politely. Afterward, faculty and students came up to him to ask about Bosnia and invite him to luncheons. He visibly loathed them. He livened up only when he realized that he had a chance to lay one of the graduate students who was willing to open her mind to "other cultures." He was gone the next week, straight back to the siege, sick of America after less than a month.

In the years after the war, only the occasional rumor reached me: Dedo had survived a massive heart attack; he'd made a deal with his physician that he would stop drinking but go on smoking; he'd released a book based on conversations with his young niece during the siege. And then—this made the news all over Bosnia—he'd married an American lawyer, who was working in Bosnia collecting war-crime evidence. The newspapers cooed over the international romance: he had wooed her by singing and writing poetry; she had taken him to mass grave sites. A picture from their wedding showed her to be a foot taller than he, a handsome woman in her forties with a long face and short hair. He consequently produced a volume of poems, titled *The Anatomy of My Love*, featuring many parts of her remarkably healthy body. There were poems about her instep and her heel, her armpit and her breasts, the small of her back and the size of her eyes, the knobs on her knees and the ridges on her spine. Her name was Rachel. I heard that they had moved to the United States—following her body, he had ended up in Madison, Wisconsin.

But I do not want to give the impression that I thought about him a lot or even often. The way you never forget a song from your childhood, the way you hear it in your mind's ear every once in a while—that's how I remembered him. He was well outside my life, a past horizon visible only when the sky of the present was particularly clear.

As it was on the cloudless morning of September 11, 2001, when I was on a plane to D.C. The flight attendant was virginally blond. The man sitting next to me had a ring of biblical proportions on his pinkie. The woman on my right was immensely pregnant, squeezed into a tight red dress. I, of course, had no idea what was going on—the plane simply landed in Detroit and we disembarked. The Twin Towers were going down simultaneously on every screen at the unreal airport; maintenance personnel wept, leaning on their brooms; teenage girls screamed into their cell phones; forlorn pilots sat at closed gates. I wandered around the airport, recalling the lines from Dedo's poem: *Alive, I will be, when everybody's dead. / But there will be no joy in that, for all those / undone by death need to pass / through me to reach hell.*

While America settled into its mold of patriotic vulgarity, I began to despair, for everything reminded me of Bosnia in 1991. The War on Terror took me to the verge of writing poetry again, but I knew better. Nevertheless, I kept having imaginary arguments with Dedo, alternately explaining to him why I had to write and why I should not write poetry, while he tried to either talk me out of writing or convince me that it was my duty. Then, last winter, I was invited to read in Madison and hesitantly accepted. Dedo was the reason for both the hesitation and the acceptance, for I was told that he would be one of the other readers.

So there I was, entering the large university auditorium. I recognized Dedo in the crowd by his conspicuous shortness, his bald dome reflecting the stage lights. He was changed: he'd lost weight; everything on him, from his limbs to his clothes, seemed older and more worn; he wiped his hands on his corduroy pants, nervously glancing up at the people around him. He was clearly dying to smoke, and I could tell that he was not drunk enough to enjoy the spotlight. He was so familiar to me, so related to everything I used to know in Sarajevo: the view from my window; the bell of the dawn streetcar; the smell of smog in February; the shape that the lips assume when people pronounce their soft Slavic consonants.

"Dedo," I said. "*Šta ima?*"

He turned to me in a snap, as if I had just woken him up, and he did not smile. He didn't recognize me, of course. It was a painful moment, as the past was rendered both imaginary and false, as though I had never lived or loved. Even so, I introduced myself, told him how we used to drink together at the Writers' Club; how he used to sing beautifully; how often I remembered those times. He still couldn't recall me. I proceeded with flattery: I had read everything he'd ever written; I admired him, and as a fellow Bosnian, I was so proud of him—I had no doubt that a Nobel Prize was around the corner. He liked all that and nodded along, but I still did not exist in his memory. I told him, finally, that he used to think I was a conductor. "*Dirigent!*" he exclaimed, smiling at last, and here I emerged into the light. He embraced me, awkwardly pressing his cheek against my chest. Before I could tell him that I had never conducted and still was not conducting, we were called up to the stage. He had a rotten-fruit smell, as if his flesh had fermented; he went up the stairs with a stoop. Onstage, I poured him a glass of ice water, and instead of thanking me, he said, "You know, I wrote a poem about you."

I do not like reading in front of an audience, because I am conscious of my accent and I keep imagining some American listener collecting my mispronunciations, giggling at my muddled sentences. I read carefully, slowly, avoiding dialogue, and I always read the same passage. Often, I do it like a robot—I just read without even thinking about it, my lips moving but my mind elsewhere. So it was this time: I felt Dedo's gaze on my back; I thought about his mistaken memories of me conducting a nonexistent orchestra; I wondered about the poem that he had written about me. It could not have been the poem with the spider-conductor, for surely he knew that I was not in Sarajevo during the siege. Who was I in his poem? Did I force the musicians to go beyond themselves, to produce sublime beauty on mistuned instruments? What were we playing? Beethoven's Ninth? *The Rite of Spring? Death and Transfiguration?* I sure as hell was not conducting the Madison audience well. They applauded feebly, having all checked out after the first paragraph or so, and I feebly thanked them. "Super," Dedo said when I crawled back into my seat, and I could not tell whether he was being generous or whether he just had no idea how bad it really was.

Dedo was barely visible behind the lectern. Bending the microphone down like a horribly wilted flower, he announced that he was going to read a few poems translated into English by his "angel wife." He started from a deep register; then his voice rose steadily until it boomed. His vowels were flat, no diphthongs audible; his consonants were hard, maximally consonanty; *the*s were *duh*s; no *r*'s were rolled. His accent was atrocious, and I was happy to discover that his English was far worse than mine. But the bastard scorched through his verses, unfettered by self-consciousness. He flung his arms like a real conductor; he pointed his finger at the audience and stamped his foot, leaning toward and away from the microphone, as two young black women in the first row followed the rhythm of his sway. Then he read as if to seduce them, whispering, slowly:

> *Nobody is old anymore—dead or young, we are.*
> *The wrinkles straighten up, the feet no longer flat.*
> *Cowering behind garbage containers, flying away*
> *from the snipers, everybody is a gorgeous body*
> *stepping over the corpses, knowing:*
> *We are never as beautiful as now.*

Later I bought him a series of drinks at a bar full of Badgers pennants and kids in college-sweatshirt uniforms, blaring TVs showing helmeted morons colliding head-on. We huddled in the corner, close to the toilets, and drank bourbon upon bourbon; we exchanged gossip about various people from Sarajevo: Sem was in D.C., Goran in Toronto; someone I knew but he could not remember was in New Zealand; someone I had never known was in South Africa. At a certain point he fell silent; I was the only one talking, and all the suppressed misery of living in America surged from me. Oh, how many times I had wished death to entire college football teams. It was impossible to meet a friend without arranging a fucking appointment weeks in advance, and there were no coffee gardens where you could sit and watch people walk by. I was sick of being asked where I was from, and I hated Bush and his Jesus freaks. With every particle of my being I hated the word "carbs" and the systematic extermination of joy from American life, et cetera.

I don't know whether he heard me at all. His head hung low and he could have been asleep, until he looked up and noticed a young woman with long blond hair passing on her way to the toilet. He kept his gaze on her backpack, then on the toilet door, as if waiting for her.

"Cute," I said.

"She is crying," Dedo said.

We went to another bar, drank more, and left after midnight. Drunk out of my mind, I slipped and sat in a snow pile. We laughed, choking, at the round stain that made it seem as if I had soiled my pants. The air was scented with burnt burgers and patchouli. My butt was cold. Dedo was drunk too, but he walked better than I, skillfully avoiding tumbles. I do not know why I agreed to go home with him to meet his wife. We wobbled down quiet streets, where the trees were lined up as if dancing a quadrille. He made me sing, and so I sang: *Put putuje Latif-aga / Sa jaranom Sulejmanom.* We passed a house as big as a castle; a Volvo stickered with someone else's thought; Christmas lights and plastic angels eerily aglow. "How the fuck did we get here?" I asked him. "Everywhere is here," he said. Suddenly he pulled a cell phone out of his pocket, as if by magic—he belonged to a time before cell phones. He was calling home to tell Rachel that we were coming, he said, so that she could get some food ready for us. Rachel did not answer, so he kept redialing.

We stumbled up the porch, past a dwarf figure and a snow-covered rocking chair. Before Dedo could find his keys, Rachel opened the door. She was a burly woman, with austere hair and eventful earrings, her chin tucked into her underchin. She glared at us, and I have to say I was scared. As Dedo crossed the threshold, he professed his love to her with an accent so horrible that I thought for an instant he was kidding. The house smelled of chemical lavender; a drawing of a large-eyed mule hung on the wall. Rachel kept saying nothing, her cheeks puckering with obvious fury. I was willing now to give my life for friendship—I might have abandoned him in Sarajevo, but now we were facing Rachel together.

"This is my friend, Dirigent," he said, propping himself up on his toes to land a hapless kiss on her taut lips. "He is conductor." I made ridiculous conducting moves, as if to prove that I could still do it. She didn't even look at me; her eyes were pinned on Dedo.

"You're drunk," she said. "Again."

"Because I love you," he said. I nodded.

"Excuse us," she said, and pulled him deeper into the house, while I stood in the hallway deliberating over whether to take my shoes off. A little ball of dust moved down the hall, away from the door, like a scared dog. I recalled Dedo's poem about the shoes he had bought the day before the siege started, which he would never wear, for *they get dirty on the streets filthy with death*. Every day he polished his new shoes with what could be his last breath, *hoping for blisters*.

He emerged from the house depths and said, "*Daj pomozi*"—Help me.

"Get the hell out, you drunken pig," Rachel snarled in his wake. "And take your stupid friend with you."

I decided not to remove my shoes and, stupidly, said, "It's O.K."

"It is not O.K.!" Rachel shouted. "It has never been O.K. It will never be O.K."

"You must be nice to him," Dedo screamed at her. "You must respect."

"It's O.K.," I said.

"Not O.K. Never O.K. This is my friend." Dedo stabbed himself with his stubby finger. "Do you know me? Do you know who am I? I am biggest Bosnian poet alive."

"He is the greatest," I said.

"You're a fucking midget, is what you are!" She leaned into him, and I could see his pointed-finger hand unfolding and swinging for a slap.

"Come on, midget," Rachel bellowed. "Hit me. Yeah, sure. Hit me. Let's have Officer Johnson for coffee and cookies again."

Detergentlike snow had already covered our footprints. We stood outside on the street, Dedo fixated on the closed door, as though his gaze could burn through it, cursing in the most beautiful Bosnian and listing all her sins against him: her bastard son, her puritanism, her president, her decaf coffee. Panting, he bent over and grabbed a handful of snow, shaped it into a frail snowball, and threw it at the house. It disintegrated into a little blizzard and sprinkled the dwarf's face. He was about to make another wretched snowball when I spotted a pair of headlights creeping down the street. It looked like a police vehicle, and I did not want to risk coffee and cookies with Officer Johnson, so I started running.

Dedo caught up to me around the corner, and we staggered down an alley in an unknown direction: the alley was deserted except for a sofa with a stuffed giraffe leaning on it. There were weak tire-mark gullies and fresh traces of what appeared to be a three-legged dog. We saw a woman in the kitchen window of one of the nearby houses. She was circling around something we could not see, a glass full of red wine in her hand. The snow was ankle-deep; we watched her, mesmerized: a long, shiny braid stretched down her back. The three-legged dog must have vanished, for the prints just stopped in the middle of the alley. We could go neither forward nor back, so we sat down right there. I felt the intense pleasure of giving up, the expansive freedom of utter defeat. *Whichever way I go, now, I'll reach the other shore.* Dedo was humming a Bosnian song I didn't recognize, snowflakes melting on his lips. It was clear to me that we could freeze to death in a Madison back alley—it would be a famous way to die. I wanted to ask Dedo about the poem he had written about me, but he said, "This is like Sarajevo in 'ninety-three." Perhaps because of what he had said, or perhaps because I thought I saw Officer Johnson's car passing the alley, I got up and helped him to his feet.

In the cab, it was only a question of time before someone vomited. The Arab cabbie despised us, but Dedo tried to tell him that he was a fellow Muslim. Madison was deserted.

"You are my brother," Dedo said, and squeezed my hand. "I wrote a poem about you."

I tried to kiss his cheek, as the cabbie glared at us in the rear-view mirror, but awkwardly managed only to leave some saliva on his forehead.

"I wrote a good poem about you," Dedo said again, and I asked him to tell it to me.

He dropped his chin to his chest. He seemed to have passed out, so I shook him, and like a talking doll, he said, "He whips butterflies with his baton. . . ." But then we arrived at my hotel. Dedo kept reciting as I paid for the cab, and I didn't catch another word.

I dragged him to the elevator, his knees buckling, the snow thawing on his coat, releasing a closet-and-naphthalene smell. I could not tell whether he was still reciting or simply mumbling and cursing. I dropped him to the floor in the elevator and he fell asleep. He sat there in a pile, while I was unlocking the door to my room, and the elevator closed its doors and took him away. The thought of his being discovered in the elevator, drooling and gibbering, gave me a momentary pleasure. But I pressed the call button, and the elevator carrying Dedo obediently came back. *We are never as beautiful as now.*

The crushing sadness of hotel rooms; the gelid lights and clean notepads; the blank walls and particles of someone else's erased life: I rolled him into this as if into hell. I hoisted him onto the bed, took off his shoes and socks. His toes were frostbitten, his heels brandished a pair of blisters. I peeled off his coat and pants, and he was shivering, his skin goosebumped, his navel hidden in a hair tuft. I wrapped the bed-covers around him and threw a blanket on top. Then I lay down next to him, smelling his sweat and infected gums. He grunted and murmured, until his face calmed, the eyelids smoothing into slumber, the brows unfurrowing. A deep sigh, as when dusk falls, settled in his body. He was a beautiful human being.

And then on Tuesday, last Tuesday, he died.

ST. LUCY'S HOME
FOR GIRLS RAISED
BY WOLVES

Karen Russell • 2007

Stage 1: The initial period is one in which
everything is new, exciting, and interesting for
your students. It is fun for your students to explore
their new environment.

—*FROM* THE JESUIT HANDBOOK ON
LYCANTHROPIC CULTURE SHOCK

At first, our pack was all hair and snarl and floor-thumping joy.
We forgot the barked cautions of our mothers and fathers, all
the promises we'd made to be civilized and ladylike, couth and
kempt. We tore through the austere rooms, overturning dresser drawers, pawing through the neat piles of the Stage 3 girls' starched underwear, smashing lightbulbs with our bare fists. Things felt less foreign in
the dark. The dim bedroom was windowless and odorless. We reme-
died this by spraying exuberant yellow streams all over the bunks. We
jumped from bunk to bunk, spraying. We nosed each other midair, our
bodies buckling in kinetic laughter. The nuns watched us from the corner of the bedroom, their tiny faces pinched with displeasure.

"*Ay caramba*," Sister Maria de la Guardia sighed. "*Que barbaridad!*" She made the Sign of the Cross. Sister Maria came to St. Lucy's from a halfway home in Copacabana. In Copacabana, the girls are fat and languid and eat pink slivers of guava right out of your hand. Even at Stage 1, their pelts are silky, sun-bleached to near invisibility. Our pack was hirsute and sinewy and mostly brunette. We had terrible posture. We went knuckling along the wooden floor on the calloused pads of our fists, baring row after row of tiny, wood-rotted teeth. Sister Josephine sucked in her breath. She removed a yellow wheel of floss from under her robes, looping it like a miniature lasso.

"The girls at our facility are *backwoods*," Sister Josephine whispered to Sister Maria de la Guardia with a beatific smile. "You must be patient with them." I clamped down on her ankle, straining to close my jaws around the woolly XXL sock. Sister Josephine tasted like sweat and freckles. She smelled easy to kill.

We'd arrived at St. Lucy's that morning, part of a pack fifteen-strong. We were accompanied by a mousy, nervous-smelling social worker; the baby-faced deacon; Bartholomew, the blue wolfhound; and four burly woodsmen. The deacon handed out some stale cupcakes and said a quick prayer. Then he led us through the woods. We ran past the wild apiary, past the felled oaks, until we could see the white steeple of St. Lucy's rising out of the forest. We stopped short at the edge of a muddy lake. Then the deacon took our brothers. Bartholomew helped him to herd the boys up the ramp of a small ferry. We girls ran along the shore, tearing at our new jumpers in a plaid agitation. Our brothers stood on the deck, looking small and confused.

Our mothers and fathers were werewolves. They lived an outsider's existence in caves at the edge of the forest, threatened by frost and pitchforks. They had been ostracized by the local farmers for eating their silled fruit pies and terrorizing the heifers. They had ostracized the local wolves by having sometimes-thumbs, and regrets, and human children. (Their condition skips a generation.) Our pack grew up in a green purgatory. We couldn't keep up with the purebred wolves, but we never stopped crawling. We spoke a slab-tongued pidgin in the cave, inflected with frequent howls. Our parents wanted something better for us; they wanted us to get braces, use towels, be fully bilingual. When the nuns showed up, our parents couldn't refuse their offer. The nuns, they said, would make us naturalized citizens of human society. We would go to St. Lucy's to study a better culture. We didn't know at the time that our parents were sending us away for good. Neither did they.

That first afternoon, the nuns gave us free rein of the grounds. Everything was new, exciting, and interesting. A low granite wall surrounded St. Lucy's, the blue woods humming for miles behind it. There was a stone fountain full of delectable birds. There was a statue of St. Lucy. Her marble skin was colder than our mother's nose, her pupil-less eyes rolled heavenward. Doomed squirrels gamboled around her stony toes. Our diminished pack threw back our heads in a celebratory howl— an exultant and terrible noise, even without a chorus of wolf brothers in the background. There were holes everywhere!

We supplemented these holes by digging some of our own. We interred sticks, and our itchy new jumpers, and the bones of the friendly, unfortunate squirrels. Our noses ached beneath an invisible assault. Everything was smudged with a human odor: baking bread, petrol, the nuns' faint woman-smell sweating out beneath a dark perfume of tallow and incense. We smelled one another, too, with the same astounded fascination. Our own scent had become foreign in this strange place.

We had just sprawled out in the sun for an afternoon nap, yawning into the warm dirt, when the nuns reappeared. They conferred in the shadow of the juniper tree, whispering and pointing. Then they started towards us. The oldest sister had spent the past hour twitching in her sleep, dreaming of fatty and infirm elk. (The pack used to dream the same dreams back then, as naturally as we drank the same water and slept on the same red scree.) When our oldest sister saw the nuns approaching, she instinctively bristled. It was an improvised bristle, given her new, human limitations. She took clumps of her scraggly, nut-brown hair and held it straight out from her head.

Sister Maria gave her a brave smile.

"And what is your name?" she asked.

The oldest sister howled something awful and inarticulable, a distillate of hurt and panic, half-forgotten hunts and eclipsed moons. Sister Maria nodded and scribbled on a yellow legal pad. She slapped on a name tag: HELLO, MY NAME IS _____! "Jeanette it is."

The rest of the pack ran in a loose, uncertain circle, torn between our instinct to help her and our new fear. We sensed some subtler danger afoot, written in a language we didn't understand.

Our littlest sister had the quickest reflexes. She used her hands to flatten her ears to the side of her head. She backed towards the far corner of the garden, snarling in the most menacing register that an eight-year-old wolf-girl can muster. Then she ran. It took them two hours to pin her down and tag her: HELLO, MY NAME IS MIRABELLA!

"Stage 1," Sister Maria sighed, taking careful aim with her tranquilizer dart. "It can be a little overstimulating."

> Stage 2: After a time, your students realize that they must work to adjust to the new culture. This work may be stressful and students may experience a strong sense of dislocation. They may miss certain foods. They may spend a lot of time daydreaming during this period. Many students feel isolated, irritated, bewildered, depressed, or generally uncomfortable.

Those were the days when we dreamed of rivers and meat. The full-moon nights were the worst! Worse than cold toilet seats and boiled tomatoes, worse than trying to will our tongues to curl around our false new names. We would snarl at one another for no reason. I remember how disorienting it was to look down and see two square-toed shoes instead of my own four feet. Keep your mouth shut, I repeated during our walking drills, staring straight ahead. Keep your shoes on your feet. Mouth shut, shoes on feet. Do not chew on your new penny loafers. Do not. I stumbled around in a daze, my mouth black with shoe polish. The whole pack was irritated, bewildered, depressed. We were all uncomfortable, and between languages. We had never wanted to run away so badly in our lives; but who did we have to run back to? Only the curled black grimace of the mother. Only the father, holding his tawny head between his paws. Could we betray our parents by going back to them? After they'd given us the choicest part of the woodchuck, loved us at our hairless worst, nosed us across the ice floes and abandoned us at St. Lucy's for our own betterment?

Physically, we were all easily capable of clearing the low stone walls. Sister Josephine left the wooden gates wide open. They unslatted the windows at night so that long fingers of moonlight beckoned us from the woods. But we knew we couldn't return to the woods; not till we were civilized, not if we didn't want to break the mother's heart. It all felt like a sly, human taunt.

It was impossible to make the blank, chilly bedroom feel like home. In the beginning, we drank gallons of bathwater as part of a collaborative effort to mark our territory. We puddled up the yellow carpet of old newspapers. But later, when we returned to the bedroom, we were dismayed to find all trace of the pack musk had vanished. Someone was coming in and erasing us. We sprayed and sprayed every morning; and every night, we returned to the same ammonia eradication. We couldn't make our scent stick here; it made us feel invisible. Eventually we gave up. Still, the pack seemed to be adjusting on the same timetable. The advanced girls could already alternate between two speeds: "slouch" and "amble." Almost everybody was fully bipedal.

Almost.

The pack was worried about Mirabella.

Mirabella would rip foamy chunks out of the church pews and re-place them with ham bones and girl dander. She loved to roam the grounds wagging her invisible tail. (We all had a hard time giving that up. When we got excited, we would fall to the ground and start pump-ing our backsides. Back in those days we could pump at rabbity veloci-ties. *Que horror!* Sister Maria frowned, looking more than a little jealous.) We'd give her scolding pinches. "Mirabella," we hissed, imitat-ing the nuns. "No." Mirabella cocked her ears at us, hurt and confused.

Still, some things remained the same. The main commandment of wolf life is Know Your Place, and that translated perfectly. Being around other humans had awakened a slavish-dog affection in us. An abasing, belly-to-the-ground desire to please. As soon as we realized that some-one higher up in the food chain was watching us, we wanted only to be pleasing in their sight. Mouth shut, I repeated, shoes on feet. But if Mirabella had this latent instinct, the nuns couldn't figure out how to activate it. She'd go bounding around, gleefully spraying on their gilded statue of St. Lucy, mad-scratching at the virulent fleas that survived all of their powders and baths. At Sister Maria's tearful insistence, she'd stand upright for roll call, her knobby, oddly muscled legs quivering from the effort. Then she'd collapse right back to the ground with an ecstatic *oomph!* She was still loping around on all fours (which the nuns had taught us to see looked unnatural and ridiculous—we could barely believe it now, the shame of it, that we used to locomote like that!), her fists blue-white from the strain. As if she were holding a secret tight to the ground. Sister Maria de la Guardia would sigh every time she saw her. "*Caramba!*" She'd sit down with Mirabella and pry her fingers apart. "You see?" she'd say softly, again and again. "What are you hold-ing on to? Nothing, little one. Nothing."

Then she would sing out the standard chorus, "Why can't you be more like your sister Jeanette?"

The pack hated Jeanette. She was the most successful of us, the one furthest removed from her origins. Her real name was GWARR!, but she wouldn't respond to this anymore. Jeanette spiffed her penny loafers until her very shoes seemed to gloat. (Linguists have since traced the colloquial origins of "goody two-shoes" back to our facilities.) She could even growl out a demonic-sounding precursor to "Pleased to meet you." She'd delicately extend her former paws to visitors, wearing white kid gloves.

"Our little wolf, disguised in sheep's clothing!" Sister Ignatius liked to joke with the visiting deacons, and Jeanette would surprise everyone by laughing along with them, a harsh, inhuman, barking sound. Her hearing was still twig-snap sharp. Jeanette was the first among us to apologize; to drink apple juice out of a sippy cup; to quit eyeballing the cleric's jugular in a disconcerting fashion. She curled her lips back into a cousin of a smile as the traveling barber cut her pelt into bangs. Then she swept her coarse black curls under the rug. When we entered a room, our nostrils flared beneath the new odors: onion and bleach, candle wax, the turnipy smell of unwashed bodies. Not Jeanette. Jeanette smiled and pretended like she couldn't smell a thing.

I was one of the good girls. Not great and not terrible, solidly middle of the pack. But I had an ear for languages, and I could read before I could adequately wash myself. I probably could have vied with Jeanette for the number one spot, but I'd seen what happened if you gave in to your natural aptitudes. This wasn't like the woods, where you had to be your fastest and your strongest and your bravest self. Different sorts of calculations were required to survive at the home.

The pack hated Jeanette, but we hated Mirabella more. We began to avoid her, but sometimes she'd surprise us, curled up beneath the beds or gnawing on a scapula in the garden. It was scary to be ambushed by your sister. I'd bristle and growl, the way that I'd begun to snarl at my own reflection as if it were a stranger.

"Whatever will become of Mirabella?" we asked, gulping back our own fear. We'd heard rumors about former wolf-girls who never adapted to their new culture. It was assumed that they were returned to our native country, the vanishing woods. We liked to speculate about this before bedtime, scaring ourselves with stories of catastrophic bliss. It was the disgrace, the failure that we all guiltily hoped for in our hard beds. Twitching with the shadow question: *Whatever will become of me?*

We spent a lot of time daydreaming during this period. Even Jeanette. Sometimes I'd see her looking out at the woods in a vacant way. If you interrupted her in the midst of one of these reveries, she would lunge at you with an elder-sister ferocity, momentarily forgetting her human catechism. We liked her better then, startled back into being foamy old Jeanette.

In school, they showed us the St. Francis of Assisi slide show, again and again. Then the nuns would give us bags of bread. They never announced these things as a test; it was only much later that I realized that we were under constant examination. "Go feed the ducks," they urged us. "Go practice compassion for all God's creatures." *Don't pair me with Mirabella*, I prayed, *anybody but Mirabella*. "Claudette"—Sister Josephine beamed—"why don't you and Mirabella take some pumpernickel down to the ducks?"

"Ohhkaaythankyou," I said. (It took me a long time to say anything; first I had to translate it in my head from the Wolf.) It wasn't fair. They knew Mirabella couldn't make bread balls yet. She couldn't even undo the twist tie of the bag. She was sure to eat the birds; Mirabella didn't even try to curb her desire to kill things—and then who would get blamed for the dark spots of duck blood on our Peter Pan collars? Who would get penalized with negative Skill Points? Exactly.

As soon as we were beyond the wooden gates, I snatched the bread away from Mirabella and ran off to the duck pond on my own. Mirabella gave chase, nipping at my heels. She thought it was a game. "Stop it," I growled. I ran faster, but it was Stage 2 and I was still unsteady on my two feet. I fell sideways into a leaf pile, and then all I could see was my sister's blurry form, bounding towards me. In a moment, she was on top of me, barking the old word for tug-of-war. When she tried to steal the bread out of my hands, I whirled around and snarled at her, pushing my ears back from my head. I bit her shoulder, once, twice, the only language she would respond to. I used my new motor skills. I threw dirt, I threw stones. "Get away!" I screamed, long after she had made a cringing retreat into the shadows of the purple saplings. "Get away, get away!"

Much later, they found Mirabella wading in the shallows of a distant river, trying to strangle a mallard with her rosary beads. I was at the lake; I'd been sitting there for hours. Hunched in the long cattails, my yellow eyes flashing, shoving ragged hunks of bread into my mouth.

I don't know what they did to Mirabella. Me they separated from my sisters. They made me watch another slideshow. This one showed images of former wolf-girls, the ones who had failed to be rehabilitated. Long-haired, sad-eyed women, limping after their former wolf packs in white tennis shoes and pleated culottes. A wolf-girl bank teller, her makeup smeared in oily rainbows, eating a raw steak on the deposit slips while her colleagues looked on in disgust. Our parents. The final slide was a bolded sentence in St. Lucy's prim script: DO YOU WANT TO END UP SHUNNED BY BOTH SPECIES?

After that, I spent less time with Mirabella. One night she came to me, holding her hand out. She was covered with splinters, keening a high, whining noise through her nostrils. Of course I understood what she wanted; I wasn't that far removed from our language (even though I was reading at a fifth-grade level, halfway into Jack London's *The Son of the Wolf*).

"Lick your own wounds," I said, not unkindly. It was what the nuns had instructed us to say; wound licking was not something you did in polite company. Etiquette was so confounding in this country. Still, looking at Mirabella—her fists balled together like small, white porcupines, her brows knitted in animal confusion—I felt a throb of compassion. *How can people live like they do?* I wondered. Then I congratulated myself. This was a Stage 3 thought.

Stage 3: It is common that students who start living in a new and different culture come to a point where they reject the host culture and withdraw into themselves. During this period, they make generalizations about the host culture and wonder how the people can live like they do. Your students may feel that their own culture's lifestyle and customs are far superior to those of the host country.

The nuns were worried about Mirabella, too. To correct a failing, you must first be aware of it as a failing. And there was Mirabella, shucking her plaid jumper in full view of the visiting cardinal. Mirabella, battling a raccoon under the dinner table while the rest of us took dainty bites of peas and borscht. Mirabella, doing belly flops into compost.

"You have to pull your weight around here," we overheard Sister Josephine saying one night. We paused below the vestry window and peered inside.

"Does Mirabella try to earn Skill Points by shelling walnuts and polishing Saint-in-the-Box? No. Does Mirabella even know how to say the word *walnut*? Has she learned how to say anything besides a sinful 'HraaaHA!' as she commits frottage against the organ pipes? No."

There was a long silence.

"Something must be done," Sister Ignatius said firmly. The other nuns nodded, a sea of thin, colorless lips and kettle-black brows. "Something must be done," they intoned. That ominously passive construction; a something so awful that nobody wanted to assume responsibility for it.

I could have warned her. If we were back home, and Mirabella had come under attack by territorial beavers or snow-blind bears, I would have warned her. But the truth is that by Stage 3 I wanted her gone. Mirabella's inability to adapt was taking a visible toll. Her teeth were ground down to nubbins; her hair was falling out. She hated the spongy, long-dead foods we were served, and it showed—her ribs were poking through her uniform. Her bright eyes had dulled to a sour whiskey color. But you couldn't show Mirabella the slightest kindness anymore—she'd never leave you alone! You'd have to sit across from her at meals, shoving her away as she begged for your scraps. I slept fitfully during that period, unable to forget that Mirabella was living under my bed, gnawing on my loafers.

It was during Stage 3 that we met our first purebred girls. These were girls raised in captivity, volunteers from St. Lucy's School for Girls. The apple-cheeked fourth-grade class came to tutor us in playing. They had long golden braids or short, severe bobs. They had frilly-duvet names like Felicity and Beulah; and pert, bunny noses; and terrified smiles. We grinned back at them with genuine ferocity. It made us nervous to meet new humans. There were so many things that we could do wrong! And the rules here were different depending on which humans we were with: dancing or no dancing, checkers playing or no checkers playing, pumping or no pumping.

The purebred girls played checkers with us.

"These girl-girls sure is dumb," my sister Lavash panted to me between games. "I win it again! Five to none."

She was right. The purebred girls were making mistakes on purpose, in order to give us an advantage. "King me," I growled, out of turn. "*I say king me!*" and Felicity meekly complied. Beulah pretended not to mind when we got frustrated with the oblique, fussy movement from square to square and shredded the board to ribbons. I felt sorry for them. I wondered what it would be like to be bred in captivity, and always homesick for a dimly sensed forest, the trees you've never seen.

Jeanette was learning how to dance. On Holy Thursday, she mastered a rudimentary form of the Charleston. "*Brava!*" The nuns clapped. "*Brava!*"

Every Friday, the girls who had learned how to ride a bicycle celebrated by going on chaperoned trips into town. The purebred girls sold seven hundred rolls of gift-wrap paper and used the proceeds to buy us a yellow fleet of bicycles built for two. We'd ride the bicycles uphill, a sanctioned pumping, a grim-faced nun pedaling behind each one of us. "Congratulations!" the nuns would huff. "Being human is like riding this bicycle. Once you've learned how, you'll never forget." Mirabella would run after the bicycles, growling out our old names. HWRAA! GWARR! TRRRRRRR! We pedaled faster.

At this point, we'd had six weeks of lessons, and still nobody could do the Sausalito but Jeanette. The nuns decided we needed an inducement to dance. They announced that we would celebrate our successful rehabilitations with a Debutante Ball. There would be brothers, ferried over from the Home for Man-Boys Raised by Wolves. There would be a photographer from the *Gazette Sophisticate*. There would be a three-piece jazz band from West Toowoomba, and root beer in tiny plastic cups. The brothers! We'd almost forgotten about them. Our invisible tails went limp. I should have been excited; instead, I felt a low mad anger at the nuns. They knew we weren't ready to dance with the brothers; we weren't even ready to talk to them. Things had been so much simpler in the woods. That night I waited until my sisters were asleep. Then I slunk into the closet and practiced the Sausalito two-step in secret, a private mass of twitch and foam. Mouth shut—shoes on feet! Mouth shut—shoes on feet! Mouthshutmouthshut . . .

One night I came back early from the closet and stumbled on Jeanette. She was sitting in a patch of moonlight on the windowsill, reading from one of her library books. (She was the first of us to sign for her library card, too.) Her cheeks looked dewy.

"Why you cry?" I asked her, instinctively reaching over to lick Jeanette's cheek and catching myself in the nick of time.

Jeanette blew her nose into a nearby curtain. (Even her mistakes annoyed us—they were always so well intentioned.) She sniffled and pointed to a line in her book: "The lakewater was reinventing the forest and the white moon above it, and wolves lapped up the cold reflection of the sky." But none of the pack besides me could read yet, and I wasn't ready to claim a common language with Jeanette.

The following day, Jeanette golfed. The nuns set up a miniature putt-putt course in the garden. Sister Maria dug four sandtraps and got old Walter, the groundskeeper, to make a windmill out of a lawn mower engine. The eighteenth hole was what they called a "doozy," a minuscule crack in St. Lucy's marble dress. Jeanette got a hole in one.

On Sundays, the pretending felt almost as natural as nature. The chapel was our favorite place. Long before we could understand what the priest was saying, the music instructed us in how to feel. The choir director—aggressively perfumed Mrs. Valuchi, gold necklaces like pineapple rings around her neck—taught us more than the nuns ever did. She showed us how to pattern the old hunger into arias. Clouds moved behind the frosted oculus of the nave, glass shadows that reminded me of my mother. The mother, I'd think, struggling to conjure up a picture. A black shadow, running behind the watery screen of pines.

We sang at the chapel annexed to the home every morning. We understood that this was the humans' moon, the place for howling beyond purpose. Not for mating, not for hunting, not for fighting, not for anything but the sound itself. And we'd howl along with the choir, hurling every pitted thing within us at the stained glass. "Sotto voce." The nuns would frown. But you could tell that they were pleased.

Stage 4: As a more thorough understanding of the host culture is acquired, your students will begin to feel more comfortable in their new environment. Your students feel more at home, and their self-confidence grows. Everything begins to make sense.

"Hey, Claudette," Jeanette growled to me on the day before the ball. "Have you noticed that everything's beginning to make sense?"

Before I could answer, Mirabella sprang out of the hall closet and snapped through Jeanette's homework binder. Pages and pages of words swirled around the stone corridor, like dead leaves off trees.

"What about you, Mirabella?" Jeanette asked politely, stooping to pick up her erasers. She was the only one of us who would still talk to Mirabella; she was high enough in the rankings that she could afford to talk to the scruggliest wolf-girl. "Has everything begun to make more sense, Mirabella?"

Mirabella let out a whimper. She scratched at us and scratched at us, raking her nails along our shins so hard that she drew blood. Then she rolled belly-up on the cold stone floor, squirming on a bed of spelling-bee worksheets. Above us, small pearls of light dotted the high, tinted window.

Jeanette frowned. "You are a late bloomer, Mirabella! Usually, everything's begun to make more sense by Month Twelve at the latest." I noticed that she stumbled on the word *bloomer*. HraaaHA! Jeanette could never fully shake our accent. She'd talk like that her whole life, I thought with a gloomy satisfaction, each word winced out like an apology for itself.

"Claudette, help me," she yelped. Mirabella had closed her jaws around Jeanette's bald ankle and was dragging her towards the closet. "Please. Help me to mop up Mirabella's mess."

I ignored her and continued down the hall. I had only four more hours to perfect the Sausalito. I was worried only about myself. By that stage, I was no longer certain of how the pack felt about anything.

At seven o'clock on the dot, Sister Ignatius blew her whistle and frog-marched us into the ball. The nuns had transformed the rectory into a very scary place. Purple and silver balloons started popping all around us. Black streamers swooped down from the eaves and got stuck in our hair like bats. A full yellow moon smirked outside the window. We were greeted by blasts of a saxophone, and fizzy pink drinks, and the brothers.

The brothers didn't smell like our brothers anymore. They smelled like pomade and cold, sterile sweat. They looked like little boys. Someone had washed behind their ears and made them wear suspendered dungarees. Kyle used to be a blustery alpha male, BTWWWR!, chewing through rattlesnakes, spooking badgers, snatching a live trout out of a grizzly's mouth. He stood by the punch bowl, looking pained and out of place.

"My stars!" I growled. "What lovely weather we've been having!"

"Yeees," Kyle growled back. "It is beginning to look a lot like Christmas." All around the room, boys and girls raised by wolves were having the same conversation. Actually, it had been an unseasonally warm and brown winter, and just that morning a freak hailstorm had sent Sister Josephina to an early grave. But we had only gotten up to Unit 7: Party Dialogue; we hadn't yet learned the vocabulary for Unit 12: How to Tactfully Acknowledge Disaster. Instead, we wore pink party hats and sucked olives on little sticks, inured to our own strangeness.

The nuns swept our hair back into high, bouffant hairstyles. This made us look more girlish and less inclined to eat people, the way that squirrels are saved from looking like rodents by their poofy tails. I was wearing a white organdy dress with orange polka dots. Jeanette was wearing a mauve organdy dress with blue polka dots. Linette was wearing a red organdy dress with white polka dots. Mirabella was in a dark corner, wearing a muzzle. Her party culottes were duct-taped to her knees. The nuns had tied little bows on the muzzle to make it more festive. Even so, the jazz band from West Toowoomba kept glancing nervously her way.

"You smell astoooounding!" Kyle was saying, accidentally stretching the diphthong into a howl and then blushing. "I mean—"

"Yes, I know what it is that you mean," I snapped. (That's probably a little narrative embellishment on my part; it must have been months before I could really "snap" out words.) I didn't smell astounding. I had rubbed a pumpkin muffin all over my body earlier that morning to mask my natural, feral scent. Now I smelled like a purebred girl, easy to kill. I narrowed my eyes at Kyle and flattened my ears, something I hadn't done for months. Kyle looked panicked, trying to remember the words that would make me act like a girl again. I felt hot, oily tears squeezing out of the red corners of my eyes. *Shoesonfeet!* I barked at myself. I tried again. "My! What lovely weather—"

The jazz band struck up a tune.

"The time has come to do the Sausalito," Sister Maria announced, beaming into the microphone. "Every sister grab a brother!" She switched on Walter's industrial flashlight, struggling beneath its weight, and aimed the beam in the center of the room.

Uh-oh. I tried to skulk off into Mirabella's corner, but Kyle pushed me into the spotlight. "No," I moaned through my teeth, "noooooo." All of a sudden the only thing my body could remember how to do was pump and pump. In a flash of white-hot light, my months at St. Lucy's had vanished, and I was just a terrified animal again. As if of their own accord, my feet started to wiggle out of my shoes. *Mouth shut*, I gasped, staring down at my naked toes, *mouthshutmouthshut.*

"Ahem. The time has come," Sister Maria coughed, "to do the Sausalito." She paused. "The Sausalito," she added helpfully, "does not in any way resemble the thing that you are doing."

Beads of sweat stood out on my forehead. I could feel my jaws gaping open, my tongue lolling out of the left side of my mouth. What were the steps? I looked frantically for Jeanette; she would help me, she would tell me what to do.

Jeanette was sitting in the corner, sipping punch through a long straw and watching me pant. I locked eyes with her, pleading with the mute intensity that I had used to beg her for weasel bones in the forest. "What are the steps?" I mouthed.

"The steps!"

"The steps?" Then Jeanette gave me a wide, true wolf smile. For an instant, she looked just like our mother. "Not for you," she mouthed back.

I threw my head back, a howl clawing its way up my throat. I was about to lose all my Skill Points, I was about to fail my Adaptive Dancing test. But before the air could burst from my lungs, the wind got knocked out of me. *Oomph!* I fell to the ground, my skirt falling softly over my head. Mirabella had intercepted my eye-cry for help. She'd chewed through her restraints and tackled me from behind, barking at unseen cougars, trying to shield me with her tiny body. "*Caramba!*" Sister Maria squealed, dropping the flashlight. The music ground to a halt. And I have never loved someone so much, before or since, as I loved my littlest sister at that moment. I wanted to roll over and lick her ears, I wanted to kill a dozen spotted fawns and let her eat first.

But everybody was watching; everybody was waiting to see what I would do. "I wasn't talking to you," I grunted from underneath her. "I didn't want your help. Now you have ruined the Sausalito! You have ruined the ball!" I said more loudly, hoping the nuns would hear how much my enunciation had improved.

"You have ruined it!" my sisters panted, circling around us, eager to close ranks. "Mirabella has ruined it!" Every girl was wild-eyed and itching under her polka dots, punch froth dribbling down her chin. The pack had been waiting for this moment for some time. "Mirabella cannot adapt! Back to the woods, back to the woods!"

The band from West Toowoomba had quietly packed their instruments into black suitcases and were sneaking out the back. The boys had fled back towards the lake, bow ties spinning, snapping suspenders in their haste. Mirabella was still snarling in the center of it all, trying to figure out where the danger was so that she could defend me against it. The nuns exchanged glances.

In the morning, Mirabella was gone. We checked under all the beds. I pretended to be surprised. I'd known she would have to be expelled the minute I felt her weight on my back. Walter came and told me this in secret after the ball, "So you can say yer good-byes." I didn't want to face Mirabella. Instead, I packed a tin lunch pail for her: two jelly sandwiches on saltine crackers, a chloroformed squirrel, a gilt-edged placard of St. Bolio. I left it for her with Sister Ignatius, with a little note: "Best wishes!" I told myself I'd done everything I could.

"Hooray!" the pack crowed. "Something has been done!" We raced outside into the bright sunlight, knowing full well that our sister had been turned loose, that we'd never find her. A low roar rippled through us and surged up and up, disappearing into the trees. I listened for an answering howl from Mirabella, heart thumping—what if she heard us and came back? But there was nothing.

We graduated from St. Lucy's shortly thereafter. As far as I can recollect, that was our last communal howl.

Stage 5: At this point your students are able to interact effectively in the new cultural environment. They find it easy to move between the two cultures.

One Sunday, near the end of my time at St. Lucy's, the sisters gave me a special pass to go visit the parents. The woodsman had to accompany me; I couldn't remember how to find the way back on my own. I wore my best dress and brought along some prosciutto and dill pickles in a picnic basket. We crunched through the fall leaves in silence, and every step made me sadder. "I'll wait out here," the woodsman said, leaning on a blue elm and lighting a cigarette.

The cave looked so much smaller than I remembered it. I had to duck my head to enter. Everybody was eating when I walked in. They all looked up from the bull moose at the same time, my aunts and uncles, my sloe-eyed, lolling cousins, the parents. My uncle dropped a thighbone from his mouth. My littlest brother, a cross-eyed wolf-boy who has since been successfully rehabilitated and is now a dour, balding children's book author, started whining in terror. My mother recoiled from me, as if I was a stranger. TRRR? She sniffed me for a long moment. Then she sank her teeth into my ankle, looking proud and sad.

THE LAST THING
WE NEED

Claire Vaye Watkins • 2010

July 28

Duane Moser
4077 Pincay Drive
Henderson, Nevada 89015

Dear Mr. Moser,
   *On the afternoon of June 25, while on my last outing to
Rhyolite, I was driving down Cane Springs Road some ten
miles outside Beatty and happened upon what looked to be
the debris left over from an auto accident. I got out of my
truck and took a look around. The valley was bone dry. A
hot west wind took the puffs of dust from where I stepped
and curled them away like ash. Near the wash I found
broken glass, deep gouges in the dirt running off the side of
the road and an array of freshly bought groceries tumbled
among the creosote. Coke cans (some full, some open and
empty, some with the tab intact but dented and half-full and*

leaking). Bud Light cans in the same shape as the Coke.
Fritos. Meat. Et cetera. Of particular interest to me were the
two almost-full prescriptions that had been filled at the
pharmacy in Tonopah only three days before, and a sealed
Ziploc bag full of letters signed M. *I also took notice of a*
bundle of photos of an old car, part primer, part rust, that I
presume was or is going to be restored. The car was a Chevy
Chevelle, a '66, I believe. I once knew a man who drove a
Chevelle. Both medications had bright yellow stickers on
their sides warning against drinking alcohol while taking
them. Enter the Bud Light, and the gouges in the dirt,
possibly. I copied your address off the prescription bottles.
What happened out there? Where is your car? Why were the
medications, food and other supplies left behind? Who are
you, Duane Moser? What were you looking for out at
Rhyolite?

    I hope this letter finds you, and finds you well. Please
write back.
    Truly,
    Thomas Grey

P.O. Box 1230
Verdi, Nevada 89439

    P.S. I left most of the debris in the desert, save for the
medications, pictures and letters from M. I also took the
plastic grocery bags, which I untangled from the bushes and
recycled on my way through Reno. It didn't feel right to just
leave them out there.

August 16

Duane Moser
4077 Pincay Drive
Henderson, Nevada 89015

Dear Mr. Moser,

This morning as I fed the horses, clouds were just beginning to slide down the slope of the Sierras, and I was reminded once again of Rhyolite. When I came inside I borrowed my father's old copy of the Physician's Desk Reference *from his room. From that book I have gathered that before driving out to Rhyolite you may have been feeling out of control, alone or hopeless. You were possibly in a state of extreme depression; perhaps you were even considering hurting yourself. Judging by the date the prescriptions were filled and the number of pills left in the bottles—which I have counted, sitting out in the fields atop a tractor that I let sputter and die, eating the sandwich my wife fixed me for lunch—you had not been taking the medications long enough for them to counteract your possible feelings of despair. "Despair," "depression," "hopeless," "alone." These are the words of the* PDR, *forty-first edition, which I returned to my father promptly, as per his request. My father can be difficult. He spends his days shut up in his room, reading old crime novels populated by dames and Negroes, or watching the TV we bought him with the volume up too high. Some days he refuses to eat. Duane Moser, my father never thought he would live this long.*

I think there will be lightning tonight; the air has that feel. Please, write back.

Truly,
Thomas Grey

P.O. Box 1230
Verdi, Nevada 89439

September 1

Duane Moser
4077 Pincay Drive
Henderson, Nevada 89015

Dear Mr. Moser,

*I slept terribly last night, dreamed dreams not easily
identified as such. Had I told my wife about them, she might
have given me a small quartz crystal or amethyst and
insisted I carry it around in my pocket all day, to cleanse my
mind and spirit. She comes from California. Here is a story
she likes to tell. On one of our first dates, we walked arm in
arm around downtown Reno, where she was a clerk at a
grocery store and I was a student of agriculture and business.
There she tried to pull me down a little flight of steps to the
red-lit underground residence of a palm reader and psychic. I
declined. Damn near an hour she pulled on me, saying what
was I afraid of, asking what was the big deal. I am not a
religious man but, as I told her then, there are some things
I'd rather not fuck with. Now she likes to say it's a good
thing I wouldn't go in, because if that psychic had told her
she'd be stuck with me for going on fourteen years now, she
would have turned and headed for the hills. Ha! And I say,*

Honey, not as fast as I would've, ha, ha! This is our old joke. Like all our memories, we like to take it out once in a while and lay it flat on the kitchen table, the way my wife does with her sewing patterns, where we line up the shape of our life against that which we thought it would be by now.

I'll tell you what I don't tell her, that there is something shameful in this, the buoying of our sinking spirits with old stories.

I imagine you a man alone, Duane Moser, with no one asking after your dreams in the morning, no one slipping healing rocks into your pockets. A bachelor. It was the Fritos, finally, which reminded me of the gas station in Beatty where I worked when I was in high school and where I knew a man who owned a Chevelle like yours, a '66. But it occurs to me that perhaps this assumption is foolish; surely there are wives out there who have not banned trans fats and processed sugar, as mine has. I haven't had a Frito in eleven years. Regardless, I write to inquire about your family, should you reply.

Our children came to us later in life than most. My oldest, Danielle, has just started school. Her little sister, Layla, is having a hard time with it. She wants so badly to go to school with Danielle that she screams and cries as the school bus pulls away in the morning. Sometimes she throws herself down to the ground, embedding little pieces of rock in the flesh of her fists. Then she is sullen and forlorn for the rest of the day. My wife worries for her, but truth be told, I am encouraged. The sooner Layla understands that we are nothing but the sum of that which we endure, the better. But my father has taken to walking Layla to the end of our gravel road in the afternoon to wait for Danielle at the bus stop. Layla likes to go as early as she is allowed, as if her being there will bring the bus sooner. She would stand at the end of the road all day if we let her. She pesters my father so that he sometimes stands there in the heat with her for an hour or more, though his heart is in no condition to be doing so. In many ways he is better to my girls than I am. He is far better to them than he was to me. I am not a religious man but I do thank God for that.

I am beginning to think I dreamed you up. Please, write soon.

   Truly,

   Thomas Grey

P.O. Box 1230
Verdi, Nevada 89439

October 16

Duane Moser
4077 Pincay Drive
Henderson, Nevada 89015

Dear Mr. Moser,

I have read the letters from M, the ones you kept folded in the Ziploc bag. Forgive me, but for all I know you may be dead, and I could not resist. I read them in my shed, where the stink and thickness of the air were almost unbearable, and then again in my truck in the parking lot of the Verdi post office. I was struck, as I was when I first found them out near Rhyolite on Cane Springs Road, by how new the letters looked. Though most were written nearly twenty years ago,

*the paper is clean, the creases sharp. Duane Moser, what I do
not understand is this: why a Ziploc bag? Did you worry
they might get wet on your journey through the desert in the
middle of summer? Then again, I am reminded of the Coke
and Bud Light. Or am I to take the Ziploc bag as an
indication of your fierce, protective love for M? Is it a sign,
as M suggests, that little by little you sealed your whole self
off, until there was nothing left for her? Furthermore, I have
to ask whether you committed this sealing purposefully. She
says she thinks she was always asking too much of you. She is
generous that way, isn't she? She says you didn't mean to
become "so very alien" to her. I am not so sure. I love my
wife. But I've never told her how I once knew a man in
Beatty with a '66 Chevelle. I know what men like us are
capable of.*

*Duane Moser, what I come back to is this: how could you
have left M's letters by the side of Cane Springs Road near the
ghost town Rhyolite where hardly anyone goes anymore? (In fact,
I have never seen another man out on Cane Springs Road. I
drive out there to be alone. Maybe you do, too. Or you did,
anyway.) Did you not realize that someone just like you might
find them?*

*I have called the phone number listed on the prescription
bottles, finally, though all I heard was the steady rising tones
of the disconnected signal. Still, I found myself listening for
you there. Please, write soon.*

Truly,

Thomas Grey

P.O. Box 1230
Verdi, Nevada 89439

*P.S. On second thought, perhaps sometimes these things
are best left by the side of the road, as it were. Sometimes
a person wants a part of you that's no good. Sometimes
love is a wound that opens and closes, opens and closes,
all our lives.*

November 2

Duane Moser
4077 Pincay Drive
Henderson, Nevada 89015

Dear Mr. Moser,
     *My wife found your pictures, the ones of the Chevelle.
The one you maybe got from a junkyard or from a friend, or
maybe it's been in your family for years, rotting in a garage
somewhere because after what happened nobody wanted to
look at it. I kept the pictures tucked behind the visor in my
truck, bound with a rubber band. I don't know why I kept
them. I don't know why I've kept your letters from M, or
your medications. I don't know what I would do if I found
what I am looking for.*
          *When I was in high school I worked the graveyard shift at a
gas station in Beatty. It's still there, on the corner of I-95 and
Highway 374, near the hot springs. Maybe you've been there.
It's a Shell station now, but back then it was called Hadley's
Fuel. I worked there forty, fifty hours a week. Bill Hadley was
a friend of my father's. He was a crazy son of a bitch, as my
father would say, who kept a shotgun under the counter and
always accused me of stealing from the till or sleeping on*

the job when I did neither. I liked the graveyard shift, liked being up at night, away from Pop, listening to the tremors of the big walk-in coolers, the hum of the fluorescent lights outside.

Late that spring, a swarm of grasshoppers moved through Beatty on their way out to the alfalfa fields down south. They were thick and fierce, roaring like a thunderstorm in your head. The hoppers ate anything green. In two days they stripped the leaves from all the cottonwoods and willows in town, then they moved on to the juniper and pine, the cheatgrass and bitter salt cedar. A swarm of them ate the wool right off of Abel Prince's live sheep. Things got so bad that the trains out to the mines shut down for a week because the guts of the bugs made the rails too slippery.

The grasshoppers were drawn to the fluorescent lights at Hadley's. For weeks the parking lot pulsed with them. I would have felt them crunch under my feet when I walked out to the pumps that night, dead and dying under my shoes, only I never made it out to the pumps. I was doing schoolwork at the counter. Calculus, for God's sake. I looked up and the guy was already coming through the door at me. I looked outside and saw the '66 Chevelle, gleaming under the lights, grasshoppers falling all around it like rain.

I tried to stop him but he muscled back behind the counter. He had a gun, held it like it was his own hand. He said, You see this?

There was a bandanna over his face. But Beatty is a small town, and it was even smaller then. I knew who he was. I knew his mother worked as a waitress at the Stagecoach and that his sister had graduated the year before me. The money, he was saying. His name was Frankie. The fucking money, Frankie said.

I'd barely touched a gun before that night. I don't know how I did it. I only felt my breath go out of me and reached under the counter to where the shotgun was and tried. I shot him in the head.

Afterward, I called the cops. I did the right thing, they told me, the cops and Bill Hadley in his pajamas, even my father. They said it over and over again. I sat on the curb outside the store, listening to them inside, their boots squeaking on the tile. The deputy sheriff, Dale Sullivan, who was also the assistant coach of the basketball team, came and sat beside me. I had my hands over my head to keep the grasshoppers away. *Kid, it was bound to happen,* Dale said. *The boy was a troublemaker. A waste of skin.*

He told me I could go on home. I didn't ask what would happen to the car.

That night, I drove out on Cane Springs Road to Rhyolite. I drove around that old ghost town with the windows rolled down, listening to the gravel pop under my tires. The sun was coming up. There, in the milky light of dawn, I hated Beatty more than I ever had. The Stagecoach, the hot springs, all the trees looking so naked against the sky. I never wanted to see any of it ever again.

I was already on my way to college and everyone knew it. I didn't belong in Beatty. The boy's family, his mother and sister and stepfather, moved away soon after it happened. I'd never see them around town, or at Hadley's. For those last few weeks of school no one talked about it, at least not to me. Soon it was as though it had never happened. But—and I think I realized this then, up in Rhyolite, that dead town picked clean—Beatty would never be a place I could come home to.

When my wife asked about your pictures, she said she didn't

realize I knew so much about cars. I said, Yeah, sure. Well, some. See the vents there? On the hood? See the blackout grille? That's how you know it's a '66. I told her I'd been thinking about buying an old car, fixing it up, maybe this one. Right then she just started laughing her head off. Sure, she managed through all her laughter, fix up a car. She kept on laughing. She tossed the bundle of photos on the seat of the truck and said, You're shitting me, Tommy.

It's not her fault. That man, the one who knows a '66 when he sees one, that's not the man she married. That's how it has to be. You understand, don't you?

I smiled at her. No, ma'am, I said. I wouldn't shit you. You're my favorite turd.

She laughed—she's generous that way—and said, A car. That's the last thing we need around here.

When I was a boy, my father took me hunting. Quail mostly and, one time, elk. But I was no good at it and he gave up. I didn't have it in me, my father said, sad and plain as if it were a birth defect, the way I was. Even now, deer come down from the mountains and root in our garden, stripping our tomatoes from the vine, eating the hearts of our baby cabbages. My father says, Kill one. String it up. They'll learn. I tell him I can't do that. I spend my Sundays patching the holes in the fence, or putting up a taller one. The Church of the Compassionate Heart, my wife calls it. It makes her happy, this life of ours, the man I am. Layla helps me mend the fence. She stands behind me and hands me my pliers or my wire cutters when I let her.

But here's the truth, Duane Moser. Sometimes I see his eyes above that bandanna, see the grasshoppers leaping in the lights, hear them vibrating. I feel the kick of the rifle butt in my sternum. I would do it again.

Truly,
Thomas Grey

P.O. Box 1230
Verdi, Nevada 89439

———————————

December 20

Duane Moser
4077 Pincay Drive
Henderson, Nevada 89015

Dear Duane Moser,
    This will be the last I write to you. I went back to
Rhyolite. I told my wife I was headed south to camp and hike
for a few days. She said, Why don't you take Layla with you?
It would be good for her.
    Layla slept nearly the whole drive. Six hours. When I slowed
the car and pulled onto Cane Springs Road she sat up and said,
Dad, where are we?
    I said, We're here.
    I helped her with her coat and mittens, and we took a walk
through the ruins. I told her what they once were. Here, I said,
was the schoolhouse. They finished it in 1909. By then there
weren't enough children in town to fill it. It burned the next
year. She wanted to go closer.
    I said, Stay where I can see you.
    Why? she said.
    I didn't know how to say it. Crumbling buildings, rotted-out

*floors, sinkholes, open mine shafts. Coyotes, rattlesnakes,
mountain lions.*

Because, I said. It's not safe for little girls.

*We went on. There behind the fence is the post office,
completed in 1908. This slab, these beams, that wall of brick,
that was the train station. It used to have marble floors,
mahogany woodworking, one of the first telephones in the state.
But those have been sold or stolen over the years.*

Why? she said.

That's what happens when a town dies.

Why?

Because, sweetheart. Because.

*At dusk I tried to show Layla how to set up a tent and build
a fire, but she wasn't interested. Instead, she concentrated on
filling her pink vinyl backpack with stones and using them to
build little pyramids along the path that led out to the town. She
squatted over them, gingerly turning the stones to find a flat
side, a stable base. What are those for? I asked.*

For if we get lost, she said. Pop Pop showed me.

*When it got dark we sat together, listening to the hiss of the
hot dogs at the ends of our sticks, the violent sizzle of sap
escaping the firewood. Layla fell asleep in my lap. I carried her
to the tent and zipped her inside a sleeping bag. I stayed and
watched her there, her chest rising and falling, hers the small
uncertain breath of a bird.*

*When I bent to step out through the opening of the tent
something fell from the pocket of my overalls. I held it up in the
firelight. It was a cloudy stump of amethyst, as big as a horse's
tooth.*

*I've tried, Duane Moser, but I can't picture you at 4077
Pincay Drive. I can't see you in Henderson, period, out in the*

suburbs, on a cul-de-sac, in one of those prefab houses with the stucco and the garage gaping off the front like a mouth. I can't see you standing like a bug under those streetlights the color of antibacterial soap. At home at night I sit on my porch and watch the lights of Reno over the hills, the city marching out at us like an army. It's no accident that the first step in what they call developing a plot of land is to put a fence around it.

I can't see you behind a fence. When I see you, I see you here, at Rhyolite, harvesting sticks of charcoal from the half-burnt schoolhouse and writing your name on the exposed concrete foundation. Closing one eye to look through the walls of Jim Kelly's bottle house. No, that's my daughter. That's me as a boy getting charcoal stains on my blue jeans. That's you in your Chevelle, the '66, coming up Cane Springs Road, tearing past what was once the Porter brothers' store. I see you with M, flinging Fritos and meat and half-full cans of Coke and Bud Light from the car like a goddamn celebration, a shedding of your old selves.

It's almost Christmas. I've looked at the prescriptions, the letters, the photos. You're not Frankie, I know this. It's just a coincidence, a packet of pictures flung from a car out in the middle of nowhere. The car is just a car. The world is full of Chevelles, a whole year's worth of the '66. You know nothing of Hadley's Fuel in Beatty, of a boy who was killed there one night in late spring when the grasshoppers sounded like a thunderstorm in your head. I don't owe you anything.

When I woke this morning there was snow on the ground and Layla was gone. She'd left no tracks. I pulled on my boots and walked around the camp. A layer of white covered the hills and the valley and the skeletons of the old buildings, lighting the valley fluorescent. It was blinding. I called my daughter's name. I listened, pressing the sole of my shoe against the blackened rocks *lining the fire pit. I watched the snow go watery within my boot print. There was no answer.*

I checked the truck. It was empty. In the tent I found her coat and mittens. Her shoes had been taken. I scrambled up a small hill and looked for her from there. I scanned for the shape of her among the old buildings, on the hills, along Cane Springs Road. Fence posts, black with moisture, strung across the valley like tombstones. Sickness thickened in my gut and my throat. She was gone.

I called for her again and again. I heard nothing, though surely my own voice echoed back to me. Surely the snow creaked under my feet when I walked through our camp and out to the ruins. Surely the frozen tendrils of creosote whipped against my legs when I began to run through the ghost town, up and down the gravel path. But all sound had left me except for a low, steady roaring, the sound of my own blood in my ears, of a car rumbling up the old road.

Suddenly my chest was burning. I couldn't breathe. Layla. Layla. I crouched and pressed my bare palms against the frozen earth. The knees of my long johns soaked through, my fingers began to sting.

Then I saw a shape near the burnt remains of the schoolhouse. A panic as hot and fierce as anything—fiercer—rose in me. The slick pink vinyl of her backpack. I ran to it.

When I bent to pick it up, I heard something on the wind. Something like the high, breathy language my daughters speak to each other when they play. I followed the sound around behind the schoolhouse and found Layla squatting there in her pajamas, softly stacking one of her stone markers in the snow.

Hi, Dad, she said. The snow had reddened her hands and cheeks as though she'd been burned. She handed me a stone. Here you go, she said.

I took my daughter by the shoulders and stood her up. I raised her sweet chin so her eyes met mine, and then I slapped her across the face. She began to cry. I held her. The Chevelle drove up and down Cane Springs Road, the gravel under its tires going pop pop pop. *I said,* Shh. That's enough. A child means nothing out here.

    Truly,

    Thomas Grey

THE PAPER MENAGERIE

Ken Liu · 2011

One of my earliest memories starts with me sobbing. I refused to be soothed no matter what Mom and Dad tried.

Dad gave up and left the bedroom, but Mom took me into the kitchen and sat me down at the breakfast table.

"*Kan, kan*," she said, as she pulled a sheet of wrapping paper from on top of the fridge. For years, Mom carefully sliced open the wrappings around Christmas gifts and saved them on top of the fridge in a thick stack.

She set the paper down, plain side facing up, and began to fold it. I stopped crying and watched her, curious.

She turned the paper over and folded it again. She pleated, packed, tucked, rolled, and twisted until the paper disappeared between her cupped hands. Then she lifted the folded-up paper packet to her mouth and blew into it, like a balloon.

"*Kan*," she said. "*Laohu.*" She put her hands down on the table and let go.

A little paper tiger stood on the table, the size of two fists placed together. The skin of the tiger was the pattern on the wrapping paper, white background with red candy canes and green Christmas trees.

I reached out to Mom's creation. Its tail twitched, and it pounced playfully at my finger. "*Rawrr-sa*," it growled, the sound somewhere between a cat and rustling newspapers.

I laughed, startled, and stroked its back with an index finger. The paper tiger vibrated under my finger, purring.

"*Zhe jiao zhèzhi*," Mom said. *This is called origami.*

I didn't know this at the time, but Mom's kind was special. She breathed into them so that they shared her breath, and thus moved with her life. This was her magic.

Dad had picked Mom out of a catalog.

One time, when I was in high school, I asked Dad about the details. He was trying to get me to speak to Mom again.

He had signed up for the introduction service back in the spring of 1973. Flipping through the pages steadily, he had spent no more than a few seconds on each page until he saw the picture of Mom.

I've never seen this picture. Dad described it: Mom was sitting in a chair, her side to the camera, wearing a tight green silk cheongsam. Her head was turned to the camera so that her long black hair was draped artfully over her chest and shoulder. She looked out at him with the eyes of a calm child.

"That was the last page of the catalog I saw," he said.

The catalog said she was eighteen, loved to dance, and spoke good English because she was from Hong Kong. None of these facts turned out to be true.

He wrote to her, and the company passed their messages back and forth. Finally, he flew to Hong Kong to meet her.

"The people at the company had been writing her responses. She didn't know any English other than 'hello' and 'good-bye.'"

What kind of woman puts herself into a catalog so that she can be bought?
The high school me thought I knew so much about everything. Contempt felt good, like wine.

Instead of storming into the office to demand his money back, he paid a waitress at the hotel restaurant to translate for them.

"She would look at me, her eyes halfway between scared and hopeful, while I spoke. And when the girl began translating what I said, she'd start to smile slowly."

He flew back to Connecticut and began to apply for the papers for her to come to him. I was born a year later, in the Year of the Tiger.

At my request, Mom also made a goat, a deer, and a water buffalo out of wrapping paper. They would run around the living room while Laohu chased after them, growling. When he caught them he would press down until the air went out of them and they became just flat, folded-up pieces of paper. I would then have to blow into them to re-inflate them so they could run around some more.

Sometimes, the animals got into trouble. Once, the water buffalo jumped into a dish of soy sauce on the table at dinner. (He wanted to wallow, like a real water buffalo.) I picked him out quickly but the capillary action had already pulled the dark liquid high up into his legs. The sauce-softened legs would not hold him up, and he collapsed onto the table. I dried him out in the sun, but his legs became crooked after that, and he ran around with a limp. Mom eventually wrapped his legs in saran wrap so that he could wallow to his heart's content (just not in soy sauce).

Also, Laohu liked to pounce at sparrows when he and I played in the backyard. But one time, a cornered bird struck back in desperation and tore his ear. He whimpered and winced as I held him and Mom patched his ear together with tape. He avoided birds after that.

And then one day, I saw a TV documentary about sharks and asked

Mom for one of my own. She made the shark, but he flapped about on the table unhappily. I filled the sink with water, and put him in. He swam around and around happily. However, after a while he became soggy and translucent, and slowly sank to the bottom, the folds coming undone. I reached in to rescue him, and all I ended up with was a wet piece of paper.

Laohu put his front paws together at the edge of the sink and rested his head on them. Ears drooping, he made a low growl in his throat that made me feel guilty.

Mom made a new shark for me, this time out of tinfoil. The shark lived happily in a large goldfish bowl. Laohu and I liked to sit next to the bowl to watch the tinfoil shark chasing the goldfish, Laohu sticking his face up against the bowl on the other side so that I saw his eyes, magnified to the size of coffee cups, staring at me from across the bowl.

When I was ten, we moved to a new house across town. Two of the women neighbors came by to welcome us. Dad served them drinks and then apologized for having to run off to the utility company to straighten out the prior owner's bills. "Make yourselves at home. My wife doesn't speak much English, so don't think she's being rude for not talking to you."

While I read in the dining room, Mom unpacked in the kitchen. The neighbors conversed in the living room, not trying to be particularly quiet.

"He seems like a normal enough man. Why did he do that?"

"Something about the mixing never seems right. The child looks unfinished. Slanty eyes, white face. A little monster."

"Do you think *he* can speak English?"

The women hushed. After a while they came into the dining room. "Hello there! What's your name?"

"Jack," I said.

"That doesn't sound very Chinesey."

Mom came into the dining room then. She smiled at the women. The three of them stood in a triangle around me, smiling and nodding at each other, with nothing to say, until Dad came back.

Mark, one of the neighborhood boys, came over with his *Star Wars* action figures. Obi-Wan Kenobi's lightsaber lit up and he could swing his arms and say, in a tinny voice, "Use the Force!" I didn't think the figure looked much like the real Obi-Wan at all.

Together, we watched him repeat this performance five times on the coffee table. "Can he do anything else?" I asked.

Mark was annoyed by my question. "Look at all the details," he said.

I looked at the details. I wasn't sure what I was supposed to say.

Mark was disappointed by my response. "Show me your toys."

I didn't have any toys except my paper menagerie. I brought Laohu out from my bedroom. By then he was very worn, patched all over with tape and glue, evidence of the years of repairs Mom and I had done on him. He was no longer as nimble and sure-footed as before. I sat him down on the coffee table. I could hear the skittering steps of the other animals behind in the hallway, timidly peeking into the living room.

"*Xiao laohu*," I said, and stopped. I switched to English. "This is Tiger." Cautiously, Laohu strode up and purred at Mark, sniffing his hands.

Mark examined the Christmas-wrap pattern of Laohu's skin. "That doesn't look like a tiger at all. Your Mom makes toys for you from trash?"

I had never thought of Laohu as *trash*. But looking at him now, he was really just a piece of wrapping paper.

Mark pushed Obi-Wan's head again. The lightsaber flashed; he moved his arms up and down. "Use the Force!"

Laohu turned and pounced, knocking the plastic figure off the table. It hit the floor and broke, and Obi-Wan's head rolled under the couch. "*Rawwww*," Laohu laughed. I joined him.

Mark punched me, hard. "This was very expensive! You can't even find it in the stores now. It probably cost more than what your Dad paid for your Mom!"

I stumbled and fell to the floor. Laohu growled and leapt at Mark's face.

Mark screamed, more out of fear and surprise than pain. Laohu was only made of paper, after all.

Mark grabbed Laohu and his snarl was choked off as Mark crumpled him in his hand and tore him in half. He balled up the two pieces of paper and threw them at me. "Here's your stupid cheap Chinese garbage."

After Mark left, I spent a long time trying, without success, to tape together the pieces, smooth out the paper, and follow the creases to re-fold Laohu. Slowly, the other animals came into the living room and gathered around us, me and the torn wrapping paper that used to be Laohu.

My fight with Mark didn't end there. Mark was popular at school. I never want to think again about the two weeks that followed.

I came home that Friday at the end of the two weeks. "*Xuexiao hao ma?*" Mom asked. I said nothing and went to the bathroom. I looked into the mirror. *I look nothing like her, nothing.*

At dinner I asked Dad, "Do I have a chink face?"

Dad put down his chopsticks. Even though I had never told him what happened in school, he seemed to understand. He closed his eyes and rubbed the bridge of his nose. "No, you don't."

Mom looked at Dad, not understanding. She looked back at me. "*Sha jiao* chink?"

"English," I said. "Speak English."

She tried. "What happen?"

I pushed the chopsticks and the bowl before me away: stir-fried green peppers with five-spice beef. "We should eat American food."

Dad tried to reason. "A lot of families cook Chinese sometimes."

"We are not other families." I looked at him. *Other families don't have Moms who don't belong.*

He looked away. And then he put a hand on Mom's shoulder. "I'll get you a cookbook."

Mom turned to me. "*Bu haochi?*"

"English," I said, raising my voice. "Speak English."

Mom reached out to touch my forehead, feeling for my temperature. "*Fashao la?*"

I brushed her hand away. "I'm fine. Speak English!" I was shouting.

"Speak English to him," Dad said to Mom. "You knew this was going to happen someday. What did you expect?"

Mom dropped her hands to her sides. She sat, looking from Dad to me, and back to Dad again. She tried to speak, stopped, and tried again, and stopped again.

"You have to," Dad said. "I've been too easy on you. Jack needs to fit in."

Mom looked at him. "If I say 'love,' I feel here." She pointed to her lips. "If I say '*ai*,' I feel here." She put her hand over her heart.

Dad shook his head. "You are in America."

Mom hunched down in her seat, looking like the water buffalo when Laohu used to pounce on him and squeeze the air of life out of him.

"And I want some real toys."

Dad bought me a full set of Star Wars action figures. I gave the Obi-Wan Kenobi to Mark.

I packed the paper menagerie in a large shoebox and put it under the bed.

The next morning, the animals had escaped and taken over their old favorite spots in my room. I caught them all and put them back into the shoebox, taping the lid shut. But the animals made so much noise in the box that I finally shoved it into the corner of the attic as far away from my room as possible.

If Mom spoke to me in Chinese, I refused to answer her. After a while, she tried to use more English. But her accent and broken sentences embarrassed me. I tried to correct her. Eventually, she stopped speaking altogether if I was around.

Mom began to mime things if she needed to let me know something. She tried to hug me the way she saw American mothers do on TV. I thought her movements exaggerated, uncertain, ridiculous, graceless. She saw that I was annoyed, and stopped.

"You shouldn't treat your mother that way," Dad said. But he couldn't look me in the eyes as he said it. Deep in his heart, he must have realized that it was a mistake to have tried to take a Chinese peasant girl and expect her to fit in the suburbs of Connecticut.

Mom learned to cook American style. I played video games and studied French.

Every once in a while, I would see her at the kitchen table studying the plain side of a sheet of wrapping paper. Later a new paper animal would appear on my nightstand and try to cuddle up to me. I caught them, squeezed them until the air went out of them, and then stuffed them away in the box in the attic.

Mom finally stopped making the animals when I was in high school. By then her English was much better, but I was already at that age when I wasn't interested in what she had to say whatever language she used.

Sometimes, when I came home and saw her tiny body busily moving about in the kitchen, singing a song in Chinese to herself, it was hard for me to believe that she gave birth to me. We had nothing in common. She might as well be from the Moon. I would hurry on to my room, where I could continue my all-American pursuit of happiness.

D ad and I stood, one on each side of Mom, lying on the hospital bed. She was not yet even forty, but she looked much older.

For years she had refused to go to the doctor for the pain inside her that she said was no big deal. By the time an ambulance finally carried her in, the cancer had spread far beyond the limits of surgery.

My mind was not in the room. It was the middle of the on-campus recruiting season, and I was focused on resumes, transcripts, and strategically constructed interview schedules. I schemed about how to lie to the corporate recruiters most effectively so that they'd offer to buy me. I understood intellectually that it was terrible to think about this while your mother lay dying. But that understanding didn't mean I could change how I felt.

She was conscious. Dad held her left hand with both of his own. He leaned down to kiss her forehead. He seemed weak and old in a way that startled me. I realized that I knew almost as little about Dad as I did about Mom.

Mom smiled at him. "I'm fine."

She turned to me, still smiling. "I know you have to go back to school." Her voice was very weak and it was difficult to hear her over the hum of the machines hooked up to her. "Go. Don't worry about me. This is not a big deal. Just do well in school."

I reached out to touch her hand, because I thought that was what I was supposed to do. I was relieved. I was already thinking about the flight back, and the bright California sunshine.

She whispered something to Dad. He nodded and left the room.

"Jack, if—" she was caught up in a fit of coughing, and could not speak for some time. "If I . . . don't make it, don't be too sad and hurt your health. Focus on your life. Just keep that box you have in the attic with you, and every year, at *Qingming*, just take it out and think about me. I'll be with you always."

Qingming was the Chinese Festival for the Dead. When I was very young, Mom used to write a letter on *Qingming* to her dead parents back in China, telling them the good news about the past year of her life in America. She would read the letter out loud to me, and if I made a comment about something, she would write it down in the letter too. Then she would fold the letter into a paper crane, and release it, facing west. We would then watch, as the crane flapped its crisp wings on its long journey west, toward the Pacific, toward China, toward the graves of Mom's family.

It had been many years since I last did that with her.

"I don't know anything about the Chinese calendar," I said. "Just rest, Mom."

"Just keep the box with you and open it once in a while. Just open—" She began to cough again.

"It's okay, Mom." I stroked her arm awkwardly.

"*Haizi, mama ai ni*—" Her cough took over again. An image from years ago flashed into my memory: Mom saying *ai* and then putting her hand over her heart.

"All right, Mom. Stop talking."

Dad came back, and I said that I needed to get to the airport early because I didn't want to miss my flight.

She died when my plane was somewhere over Nevada.

Dad aged rapidly after Mom died. The house was too big for him and had to be sold. My girlfriend Susan and I went to help him pack and clean the place.

Susan found the shoebox in the attic. The paper menagerie, hidden in the uninsulated darkness of the attic for so long, had become brittle, and the bright wrapping paper patterns had faded.

"I've never seen origami like this," Susan said. "Your Mom was an amazing artist."

The paper animals did not move. Perhaps whatever magic had animated them stopped when Mom died. Or perhaps I had only imagined that these paper constructions were once alive. The memory of children could not be trusted.

It was the first weekend in April, two years after Mom's death. Susan was out of town on one of her endless trips as a management consultant and I was home, lazily flipping through the TV channels.

I paused at a documentary about sharks. Suddenly I saw, in my mind, Mom's hands as they folded and refolded tinfoil to make a shark for me, while Laohu and I watched.

A rustle. I looked up and saw that a ball of wrapping paper and torn tape was on the floor next to the bookshelf. I walked over to pick it up for the trash.

The ball of paper shifted, unfurled itself, and I saw that it was Laohu, who I hadn't thought about in a very long time. "*Rawrr-sa*." Mom must have put him back together after I had given up.

He was smaller than I remembered. Or maybe it was just that back then my fists were smaller.

Susan had put the paper animals around our apartment as decoration. She probably left Laohu in a pretty hidden corner because he looked so shabby.

I sat down on the floor, and reached out a finger. Laohu's tail twitched, and he pounced playfully. I laughed, stroking his back. Laohu purred under my hand.

"How've you been, old buddy?"

Laohu stopped playing. He got up, jumped with feline grace into my lap, and proceeded to unfold himself.

In my lap was a square of creased wrapping paper, the plain side up. It was filled with dense Chinese characters. I had never learned to read Chinese, but I knew the characters for *son*, and they were at the top, where you'd expect them in a letter addressed to you, written in Mom's awkward, childish handwriting.

I went to the computer to check the Internet. Today was *Qingming*.

I took the letter with me downtown, where I knew the Chinese tour buses stopped. I stopped every tourist, asking, *"Nin hui du zhongwen ma?"* *Can you read Chinese?* I hadn't spoken Chinese in so long that I wasn't sure if they understood.

A young woman agreed to help. We sat down on a bench together, and she read the letter to me aloud. The language that I had tried to forget for years came back, and I felt the words sinking into me, through my skin, through my bones, until they squeezed tight around my heart.

> *Son,*
>
> *We haven't talked in a long time. You are so angry when I try to touch you that I'm afraid. And I think maybe this pain I feel all the time now is something serious.*
>
> *So I decided to write to you. I'm going to write in the paper animals I made for you that you used to like so much.*
>
> *The animals will stop moving when I stop breathing. But if I write to you with all my heart, I'll leave a little of myself behind on this paper, in these words. Then, if you think of me on* Qingming, *when the spirits of the departed are allowed to visit their families, you'll make the parts of myself I leave behind come alive too. The creatures I made for you will again leap and run and pounce, and maybe you'll get to see these words then.*
>
> *Because I have to write with all my heart, I need to write to you in Chinese.*
>
> *All this time I still haven't told you the story of my life. When you were little, I always thought I'd tell you the story*

*when you were older, so you could understand. But somehow
that chance never came up.*

*I was born in 1957, in Sigulu Village, Hebei Province.
Your grandparents were both from very poor peasant families
with few relatives. Only a few years after I was born, the
Great Famines struck China, during which thirty million
people died. The first memory I have was waking up to see
my mother eating dirt so that she could fill her belly and
leave the last bit of flour for me.*

*Things got better after that. Sigulu is famous for its
zhezhi papercraft, and my mother taught me how to make
paper animals and give them life. This was practical magic
in the life of the village. We made paper birds to chase
grasshoppers away from the fields, and paper tigers to keep
away the mice. For Chinese New Year my friends and I
made red paper dragons. I'll never forget the sight of all those
little dragons zooming across the sky overhead, holding up
strings of exploding firecrackers to scare away all the bad
memories of the past year. You would have loved it.*

*Then came the Cultural Revolution in 1966. Neighbor
turned on neighbor, and brother against brother. Someone
remembered that my mother's brother, my uncle, had left for
Hong Kong back in 1946, and became a merchant there.
Having a relative in Hong Kong meant we were spies and
enemies of the people, and we had to be struggled against in
every way. Your poor grandmother—she couldn't take the
abuse and threw herself down a well. Then some boys with
hunting muskets dragged your grandfather away one day
into the woods, and he never came back.*

*There I was, a ten-year-old orphan. The only relative I
had in the world was my uncle in Hong Kong. I snuck away
one night and climbed onto a freight train going south.*

Down in Guangdong Province a few days later, some men caught me stealing food from a field. When they heard that I was trying to get to Hong Kong, they laughed. "It's your lucky day. Our trade is to bring girls to Hong Kong."

They hid me in the bottom of a truck along with other girls, and smuggled us across the border.

We were taken to a basement and told to stand up and look healthy and intelligent for the buyers. Families paid the warehouse a fee and came by to look us over and select one of us to "adopt."

The Chin family picked me to take care of their two boys. I got up every morning at four to prepare breakfast. I fed and bathed the boys. I shopped for food. I did the laundry and swept the floors. I followed the boys around and did their bidding. At night I was locked into a cupboard in the kitchen to sleep. If I was slow or did anything wrong I was beaten. If the boys did anything wrong I was beaten. If I was caught trying to learn English I was beaten.

"Why do you want to learn English?" Mr. Chin asked. "You want to go to the police? We'll tell the police that you are a mainlander illegally in Hong Kong. They'd love to have you in their prison."

Six years I lived like this. One day, an old woman who sold fish to me in the morning market pulled me aside.

"I know girls like you. How old are you now, sixteen? One day, the man who owns you will get drunk, and he'll look at you and pull you to him and you can't stop him. The wife will find out, and then you will think you really have gone to hell. You have to get out of this life. I know someone who can help."

She told me about American men who wanted Asian wives. If I can cook, clean, and take care of my American *husband, he'll give me a good life. It was the only hope I had. And that was how I got into the catalog with all those lies and met your father. It is not a very romantic story, but it is my story.*

In the suburbs of Connecticut, I was lonely. Your father was kind and gentle with me, and I was very grateful to him. But no one understood me, and I understood nothing.

But then you were born! I was so happy when I looked into your face and saw shades of my mother, my father, and myself. I had lost my entire family, all of Sigulu, everything I ever knew and loved. But there you were, and your face was proof that they were real. I hadn't made them up.

Now I had someone to talk to. I would teach you my language, and we could together remake a small piece of everything that I loved and lost. When you said your first words to me, in Chinese that had the same accent as my mother and me, I cried for hours. When I made the first zhezhi animals for you, and you laughed, I felt there were no worries in the world.

You grew up a little, and now you could even help your father and me talk to each other. I was really at home now. I finally found a good life. I wished my parents could be here, so that I could cook for them, and give them a good life too. But my parents were no longer around. You know what the Chinese think is the saddest feeling in the world? It's for a child to finally grow the desire to take care of his parents, only to realize that they were long gone.

Son, I know that you do not like your Chinese eyes, which are my eyes. I know that you do not like your Chinese hair, which is my hair. But can you understand how much joy your very existence brought to me? And can you understand how it felt when you stopped talking to me and

won't let me talk to you in Chinese? I felt I was losing
everything all over again.
    Why won't you talk to me, son? The pain makes it hard
to write.

The young woman handed the paper back to me. I could not bear to look into her face.

Without looking up, I asked for her help in tracing out the character for *ai* on the paper below Mom's letter. I wrote the character again and again on the paper, intertwining my pen strokes with her words.

The young woman reached out and put a hand on my shoulder. Then she got up and left, leaving me alone with my mother.

Following the creases, I refolded the paper back into Laohu. I cradled him in the crook of my arm, and as he purred, we began the walk home.

THE DUNE

Stephen King · 2011

As the Judge climbs into the kayak beneath a bright morning sky, a slow and clumsy process that takes him almost five minutes, he reflects that an old man's body is nothing but a sack filled with aches and indignities. Eighty years ago, when he was ten, he jumped into a wooden canoe and cast off, with no bulky life jacket, no worries, and certainly with no pee dribbling into his underwear. Every trip out to the little unnamed island began with a great and uneasy excitement. Now there is only unease. And pain that seems centered deep in his guts and radiates everywhere. But he still makes the trip. Many things have lost their allure in these shadowy later years—most things, really—but not the dune on the far side of the island. Never the dune.

In the early days of his exploration, he expected the dune to be gone after every big storm, and following the 1944 hurricane that sank the USS *Raleigh* off Siesta Key, he was sure it would be. But when the skies cleared, the island was still there. So was the dune, although the hundred-mile-an-hour winds should have blown all the sand away, leaving only the bare rocks. Over the years he has debated back and forth about whether the magic is in him or in the dune. Perhaps it's both, but surely most of it is in the dune.

Since 1932, he has crossed this short stretch of water thousands of times. Usually there's nothing but rocks and bushes and sand, but sometimes there is something else.

Settled in the kayak at last, he paddles slowly from the beach to the island, his frizz of white hair blowing around his mostly bald skull. A few turkey buzzards wheel overhead, making their ugly conversation. Once he was the son of the richest man on the Florida Gulf coast, then he was a lawyer, then he was a judge on the Pinellas County Circuit, then he was appointed to the State Supreme Court. There was talk, during the Reagan years, of a nomination to the United States Supreme Court, but that never happened, and a week after the idiot Clinton became president, Judge Harvey Beecher—just Judge to his many acquaintances (he has no real friends) in Sarasota, Osprey, Nokomis, and Venice—retired. Hell, he never liked Tallahassee, anyway. It's cold up there.

Also, it's too far from the island, and its peculiar dune. On these early morning kayak trips, paddling the short distance on smooth water, he's willing to admit that he's addicted to it. But who wouldn't be addicted to a thing like this?

On the rocky east side, a gnarled bush juts from the split in a guano-splattered rock. This is where he ties up, and he's always careful with the knot. It wouldn't do to be stranded out here; his father's estate (that's how he still thinks of it, although the elder Beecher has been gone for forty years now) covers almost two miles of prime Gulf-front property, the main house is far inland, on the Sarasota Bay side, and there would be no one to hear him yelling. Tommy Curtis, the caretaker, might notice him gone and come looking; more likely, he would just assume the Judge was locked up in his study, where he often spends whole days, supposedly working on his memoirs.

Once upon a time, Mrs. Riley might have gotten nervous when he didn't come out of the study for lunch, but now he hardly ever eats at noon (she calls him "nothing but a stuffed string," but never to his face). There's no other staff, and both Curtis and Riley know he can be cross when he's interrupted. Not that there's really much to interrupt; he hasn't added so much as a line to the memoirs in two years, and in his heart he knows they will never be finished. The unfinished recollections of a Florida judge? No great loss there. The one story he *could* write is the one he never will. The Judge wants no talk at his funeral about how, in his last years, a previously fine intellect was corrupted by senility.

He's even slower getting out of the kayak than he was getting in, and turns turtle once, wetting his shirt and pants in the little waves that run up the gravelly shingle. Beecher is not discommoded. It isn't the first time he's fallen, and there's no one to see him. He supposes it's unwise to continue these trips at his age, even though the island is so close to the mainland, but stopping isn't an option. An addict is an addict is an addict.

Beecher struggles to his feet and clutches his belly until the last of the pain subsides. He brushes sand and shells from his pants, double-checks his mooring rope, then spots one of the turkey buzzards perched on the island's largest rock, peering down at him.

"Hi!" he shouts in the voice he now hates—cracked and wavering, the voice of a fishwife. "Hi, you bugger! Get on about your business."

After a brief rustle of its raggedy wings, the turkey buzzard sits right where it is. Its beady eyes seem to say, *But Judge—today you* are *my business.*

Beecher stoops, picks up a larger shell, and shies it at the bird. This time it does fly away, the sound of its wings like rippling cloth. It soars across the short stretch of water and lands on his dock. *Still*, the Judge thinks, *a bad omen.* He remembers a fellow on the Florida State Patrol telling him once that turkey buzzards didn't just know where carrion was; they also know where carrion *would be.*

"I can't tell you," the patrolman said, "how many times I've seen those ugly bastards circling a spot on the Tamiami where there's a fatal wreck a day or two later. Sounds crazy, I know, but just about any Florida road cop will tell you the same."

There are almost always turkey buzzards out here on the little no-name island. He supposes it smells like death to them, and why not? What else?

The Judge sets off on the little path he has beaten over the years. He will check the dune on the other side, where the sand is beach-fine instead of stony and shelly, and then he will return to the kayak and drink his little jug of cold tea. He may doze awhile in the morning sun (he dozes often these days, supposes most nonagenarians do), and when he wakes (*if* he wakes), he'll make the return trip. He tells himself that the dune will be just a smooth blank upslope of sand, as it is most days, but he knows better.

That damned buzzard knew better, too.

He spends a long time on the sandy side, with his age-warped fingers clasped in a knot behind him. His back aches, his shoulders ache, his hips ache, his knees ache; most of all, his gut aches. But he pays these things no mind. Perhaps later, but not now.

He looks at the dune, and what is written there.

Anthony Wayland arrives at Beecher's Pelican Point estate bang on seven p.m., just as promised. One thing the Judge has always appreciated—both in the courtroom and out of it—is punctuality, and the boy is punctual. He reminds himself never to call Wayland *boy* to his face (although, this being the South, *son* is okay). Wayland wouldn't understand that, when you're ninety, any fellow under the age of forty looks like a boy.

"Thank you for coming," the Judge says, ushering Wayland into his study. It's just the two of them; Curtis and Mrs. Riley have long since gone to their homes in Nokomis Village. "You brought the necessary document?"

"Yes indeed, Judge," Wayland says. He opens his attorney's briefcase and removes a thick document bound by a large steel clip. The pages aren't vellum, as they would have been in the old days, but they are rich and heavy just the same. At the top of the first, in forbidding gothic type (what the Judge has always thought of as graveyard type), are the words LAST WILL AND TESTAMENT OF HARVEY L. BEECHER.

"You know, I'm kind of surprised you didn't draft this document yourself. You've probably forgotten more Florida probate law than I've ever learned."

"That might be true," the Judge says in his driest tone. "At my age, folks tend to forget a great deal."

Wayland flushes to the roots of his hair. "I didn't mean—"

"I know what you mean, son," the Judge says. "No offence taken. Not a mite. But since you ask . . . you know that old saying about how a man who serves as his own lawyer has a fool for a client?"

Wayland grins. "Heard it and used it plenty of times when I'm wearing my public defender hat and some sad-sack wife-abuser or hit-and-runner tells me he's going to go the DIY route in court."

"I'm sure you have, but here's the other half: a lawyer who serves as his own lawyer has a *great* fool for a client. Goes for criminal, civil, and probate law. So shall we get down to business? Time is short." This is something he means in more ways than one.

They get down to business. Mrs. Riley has left decaf coffee, which Wayland rejects in favor of a Co'Cola. He makes copious notes as the Judge dictates the changes in his dry courtroom voice, adjusting old bequests and adding new ones. The major new one—four million dollars—is to the Sarasota County Beach and Wildlife Preservation Society. In order to qualify, they must successfully petition the State Legislature to have a certain island just off the coast of Pelican Point declared forever wild.

"They won't have a problem getting that done," the Judge says. "You can handle the legal for them yourself. I'd prefer *pro bono*, but of course that's up to you. One trip to Tallahassee should do it. It's a little spit of a thing, nothing growing there but a few bushes. Governor Scott and his Tea Party cronies will be delighted."

"Why's that, Judge?"

"Because the next time Beach and Preservation comes to them, begging money, they can say, 'Didn't old Judge Beecher just give you four million? Get out of here, and don't let the door hit you in the ass on your way out!'"

Wayland agrees that this is probably just how it will go—Scott and his friends are all for giving if they're not the ones doing it—and the two men move on to the smaller bequests.

"Once I get a clean draft, we'll need two witnesses, and a notary," Wayland says when they've finished.

"I'll get all that done with this draft here, just to be safe," the Judge says. "If anything happens to me in the interim, it should stand up. There's no one to contest it; I've outlived them all."

"A wise precaution, Judge. It would be good to take care of it tonight. I don't suppose your caretaker and housekeeper—"

"Won't be back until eight tomorrow," Beecher says, "but I'll make it the first order of business. Harry Staines on Vamo Road's a notary, and he'll be glad to come over before he goes in to his office. He owes me a favor or six. You give that document to me, son. I'll lock it in my safe."

"I ought to at least make a . . ." Wayland looks at the gnarled, outstretched hand and trails off. When a State Supreme Court judge (even a retired one) holds out his hand, demurrals must cease. What the hell, it's only an annotated draft, anyway, soon to be replaced by a clean version. He passes the unsigned will over and watches as Beecher rises (painfully) and swings a picture of the Florida Everglades out on a hidden hinge. The Judge enters the correct combination, making no attempt to hide the touchpad from view, and deposits the will on top of what looks to Wayland like a large and untidy heap of cash. Yikes.

"There!" Beecher says. "All done and buttoned up! Except for the signing part, that is. How about a drink to celebrate? I have some fine single-malt Scotch."

"Well . . . I guess one wouldn't hurt."

"It never hurt me when I was your age, although it does now, so you'll have to pardon me for not joining you. Decaf coffee and a little sweet tea are the strongest drinks I take these days. Ice?"

Wayland holds up two fingers, and Beecher adds two cubes to the drink with the slow ceremony of old age. Wayland takes a sip, and high color rises into his cheeks. It is the flush, Judge Beecher thinks, of a man who enjoys his tipple. As Wayland sets his glass down, he says, "Do you mind if I ask what the hurry is? You're all right, I take it?"

The Judge doubts if young Wayland takes it that way at all. He's not blind.

"A-country fair," he says, seesawing one hand in the air and sitting down with a grunt and a wince. Then, after consideration, he says, "Do you really want to know what the hurry is?"

Wayland considers the question, and Beecher likes him for that. Then he nods.

"It has to do with that island we took care of just now. Probably never even noticed it, have you?"

"Can't say that I have."

"Most people don't. It barely sticks out of the water. The sea-turtles don't even bother with that old island. Yet it's special. Did you know my grandfather fought in the Spanish-American war?"

"No, sir, I did not." Wayland speaks with exaggerated respect, and Beecher knows the boy believes his mind is wandering. The boy is wrong. Beecher's mind has never been clearer, and now that he's begun, he finds that he wants to tell this story at least once before . . .

Well, before.

"Yes. There's a photograph of him standing on top of San Juan Hill. It's around here someplace. Grampy claimed to have fought in the Civil War as well, but my research—for my memoirs, you understand—proved conclusively that he couldn't have. He would have been a mere child, if born at all. But he was quite the fanciful gentleman, and he had a way of making me believe the wildest tales. Why would I not? I was only a child, not long from believing in Kris Kringle and the tooth fairy."

"Was he a lawyer, like you and your father?"

"No, son, he was a thief. The original Light-Finger Harry. Anything that wasn't nailed down. Only like most thieves who don't get caught—our current governor might be a case in point—he called himself a businessman. His chief business—and chief thievery—was land. He bought bug-and-gator-infested Florida acreage cheap and sold it dear to folks who must have been as gullible as I was as a child. Balzac once said, 'Behind every great fortune there is a crime.' That's certainly true of the Beecher family, and please remember that you're my lawyer. Anything I say to you must be held in confidence."

"Yes, Judge." Wayland takes another sip of his drink. It is by far the finest Scotch he has ever drunk.

"Grampy Beecher was the one who pointed that island out to me. I was ten. He had care of me for the day, and I suppose he wanted some peace and quiet. Or maybe what he wanted was a bit noisier. There was a pretty housemaid, and he may have been in hopes of investigating beneath her petticoats. So he told me that Edward Teach—better known as Blackbeard—had supposedly buried a great treasure out there. 'Nobody's ever found it, Havie,' he said—Havie's what he called me—'but you might be the one. A fortune in jewels and gold doubloons.' You'll know what I did next."

"I suppose you went out there and left your grandfather to cheer up the maid."

The Judge nods, smiling. "I took the old wooden canoe we had tied up to the dock. Went like my hair was on fire and my tailfeathers were catching. Didn't take but five minutes to paddle out there. Takes me three times as long these days, and that's if the water's smooth. The island's all rock and brush on the landward side, but there's a dune of fine beach sand on the Gulf side. It never goes away. In the eighty years I've been going out there, it never seems to change. At least not geographically."

"Didn't find any treasure, I suppose?"

"I did, in a way, but it wasn't jewels and gold. It was a name, written in the sand of that dune. As if with a stick, you know, only I didn't see any stick. The letters were drawn deep, and the sun struck shadows into them, making them stand out. Almost as if they were floating."

"What was the name, Judge?"

"I think you have to see it written to understand."

The Judge takes a sheet of paper from the top drawer of his desk, prints carefully, then turns the paper around so Wayland can read it: ROBIE LADOOSH.

"All right . . ." Wayland says cautiously.

"On any other day, I would have gone treasure-hunting with this very boy, because he was my best friend, and you know how boys are when they're best friends."

"Joined at the hip," Wayland says, smiling.

"Tight as a new key in a new lock," Wayland agrees. "But it was summer and he'd gone off with his parents to visit his mama's people in Virginia or Maryland or some such northern clime. So I was on my own. But attend me closely, counselor. The boy's *actual* name was Robert LaDoucette."

Again Wayland says, "All right . . ." The Judge thinks that sort of leading drawl could become annoying over time, but it isn't a thing he'll ever have to actually find out, so he lets it go.

"He was my best friend and I was his, but there was a whole gang of boys we ran around with, and everyone called him Robbie LaDoosh. You follow?"

"I guess," Wayland says, but the Judge can see he doesn't. That's understandable; Beecher has had a lot more time to think about these things. Often on sleepless nights.

"Remember that I was ten. If I had been asked to spell my friend's nickname, I would have done it just this way." He taps ROBIE LA-DOOSH. Speaking almost to himself, he adds: "So some of the magic comes from me. It *must* come from me. The question is, how much?"

"You're saying you didn't write that name in the sand?"

"No. I thought I made that clear."

"One of your other friends, then?"

"They were all from Nokomis Village, and didn't even know about that island. We never would have paddled out to such an uninteresting little rock on our own. Robbie knew it was there, he was also from the Point, but he was hundreds of miles north."

"All right . . ."

"My chum Robbie never came back from that vacation. We got word a week or so later that he'd taken a fall while out horseback riding. He broke his neck. Killed instantly. His parents were heartbroken. So was I, of course."

There is silence while Wayland considers this. While they both consider it. Somewhere far off, a helicopter beats at the sky over the Gulf. The DEA looking for drug-runners, the Judge supposes. He hears them every night. It's the modern age, and in some ways—in many—he'll be glad to be shed of it.

At last Wayland says, "Are you saying what I think you're saying?"

"Well, I don't know," the Judge says. "What do you think I'm saying?"

But Anthony Wayland is a lawyer, and refusing to be drawn in is an ingrained habit with him. "Did you tell your grandfather?"

"On the day the telegram about Robbie came, he wasn't there to tell. He never stayed in one place for long. We didn't see him again for six months or more. No, I kept it to myself. And like Mary after she gave birth to Jesus, I considered these things in my heart."

"And what conclusion did you draw?"

"I kept canoeing out to that island to look at the dune, and that should answer your question. There was nothing . . . and nothing . . .

and nothing. I guess I was on the verge of forgetting all about it, but then I went out one afternoon after school and there was another name written in the sand. *Printed* in the sand, to be courtroom-exact. No sign of a stick that time, either, although I suppose a stick could have been thrown into the water. This time the name was Peter Alderson. It meant nothing to me until a few days later. It was my chore to go out to the end of the road and get the paper, and it was my habit to scan the front page while I walked back up the drive—which, as you know from driving it yourself, is a good quarter-mile long. In the summer I'd also check on how the Washington Senators had done, because back then they were as close to a southern team as we had.

"This particular day, a headline on the bottom of the front page caught my eye: WINDOW WASHER KILLED IN FALL. The poor guy was doing the third-floor windows of the Sarasota Public Library when the scaffolding he was standing on gave way. His name was Peter Alderson."

The Judge can see from Wayland's face that he believes this is either a prank or some sort of elaborate fantasy the Judge is spinning out. He can also see that Wayland is enjoying his drink, and when the Judge moves to top it up, Wayland doesn't say no. And really, the young man's belief or disbelief is beside the point. It's just such a luxury to tell it.

"Maybe you see why I go back and forth in my mind about where the magic lies," Beecher says. "I *knew* Robbie, and the misspelling of his name was my misspelling. But I didn't know this window washer from Adam. In any case, that's when the dune really started to get a hold on me. I began going out every day when I was here, a habit that's continued into my very old age. I respect the place, I fear the place, but most of all, I'm addicted to the place.

"Over the years, many names have appeared on that dune, and the people the names belong to always die. Sometimes it's within the week, sometimes it's two, but it's never more than a month. Some have been people I knew, and if it's by a nickname I knew them, it's the nickname I see. One day in 1940 I paddled out there and saw GRAMPY BEECHER drawn into the sand. He died in Key West three days later. Heart attack."

With the air of someone humoring a man who is mentally unbalanced but not actually dangerous, Wayland asks, "Did you never try to interfere with this . . . this process? Call your grandfather, for instance, and tell him to see a doctor?"

Beecher shakes his head. "I didn't *know* it was a heart attack until we got word from the Monroe County medical examiner, did I? It could have been an accident, or even a murder. Certainly there were people who had reasons to hate my grandfather; his dealings were not of the purest sort."

"Still . . . he was your grandfather and all . . ."

"The truth, counselor, is that I was afraid. I felt—I still feel—as if there on that island, there's a hatch that's come ajar. On this side is what we're pleased to call 'the real world.' On the other is all the machinery of the universe, running at top speed. Only a fool would stick his hand into such machinery in an attempt to stop it."

"Judge Beecher, if you want your paperwork to sail through probate, I'd keep quiet about all this. You might think there's no one to contest your will, but when large amounts of money are at stake, third and fourth cousins have a way of coming out of the woodwork. And you know the criterion: 'Being of sound mind and body.'"

"I've kept it to myself for eighty years," Beecher says, and in his voice Wayland can hear *objection overruled.* "Never a word until now. And I'm sure *you* won't talk."

"Of course not," Wayland says.

"I was always excited on days when names appeared in the sand— unhealthily excited, I'm sure—but terrified of the phenomenon only once. That single time I was *deeply* terrified, and fled back to the Point in my canoe as if devils were after me. Shall I tell you?"

"Please." Wayland lifts his drink and sips. Why not? Billable hours are, after all, billable hours.

"It was 1959. I was still on the Point. I've always lived here except for the years in Tallahassee, and it's better not to speak of them . . . although I now think part of the hate I felt for that provincial backwater of a town, perhaps even most of it, was simply a masked longing for the island, and the dune. I kept wondering what I was missing, you see. *Who* I was missing. Being able to read obituaries in advance gives a man an extraordinary sense of power. Perhaps you find that unlovely. The truth often is.

"So. 1959. Harvey Beecher lawyering in Sarasota and living at Pelican Point. If it wasn't pouring down rain when I got home, I'd always change into old clothes and paddle out to the island for a look-see before supper. On this particular day I'd been kept at the office late, and by the time I'd gotten out to the island, tied up, and walked over to the dune side, the sun was going down big and red, as it so often does over the Gulf. What I saw stunned me. I literally could not move.

"There wasn't just one name written in the sand that evening but many, and in that red sunset light they looked as if they had been written in blood. They were crammed together, they wove in and out, they were written over and above and up and down. The whole length and breadth of the dune was covered with a tapestry of names. The ones down by the water had been half-erased."

Wayland looks awed in spite of his core disbelief.

"I think I screamed. I can't remember for sure, but yes, I think so. What I *do* remember is breaking the paralysis and running away as fast as I could, down the path to where my canoe was tied up. It seemed to take me forever to unpluck the knot, and when I did, I pushed the canoe out into the water before I climbed in. I was soaked from head to toe, and it's a wonder I didn't tip over. Although in those days I could have easily swum to shore, pushing the canoe ahead of me. Not these days; if I tipped my kayak over now, that would be all she wrote."

"Then I suggest you stay onshore, at least until your will is signed, witnessed, and notarized."

Judge Beecher gives the young man a wintery smile. "You needn't worry about that, son," he says. He looks toward the window, and the Gulf beyond. His face is long and thoughtful. "Those names . . . I can see them yet, jostling each other for place on that blood-red dune. Two days later, a TWA plane on its way to Miami crashed in the Glades. All one hundred and nineteen souls on board were killed. The passenger list was in the paper. I recognized some of the names. I recognized *many* of them."

"You *saw* this. You saw those names."

"Yes. For several months after that I stayed away from the island, and I promised myself I would stay away for good. I suppose drug addicts make the same promises to themselves about their dope, don't they? And like them, I eventually weakened and resumed my old habit. Now, counselor: do you understand why I called you out here to finish the work on my will, and why it had to be tonight?"

Wayland doesn't believe a word of it, but like many fantasies, this one has its own internal logic. It's easy enough to follow. The Judge is ninety, his once ruddy complexion has gone the color of clay, his formerly firm step has become shuffling and tentative. He's clearly in pain, and he's lost weight he can't afford to lose.

"I suppose that today you saw your name in the sand," Wayland says.

Judge Beecher looks momentarily startled, and then he smiles. It is a terrible smile, transforming his narrow, pallid face into a death's head grin.

"Oh no," he says. "Not *mine*."

DIEM PERDIDI

Julie Otsuka • 2011

She remembers her name. She remembers the name of the president. She remembers the name of the president's dog. She remembers what city she lives in. And on which street. And in which house. *The one with the big olive tree where the road takes a turn.* She remembers what year it is. She remembers the season. She remembers the day on which you were born. She remembers the daughter who was born before you—*She had your father's nose, that was the first thing I noticed about her*—but she does not remember that daughter's name. She remembers the name of the man she did not marry—Frank—and she keeps his letters in a drawer by her bed. She remembers that you once had a husband, but she refuses to remember your ex-husband's name. *That man*, she calls him.

She does not remember how she got the bruises on her arms or going for a walk with you earlier this morning. She does not remember bending over, during that walk, and plucking a flower from a neighbor's front yard and slipping it into her hair. *Maybe your father will kiss me now.* She does not remember what she ate for dinner last night, or when she last took her medicine. She does not remember to drink enough water. She does not remember to comb her hair.

She remembers the rows of dried persimmons that once hung from the eaves of her mother's house in Berkeley. *They were the most beautiful shade of orange.* She remembers that your father loves peaches. She remembers that every Sunday morning, at ten, he takes her for a drive down to the sea in the brown car. She remembers that every evening, right before the eight o'clock news, he sets out two fortune cookies on a paper plate and announces to her that they are having a party. She remembers that on Mondays he comes home from the college at four, and if he is even five minutes late she goes out to the gate and begins to wait for him. She remembers which bedroom is hers and which is his. She remembers that the bedroom that is now hers was once yours. She remembers that it wasn't always like this.

She remembers the first line of the song, *How High the Moon*. She remembers the Pledge of Allegiance. She remembers her Social Security number. She remembers her best friend Jean's telephone number even though Jean has been dead for six years. She remembers that Margaret is dead. She remembers that Betty is dead. She remembers that Grace has stopped calling. She remembers that her own mother died nine years ago, while spading the soil in her garden, and she misses her more and more every day. *It doesn't go away.* She remembers the number assigned to her family by the government right after the start of the war. *13611.* She remembers being sent away to the desert with her mother and brother during the fifth month of that war and taking her first ride on a train. She remembers the day they came home. *September 9, 1945.* She remembers the sound of the wind hissing through the sagebrush. She remembers the scorpions and red ants. She remembers the taste of dust.

· · ·

Whenever you stop by to see her she remembers to give you a big hug, and you are always surprised at her strength. She remembers to give you a kiss every time you leave. She remembers to tell you, at the end of every phone call, that the FBI will check up on you again soon. She remembers to ask you if you would like her to iron your blouse for you before you go out on a date. She remembers to smooth down your skirt. *Don't give it all away.* She remembers to brush aside a wayward strand of your hair. She does not remember eating lunch with you twenty minutes ago and suggests that you go out to Marie Callender's for sandwiches and pie. She does not remember that she herself once used to make the most beautiful pies with perfectly fluted crusts. She does not remember how to iron your blouse for you or when she began to forget. *Something's changed.* She does not remember what she is supposed to do next.

She remembers that the daughter who was born before you lived for half an hour and then died. *She looked perfect from the outside.* She remembers her mother telling her, more than once, *Don't you ever let anyone see you cry.* She remembers giving you your first bath on your third day in the world. She remembers that you were a very fat baby. She remembers that your first word was *No.* She remembers picking apples in a field with Frank many years ago in the rain. *It was the best day of my life.* She remembers that the first time she met him she was so nervous she forgot her own address. She remembers wearing too much lipstick. She remembers not sleeping for days.

When you drive past Hesse Park, she remembers being asked to leave her exercise class by her teacher after being in that class for more than ten years. *I shouldn't have talked so much.* She remembers touching her toes and doing windmills and jumping jacks on the freshly mown grass. She remembers being the highest kicker in her class. She does not remember how to use the "new" coffee maker, which is now three years old, because it was bought after she began to forget. She does not remember asking your father, ten minutes ago, if today is Sunday, or if it is time to go for her ride. She does not remember where she last put her sweater or how long she has been sitting in her chair. She does not always remember how to get out of that chair, and so you gently push down on the footrest and offer her your hand, which she does not always remember to take. *Go away*, she sometimes says. Other times, she just says, *I'm stuck*. She does not remember saying to you, the other night, right after your father left the room, *He loves me more than I love him*. She does not remember saying to you, a moment later, *I can hardly wait until he comes back*.

She remembers that when your father was courting her he was always on time. She remembers thinking that he had a nice smile. *He still does*. She remembers that when they first met he was engaged to another woman. She remembers that that other woman was white. She remembers that that other woman's parents did not want their daughter to marry a man who looked like the gardener. She remembers that the winters were colder back then, and that there were days on which you actually had to put on a coat and scarf. She remembers her mother bowing her head every morning at the altar and offering her ancestors a bowl of hot rice. She remembers the smell of incense and pickled cabbage in the kitchen. She remembers that her father always wore nice shoes. She remembers that the night the FBI came for him, he and her mother had just had another big fight. She remembers not seeing him again until after the end of the war.

She does not always remember to trim her toenails, and when you soak her feet in the bucket of warm water she closes her eyes and leans back in her chair and reaches out for your hand. *Don't give up on me.* She does not remember how to tie her shoelaces, or fasten the hooks on her bra. She does not remember that she has been wearing her favorite blue blouse for five days in a row. She does not remember your age. *Just wait till you have children of your own*, she says to you, even though you are now too old to do so.

She remembers that after the first girl was born and then died, she sat in the yard for days, just staring at the roses by the pond. *I didn't know what else to do.* She remembers that when you were born you, too, had your father's long nose. *It was as if I'd given birth to the same girl twice.* She remembers that you are a Taurus. She remembers that your birthstone is green. She remembers to read you your horoscope from the newspaper whenever you come over to see her. *Someone you were once very close to may soon reappear in your life*, she tells you. She does not remember reading you that same horoscope five minutes ago or going to the doctor with you last week after you discovered a bump on the back of her head. *I think I fell.* She does not remember telling the doctor that you are no longer married, or giving him your number and asking him to please call. She does not remember leaning over and whispering to you, the moment he stepped out of the room, *I think he'll do.*

She remembers another doctor asking her, fifty years ago, minutes after the first girl was born and then died, if she wanted to donate the baby's body to science. *He said she had a very unusual heart.* She remembers being in labor for thirty-two hours. She remembers being too tired to think. *So I told him yes.* She remembers driving home from the hospital in the sky blue Chevy with your father and neither one of them saying a word. She remembers knowing she'd made a big mistake. She does not remember what happened to the baby's body and worries that it might be stuck in a jar. She does not remember why they didn't just bury her. *I wish she were under a tree.* She remembers wanting to bring her flowers every day.

She remembers that even as a young girl you said you did not want to have children. She remembers that you hated wearing dresses. She remembers that you never played with dolls. She remembers that the first time you bled you were thirteen years old and wearing bright yellow pants. She remembers that your childhood dog was named Shiro. She remembers that you once had a cat named Gasoline. She remembers that you had two turtles named Turtle. She remembers that the first time she and your father took you to Japan to meet his family you were eighteen months old and just beginning to speak. She remembers leaving you with his mother in the tiny silkworm village in the mountains while she and your father travelled across the island for ten days. *I worried about you the whole time.* She remembers that when they came back you did not know who she was and that for many days afterwards you would not speak to her, you would only whisper in her ear.

She remembers that the year you turned five you refused to leave the house without tapping the door frame three times. She remembers that you had a habit of clicking your teeth repeatedly, which drove her up the wall. She remembers that you could not stand it when different-colored foods were touching on the plate. *Everything had to be just so.* She remembers trying to teach you to read before you were ready. She remembers taking you to Newberry's to pick out patterns and fabric and teaching you how to sew. She remembers that every night, after dinner, you would sit down next to her at the kitchen table and hand her the bobby pins one by one as she set the curlers in her hair. She remembers that this was her favorite part of the day. *I wanted to be with you all the time.*

She remembers that you were conceived on the first try. She remembers that your brother was conceived on the first try. She remembers that your other brother was conceived on the second try. *We must not have been paying attention.* She remembers that a palm reader once told her that she would never be able to bear children because her uterus was tipped the wrong way. She remembers that a blind fortune-teller once told her that she had been a man in her past life, and that Frank had been her sister. She remembers that everything she remembers is not necessarily true. She remembers the horse-drawn garbage carts on Ashby, her first pair of crepe-soled shoes, scattered flowers by the side of the road. She remembers that the sound of Frank's voice always made her feel calmer. She remembers that every time they parted he turned around and watched her walk away. She remembers that the first time he asked her to marry him she told him she wasn't ready. She remembers that the second time she said she wanted to wait until she was finished with school. She remembers walking along the water with him one warm summer evening on the boardwalk and being so happy she could not remember her own name. She remembers not knowing that it wouldn't be like this with any of the others. She remembers thinking she had all the time in the world.

She does not remember the names of the flowers in the yard whose names she has known for years. *Roses? Daffodils? Immortelles?* She does not remember that today is Sunday, and she has already gone for her ride. She does not remember to call you, even though she always says that she will. She remembers how to play *Clair de Lune* on the piano. She remembers how to play *Chopsticks* and scales. She remembers not to talk to telemarketers when they call on the telephone. *We're not interested.* She remembers her grammar. *Just between you and me.* She remembers her manners. She remembers to say thank you and please. She remembers to wipe herself every time she uses the toilet. She remembers to flush. She remembers to turn her wedding ring around whenever she pulls on her silk stockings. She remembers to reapply her lipstick every time she leaves the house. She remembers to put on her anti-wrinkle cream every night before climbing into bed. *It works while you sleep.* In the morning, when she wakes, she remembers her dreams. *I was walking through a forest. I was swimming in a river. I was looking for Frank in a city I did not know and no one would tell me where he was.*

On Halloween day, she remembers to ask you if you are going out trick-or-treating. She remembers that your father hates pumpkin. *It's all he ate in Japan during the war.* She remembers listening to him pray, every night, when they first got married, that he would be the one to die first. She remembers playing marbles on a dirt floor in the desert with her brother and listening to the couple at night on the other side of the wall. *They were at it all the time.* She remembers the box of chocolates you brought back to her after your honeymoon in Paris. "But will it last?" you asked her. She remembers her own mother telling her, "The moment you fall in love with someone, you are lost."

She remembers that when her father came back after the war he and her mother fought even more than they had before. She remembers that he would spend entire days shopping for shoes in San Francisco while her mother scrubbed other people's floors. She remembers that some nights he would walk around the block three times before coming into the house. She remembers that one night he did not come in at all. She remembers that when your own husband left you, five years ago, you broke out in hives all over your body for weeks. She remembers thinking he was trouble the moment she met him. *A mother knows.* She remembers keeping that thought to herself. *I had to let you make your own mistakes.*

She remembers that, of her three children, you were the most delightful to be with. She remembers that your younger brother was so quiet she sometimes forgot he was there. *He was like a dream.* She remembers that her own brother refused to carry anything with him on to the train except for his rubber toy truck. *He wouldn't let me touch it.* She remembers her mother killing all the chickens in the yard the day before they left. She remembers her fifth-grade teacher, Mr. Martello, asking her to stand up in front of the class so everyone could tell her goodbye. She remembers being given a silver heart pendant by her next-door neighbor, Elaine Crowley, who promised to write but never did. She remembers losing that pendant on the train and being so angry she wanted to cry. *It was my first piece of jewelry.*

She remembers that one month after Frank joined the Air Force he suddenly stopped writing her letters. She remembers worrying that he'd been shot down over Korea or taken hostage by guerrillas in the jungle. She remembers thinking about him every minute of the day. *I thought I was losing my mind.* She remembers learning from a friend one night that he had fallen in love with somebody else. She remembers asking your father the next day to marry her. *"Shall we go get the ring?" I said to him.* She remembers telling him, *It's time.*

When you take her to the supermarket she remembers that coffee is Aisle Two. She remembers that Aisle Three is milk. She remembers the name of the cashier in the express lane who always gives her a big hug. *Diane.* She remembers the name of the girl at the flower stand who always gives her a single broken-stemmed rose. She remembers that the man behind the meat counter is Big Lou. "Well, hello, gorgeous," he says to her. She does not remember where her purse is, and begins to panic until you remind her that she has left it at home. *I don't feel like myself without it.* She does not remember asking the man in line behind her whether or not he was married. She does not remember him telling her, rudely, that he was not. She does not remember staring at the old woman in the wheelchair by the melons and whispering to you, *I hope I never end up like that.* She remembers that the huge mimosa tree that once stood next to the cart corral in the parking lot is no longer there. *Nothing stays the same.* She remembers that she was once a very good driver. She remembers failing her last driver's test three times in a row. *I couldn't remember any of the rules.* She remembers that the day after her father left them her mother sprinkled little piles of salt in the corner of every room to purify the house. She remembers that they never spoke of him again.

She does not remember asking your father, when he comes home from the pharmacy, what took him so long, or who he talked to, or whether or not the pharmacist was pretty. She does not always remember his name. She remembers graduating from high school with high honors in Latin. She remembers how to say, "I came, I saw, I conquered." *Veni, vidi, vici.* She remembers how to say, "I have lost the day." *Diem perdidi.* She remembers the words for "I'm sorry" in Japanese, which you have not heard her utter in years. She remembers the words for "rice" and "toilet." She remembers the words for "Wait." *Chotto matte kudasai.* She remembers that a white-snake dream will bring you good luck. She remembers that it is bad luck to pick up a dropped comb. She remembers that you should never run to a funeral. She remembers that you shout the truth down into a well.

She remembers going to work, like her mother, for the rich white ladies up in the hills. She remembers Mrs. Tindall, who insisted on eating lunch with her every day in the kitchen instead of just leaving her alone. She remembers Mrs. Edward deVries, who fired her after one day. *"Who taught you how to iron?" she asked me.* She remembers that Mrs. Cavanaugh would not let her go home on Saturdays until she had baked an apple pie. She remembers Mrs. Cavanaugh's husband, Arthur, who liked to put his hand on her knee. She remembers that he sometimes gave her money. She remembers that she never refused. She remembers once stealing a silver candlestick from a cupboard but she cannot remember whose it was. She remembers that they never missed it. She remembers using the same napkin for three days in a row. She remembers that today is Sunday, which six days out of seven is not true.

When you bring home the man you hope will become your next husband, she remembers to take his jacket. She remembers to offer him coffee. She remembers to offer him cake. She remembers to thank him for the roses. *So you like her?* she asks him. She remembers to ask him his name. *She's my first-born, you know.* She remembers, five minutes later, that she has already forgotten his name, and asks him again what it is. *That's my brother's name,* she tells him. She does not remember talking to her brother on the phone earlier that morning— *He promised me he'd call*—or going for a walk with you in the park. She does not remember how to make coffee. She does not remember how to serve cake.

S he remembers sitting next to her brother many years ago on a train to the desert and fighting about who got to lie down on the seat. She remembers hot white sand, the wind on the water, someone's voice telling her, *Hush, it's all right.* She remembers where she was the day the men landed on the moon. She remembers the day they learned that Japan had lost the war. *It was the only time I ever saw my mother cry.* She remembers the day she learned that Frank had married somebody else. *I read about it in the paper.* She remembers the letter she got from him not long after, asking if he could please see her. *He said he'd made a mistake.* She remembers writing him back, "It's too late." She remembers marrying your father on an unusually warm day in December. She remembers having their first fight, three months later, in March. *I threw a chair.* She remembers that he comes home from the college every Monday at four. She remembers that she is forgetting. She remembers less and less every day.

W hen you ask her your name, she does not remember what it is. *Ask your father. He'll know.* She does not remember the name of the president. She does not remember the name of the president's dog. She does not remember the season. She does not remember the day or the year. She remembers the little house on San Luis Avenue that she first lived in with your father. She remembers her mother leaning over the bed she once shared with her brother and kissing the two of them goodnight. She remembers that as soon as the first girl was born she knew that something was wrong. *She didn't cry.* She remembers holding the baby in her arms and watching her go to sleep for the first and last time in her life. She remembers that they never buried her. She remembers that they did not give her a name. She remembers that the baby had perfect fingernails and a very unusual heart. She remembers that she had your father's long nose. She remembers knowing at once that she was his. She remembers beginning to bleed two days later when she came home from the hospital. She remembers your father catching her in the bathroom as she began to fall. She remembers a desert sky at sunset. *It was the most beautiful shade of orange.* She remembers scorpions and red ants. She remembers the taste of dust. She remembers once loving someone more than anyone else. She remembers giving birth to the same girl twice. She remembers that today is Sunday, and it is time to go for her ride, and so she picks up her purse and puts on her lipstick and goes out to wait for your father in the car.

THE GREAT SILENCE

Ted Chiang • 2015

The humans use Arecibo to look for extraterrestrial intelligence. Their desire to make a connection is so strong that they've created an ear capable of hearing across the universe.

But I and my fellow parrots are right here. Why aren't they interested in listening to our voices?

We're a nonhuman species capable of communicating with them. Aren't we exactly what humans are looking for?

The universe is so vast that intelligent life must surely have arisen many times. The universe is also so old that even one technological species would have had time to expand and fill the galaxy. Yet there is no sign of life anywhere except on Earth. Humans call this the Fermi Paradox.

One proposed solution to the Fermi Paradox is that intelligent species actively try to conceal their presence, to avoid being targeted by hostile invaders.

Speaking as a member of a species that has been driven nearly to extinction by humans, I can attest that this is a wise strategy.

It makes sense to remain quiet and avoid attracting attention.

The Fermi Paradox is sometimes known as the Great Silence. The universe ought to be a cacophony of voices, but instead it is disconcertingly quiet.

Some humans theorize that intelligent species go extinct before they can expand into outer space. If they're correct, then the hush of the night sky is the silence of a graveyard.

Hundreds of years ago, my kind was so plentiful that the Río Abajo Forest resounded with our voices. Now we're almost gone. Soon this rain forest may be as silent as the rest of the universe.

There was an African gray parrot named Alex. He was famous for his cognitive abilities. Famous among humans, that is.

A human researcher named Irene Pepperberg spent thirty years studying Alex. She found that not only did Alex know the words for shapes and colors, he actually understood the concepts of shape and color.

Many scientists were skeptical that a bird could grasp abstract concepts. Humans like to think they're unique. But eventually Pepperberg convinced them that Alex wasn't just repeating words, that he understood what he was saying.

Out of all my cousins, Alex was the one who came closest to being taken seriously as a communication partner by humans.

Alex died suddenly, when he was still relatively young. The evening before he died, Alex said to Pepperberg, "You be good. I love you."

If humans are looking for a connection with a nonhuman intelligence, what more can they ask for than that?

E very parrot has a unique call that it uses to identify itself; biologists refer to this as the parrot's "contact call."

In 1974, astronomers used Arecibo to broadcast a message into outer space intended to demonstrate human intelligence. That was humanity's contact call.

In the wild, parrots address each other by name. One bird imitates another's contact call to get the other bird's attention.

If humans ever detect the Arecibo message being sent back to Earth, they will know someone is trying to get their attention.

P arrots are vocal learners: we can learn to make new sounds after we've heard them. It's an ability that few animals possess. A dog may understand dozens of commands, but it will never do anything but bark.

Humans are vocal learners, too. We have that in common. So humans and parrots share a special relationship with sound. We don't simply cry out. We pronounce. We enunciate.

Perhaps that's why humans built Arecibo the way they did. A receiver doesn't have to be a transmitter, but Arecibo is both. It's an ear for listening, and a mouth for speaking.

H umans have lived alongside parrots for thousands of years, and only recently have they considered the possibility that we might be intelligent.

I suppose I can't blame them. We parrots used to think humans weren't very bright. It's hard to make sense of behavior that's so different from your own.

But parrots are more similar to humans than any extraterrestrial species will be, and humans can observe us up close; they can look us in the eye. How do they expect to recognize an alien intelligence if all they can do is eavesdrop from a hundred light-years away?

It's no coincidence that "aspiration" means both hope and the act of breathing.

When we speak, we use the breath in our lungs to give our thoughts a physical form. The sounds we make are simultaneously our intentions and our life force.

I speak, therefore I am. Vocal learners, like parrots and humans, are perhaps the only ones who fully comprehend the truth of this.

There's a pleasure that comes with shaping sounds with your mouth. It's so primal and visceral that, throughout their history, humans have considered the activity a pathway to the divine.

Pythagorean mystics believed that vowels represented the music of the spheres, and chanted to draw power from them.

Pentecostal Christians believe that when they speak in tongues, they're speaking the language used by angels in heaven.

Brahman Hindus believe that by reciting mantras, they are strengthening the building blocks of reality.

Only a species of vocal learners would ascribe such importance to sound in their mythologies. We parrots can appreciate that.

According to Hindu mythology, the universe was created with a sound: "om." It is a syllable that contains within it everything that ever was and everything that will be.

When the Arecibo telescope is pointed at the space between stars, it hears a faint hum.

Astronomers call that the cosmic microwave background. It's the residual radiation of the Big Bang, the explosion that created the universe fourteen billion years ago.

But you can also think of it as a barely audible reverberation of that original "om." That syllable was so resonant that the night sky will keep vibrating for as long as the universe exists.

When Arecibo is not listening to anything else, it hears the voice of creation.

We Puerto Rican parrots have our own myths. They're simpler than human mythology, but I think humans would take pleasure from them.

Alas, our myths are being lost as my species dies out. I doubt the humans will have deciphered our language before we're gone.

So the extinction of my species doesn't just mean the loss of a group of birds. It's also the disappearance of our language, our rituals, our traditions. It's the silencing of our voice.

Human activity has brought my kind to the brink of extinction, but I don't blame them for it. They didn't do it maliciously. They just weren't paying attention.

And humans create such beautiful myths; what imaginations they have. Perhaps that's why their aspirations are so immense. Look at Arecibo. Any species who can build such a thing must have greatness within them.

My species probably won't be here for much longer; it's likely that we'll die before our time and join the Great Silence. But before we go, we are sending a message to humanity. We just hope the telescope at Arecibo will enable them to hear it.

The message is this:

You be good. I love you.

THE MIDNIGHT ZONE

Lauren Groff · 2016

It was an old hunting camp shipwrecked in twenty miles of scrub. Our friend had seen a Florida panther sliding through the trees there a few days earlier. But things had been fraying in our hands, and the camp was free and silent, so I walked through the resistance of my cautious husband and my small boys, who had wanted hermit crabs and kites and wakeboards and sand for spring break. Instead, they got ancient sinkholes filled with ferns, potential death by cat.

One thing I liked was how the screens at night pulsed with the tender bellies of lizards.

Even in the sleeping bag with my smaller son, the golden one, the March chill seemed to blow through my bones. I loved eating, but I'd lost so much weight by then that I carried myself delicately, as if I'd gone translucent.

There was sparse electricity from a gas-powered generator and no Internet, and you had to climb out through the window in the loft and stand on the roof to get a cell signal. On the third day, the boys were asleep and I'd dimmed the lanterns when my husband went up and out, and I heard him stepping on the metal roof, a giant brother to the raccoons that woke us thumping around up there at night like burglars.

Then my husband stopped moving, and stood still for so long I forgot where he was. When he came down the ladder from the loft, his face had blanched.

Who died? I said lightly, because if anyone was going to die it was going to be us, our skulls popping in the jaws of an endangered cat. It turned out to be a bad joke, because someone actually had died, that morning, in one of my husband's apartment buildings. A fifth-floor occupant had killed herself, maybe on purpose, with aspirin and vodka and a bathtub. Floors four, three, and two were away somewhere with beaches and alcoholic smoothies, and the first floor had discovered the problem only when the water of death had seeped into the carpet.

My husband had to leave. He'd just fired one handyman, and the other was on his own Caribbean adventure, eating buffet foods to the sound of cruise-ship calypso. Let's pack, my husband said, but my rebelliousness at the time was like a sticky fog rolling through my body and never burning off, there was no sun inside, and so I said that the boys and I would stay. He looked at me as if I were crazy and asked how we'd manage with no car. I asked if he thought he'd married an incompetent woman, which cut to the bone, because the source of our problems was that, in fact, he had. For years at a time I was good only at the things that interested me, and since all that interested me was my books and my children, the rest of life had sort of inched away. And while it's true that my children were endlessly fascinating, two petri dishes growing human cultures, being a mother never had been, and all that seemed assigned by default of gender I would not do because it felt insulting. I would not buy clothes, I would not make dinner, I would not keep schedules, I would not make playdates, never ever. Motherhood meant, for me, that I would take the boys on monthlong adventures to Europe, teach them to blast off rockets, to swim for glory. I taught them how to read, but they could make their own lunches. I would hug them as long as they wanted to be hugged, but that was just being human. My husband had to be the one to make up for the depths of my lack. It is exhausting, living in debt that increases every day but that you have no intention of repaying.

Two days, he promised. Two days and he'd be back by noon on the third. He bent to kiss me, but I gave him my cheek and rolled over when the headlights blazed then dwindled on the wall. In the banishing of the engine, the night grew bold. The wind was making a low, inhuman muttering in the pines, and, inspired, the animals let loose in call-and-response. Everything kept me alert until shortly before dawn, when I slept for a few minutes until the puppy whined and woke me. My older son was crying because he'd thrown off his sleeping bag in the night and was cold but too sleepy to fix the situation.

I made scrambled eggs with a vengeful amount of butter and cheddar, also cocoa with an inch of marshmallow, thinking I would stupefy my children with calories, but the calories only made them stronger.

Our friend had treated the perimeter of the clearing with panther deterrent, some kind of synthetic super-predator urine, and we felt safe-ish near the cabin. We ran footraces until the dog went wild and leapt up and bit my children's arms with her puppy teeth, and the boys screamed with pain and frustration and showed me the pink stripes on their skin. I scolded the puppy harshly and she crept off to the porch to watch us with her chin on her paws. The boys and I played soccer. We rocked in the hammock. We watched the circling red-winged hawks. I made my older son read *Alice's Adventures in Wonderland* to the little one, which was a disaster, a book so punny and Victorian for modern cartoonish children. We had lunch, then the older boy tried to make fire by rubbing sticks together, his little brother attending solemnly, and they spent the rest of the day constructing a hut out of branches. Then dinner, singing songs, a bath in the galvanized-steel horse trough someone had converted to a cold-water tub, picking ticks and chiggers off with tweezers, and that was it for the first day.

There had been a weight on us as we played outside, not as if something were actually watching, but merely the possibility that something could be watching when we were so far from humanity in all that Florida waste.

The second day should have been like the first. I doubled down on calories, adding pancakes to breakfast, and succeeded in making the boys lie in pensive digestion out in the hammock for a little while before they ricocheted off the trees.

But in the afternoon the one lightbulb sizzled out. The cabin was all dark wood, and I couldn't see the patterns on the dishes I was washing. I found a new bulb in a closet and dragged over a stool from the bar area and made the older boy hold the spinning seat as I climbed aboard. The old bulb was hot, and I was passing it from hand to hand, holding the new bulb under my arm, when the puppy leapt up at my older son's face. He let go of the stool to whack at her, and I did a quarter spin, then fell and hit the floor with my head, and then I surely blacked out.

After a while, I opened my eyes. Two children were looking down at me. They were pale and familiar. One fair, one dark; one small, one big.

Mommy? the little boy said, through water.

I turned my head and threw up on the floor. The bigger boy dragged a puppy, who was snuffling my face, out the door.

I knew very little except that I was in pain and that I shouldn't move. The older boy bent over me, then lifted an intact lightbulb from my armpit triumphantly; I a chicken, the bulb an egg.

The smaller boy had a wet paper towel in his hand and he was patting my cheeks. The pulpy smell made me ill again. I closed my eyes and felt the dabbing on my forehead, on my neck, around my mouth. The small child's voice was high. He was singing a song.

I started to cry with my eyes closed and the tears went hot across my temples and into my ears.

Mommy! the older boy, the solemn dark one, screamed, and when I opened my eyes, both of the children were crying, and that was how I knew them to be mine.

Just let me rest here a minute, I said. They took my hands. I could feel the hot hands of my children, which was good. I moved my toes, then my feet. I turned my head back and forth. My neck worked, though fireworks went off in the corners of my eyes.

I can walk to town, the older boy was saying to his brother through wadding, but the nearest town was twenty miles away. Safety was twenty miles away and there was a panther between us and there, but also possibly terrible men, sinkholes, alligators, the end of the world. There was no landline, no umbilicus, and small boys using cell phones would easily fall off such a slick, pitched metal roof.

But what if she's all a sudden dead and I'm all a sudden alone? the little boy was saying.

Okay, I'm sitting up now, I said.

The puppy was howling at the door.

I lifted my body onto my elbows. Gingerly, I sat. The cabin dipped and spun, and I vomited again.

The big boy ran out and came back with a broom to clean up. No! I said. I am always too hard on him, this beautiful child who is so brilliant, who has no logic at all.

Sweetness, I said, and I couldn't stop crying, because I'd called him Sweetness instead of his name, which I couldn't remember just then. I took five or six deep breaths. Thank you, I said in a calmer voice. Just throw a whole bunch of paper towels on it and drag the rug over it to keep the dog off. The little one did so, methodically, which was not his style; he has always been adept at cheerfully watching other people work for him.

The bigger boy tried to get me to drink water, because this is what we do in our family in lieu of applying Band-Aids, which I refuse to buy because they are just flesh-colored landfill.

Then the little boy screamed, because he'd moved around me and seen the bloody back of my head, and then he dabbed at the cut with the paper towel he had previously dabbed at my pukey mouth. The paper disintegrated in his hands. He crawled into my lap and put his face on my stomach. The bigger boy held something cold on my wound, which I discovered later to be a beer can from the fridge.

They were quiet like this for a very long time. The boys' names came back to me, at first dancing coyly out of reach, then, when I seized them in my hands, mine.

I'd been a soccer player in high school, a speedy and aggressive midfielder, and head trauma was an old friend. I remembered this constant lability from one concussive visit to the emergency room. The confusion and the sense of doom were also familiar. I had a flash of my mother sitting beside my bed for an entire night, shaking me awake whenever I tried to fall asleep, and I wanted my mother, not in her diminished current state, brittle retiree, but as she had been when I was young, a small person but gigantic, a person who had blocked out the sun.

I sent the little boy off to get a roll of dusty duct tape, the bigger boy to get gauze from my toiletry kit, and when they wandered back, I ducttaped the gauze to my head, already mourning my long hair, which had been my most expensive pet.

I inched myself across the room to the bed and climbed up, despite the sparklers behind my eyeballs. The boys let the forlorn puppy in, and when they opened the door they also let the night in, because my fall had taken hours from our lives.

It was only then, when the night entered, that I understood the depth of time we had yet to face. I had the boys bring me the lanterns, then a can opener and the tuna and the beans, which I opened slowly, because it is not easy, supine, and we made a game out of eating, though the thought of eating anything gave me chills. The older boy brought over mason jars of milk. I let my children finish the entire half gallon of ice cream, which was my husband's, his one daily reward for being kind and good, but by this point the man deserved our disloyalty, because he was not there.

It had started raining, at first a gentle thrumming on the metal roof.

I tried to tell my children a cautionary tale about a little girl who fell into a well and had to wait a week until firefighters could figure out a way to rescue her, something that maybe actually took place back in the dimness of my childhood, but the story was either too abstract for them or I wasn't making much sense, and they didn't seem to grasp my need for them to stay in the cabin, to not go anywhere, if the very worst happened, the unthinkable that I was skirting, like a pit that opened just in front of each sentence I was about to utter. They kept asking me if the girl got lots of toys when she made it out of the well. This was so against my point that I said, out of spite, Unfortunately, no, she did not.

I made the boys keep me awake with stories. The younger one was into a British television show about marine life, which the older one maintained was babyish until I pretended not to believe what they were telling me. Then they both told me about cookie-cutter sharks, which bore perfect round holes in whales, as if their mouths were cookie cutters. They told me about a fish called the humuhumunukunukuāpua'a, a beautiful name that I couldn't say correctly, even though they sang it to me over and over, laughing, to the tune of "Twinkle, Twinkle, Little Star." They told me about the walking catfish, which can stay out of water for three days, meandering about in the mud. They told me about the sunlight, the twilight, and the midnight zones, the three densities of water, where there is transparent light, then a murky darkish light, then no light at all. They told me about the World Pool, in which one current goes one way, another goes another way, and where they meet they make a tornado of air, which stretches, said my little one, from the midnight zone, where the fish are blind, all the way up up up to the birds.

I had begun shaking very hard, which my children, sudden gentlemen, didn't mention. They piled all the sleeping bags and blankets on me, then climbed under and fell asleep without bathing or toothbrushing or getting out of their dirty clothes, which, anyway, they sweated through within an hour.

The dog did not get dinner but she didn't whine about it, and though she wasn't allowed to, she came up on the bed and slept with her head on my older son's stomach, because he was her favorite, being the biggest puppy of all.

Now I had only myself to sit vigil with me, though it was still early, nine or ten at night.

I had a European novel on the nightstand that filled me with bleach and fret, so I tried to read *Alice's Adventures in Wonderland*, but it was incomprehensible with my scrambled brains. Then I looked at a hunting magazine, which made me remember the Florida panther. I hadn't truly forgotten it, but I could manage only a few terrors at a time, and others, when my children had been awake, were more urgent. We had seen some scat in the woods on a walk three days earlier, enormous scat, either a bear's or the panther's, but certainly a giant carnivore's. The danger had been abstract until we saw this bodily proof of existence, and my husband and I led the children home, singing a round, all four of us holding hands, and we let the dog off the leash to circle us joyously, because, as small as she was, it was bred in her bones that in the face of peril she would sacrifice herself first.

The rain increased until it was loud and still my sweaty children slept. I thought of the waves of sleep rushing through their brains, washing out the tiny unimportant flotsam of today so that tomorrow's heavier truths could wash in. There was a nice solidity to the rain's pounding on the roof, as if the noise were a barrier that nothing could enter, a stay against the looming night.

I tried to bring back the poems of my youth, and could not remember more than a few floating lines, which I put together into a strange, sad poem, Blake and Dickinson and Frost and Milton and Sexton, a tag-sale poem in clammy meter that nonetheless came alive and held my hand for a little while.

Then the rain diminished until all that was left were scattered clicks from the drops drifting off the pines. The batteries of one lantern went out and the light from the remaining lantern was sparse and thwarted. I could hardly see my hand or the shadow it made on the wall when I held it up. This lantern was my sister; at any moment it, too, could go dark. I feasted my eyes on the cabin, which in the oncoming black had turned into a place made of gold, but the shadows seemed too thick now, fizzy at the edges, and they moved when I shifted my eyes away from them. It felt safer to look at the cheeks of my sleeping children, creamy as cheeses.

It was elegiac, that last hour or so of light, and I tried to push my love for my sons into them where their bodies were touching my own skin.

The wind rose again and it had personality; it was in a sharpish, meanish mood. It rubbed itself against the little cabin and played at the corners and broke sticks off the trees and tossed them at the roof so they jigged down like creatures with strange and scrabbling claws. The wind rustled its endless body against the door.

Everything depended on my staying still, but my skin was stuffed with itches. Something terrible in me, the darkest thing, wanted to slam my own head back against the headboard. I imagined it over and over, the sharp backward crack, and the wash and spill of peace.

I counted slow breaths and was not calm by two hundred; I counted to a thousand.

The lantern flicked itself out and the dark poured in.

The moon rose in the skylight and backed itself across the black.

When it was gone and I was alone again, I felt the disassociation, a physical shifting, as if the best of me were detaching from my body and sitting down a few feet distant. It was a great relief.

For a few moments, there was a sense of mutual watching, a wait for something definitive, though nothing definitive came, and then the bodiless me stood and circled the cabin. The dog shifted and gave a soft whine through her nose, although she remained asleep. The floors were cool underfoot. My head brushed the beams, though they were ten feet up. Where my body and those of my two sons lay together was a black and pulsing mass, a hole of light.

I passed outside. The path was pale dirt and filled with sandspurs and was cold and wet after the rain. The great drops from the tree branches left a pine taste in me. The forest was not dark, because darkness has nothing to do with the forest—the forest is made of life, of light—but the trees moved with wind and subtle creatures. I wasn't in any single place. I was with the raccoons of the rooftop that were now down fiddling with the bicycle lock on the garbage can at the end of the road, with the red-winged hawk chicks breathing alone in the nest, with the armadillo forcing its armored body through the brush. I hadn't realized that I'd lost my sense of smell until it returned hungrily now; I could smell the worms tracing their paths under the pine needles and the mold breathing out new spores, shaken alive by the rain.

I was vigilant, moving softly in the underbrush, and the palmettos' nails scraped down my body.

The cabin was not visible, but it was present, a sore at my side, a feeling of density and airlessness. I couldn't go away from it, I couldn't return, I could only circle the cabin and circle it. With each circle, a terrible, stinging anguish built in me and I had to move faster and faster, each pass bringing up ever more wildness. What had been built to seem so solid was fragile in the face of time because time is impassive, more animal than human. Time would not care if you fell out of it. It would continue on without you. It cannot see you; it has always been blind to the human and the things we do to stave it off, the taxonomies, the cleaning, the arranging, the ordering. Even this cabin with its perfectly considered angles, its veins of pipes and wires, was barely more stable than the rake marks we made in the dust that morning, which time had already scrubbed away.

The self in the woods ran and ran, but the running couldn't hold off the slow shift. A low mist rose from the ground and gradually came clearer. The first birds sent their questions into the chilly air. The sky developed its blue. The sun emerged.

The drawing back was gradual. My older son opened his brown eyes and saw me sitting above him.

You look terrible, he said, patting my face, and my hearing was only half underwater now.

My head ached, so I held my mouth shut and smiled with my eyes and he padded off to the kitchen and came back with peanut-butter-and-jelly sandwiches, with a set of Uno cards, with cold coffee from yesterday's pot for the low and constant thunder of my headache, with the dog whom he'd let out and then fed all by himself.

I watched him. He gleamed. My little son woke but didn't get up, as if his face were attached to my shoulder by the skin. He was rubbing one unbloodied lock of my hair on his lips, the way he did after he nursed when he was a baby.

My boys were not unhappy. I was usually a preoccupied mother, short with them, busy, working, until I burst into fun, then went back to my hole of work; now I could only sit with them, talk to them. I could not even read. They were gentle with me, reminded me of a golden retriever I'd grown up with, a dog with a mouth so soft she would go down to the lake and steal ducklings and hold them intact on her tongue for hours until we noticed her sitting unusually erect in the corner, looking sly. My boys were like their father; they would one day be men who would take care of the people they loved.

I closed my eyes as the boys played game after game after game of Uno.

Noon arrived, noon left, and my husband did not come.

At one point, something passed across the woods outside like a shudder, and everything went quiet, and the boys and the dog all looked at me and their faces were like pale birds taking flight, but my hearing had mercifully shut off whatever had occasioned such swift terror over all creatures of the earth, save me.

When we heard the car from afar at four in the afternoon, the boys jumped up. They burst out of the cabin, leaving the door wide open to the blazing light that hurt my eyes. I heard their father's voice, and then his footsteps, and he was running, and behind him the boys were running, the dog was running. Here were my husband's feet on the dirt drive. Here were his feet heavy on the porch.

For a half breath, I would have vanished myself. I was everything we had fretted about, this passive Queen of Chaos with her bloody duct-tape crown. My husband filled the door. He is a man born to fill doors. I shut my eyes. When I opened them, he was enormous above me. In his face was a thing that made me go quiet inside, made a long, slow sizzle creep up my arms from the fingertips, because the thing I read in his face was the worst, it was fear, and it was vast, it was elemental, like the wind itself, like the cold sun I would soon feel on the silk of my pelt.

ANYONE CAN DO IT

Manuel Muñoz • 2019

Her immediate concern was money. It was a Friday when the men didn't come home from the fields and, true, sometimes the men wouldn't return until late, the headlights of the neighborhood worktruck turning the corner, the men drunk and laughing from the bed of the pickup. And, true, other women might have thought first about the green immigration vans prowling the fields and the orchards all around the Valley, ready to take away the men they might not see again for days if good luck held, or even longer if they found no luck at all.

When the street fell silent at dusk, the screen doors of the dark houses opened one by one and the shadows of the women came to sit out on the concrete steps. Delfina was one of them, but her worry was a different sort. She didn't know these women yet and these women didn't know her: she and her husband and her little boy had been in the neighborhood for only a month, renting a two-room house at the end of the street, with a narrow screened-in back porch, a tight bathroom with no insulation, and a mildewed kitchen. There was only a dirt yard for the boy to play in and they had to drive into the town center to use the payphone to call back to Texas, where Delfina was from. They had been here just long enough for Delfina's husband to be welcomed along to the fieldwork, the pay split among all the neighborhood men, the worktruck chugging away from the street before the sun even rose.

When Delfina saw the first shadow rise in defeat, she thought of the private turmoil these other women felt in the absence of their men, and she knew that her own house held none of that. Just days before the end of June, with the rent due soon, she thought that all the women on the front steps might believe that nothing could be any different until the men returned, that nothing could change until they arrived back from wherever they had been taken. She was alert to her worry, to be sure, but she sensed a resolve all her own that was absent in the women putting out last cigarettes and retreating behind the screen doors. She watched as the street went dark past sundown and the neighborhood children were all sent inside to bed. The longer she held her place on her front steps, the stronger she felt.

From the far end of the street, one of the women emerged from a porch and Delfina saw her moving along toward her house, guided by a few dim porchlights and the wan blur of television sets glowing through the windows. When the woman, tall and slender, arrived at her front yard, Delfina could make out the long sleeves of a husband's workshirt and wisps of hair falling from her neighbor's bun. Buenas tardes, the woman said.

Buenas tardes, Delfina answered and, rather than invite her forward, she rose from the steps and met her at the edge of the yard.

Sometimes they don't come back right away, the neighbor woman said in Spanish. But don't worry. They'll be back soon. All of them. If they take them together, they come back together.

The woman extended her hand. Me llamo Lis, she said.

Delfina, she answered and Lis emerged fully out of the street shadow, Delfina seeing a face about the same age as hers.

Your house was empty for about three months, said Lis, before you arrived. That's a long time for a house around here, even for our neighborhood. Everything costs so much these days.

It does, Delfina agreed.

Was it expensive in Texas? Lis asked. Is that why you moved?

Delfina looked at her placidly, betraying nothing. She had not told this woman that she was from Texas, and she began to wonder what her husband might have said to the other men in the worktruck, or in the parking lot of the little corner store near Gold Street, where the owner said nothing about the men's loitering as long as they kept buying beer after a day in the fields.

Your car, Lis said, pointing to the Ford Galaxie parked on the dirt yard. I noticed the Texas license plates when you first came.

We drove it from Texas, Delfina answered.

You're lucky your husband didn't take that car to the fields. They impound them, you know, and it's tough to get them back.

The woman reminded Delfina of her sister back in Texas, who had always tried to talk her into things she didn't want to do. It was her sister who had told her that moving to California was a bad idea, and who had repeated terrible stories about the people who lived there, though she had never been there herself. Her sister had given all the possible reasons why she should stay except for the true one, that she had not wanted to be left alone with their mother.

My husband says they stop you if you don't have California plates, Delfina said. So I try not to drive the car unless I have to.

On the long drive from Texas, she had learned that strangers only approached when they needed something. She could refuse Lis money if she asked, but it would be hard to deny her a ride into town if she needed it.

Even in the dark, she could tell that Lis was coming up with an answer to that. She had turned her head to look at the Galaxie, her face back in shadow under the streetlight.

Gas is expensive, Lis said, drawn out and final, as if she had realized that whatever she had wanted to request was no longer worth asking about. But she kept her sight on the car and said nothing more, which only convinced Delfina that she would, in time, come out with it.

We got our worktruck very cheap before the gas lines started and we didn't realize how much it would take to keep it filled up. Did you have to stand in line for gas in Texas?

We did, said Delfina. It was like that everywhere, I heard.

Not everywhere, said Lis. They tell me that Mexico is okay again, but family will always tell you whatever they need to get you home.

Where are you from?

Guanajuato. And you?

From Texas, said Delfina. Where we drove from, she added, as if to remind her.

Lis's face had fallen back into shadow, making it hard to see if she was pressing her lips into a vague smile about the fact that Delfina's husband had been rounded up with the rest of them. The old man who used to live in your house a long time ago was from Texas, from the Matamoros side, she said. He lived here so long he said this street used to be the real edge of town and that it backed up to a grape vineyard.

Is that right?

He passed away a while back but he was too old to work by then. He always said he wished he could go back to Mexico because he was all alone. Pobrecito. Sometimes I think he had the right idea. It's a terrible thing to be alone.

If she knew this woman better, if this woman knew her better, Delfina thought, she would tell her that this was only half true, that it was hard to make a go of it alone, but that it could be just as hard to live in a house without kindness.

But then you two came. With your niño. How old is he?

He is four.

So little, said Lis. How sweet. My girl is a little older. Ten.

I think I've seen her before, said Delfina, though she didn't remember.

Children never understand the circumstances, said Lis.

No, they don't, said Delfina. I don't think they should ever learn that.

It's part of life, said Lis. Ni modo. You know, that old man, I think he would've liked what we were doing with the worktruck. All of us going together, as many people as we could load in the back. He always said people were better neighbors in Mexico.

The Texas side?

Claro, said Lis, half-smiling. Listen, our rent is due on the first, she said. Yours, too, no?

Delfina didn't want to say yes, not even in the dark, but only "no" would mean this wasn't true.

Lis looked over at the Galaxie. I learned something the last time this happened, that I had to keep working instead of waiting. It's not good to run low on money.

Delfina could hear her voice press in the same way her sister's used to, her sister who talked and talked, who thought that the more you talked, the more convincing you sounded. Her husband had said that anyone who asked too hard about anything really wanted something else.

What would you say about taking the car out to the peach orchards and splitting what we get? I'd pay for half the gas.

Oh, I don't know . . . , Delfina began.

My girl is old enough to care for your niño, if you trust her, Lis offered. It could be just us, she said, if you don't want to bring along anyone else in the neighborhood.

I don't know . . . , Delfina hesitated, though she knew she could not say that more than twice and she steeled herself to say no.

I know the farmer, said Lis. We could go out to the orchards and pick up a few rows before he gives all that work away.

I'll have to think about it, said Delfina. My husband doesn't like me driving the car. She remembered what her neighbor had said about impoundment and she tried that: If they take the car . . .

You're from Texas, said Lis, but she pressed no further. Her face was clear and open, but the way she said these words stung, as if being from one side or the other meant anything about how easy or hard things could be. It was none of any stranger's business, but Delfina's husband had never allowed her to work and she knew what women like Lis thought about women like her.

I don't know the first thing about working in the fields anyway, Delfina said. She tried to say it in a way that meant it was the truth and not at all a reply to what Lis had said about Texas.

It's easy but hard at the same time, said Lis. Anyone can do it. It's just that no one really wants to.

I'll have to think about it, said Delfina.

I understand, Lis answered and backed a step out to the street, her arms folded in a way that Delfina recognized from her sister, the way she had stood on the Texas porch in defeat and resignation. Que pases buenas noches, Lis said and began walking away before Delfina had a chance to reply in kind. When she did, she felt her voice carry along the street, as if everyone else on the block had overheard this refusal, and she went back into the house with an unexpected sense of shame.

Very early the next morning, after a restless night, Delfina woke her little boy from the pallet of blankets on the living room floor. We're going into town, she told him, when Kiki resisted her with grogginess as she struggled to get him dressed. She was about to lead him to the car when she pictured herself driving past Lis's house, how that would look to a woman she had just refused, and her pride took over. She grasped Kiki's hand in her own with such ferocity that he knew that she meant business and he walked quickly beside her down the street and around the corner, past the little white church empty on a Saturday morning and toward town. The boy kept pace with her somehow and, to her surprise, he made no more protests, and twenty minutes later, when they reached the TG&Y, she deposited Kiki in the toy aisle without saying a word and marched to the payphone at the back of the store to call her mother in Texas.

He left you, her mother's voice said over the line. Nothing keeps a good father from his family.

They took other men in the neighborhood, too, Delfina said. He wasn't alone.

How many times did he go out to work here in Texas and he came home just fine? I told you that you shouldn't have gone. Your sister was absolutely right . . .

Delfina pulled the phone away from her ear and the vague hectoring of her mother barely rippled out along the bolts of fabric and the sewing notions hanging on the back wall of the store. Delfina gripped the remaining dimes in her hands, slick and damp in her palm, and clicked one of them into the phone, the sound cutting out for a moment as the coin went through.

How's the niño? Is he dreaming about his father yet? That's how you'll know if he's coming back or not.

Did you hear that? she interrupted her mother, dropping another coin. I don't have much time left.

Why are you calling? For money? Of course, you're calling for money. If he's a good father, he'll find a way to send some if he can't get back.

If you were a good mother, Delfina began, but it came as hardly even a whisper, and she lacked the real courage to talk back this way, to summon the memory of her white-haired father who had died years ago and taken with him, it seemed, any criticism of his late-night ways. Her voice was lost anyway as her mother yelled out to trade the phone over to Delfina's sister, and in the moment when the exchange left them all suspended in static, Delfina hung up the receiver. She had not even given them the address for the Western Union office and she would have to apologize, she knew, when the worst of the financial troubles would be upon her. But for the moment, she relished how she had left her older sister calling into the phone, staring back incredulous at her mother.

Come along, she said to Kiki, when she went to collect him from the toy aisle, where he had quietly scattered the pieces of a board game without the notice of the clerk. He started to cry out in protest, now that he was in the cool and quiet of the five-and-dime and she was pulling him away from the bins of marbles and plastic army men. Delfina imagined the footsteps of the clerk coming to check on the commotion and, in her hurry to shove the board game back onto the shelf, she let slip the payphone dimes, Kiki frozen in surprise by their clatter before he stooped to pick them up.

Come along, she said again, letting him have the dimes. Ice cream, she whispered in encouragement, and led on by this suggestion, he followed her out of the store. Kiki fell meek and quiet once again, as if he knew not to jeopardize his sudden fortune. It was only right to reward him with the truth and she led him down the street to the drugstore with its ice cream stand visible from the large front window. It was only ten in the morning and the young woman at the main register had to come around to serve them two single scoops, but Delfina didn't even take the money from Kiki's hands to pay for it. She had a single folded dollar bill in her pocket and she handed it to the clerk, foolish, she thought, to be spending so frivolously. But her boy didn't need to know those troubles. His Saturday was coming along like any other, his father sometimes not home at sundown and always gone at sunrise. There was no reason to get him wondering about things he wasn't wondering about.

Come along, Delfina said, and led him to the little park across the street from the town bank. He gripped his cone tightly and his other hand held the fist of dimes. She motioned him to pocket the change for safekeeping. Put it away, she said, sitting on one of the benches. But her little boy kept them in his grip and so she patted his pocket more firmly to encourage him and that's when she felt it, a hard little object that she knew instantly was something he had stolen from the toy aisle.

Let me see, she said, or I will take away your coins. Kiki struggled against her, smearing some of the ice cream on his pants, which finally distressed him enough into actual tears. Ya, ya, Delfina said, calming him, and fished what was in his pocket, a little green car, metal and surprisingly heavy. Her little boy was inconsolable and the Saturday shoppers along the sidewalk stopped to look in their direction. Sssh, she told him, there, there, and took the time to show him the car in the palm of her hand before she slipped it back into his pocket. Ya, ya, she said one more time, and leaned back on the bench, the Saturday morning going by.

Later, when they rounded the corner back into the neighborhood, she saw Lis out in her dirt yard. She was tending to a small bed of wild sunflowers, weeding around them with a hoe, her back turned to the street. The closer they got to Lis's yard, the harder the scuffling of Kiki's shoes became and Lis turned around to the noise.

Buenos dias, Delfina greeted her. She wanted to keep walking but Lis made her way toward her and she knew she would have to stop and listen, much like the time in Arizona on the trip out here, when she had accidently locked eyes with a man at a gas station, and he had walked over to rap on the window of the Galaxie and beg for some change.

Good thing we didn't go to the orchards after all, said Lis. I would've felt terrible if your car had stalled out there.

No . . . , Delfina began. I . . . The more she stumbled, the less it made sense to make up any story at all. There was no reason to be anything but honest.

The car is fine, she said. I just wanted him to walk a bit. We got ice cream.

For breakfast, Lis said, looking down at Kiki and smiling. What a Saturday! The morning's sweat matted her hair down on her forehead and she wore no gloves, her fingers a bit raw from the metal handle of the hoe, but she was cheerful with Kiki, recognizing his exhaustion. Her daughter, Delfina realized, was not out helping her, but inside the cool of the house, and she took this as a sign of the same propensity for sacrifice that she believed herself to hold.

I've thought about it, Delfina said, though she really hadn't. I think it's a good idea.

I'm glad, said Lis.

I wish I had said so last night. We could've put in a day's work. But I'm happy to go tomorrow.

Tomorrow's Sunday, said Lis, and when Delfina put her hand up to her mouth as if she'd forgotten, as if she might change her mind, Lis moved even closer to her, looking down at Kiki. But work never waits, she said.

El día de Dios, said Delfina. I didn't even think of it.

People work, said Lis. Don't worry about it.

We can wait until Monday. That way the children can be at school.

Like I told you, my daughter is old enough to watch him, if you trust her. I leave her alone sometimes. Or we can bring them out with us and stay longer.

Delfina could make out the shadow of a child watching from behind the screen door and, catching her glance past her shoulder, Lis turned to look. She called her forth and her daughter stepped out, a girl very tall for ten years old. This is our neighbor, Lis explained, and we'll need you to watch her little boy tomorrow. Will you do that?

The girl nodded and she stuck out her hand to Delfina in awkward politeness.

What's your name? Delfina asked.

Irma, the girl said, very quietly, her voice deferential. She had very small eyes that she squinted as if in embarrassment and Delfina wondered if she needed glasses but was too afraid to say.

We can trust you, can't we, said Lis, to take care of the little boy? If I leave you some food, you can feed him, can't you?

Oh, I can leave them something . . .

Don't worry, said Lis. I can leave something easy to fix and you can bring out something for us in the orchard. I have a little ice chest to keep everything out of the sun.

After Delfina nodded her head in agreement, Lis made as if to go back to her yard work. At dawn, then, Lis said. I'll bring everything we need.

For the rest of the day, Delfina was restless, anxious that every noise on the street might signal the return of the men. To have them come back would mean the lull of normalcy, of what had been and would continue to be, just when she was on the brink of doing something truly on her own. But the street stayed quiet. The afternoon heat swallowed the houses and by evening, some of the shadows resumed their evening watch, sitting stiffly but without much hope or expectation. They turned back in before night had fully come and Delfina went to bed early, too.

At dawn, she roused Kiki from the blankets strewn on the living room floor and poured him some cereal. He blinked against the harshness of the kitchen light at such an early hour, surprised at his mother wearing one of his father's long-sleeved workshirts, and even more surprised by the knock at the door. Lis stood there, her daughter behind her. Buenos dias, Delfina said and waved the girl Irma inside. She poured her a bowl of cereal, too, and Irma sat quietly at the table without having to be told to do so.

Thank you for taking care of him, Delfina said. We'll be back in the middle of the afternoon. She knew she didn't have to say more than that, trusted that Lis had spoken with the same motherly sense of warning that she used. Still, it was only now, on the brink of leaving them alone for the day, that she wished she had asked Kiki if he had been dreaming about his father, if he might have communicated something about what was true for him while he slept.

Lis showed her the gloves and the work knives and then the two costales to hold the fruit, a sturdy one of thick canvas with a hearty shoulder strap and a smaller one of nylon mesh. Her other hand balanced a water jug and a small ice chest, where Delfina put in a bundle of foil-wrapped bean tacos that would keep through the heat of the day.

In the car, Lis pointed her south of town and toward the orchards and Delfina drove along. They kept going south, the orchards endless, cars parked over on the side of the road and pickers approaching foremen, work already getting started even though the dawn's light hadn't yet seeped into the trees.

Up there, Lis said, where a few cars had already lined up and several workers had gathered around a man sitting on the open tailgate of his worktruck. Wait here, she said.

Before Delfina could ask why, Lis had exited, approaching the man with a handshake. He seemed to recognize her and then looked back at Delfina in the car. Lis finished what she had needed to say and the man took one more look at Delfina and then pointed down the rows.

Lis motioned her to get out of the car.

He says he'll give us two rows for now and we do what we can. If we're fast, he'll give us more. And he's letting us use a ladder free of charge.

That's kind of him . . .

They charge sometimes, Lis said. She took one end of a heavy-looking wooden ladder, the tripod hinge rusty and the rungs worn smooth in the middle. So fifty-fifty?

Half and half, Delfina agreed.

I can pick the tops and you can do the bottoms, if you're afraid of heights. Or you can walk the costales back to the crates for weighing. Give them your name if you want to, but make sure the foreman tells you exactly how much we brought in.

They worked quickly, the morning still cool. Delfina parted the leaves where the peaches sat golden among the boughs and the work felt easy at first. The fruit came down with scarcely more than a tug and when she yanked hard enough to rustle the branches, Lis spoke her advice from the ladder above. Just the redder ones and not too hard. Feel them, she said. If they're too hard, leave them. Someone else will come back around in a few days and they'll be riper then.

They did a few rounds like this, Delfina taking the costales back to the road to have them weighed. Sometimes Lis was ready with the smaller nylon sack and sometimes Delfina had to wait for other pickers to have their fruit accounted for. The morning moved on, a brighter white light coming into the orchard as they got closer to noon. As they picked the trees near clean, they moved deeper and deeper into the orchard and the walk back to the crates took longer, Lis almost lost to her among the leaves.

They had not quite finished the row when the sun finally peaked directly overhead and their end of the orchard sank into quiet. Delfina let out a sigh upon her return.

I should've brought the ice chest while I was there.

I can get it, said Lis. You've walked enough. She came down with the half-empty nylon costal and pulled a few more peaches from the bottom boughs as Delfina rested. She started walking toward the road, then turned around. The keys, she said, and held out her hand.

Delfina watched her go. Lis walked quickly with the nylon costal dangling over her shoulder. Maybe the weight of Lis's work was all in her arms from stretching and pulling, and not heavy and burning in the thighs like hers. Delfina sat in the higher bank of the orchard row, catching her breath, massaging her upper legs and resting. It was a Sunday, she remembered, and Lis had been right after all. People did work on this day, even if it felt as tranquil and lonely as Sundays always did, here among the trees with the leaves growing more and more still, the orchard quiet and then quieter. Sundays were always so peaceful,

Delfina thought, no matter where you were, so serene she imagined the birds themselves had gone dumb. El día de Dios, she thought, and remembered Sundays when her white-haired father had not yet slept out the drunkenness of the previous night. Her own husband had sometimes broken the sacredness of a Sunday silence and she was oddly thankful for the calm of this orchard moment that had been brought on only by his absence. Delfina looked down the row to soak in that blessed quiet and the longer she looked, the emptier and emptier it became. The empty row where, she realized, Lis had disappeared like a faraway star.

She started back toward the road. The walk was long and she couldn't hear a sound, not of the other workers, not other cars rumbling past the orchards, just the endless trees and her feet against the heavy dirt of the fields. The day's weariness slowed her and made the trees impossible to count, but she walked on, resolute, the gray of the road coming into view. She emerged onto the shoulder of the road and saw the foreman and the foreman's truck and a few other cars, but the Galaxie was gone.

Excuse me, she said, approaching the foreman, who seemed surprised to see her, though he had seen her all morning, noting down the weight of the peaches she had brought in, saying the numbers twice, tallied under the last name Arellano.

You're still here, the foreman said, very kindly, as if the fact was a surprise to him too, and his face grew into a scowl like the faces of the white men Delfina had encountered in Texas, the ones who always seemed surprised that she spoke English. But where their faces had been steely and uncaring, his softened with concern, as if he recognized that he had made a serious mistake.

I thought you were gone . . . , he said.

We were supposed to split . . . She held a hand to her head and looked up the road, one way and then the other, as if the car were on its way back, Lis having gone only to the small country store to fetch colder drinks.

Arellano, the foreman said, tapping his ledger. Arellano is the first name on the list, he said. I paid it out about a half hour ago.

That was my car, Delfina said, as if that would be enough for him to know what to do next. But the foreman only stared back at her. It was my husband's car, she said, because that was how she saw it now, what her husband would say about its loss if he ever made it back.

She told me that you two were sisters, the foreman said. If he only knew, Delfina thought, her real sister back in Texas. The mere mention made her turn back toward the orchard and walk into the row. She could sense the foreman walking to the row's opening to see where she was going, and when she reached the ladder, she folded it down and heaved it best as she could, its legs cutting a little trough behind her as she dragged it back to the road.

You didn't have to do that, the foreman said.

You did right by letting us use it, Delfina said. It's only fair. Other pickers had approached the foreman's truck and he attended to them, though he kept looking over at Delfina now and then, his face sunken in concern. None of the workers looked at her and she let go of the idea of asking any of them for a ride back into town. She sat in the dirt under the shade of a peach tree and watched while the foreman flipped out small wads of cash as the workers began to quit for the afternoon. When the last of them shook hands with the foreman and began to leave, she rose to help him load all of the wooden ladders back on to the truck.

He accepted her help and opened the door of the truck cab, motioning for her to get in. They drove slow back into town, the ladders clattering with every stop and start, the weight of them shifting and settling. Neither of them said a word, but before the orchards gave way back to the houses, the foreman cleared his throat and spoke: I think it's the first time I ever had two women come out alone like that, but I was raised to think that anybody can do anything and you don't ask questions just because something isn't normal. Even just a little bit of work is better than none at all and I kept thinking about the story she told me, that you two were sisters and that your husbands had gotten thrown over the border. You can tell a lot by a wife who wants to work as hard as her husband, you know what I mean? I wasn't sure you could finish two rows just the both of you, but you kept coming and coming with those sacks and that's how I knew you had kids to feed.

At the four-way intersection, just before the last mile into town, the foreman fished into his pocket and pulled out a bill. Take it, he said. He handed it to her, a twenty, and almost pushed it into Delfina's hands as he started the turn, needing to keep the steering wheel steady. The bill fluttered in her fingers from the breeze of the open passenger window, but the truck wasn't going to pick up much more speed. She wouldn't lose it.

Thank you, she said.

It's not your fault, he said. And I'm not defending her for what she did. But I believe any story that anybody tells me. You can't be to blame if you got faith in people.

You're right, she agreed. And though she didn't have to say it, she followed it with the words of blind acceptance before she could stop herself. I understand, she said, and it was not worth explaining that she really didn't.

Where should I take you? asked the foreman.

She didn't hesitate. There's a little store right near Gold Street, just across the tracks, she said. If you could stop, just so I can get something for my boy.

Of course, he said, though there could have been no other possible way to respond, since Delfina's request came with a small hiccup of tears, which she quickly swallowed away as the truck pulled into the store's small lot. Other workers had stopped there, too, and men from other neighborhoods lingered out front with their open cases of beer and skinny bags of sunflower seeds, staring at her as she wiped at her face with her dirty sleeves. She brought a package of bologna and a loaf of bread to the register and fished out three bottles of cola from the case at the front counter. The clerk broke the twenty into a bundle of ones, and she held them with the temporary solace of pretending there would be money enough for the days ahead and that money was going to be the least of her worries anyway.

She directed the foreman just a couple more blocks and when they turned the corner, the neighborhood held a Sunday quiet that made her think first of an empty church, but she had not been to a service in years. No, it was a quiet like the porch of the house in Texas when she and her husband had driven away, leaving her sister and her mother, a stillness that she was sure held only so long before one of them had started crying, followed by the other. A calm like that could only be broken by the bereft and that was how she understood that neither of them would ever forgive her. But that didn't matter now. The hotter days of July were coming, Delfina knew, and the work of picking all the fruit would last from sunup to sundown. Something would work out, she told herself, clear and resolute against the emptiness of her neighborhood, Lis's house stark in its vacancy. There, she said, pointing to her house, and she wasn't surprised to see Kiki sitting there on the front steps all alone.

There he is, waiting for his mama, the foreman said, as he pulled up, and Kiki looked back at them, with neither curiosity nor glee.

She handed the foreman the third cola bottle.

You know, he said, it'll work out in the end. Sisters always end up doing the right thing. She'll be back, you'll see.

What story had he figured out for himself, Delfina wondered, after she hadn't bothered to correct him about Lis not being her sister, and she decided that this also mattered little in the end, how he would explain this to his wife back home. She would not explain this to her husband when he came back. All her husband would care about was what happened to the Galaxie and that would be enough of a story. She might even tell her husband about the luck of the twenty-dollar bill but she would hold private the detail of the ring on the foreman's finger. She would hold in her mind what it felt like to be treated with a faithful kindness.

Thank you, she said, and descended from the truck cab, nodding her head goodbye.

On the steps, Kiki eyed the tall bottles of cola in her hand. But first there was the heavy field dust to pound away from her shoes and the tiredness she could suddenly feel in her bones. Delfina kicked her shoes off and sat on the front steps. She lodged one of the bottles under the water spigot to pop the cap, a trick she had seen her husband do. She handed that bottle to Kiki and he took it with both hands, full of thirst or greed for the sweetness, she couldn't tell. She took some of the bread loaf and the bologna for herself and offered him a bite, knowing he wouldn't eat one of his own. He was hungry and this was how she knew that Irma was gone, too. She was a girl who did what she was told and Delfina didn't blame her. Kiki crowded close to her knees, even in the heat of the afternoon, and so she popped the cap of the second bottle to take a sip herself and to ask her little boy of no words to tell where he thought the older girl had gone, of where he dreamed his father was. Dígame, she said, asking him to tell her a whole story, but Kiki had already taken the little metal car from his pocket and he was showing her, starting from the crook of his arm, how a car had driven away slowly, slowly, and on out past the edge of his little hand and out of their lives forever.

Chimamanda Ngozi Adichie is the author of award-winning and best-selling novels, including *Americanah* and *Half of a Yellow Sun*; the short-story collection *The Thing Around Your Neck*; and the essay collection *We Should All Be Feminists*. A recipient of a MacArthur Fellowship, she divides her time between the United States and Nigeria.

Dorothy Allison is the bestselling author of several novels, including *Bastard Out of Carolina*, *Cavedweller*, and *Two or Three Things I Know for Sure*. The recipient of numerous awards, she has been the subject of many profiles and a short documentary film of her life, *2 or 3 Things but Nothing for Sure*.

Toni Cade Bambara (1939–1995) was the author of two short-story collections, *Gorilla, My Love* and *The Seabirds Are Still Alive*, and the novels *The Salt Eaters* and *If Blessing Comes*. She also edited and contributed to *The Black Woman: An Anthology* and *Tales and Stories for Black Folks*. Her works have appeared in various periodicals and have been translated into several languages.

Rick Bass lives in northwest Montana's Yaak Valley, where he is the chair of the Yaak Valley Forest Council. He is the author of numerous books of fiction and nonfiction. Bass teaches in the University of Southern Maine's Stonecoast MFA Program as well as runs private workshops.

Lucia Berlin (1936–2004) worked brilliantly but sporadically throughout the 1960s, '70s, and '80s. Her stories are inspired by her early childhood in various Western mining towns; her glamorous teenage years in Santiago, Chile; three failed marriages; a lifelong problem with alcoholism; her years spent in Berkeley, Albuquerque, and Mexico City; and the various jobs she held to support her writing and her four sons. Sober and writing steadily by the 1990s, she took a post as a Visiting Writer at the University of Colorado, Boulder, in 1994 and was soon promoted to associate professor. In 2001, in failing health, she moved to Southern California to be near her sons. She died in 2004 in Marina del Rey.

Raymond Carver (1938–1988) was born in Clatskanie, Oregon. His first collection of stories, *Will You Please Be Quiet, Please?* (a National Book Award nominee in 1977), was followed by *What We Talk About When We Talk About Love, Cathedral* (nominated for the Pulitzer Prize in 1984), and *Where I'm Calling From* in 1988, when he was inducted into the American Academy of Arts and Letters. He died August 2, 1988, shortly after completing the poems of *A New Path to the Waterfall*.

Ted Chiang has won four Hugo Awards, four Nebula Awards, and six Locus Awards, and has been featured in *The Best American Short Stories*. His collections *Stories of Your Life and Others* (2002; republished as *Arrival* in 2016) and *Exhalation* (2019) have been translated into more than twenty languages. He was born in Port Jefferson, New York, and currently lives near Seattle, Washington.

Sandra Cisneros is a poet, short-story writer, novelist, essayist, and visual artist whose work explores the lives of Mexicans and Mexican Americans. Her numerous awards include a MacArthur Fellowship, the National Medal of Arts, a Ford Foundation Art of Change Fellowship, and the PEN/Nabokov Award for Achievement in International Literature. Her classic novel, *The House on Mango Street* (1984), has been translated into more than twenty-five languages and is required reading in schools and universities across the nation.

Edwidge Danticat is the award-winning author of many novels and story collections, including the National Book Award nominee *Krik? Krak!*; *Breath, Eyes, Memory*; *The Dew Breaker*; and *Everything Inside*. She has also written several Young Adult novels (*Behind the Mountains*; *Anacaona: Golden Flower, Haiti, 1490*; *Untwine*); picture books (*Eight Days*; *Mama's Nightingale*; *My Mommy Medicine*); memoirs (*Brother, I'm Dying*; *The Art of Death: Writing the Final Story*); and essays (*Create Dangerously: The Immigrant Artist at Work*). She is the recipient of a MacArthur Fellowship and the winner of the 2018 Neustadt International Prize for Literature.

Lydia Davis is the author of *The End of the Story: A Novel* and several story collections. *Varieties of Disturbance: Stories* was a finalist for the 2007 National Book Award. She is the recipient of a MacArthur Fellowship and the American Academy of Arts and Letters Award of Merit Medal. Named a Chevalier of the Order of Arts and Letters by the French government for her fiction and her translations of modern writers, including Maurice Blanchot, Michel Leiris, and Marcel Proust, Davis is also the winner of the 2013 Man Booker International Prize.

Junot Díaz is the author of the critically acclaimed story collections *Drown* and *This Is How You Lose Her*, and a novel, *The Brief Wondrous Life of Oscar Wao*, winner of the 2008 Pulitzer Prize and the National Book Critics Circle Award. He is also the author of an award-winning picture book, *Islandborn*. Díaz is the recipient of a MacArthur Fellowship and was inducted into the American Academy of Arts and Letters in 2017.

Stuart Dybek is the author of five books of fiction—*Ecstatic Cahoots*, *Paper Lantern*, *I Sailed with Magellan*, *The Coast of Chicago*, and *Childhood* *and Other Neighborhoods*—as well as two collections of poetry, *Brass Knuckles* and *Streets in Their Own Ink*. Dybek is the recipient of many prizes and awards, including the PEN/Malamud Award for Excellence in the Short Story, an Arts and Letters Award from the American Academy of Arts and Letters, a Whiting Writers' Award, four O. Henry Awards, a MacArthur Fellowship, and a Guggenheim Fellowship. He is Distinguished Writer in Residence at Northwestern University.

Nathan Englander is the author of the novels *The Ministry of Special Cases, Dinner at the Center of the Earth,* and *kaddish.com,* and the story collections *For the Relief of Unbearable Urges* and *What We Talk About When We Talk About Anne Frank* (winner of the 2012 Frank O'Connor International Short Story Award and a finalist for the 2013 Pulitzer Prize).

Louise Erdrich is the author of sixteen novels as well as volumes of poetry, children's books, short stories, and a memoir of early motherhood. Her novel *The Round House* won the National Book Award for Fiction. She has twice won the National Book Critics Circle Award, for her debut novel, *Love Medicine,* and *LaRose,* and was a finalist for the Pulitzer Prize for her novel *The Plague of Doves,* winner of the Anisfield-Wolf Book Award. She has received the Library of Congress Prize for American Fiction, the prestigious PEN/Saul Bellow Award for Achievement in American Fiction, and the Dayton Literary Peace Prize. Erdrich, an enrolled member of the Turtle Mountain band of Chippewa, lives in Minnesota with her daughters and is the owner of Birchbark Books, a small independent bookstore.

Percival Everett is the author of more than thirty books, including *Telephone, So Much Blue, Assumption, Erasure,* and *I Am Not Sidney Poitier.* He has received the Zora Neale Hurston/Richard Wright Legacy Award for Fiction and the PEN Center USA Award for Fiction. He lives in Los Angeles.

Lauren Groff is the author of three novels, *The Monsters of Templeton*, *Arcadia*, and *Fates and Furies*, and the short-story collections *Delicate Edible Birds* and *Florida*. She has won the Story Prize, has been a finalist for the National Book Critics Circle Award and the Los Angeles Times Book Prize, and has twice been a finalist for the National Book Award. She was a Guggenheim Fellow and named one of *Granta* magazine's 2017 Best of Young American Novelists. Her work has been published in thirty languages. Her fourth novel, *Matrix*, is forthcoming.

Aleksandar Hemon is the author of *The Question of Bruno*, *Nowhere Man*, *The Lazarus Project*, *Love and Obstacles*, *The Making of Zombie Wars*, and two collections of autobiographical essays, *The Book of My Lives* and *My Parents: An Introduction/This Does Not Belong to You*. He is the recipient of a MacArthur Fellowship.

Andrew Holleran is the author of three novels—*Dancer from the Dance*, *Nights in Aruba*, and *The Beauty of Men*—a book of essays, *Ground Zero*; and a collection of short stories, *In September, the Light Changes*.

Charles Johnson is the author of *Dr. King's Refrigerator: And Other Bedtime Stories*, *Dreamer*, *Faith and the Good Thing*, and *Middle Passage*, for which he won the National Book Award. A MacArthur Fellow, Johnson received a 2002 Arts and Letters Award in Literature from the American Academy of Arts and Letters. He is Professor Emeritus at the University of Washington in Seattle, where he lives.

Denis Johnson (1949–2017) was the author of two story collections, *Jesus' Son* and *The Largesse of the Sea Maiden*; a novella, *Train Dreams* (finalist for the 2012 Pulitzer Prize for Fiction); and several novels, including *Tree of Smoke*, which won the 2007 National Book Award and was a finalist for the 2008 Pulitzer Prize. He was posthumously awarded the Library of Congress Prize for American Fiction in 2017.

Jamaica Kincaid was born in St. John's, Antigua. Her books include *At the Bottom of the River*, *Annie John*, *Lucy*, *The Autobiography of My Mother*, *My Brother*, and *Mr. Potter*. She lives with her family in Vermont.

Stephen King is the author of more than fifty books, all of them worldwide bestsellers. His first crime thriller featuring Bill Hodges, *Mr. Mercedes*, won the Edgar Award for Best Novel and was shortlisted for the 2015 Crime Writers' Association Gold Dagger Award. Both *Mr. Mercedes* and *End of Watch* received the Goodreads Choice Award for the Best Mystery and Thriller of 2014 and 2016 respectively. King cowrote the bestselling novel *Sleeping Beauties* with his son Owen King, and many of King's books have been turned into celebrated films and television series, including *The Shawshank Redemption*, *Gerald's Game*, and *It*. King is the recipient of the 2003 National Book Foundation Medal for Distinguished Contribution to American Letters, the 2007 Grand Master Award from the Mystery Writers of America, and the 2014 National Medal of Arts. He lives with his wife, Tabitha King, in Maine.

Jhumpa Lahiri is the author of five works of fiction: *Interpreter of Maladies*, *The Namesake*, *Unaccustomed Earth*, *The Lowland*, and *Whereabouts*; and a work of nonfiction, *In Other Words*. She has received numerous awards, including the Pulitzer Prize; the PEN/Hemingway Award; the PEN/Malamud Award; the Frank O'Connor International Short Story Award; the Premio Gregor von Rezzori; the DSC Prize for South Asian Literature; a 2014 National Humanities Medal, awarded by President Barack Obama; and the Premio Internazionale Viareggio-Versilia, for *In altre parole*.

Ursula K. Le Guin (1929–2018) was the author of twenty-one novels, eleven volumes of short stories, four collections of essays, twelve children's books, six volumes of poetry, and four works of translation. She was widely known for her works of science fiction and fantasy, including the acclaimed novels *The Left Hand of Darkness* and *The Dispossessed*. Le Guin received numerous awards and honors, and her books continue to sell millions of copies worldwide. An author of singular imagination and resolve, Le Guin died in her home in Portland, Oregon.

Ken Liu is an award-winning American author of speculative fiction. His collection *The Paper Menagerie and Other Stories* has been published in more than a dozen languages. Liu's other works include *The Grace of Kings*, *The Wall of Storms*, a Star Wars tie-in (*The Legends of Luke Skywalker*), and a second collection, *The Hidden Girl and Other Stories*. He has been involved in multiple media adaptations of his work, including the short story "Good Hunting," adapted as an episode in Netflix's animated series *Love, Death + Robots*; and AMC's *Pantheon*, adapted from an interconnected series of short stories. "The Hidden Girl," "The Message," and *The Grace of Kings* have also been optioned for development. He lives with his family near Boston, Massachusetts.

Manuel Muñoz is the author of two short-story collections: *Zigzagger* and *The Faith Healer of Olive Avenue*. His debut novel, *What You See in the Dark*, was published in 2011. His writing has been recognized with a Whiting Writers' Award, three O. Henry Prizes, and an appearance in a *Best American Short Stories* anthology, among other honors. He lives and works in Tucson, Arizona.

Tim O'Brien received the 1979 National Book Award for *Going After Cacciato*. Among his other books are *The Things They Carried*, a finalist for the Pulitzer Prize and a *New York Times* Book of the Century, and *In the Lake of the Woods*, winner of the James Fenimore Cooper Prize. He was awarded the Pritzker Military Library Literature Award for Lifetime Achievement in Military Writing in 2013.

Julie Otsuka is the award-winning author of *When the Emperor Was Divine* and *The Buddha in the Attic*, winner of the PEN/Faulkner Award for Fiction and France's Prix Femina Étranger, and a finalist for the National Book Award. She lives in New York City.

Grace Paley (1922–2007) was a renowned writer and activist. Her *Collected Stories* was a finalist for both the Pulitzer Prize and the National Book Award. Her other collections include *Enormous Changes at the Last Minute* and *Just as I Thought*. A native of the Bronx, she died at age eighty-four in Thetford, Vermont.

Karen Russell has received a MacArthur Fellowship and a Guggenheim Fellowship, the 5 Under 35 prize from the National Book Foundation, the New York Public Library's Young Lion's Award, and a fellowship from the American Academy in Berlin. She lives in Portland, Oregon, with her husband, son, and daughter.

George Saunders is the author of ten books, including the novel *Lincoln in the Bardo*, which won the Man Booker Prize, and the story collections *Pastoralia* and *Tenth of December*, which was a finalist for the National Book Award. He has received fellowships from the Lannan Foundation, the American Academy of Arts and Letters, and the Guggenheim Foundation. In 2006 he was awarded a MacArthur Fellowship. In 2013 he was awarded the PEN/Malamud Award for Excellence in the Short Story and was included in *Time*'s list of the one hundred most influential people in the world. He teaches in the creative writing program at Syracuse University. His latest book is *A Swim in the Pond in the Rain: In Which Four Russians Give a Master Class on Writing, Reading, and Life*.

Isaac Bashevis Singer (1904–1991) was the author of many novels, stories, children's books, and memoirs. He was awarded the Nobel Prize in Literature in 1978.

Susan Sontag (1933–2004) was the author of numerous works of non-fiction, including the groundbreaking collection of essays *Against Interpretation*, and of four novels, including *In America*, which won the National Book Award.

Alice Walker won the Pulitzer Prize and the National Book Award for her novel *The Color Purple*. Her other novels include *By the Light of My Father's Smile* and *Possessing the Secret of Joy*. She is also the author of three collections of short stories, three collections of essays, seven volumes of poetry, and several children's books. Born in Eatonton, Georgia, Walker now lives in Northern California.

Claire Vaye Watkins is the award-winning author of the story collection *Battleborn* and the novel *Gold Fame Citrus*. In 2017 she was named one of *Granta* magazine's Best Young American Novelists.

Joy Williams is the author of four novels, five short-story collections, and the book of essays *Ill Nature: Rants and Reflections on Humanity and Other Animals*. She has been nominated for the National Book Award, the Pulitzer Prize, and the National Book Critics Circle Award. She lives in Tucson, Arizona, and Laramie, Wyoming.

Tobias Wolff lives in Northern California and teaches at Stanford University. He has received the Rea Award for the Short Story, a Los Angeles Times Book Prize, and the PEN/Faulkner Award for Fiction.

CREDITS